LOST IN SPACE

Dr. Jon Schiller

Lost In Space

a novel by

JON SCHILLER, PhD

BOOKSURGE
CHARLESTON, SC
2008

First printing

PUBLISHED BY BOOKSURGE
Charleston, SC 29418
Printed in the United States of America

Jon Schiller, Author of Trading Books
Insider's Automatic Options Strategy
The 100% Return Options Trading Strategy
Self-Adaptive Options & Currency Trading
Profit in Index Options Trading Using Decision Charts
Compilation of Jon Schiller's OEX Options Trading Newsletters

Author of Fiction Novels
Masada Never Again
Ibex
Multihulls
Ultra Taiwan Fighter

Author of a True Story:
Irrational Indictment & Imprisonment

ISBN: 0-9774305-3-7
copyright © 2008 Dr. Jon Schiller
jonsch1@verizon.net
http://www.jonschilleroptions.com/
http://wwwjonschblogger.blogspot.com/

Prologue

Lost In Space Summary

The US space shuttle delivering supplies to the US Space Station has a mechanical breakdown that prevents its return to the Earth. The remaining two US space shuttles are launched as quickly as possible to carry the needed supplies to the Space Station before the people there run out of *expendables*: air, water, etc. Both aging shuttles suffer breakdowns – one explodes on the launch pad and the other has a breakdown in orbit near the Space Station. This second shuttle is close enough to the Space Station to be secured by a cable and then winched up to the Space Station docking gate.

The hero, Dr. Donald Richards, devises two options for rescuing the stranded astronauts: use the new European space shuttle or use the Russian space shuttle. The US President over-rules NASA's recommendation to use the Russian space shuttle for the rescue, so Richards negotiates an agreement with the European Space Agency to use their shuttle to rescue the astronauts. Unfortunately, the Ariane booster to be used in the rescue explodes during launch. Reluctantly, the US President agrees that the Russians can now be asked to send their shuttle up before the Space Station crew's expendables run out. Richards goes to the Russian Space Center in Novosibirsk to assist the Russians in planning and executing the rescue.

The Russian shuttle fails just after it attempts to start its retro rocket for re-entering the Earth's atmosphere. This means the crews of the two US shuttles and the one Russian shuttle, plus the original crew of the Space Station, are all stranded in space with only enough life support expendables for a few months. Richards has to seek assistance from the European space shuttle director in Toulouse once again. The Europeans have fixed the problem with the Ariane booster by now and after three European Shuttle missions all the people lost in space are rescued. A gala welcome party for all the crew members and key rescue team members is given in the Malaga Palacio Hotel in Spain.

Dr. Jon Schiller

Author's Background

AUTHOR: JON SCHILLER received the BS in Physics from the California Institute of Technology (Caltech) and the PhD in EE & Math from the University of Southern California. He worked for major aerospace companies and received the NASA Group Achievement Award for certifying the flight readiness before the first Space Shuttle flight. As a result of this NASA service he was invited to attend the launch of the first flight of Colombia in April 1981.

After retiring from aerospace, he began designing options trading software. His experience trading options for two decades and writing options software gives him the background to write the options trading books.

The 5 novels are based on his experiences designing avionics for military aircraft and his responsibilities for Middle East business in Iran and Israel for a large aerospace company.

Jon Schiller's books include 4 option books and 5 novels which are all listed on page vi. The options trading books are available from Windsor Books. All these books are available from Amazon.com.

He skippered three Transpacific sail boat races from Los Angeles to Honolulu, trophying twice. He had to navigate using celestial navigation with a sextant, before the days of GPS.

His background of yacht racing, flying private aircraft and world-wide traveling provided the depth of experience to create the novels. The author lived in Europe, mostly in Spain, for 17 years before returning to California in 2001 and many of the places he visited provide the geographical background for creating his exciting novels.

Author's Note

Your author believes this is an important story to tell because it gives insight into how the US aerospace business operates and how international cooperation in space, even between the old Cold War enemies, the US and Russia, might be possible.

The author wishes to acknowledge the contributions of his wife, Emilie, who was the editor and made sure the text made good logical sense and was not just *science talk* which is what the author tended to write. Emilie Manns Smyth received the BS in Education from Occidental College and the MA in Education from the University of Southern California.

LIST OF CHARACTERS

HEADS OF STATE (Actions and words are fictional)
Jack Williamson US President
Mikhail S. Gorbachev Soviet Premier
Lorenzo Felipe López President of European Economic
  Community, EEC has financial control of European space
  shuttle developed as part of the *Eureka Program*

AMERICANS
Dr. Donald F. Richards
  Vice President for Space Station Operations,
  Universal Aircraft Corp. in Irvine, CA,
  reports to President of UAC
Dawn
  Live-in companion of Dr. Richards
June
  Secretary to Dr. Richards
Dr. Barbara Rosen
  Deputy Commander of space station,
  Specialist in software and computers
Buck Woods
  Retired systems engineer for Space Station,
  at UAC in Irvine, CA
General Jack Robbins
  Commander of US Space Station
Colonel Billie Joe Johnson
  Commander of space shuttle *Columbia*
Colonel Richard Rogers
  Commander of space shuttle *Atlantis*
Dr. John Davidson
  Science Advisor to US President
Lois
  Secretary to Dr. Davidson
Mary Jane
  Secretary to President Williamson

AMERICANS (Cont'd)

Gus Ford
> Director of Space Operations for space shuttle and Space Station, NASA Houston

Jim Atkins
> UAC pilot for company helicopter and Lear Jet stationed in Houston, Texas

Marie Jackson
> Blonde in Houston

Cindy Brown
> African-American in Houston

David Moore
> President of UAC, Dr. Richards' boss

Tom Rubin
> Chief Engineer, reports to Dr. Richards

Jack Kelly
> Director for External Tanks of Space Shuttle in NASA Michoud

Nancee Browne
> Administrative Assistant to Dr. Jonathon of the Smithsonian Museum

William Wiley
> Chairman of President's Investigative Commission

Seymour Bloomberg
> Shuttle Program Director at Integration Contractor's Downey Plant

Dr. Barnes
> Chairman of National Security Commission

Dr. Jonathon
> Director of Smithsonian Aerospace Museum in Washington DC

Tom Ahrons,
> CIA Agent, assigned to UAC

Jack Hill
> UAC Engineer

Elena
> UAC Front Lobby Receptionist

Joe
> UAC Chauffeur

EUROPEANS

Professora Dr. Juanita Gonzalez
>   Director of European shuttle computer and software
>   programs, Fujitsu Espana SA in Malaga, Spain

Dr. Jacques Dubois   Program Director European space shuttle,
>   Aerospatiale in Toulouse, France

Yvon Bourgain
>   Commander of European space shuttle

Dr. Enrique Rodriguez Manuelo
>   Deputy Program Director European space shuttle of Iber
>   Avion Spacio in Madrid, Spain

Professor Dr. Tom Shepherd
>   Director of European space shuttle trajectories of Cranfield
>   Institute of Technology in Milton Keynes, UK

Dr. Heinz Zinn
>   Deputy Director of European space shuttle system
>   engineering in Siemens, Munich, Germany

Jose Espejo
>   Software engineer, reporting to Dr. Gonzalez

RUSSIANS

Dr. Lina Gorlovka
>   Deputy Director of Russian space shuttle software

Colonel Georgi Andrejevich Gusev
>   Commander of Russian space shuttle

Yuli Ilyich Litvinov
>   System engineer Russian space shuttle, designer of docking
>   adapter.

Brigitte Michon (Michov)
>   KGB Agent

Professor Dr. Nikolai Chekhov
>   Program Director of Russian space shuttle, Moscow

LOST IN SPACE
TABLE OF CONTENTS

Chapter 1

Crisis in Space

The jangle of the headboard telephone on his king-sized bed startled Dr. Donald Richards from a sound sleep. The warm, nude body next to him stirred. Dawn groped for the telephone receiver and murmured sleepily, "Who is it?"

The voice at the other end of the line said apologetically, "I'm sorry, ma'am, this is the security guard down at Universal Aircraft. I'm trying to reach Dr. Richards. There's an emergency."

Dawn mumbled hoarsely, "Just a moment." She turned to Richards, "Don, it's for you. A guard down at the plant says there's an emergency."

Richards took the phone, "Yes? This Dr. Richards."

The guard said, "Doctor, there's an emergency down here at Universal. Mr. Rubin asked me to call you and have you come down to the plant right away. Something about the Space Shuttle."

"Can't I talk to Mr. Rubin directly?"

"No, sir. He's busy in the Space Station control center talking on the radio. He said he needs you right away."

"OK, OK! Tell him I'll be there in about a half hour."

Dawn asked sleepily, "Dear, what in the world is that all about? Do you realize it's two am?"

"Yes, on Tuesday the 27th of February. This is the day the Space Shuttle Columbia is supposed to return from the Space Station, but there seems to be some kind of problem. Darling, I've got to go to the plant right away!"

"OK. Then you probably won't be back for breakfast, right?"

"Right, Honey. I'll see you down at the plant!"

Dr. Don Richards was the vice president of the new American Space Station program at Universal Aircraft in Irvine, California. Dawn, his live-in girl friend, was a computer operator at Universal. After his divorce two years ago, Richard started going out with Dawn, a comely young lady some fifteen years his junior. After a period of dating, Dawn moved into his condominium in the hills of

Irvine, about twenty minutes by car from the large Universal Aircraft plant at the John Wayne Airport in Orange County California. Richards traveled frequently in his executive post and on the average was only home three nights of the week, usually on week-ends.

It was 1992 and the new American Space Station was just beginning its initial operation. The US Space Shuttle acted as a re-supply ship for the space station, carrying crew and supplies back and forth. The latest re-supply mission was in progress this week. Richards' deputy, Tom Rubin, was scheduled to work all night tonight to make sure the return of the Shuttle Columbia from the Space Station went smoothly.

As Richards drove down the winding street from his hillside condominium, he thought, "That message sounded ominous What can it be?"

Richards turned his white Datsun sports convertible onto MacArthur Boulevard heading north. Shortly he reached the turn-off to the Universal Aircraft plant, a large high rise on the south east corner of the John Wayne Airport. He drove into the building grounds, approached the guard gate, and flashed his picture ID badge.

The guard smiled and said, "Good morning, Dr. Richards. Drive right in. Sorry I had to wake you up in the middle of the night. Hope I didn't upset the missus!"

"No problem, Bill. It's just part of the job. Never a dull moment!"

Richard guided his car to the spot marked *Dr. Donald P. Richards, VP*, parked and strode to the closest entrance door. He took the elevator to the sixth floor to the Space Station Control Center. The large room was full of TV monitors and electronic control consoles. There were a half dozen operators sitting at the consoles with headphones and mouth speakers attached.

Tom Rubin rushed up to Richards, blurted out excitedly, "Don, we've got a real mess on our hands!"

"What's the problem, Tom?"

"Well, Columbia pushed off the docking port about an hour ago, started up the main engines, and the cockpit lit up with red lights and warning horns!"

"What caused the red lights?"

"We're not completely sure yet, but it looks like they lost two of the hydraulic power units."

Richards and Rubin had been friends for a long time. Previously they had worked at NASA Houston where Richards had been the chief engineer on the Space Shuttle with Rubin as his deputy. Seven year ago Richard had received a job offer from Universal Aircraft to head up their proposal effort for the new American Space Station program. Richards decided to make the career move and brought Rubin with him. Their team's proposal won the prime contract for the Space Station for Universal. As his reward, Richards was appointed VP and program director for the space program and immediately he made Rubin his deputy.

Richards responded, "As I remember, Tom, the shuttle's hydraulics are only triply redundant rather than quad redundant."

"That's right, Don. Remember, we had big debates about that during the shuttle design, but, yes, it ended up triple, not quad."

"Then, with one hydraulic system left, they should be all right, right?"

"Wrong, Don! During re-entry with the cross winds we have in the upper atmosphere, they wouldn't have enough control power. Our simulations show that we would lose the shuttle on re-entry. It would burn to a crisp!"

"Can't risk that, then!"

"Yes, that's what we all decided before we woke you up. We can't risk it. That means Columbia is stranded in space!"

"Who've we got on the video communication link now?"

"Dr. Barbara Rosen, deputy commander of the Space Station, is on watch on the space station. She's on screen two. Colonel Johnson, Columbia's commander is on screen three on the shuttle. I've got Gus Ford, down at Houston, on screen one. You want to talk to them?"

"Yeah, switch me to Dr. Rosen first."

"OK, you've got her."

"Barbara, how's it look up there?"

"Not too good, Don. As Colonel Johnson just said, 'We're up the creek without a paddle!'"

"Can't your maintenance man get at least one more system back operating? We could make the re-entry with two units working."

"Not a chance, Don. Those hydraulic power units are devils! We don't have any spares here. Besides, it takes special tooling to get 'em out. It's out of the question to fix 'em up here!"

"OK, Barbara. Let me talk to Colonel Johnson for a minute. I'll get back to you. Tom, connect me to screen two."

"OK. Don. Here's Colonel Johnson on your screen."

Richards addressed the TV image of Colonel Johnson in a friendly voice, "Hi there, Billie Joe. Barbara tells me you've got a little problem up there."

"You bet your ass we do! We can start re-entry with the main engine and the reaction jets for control but without the control power from at least two hydraulic units, we'll become a hot cinder during the re-entry. That's not healthy!"

"No, it isn't! Do you have any problem re-docking with the Space Station?"

"No, sir. We can execute the docking maneuver with hydraulics we have. We've been too busy assessing the problem to tackle the getting back exercise yet."

"OK, Billie Joe, looks like you'll be returning to the Station soon. Let me get back to Barbara for a while. Good luck!"

"We'll need it. What we really need is for Discovery or Atlantis to come and get us!"

"Barbara, this is Don, back with you. It looks like we need to get Houston to start readying one of the other shuttles to come up. How much in the way of expendables do you have aboard?"

"Well, Don, we've got ten happy souls aboard the Station now, counting Billie Joe and his other three crew men, that will make 14. I just figured we have enough up here to keep us alive through the end of May."

"In other words, you have about three months' worth of expendables – oxygen, fuel, etc. Right?"

"You've got it, Don!"

"I'll talk to Gus Ford down at NASA Houston and be back to you later, Barbara."

"OK, Don. We're on pins and needles up here! We've never had a shuttle failure in orbit before."

The big Texan who was director of space operations at NASA Houston appeared on Richards' TV screen. Gus Ford said cheerily, "This is a hell of a way to start a morning, isn't it? Glad they got you out of bed, too, Don."

"Gus, how soon can you get the next shuttle up there?"

"That's kind of a complex question, but off the top of my head I'd say about two weeks, plus or minus a couple of days. The next one would probably be Atlantis."

"Good. That leaves only one problem."

Gus queried, "What's that, Don?"

"What do we do with Columbia when Atlantis arrives at the Space Station. We only have one shuttle docking port!"

Tom Rubin interrupted, "Don, I've already thought about that problem. We can just use the tether cable that's already on board the shuttle to tie Columbia to the Station. That'll get it out of the way."

"Will that give the Space Station attitude control system any problems?"

"No, we ran a simulation of that configuration. We can do it OK."

Richards said calmly, "Tom, please connect my comset to all parties. Richards spoke authoritatively into his headset microphone, "Now, listen, lady and gentlemen, I know we have a little problem up there, but we've got several shuttles left here on Earth and three months' expendables on the Station, so nobody's going to suffer. I'm going to get our Space Station team together and work out a plan to get us out of this mess. So, don't worry!"

Dr. Barbara Rosen interjected in a calm voice, "Don, don't worry about us panicking up here. We were going to be here for a year anyway. It's just a little disconcerting to have one of our supply trucks broke!"

Gus Ford broke in, "Don, this is Gus. How soon can you get down here to Houston? We want to meet you eyeball to eyeball about the final plan details!"

"Gus, I'll fly down this afternoon. There's a commercial flight leaving Orange County at 4 pm. Gets to Houston Hobby at 8 pm."

"Good, I'll set up an 8:30 meeting in the space operations center here tomorrow morning. We'll video link to Headquarters to keep Bill Adams there up to speed. See you later. So long."

"So long, Gus. And Barbara, we should be able to give you a preliminary launch date after our meeting at Houston tomorrow."

She replied, "OK, Don. We're going to be busy up here for the next couple of hours, getting Columbia re-docked. We've also got to work out the plan for tethering Columbia when Atlantis, or whatever shuttle they send up, gets here.

Richards replied on the communications net to everyone, "So long, everybody. We'll be getting back with you just as soon as the launch plans are finalized."

Turning to Gus Ford's TV screen, Richards added, "Gus, no use waking up anybody else here in California this early in the morning.   You're going to be busy in Houston with communications during the Columbia re-docking. When everyone gets here for work this morning, I'll have my secretary, June, set up an 8:30 meeting in the big conference room to explain to all the group here what we're doing to take care of this emergency.   I assume you want to be video linked in to our meeting?"

"Right, Don. See you then."

Chapter 2

Fun & Games in Houston

Richards strode into the Universal Aircraft Space Station conference room exactly at 8:30 am. The team members were waiting expectantly. Richards walked to the head of the long, mahogany conference table ringed with his first line managers. The other key members – some fifty people - were sitting in upholstered chairs around the periphery of the room. Richard's baritone voice rang out, "Thanks for coming to the meeting. As you've probably heard, we have an emergency up at the Space Station. Columbia was all ready to begin its de-orbit maneuver this morning when the crew discovered that two of the three hydraulic power units had failed."

Tom Rubin interrupted, "Dr. Richards, we have confirmed that the motor windings on both units have shorts. They'll have to be replaced – not an easy job."

"Tom, thanks for the update. With the two systems failed, we cannot safely re-enter Earth's atmosphere using the one remaining hydraulic unit. So Columbia is stuck in space. We've got to devise a rescue plan using the other shuttles." He listed names of five men who would act as crisis team leaders.

Rubin asked, "When do we need the plan?"

"I need the first cut by three this afternoon to carry to Houston. I have a 4 pm flight. I'll meet with the crisis team leaders again next Saturday morning to finalize the plan. By then, we should have all the information we need from NASA about the status of the other three shuttles.

Richards and his engineers listed their ideas for areas of study on the whiteboard. Team members' names were placed next to each area. The topics listed included:

Docking of shuttle to Space Station with Columbia tethered
Re-supply of expendables
Repair of Columbia
Schedule of shuttle launch

Schedule for recovery of Columbia after repair

Richards closed the meeting by saying, "I would like to have a briefing, consisting of about thirty charts, to take with me to Houston this afternoon. Tom, you prepare the front end of the briefing summarizing the problem. The rest of you concentrate on the solutions in the areas assigned to you. I want to make sure the rescue shuttle carries up three more months of expendables. See you here at 3 pm."

Hurrying to his office to clean up his mail, he asked his secretary if she had made his afternoon flight reservations. He also asked June to request that Jim Atkins, the Universal Aircraft pilot stationed in Houston, pick him up in the company chopper upon arrival at the Houston Hobby Airport. Then he dialed five digits on the company intercom phone and reached Dawn's number in the computer room.

"Good morning, Darling. Sorry you had to drive in alone this morning. We have a real problem at the Space Station – Columbia is stranded in space. I've got to go to Houston this afternoon. Probably won't get back 'til Friday. I'll call you later in the week, as soon as I see how my schedule develops.

"So that's what the middle-of-the-night phone call was all about. OK. Have a good flight. See you when you get back. Hope you make it back by Friday. You promised to take me out to dinner, remember?"

"Yes, I remember. By the way, would you have time to go home at lunch and pack my carry-on bag for the trip and put it in my office?"

"Yes, I'll pack your bag, you poor, helpless thing. Goodbye, Darling."

"Goodbye, Dawn. I'll miss you."

At 3 pm Richards returned to the conference room to meet with his crisis team. Tom Rubin had the first view graph on the projector at the front of the conference table.

Richards asked him, "How's the briefing look, Tom?"

"Pretty rough, but not bad for a first cut. We ended up with thirty charts. At two minutes per chart, that's an hour long briefing."

"OK, Roll them quickly. I've got twenty minutes before I have to leave to catch my four o'clock flight."

Richards examined each view graph briefly, then remarked happily, "The charts look great! You summarized the problems very well. The solutions are logical and well presented. Good job!"

The team members looked at each other and grinned. Jack Hill, the team member responsible for expendables, added, "Dr. Richards, we included in the three months of expendables enough for another crew on the shuttle, just in case!"

"Jack, that's good conservative planning, but I don't think we have to worry about the second shuttle's crew being stranded, too. We've already had our share of bad luck with the Columbia. Remember, the last shuttle accident was way back in January 1986, over six years ago!"

Tom said, "Don, here are ten hard copies of the view graphs to give to the NASA Houston folks. You had better go now to make your 4 o'clock . Have a good flight!"

"Right, Tom. Thanks again for the great charts. They'll make me look good in the meeting at NASA Houston tomorrow."

Richards hurriedly stuffed the viewgraphs and the package of hard copies into his briefcase, grabbed the small bag Dawn had dropped by his office and dashed for the elevator down to the lobby. He was greeted by the beautiful Hispanic receptionist, Elena, who said, "Dr. Richards, your driver is waiting just outside the door. Your secretary, June, brought these down for you. She said she was sure you would forget to go by her desk to get them."

Elena handed Richards his airline tickets and $1000 cash in ten crisp one hundred dollar bills. Richards reached for them, saying, "Thanks, Elena! I was so busy I forgot about these! See you later!" and rushed out the lobby door.

The Universal Aircraft driver was holding open the back door of the black Cadillac limousine. Almost breathless, Richards greeted him while fumbling with the tickets, "Joe, I'm on Pan Am 232. Just drop me at their gate."

"Relax, Dr. Richards. June already gave me the flight number. The Pan Am boarding clerk said I can take you right to the plane. You don't need to go into the terminal. That case of

Jack Daniels I gave him for Christmas really works! Also, I have clearance from the tower to drive along the taxiways."

"Joe, that's great. I can really relax when you and June take care of things!"

The big limousine sped along the Universal Aircraft ramp inside the John Wayne Airport along the taxiways northward to the airline terminals. Because of the large number of private aircraft and commercial airliners using this airport, it was the second busiest in the world, second only to Chicago O'Hare.

Joe stopped right beside the boarding stairs of the Pan Am DC-9. The other passengers had not yet left the terminal for the plane. Richards climbed the stairs with his carry-on bag slung over his shoulder and his briefcase in hand. He was greeted by a beautiful, blonde stewardess who took his boarding pass and ticket, saying, "Welcome aboard, Dr. Richards. Here's your seat, number 2A. Would you like a glass of champagne before we depart?"

"Why, yes, thank you." Richards settled down into his first class seat while the stewardess put his bag in the small forward baggage compartment.

Hurrying back with his glass of bubbling champagne she said, "Have a good flight!"

Soon the other passengers scrambled aboard. At 4 pm sharp the DC-9 taxied to the north end of runway 19. The tower issued take off clearance to the jet and the acceleration pressed Richards into his seat. The DC-9 lifted off the runway and leapt into the air. It made a gentle right turn to avoid over-flying the expensive homes on Newport Harbor and headed south over the blue Pacific Ocean. After gaining altitude it turned inland toward Tucson.

Richards leaned back in his seat and looked once again at the view graphs his crisis team had prepared for him. He went through in his mind what he would say during his briefing at NASA Houston in the morning. The briefing had to be polished. He would have a large TV audience. The conference room would be video linked to NASA Headquarters in Washington, DC, NASA Marshall in Huntsville, NASA Michoud near New Orleans, the Universal Aircraft plant, and the fourteen souls stranded in space on the Space Station orbiting above. After finishing his mental presentation of the briefing, he fell into a deep sleep, exhausted because of his 2 am awakening the night before.

He awoke when he felt the DC-9 touch down on the runway at Houston Hobby Airport. Peering into the darkness outside his window, he picked out the rotating beacon of the UAC helicopter parked near the airline ramp and thought, *That will be Jim Atkins, to fly me to NASA Houston. Good ole Jim!*

Richards was first off the DC-9. He headed down the stairs with his bag and briefcase and dashed over to the waiting helicopter.

Atkins greeted him, "Hi. Doc. I want cha to meet two honey dolls – Marie Jackson and Cindy Brown, there in the back seat. You just slip in 'tween 'em!"

Richards took a good look in the back seat – two luscious young girls in their early twenties. Marie had honey blonde hair and very long legs, with an ample bosom. Cindy was a strikingly beautiful African-American girl with enormous breasts and a brilliant smile, highlighted by sparkling white teeth. "Hi, Girls! Pleased to meet you!"

The girls chorused, "Hi, Dr. Richards!"

Cindy, who was sitting on the outside, closest to the door, added, "Get in, Doctor. We're saving a seat for you here in the middle."

Richards responded, "Thanks, Girls, but please don't be so formal. Call me Don."

Marie said, "OK, Don, but hurry and get in. It's chilly tonight. Jim has been telling us how good looking you are. He was right."

Richards climbed into the back seat as Jim Atkins, the UAC pilot clambered into the pilot's seat in front. Atkins started the turbine engine and turned out the cabin lights. As Kelly started to reach for his safety belt, Cindy reached over and stopped him, saying, "No, no, Don! Marie and I will take care of that!"

Richards felt the seat belt being fastened around his waist. At the same time, he felt a feminine hand start massaging through his pants. Another set of hands unzipped his trousers. Richards heard the loud speaker blaring, "Chopper 72 Delta, you are cleared for immediate takeoff. Use departure corridor Alpha One to NASA Houston. Maintain one thousand. Contact Departure Control on 132 point 35 after reaching one thousand feet. Good evening, Jim!"

Atkins replied, "Roger, Chopper 72 Delta, copied clearance. So long, Slim!"

Atkins increased the engine RPM to 3500 and pulled back on the collective pitch lever, making the turbine powered helicopter rise into the dark night. Richards felt one set of hands take his swelling member out of his trouser opening and massage it rhythmically. Richard felt the helicopter begin its descent into the airport at NASA Houston. He felt the hands stuff his member back into his trousers. Another pair of hands zipped up his trousers.

Atkins set the helicopter down on a pad just outside the hanger housing the sleek UAC Lear-Gates jet. After switching off the engine, he turned around toward the back seat and asked, "How was the flight, Doc?"

With a satisfied look on his face, Richards answered eagerly, "Fabulous, Jim. Best chopper flight I've ever had. Cindy and Marie here are gorgeous and talented!"

"Doc, they're yours for the night. Right, Girls?"

The girls chorused, "Right, Jim. We just love Dr. Richards!"

Cindy corrected her, "Don, we mean."

Marie interjected, "Don, if you thought that little warm-up exercise in the air was good, wait until Cindy and I get you into bed tonight!"

"I can hardly wait!"

The quartet exited the helicopter and Atkins lead them to the white company station wagon parked just outside the hanger. He said, "Doc, I've got a motel suite for you and the girls near the NASA gate. You're on the twentieth floor of the Quality Inn overlooking NASA. Here's the key. Cindy and Marie's things are already in the suite."

"Jim, that's real service! Won't we have trouble getting Cindy and Marie out the guard gate here?"

"Hell, no, Doc! That's no problem. They both work here at NASA. Show Doc your badges, Girls."

The girls clipped their picture badges onto their blouses, as Richards put his badge on his jacket lapel for the exit through the NASA Houston guard gate. A few minutes later, Atkins pulled into the Quality Inn entrance and let Richards and the girls out. Atkins then said, cheerily, "Doc, I understand from your secretary you've been up since 2 am with the Space Station crisis and all. You'll probably want to go right to bed now. Right?"

"Right, Jim, but I don't think I'll be going to sleep right away!"

The girls chorused, "We certainly hope not!"

Richards added just before Atkins closed the limousine door, "Jim, get the Lear-Gates ready in the morning, in case we have to go to Washington or somewhere tomorrow. You know how these NASA guys like to get the blessing from Headquarters before they do anything."

Jim retorted sarcastically, "Yeah, Doc. They probably call Headquarters to get permission to take a crap. The Lear-Gates is all fuelled ready to go. I've got every conceivable flight plan stored in the area navigation computer memory. You just say where and off we go!"

"OK, Jim. Pick me up at 7:30 am. I've got a 9 o'clock meeting in the Space Operations Center over at NASA tomorrow."

"So long, see you then. Don't do anything tonight I wouldn't do!"

"That gives me a lot of latitude. So long, Jim, and thanks for everything!"

Richards lead the two girls to the gaudily gilded elevator that whizzed them up to the twentieth floor and his two room suite at the end of the hall. While Richards was unpacking and showering, the two girls stripped, showered, and were already waiting in the big queen sized bed when he arrived.

He climbed in between the two nude girls and said, "This is a new experience for me. Two at once!"

Cindy answered, "You just lie back and we'll get the show started.

In the ensuing pleasures, it never crossed Richards' mind that he had not had dinner. It seemed only an instant before the trio fell asleep into a tangled mass of satisfied flesh.

Chapter 3

NASA Houston Crisis Meeting

Richards got up early and checked out of the hotel. He and the two girls were picked up by Jim Atkins in the hotel lobby at 7:30 and driven to NASA Houston, just across the highway. Atkins dropped the two girls off at the building where they worked and proceeded on to the big, white building that housed the Space Operations Control Center and parked the white station wagon in a spot marked UAC in front. Handing the car keys to Richards, he said, "Doc, take these in case you need wheels today. I'll take the bus over to the flight line and polish up the Lear–Gates in case you need to fly anywhere. You know my extension number!"

"OK, Jim. Thanks for the ride. And for Cindy and Marie!"

"I thought you'd like 'em."

Richards carried his small bag and briefcase into the building, wearing his picture badge. The pretty young receptionist smiled recognition and waved him in past the lobby. He took the elevator up to the fourth floor to the large Space Operations Conference Room, just above the Control Center. This building was the nerve center for the control of all NASA space operations. Richards was met at the conference room by Gus Ford, a large, red-headed Texan, who had played football with the Texas Aggies while attending engineering school.

Ford's booming Texas twang rang out, "Hi, Don. Let's go in and figure out how to solve this mess we're in!"

Richards replied confidently, "We've got a pretty thorough plan worked out. I brought along a briefing to present the details!"

"Good! Knew you would. Everyone's waiting. We're video linked to NASA Headquarters and NASA Michoud. We've got a little problem with the external tanks they make down at Michoud. We'll tell you all about it."

Richards and Ford strode into the big conference room, packed with NASA people waiting to hear the plan to save the people in the Space Station orbiting high overhead. The air of excitement was palpable.

Richards handed his view graphs to the projectionist who took them into the room behind the big screen at the end of the conference room. The view graphs were back projected onto the screen, which added an aura of formality to the briefing. There were four huge back projected monitors, two on either side of the view graph screen. A group from NASA Headquarters were seen on the top left screen and a group from NASA Michoud were on the other left hand screen. The commanders of the Space Station and the stranded Columbia Space Shuttle were on one of the right hand screens and the crisis team from Universal Aircraft were on the other screen. Three large TV cameras were looking down on the assembled group to transmit images over the video link to people at other locations participating in the meeting. The idea of video linking all parties together for space program meetings had its origins during the development of the Space Shuttle back in the early 1970's. It had become an institutionalized feature of NASA now, necessary because of the vast number of management and technical people involved in space operations in the 1990's.

Gus Ford introduced Richards by saying, "Folks, this is Dr. Don Richards, VP of the Space Station program for Universal Aircraft out in Orange County, California. As you all know, we have a little problem up at the Space Station. Dr. Richards is going to summarize the problem and present UAC's recommended solution. Don, the floor is yours."

"Thank you, Gus. The problem is Columbia suffered a double failure of the hydraulic power units when Colonel Johnson left the Space Station and selected the re-entry mode. He got warning lights that indicated the failure. Attempting a re-entry of the Shuttle from orbit to Earth is too risky with only a single hydraulic system working. In fact, our simulations show that the shuttle would burn up due to lack of the hydraulic power needed to control the shuttle in the strong cross winds aloft at Mach 4 during the period when the hydraulics take over and other reaction controls, used during the early phases of re-entry, are phased out. In short, Columbia is stuck in space. Repair within the next few months is out of the question. We have expendables for three months – until the end of May. The solution is simple. Get another shuttle mission launched and bring the Columbia crew home. It is also important to take enough expendables up to the Space Station – oxygen, water, food, fuel, etc., to last for another few months –just in case of further problems."

Ford interrupted in his Texas twang, "Don, since we have only one shuttle docking port, you might tell the folks how you will manage having two shuttles at the Space Station at the same time."

"Good point, Gus. The plan is to anchor the Columbia to the Space Station using the tether cable in the cargo bay. That way, the Columbia will be out of the way and the next shuttle can use the docking port."

Dr. Barbara Rosen interrupted from the Space Station video screen, "Don, we tried out the tether yesterday and it works OK. We did note that it increases the Space Station's usage of attitude control fuel, so we re-docked. We'll tether the shuttle again just before the next shuttle arrives. Also, we like the idea of the shuttle connected to the port while it's here. It's like a security blanket, even if it is broke!"

Richards continued his briefing. "We recommend at least two of the remaining shuttles, Atlantis and Discoverer, be readied for launch – one at Cape Canaveral and the other at Vandenberg. We're lucky to have two shuttle launch sites."

Ford broke in, "Don, we have a problem with the next launch. The folks at Michoud can explain it to you."

Jack Kelly spoke up from his video screen, "Dr. Richards, Jack Kelly, here at Michoud. We have some bad news for you. We just discovered a leak in the disposable external tank we had programmed for the next launch at Canaveral. We're not sure whether this is a random failure or a design problem. We can't take any chances. Remember what happened to Challenger back in 1986."

Richards replied with a little impatience showing in his voice, "Well, Jack, what's the next step. We can't have an open ended problem like that."

"I know, Don. We're continuing our tests here at Michoud on a round-the-clock basis. We should have an answer later today. I suggest you and Gus come down here tonight so you can be here to review the test results in the morning. We can decide what the next step is tomorrow."

Ford interjected, "Jack, that sounds like a good idea. Don, let's take that Lear-Gates jet of yours down to New Orleans this evening and meet with the Michoud folks tomorrow."

"OK, Gus. We've got to solve this problem, and fast! We can't afford to let the rescue launch slip beyond our planned launch date of 11 March."

Ford then stated authoritatively, "OK, Jack. Dr. Richards and I will see you in Michoud at 9 am tomorrow."

Now a voice on the NASA Headquarters video screen piped up, "This is Bill Adams at NASA Headquarters here in Washington. When you figure out the problem down at Michoud and get the next launch date figured out, come on back here and brief us in person on the details. The NASA Administrator is getting worried about this problem. He just got a call from the President's Science Advisor saying the President heard the news reports and wants a personal briefing on the problem."

Ford replied, "OK, Bill. We'll come on into Washington after finishing at Michoud. Probably be there Friday morning. Sorry for all the interruptions Dr. Richards. Finish your briefing."

Richards continued with the details of his company's plan and ended with the summary comment, "We have a serious problem, but we do have the resources to solve it. So you folks up at the Space Station, don't worry! We'll get help up there as soon as possible."

A voice came over the speaker from the Space Station video screen, "This is General Jack Robbins, commander of this American colony up here called Space Station. Dr. Richards, on behalf of Dr. Barbara Rosen, my deputy commander, and the rest of the space community up here, I'd like to say that was a mighty fine briefing. Looks like you have a handle on everything, except the external tank problem. Be sure to plug us in tomorrow when you meet at Michoud."

"Thank you, General. We'll keep you fully informed."

Chapter 4

New Orleans

Richards finished his strenuous day of seemingly endless briefings and hectic follow-up meetings with NASA Houston personnel shortly after 4 pm. He went to Ford's office and told his secretary that he was ready to drive Mr. Ford to the flight line for their trip to Michoud. She asked Richards to wait a few minutes until Ford finished a phone call to Washington. Ten minutes later, Ford rushed out of his inner office, saying, "Sorry to keep you waiting, Don, but that was Dr. Bill Adams from NASA Headquarters. He wanted to emphasize that with the President's interest in our problems, the pressure is really building. The President's Science Advisor, Dr. John Davidson, will be in our meeting Friday morning."

In other words, our trip to Washington is firm now. Is that right?"

"Yeah, Don, that's right. Looks like we'll keep that Lear-Gates jet of yours busy."

"That's no problem, Gus. That's why UAC keeps the plane and pilot down here. To support NASA!. We better go. Jim Atkins is waiting at the plane for us."

"OK! It's lucky I keep a bag packed at the office for these unplanned trips. Otherwise, I'd have to wear dirty underwear."

Richards and Ford arrived at the flight line a few minutes before 4:30 pm. Jim Atkins had the aircraft outside the hanger with the auxiliary power unit connected, ready to start the engines. As they approached the plane, Atkins motioned Richards aside and said, "Gee, Doc, I didn't realize you were bringing a NASA wheel like Gus Ford along. I've invited Cindy and Marie to come along. Think it'll be OK? They're in the cabin now."

Richards replied nonchalantly, "Yeah, it'll be OK. I'll explain it to Gus. Since they work at NASA, I don't want to embarrass him."

As they boarded the aircraft, Richards said, "Gus, meet Cindy and Marie. They're going to ride along. You should know they're both NASA employees and also friends of our pilot, Jim. Is it OK?"

Ford eyed the girls enthusiastically and, with a touch of wariness in his voice, remarked, "How could I complain with such beauty aboard? Yes, it's OK. Just make sure they are on annual leave. I don't want them being paid by NASA for being 'sick'."

Cindy piped up, "Don't worry, Mr. Ford. Marie and I got permission from our supervisor to be on annual leave for the rest of the week. Jim's asked me to be his co-pilot. I have a commercial pilot's license. Marie will serve you coffee and drinks during the flight."

Ford replied, "Cindy, you're the best looking pilot I've ever flown with. Marie, I'll take a Jack Daniels Green Label right after take off."

Richards added, "Marie, I'll have a Tanqueray on the rocks, a double."

Meanwhile Atkins had started the engines and was taxiing to the active runway. A few minutes later, they heard the tower say, over the cabin loud speaker, "Lear-Gates one uniform alpha, you are cleared for take-off. Contact departure control on one twenty seven point seven five after reaching one thousand five hundred. So long, Jim."

Atkins answered, "Roger, one uniform alpha. We're rolling. So long, Tim."

Richards reached up and switched off the tower and turned on a classical music tape playing Bruchner's Symphony Number One in A minor. He said to Ford in a relaxed voice. "We've had enough official communication for one day. Let's listen to good music and relax with our drinks during the flight to New Orleans."

"I'll buy that! This is a bad time. This Columbia accident is the first major problem we've had with the shuttle since Challenger blew up shortly after launch in January '86. Boy, Don, you were lucky to be out of NASA then. We had to work around the clock to figure out what went wrong."

Sarcastically, Richards replied, "Yeah, I was lucky. I was working around the clock on the proposal that won the Space

Station contract for Universal Aircraft. I've been on the ole treadmill every since."

"Your work schedule probably contributed to your breaking up with Joannie."

"Yes, Gus. I was never home. Joannie took up with a younger teacher at the school where she worked. I couldn't give her the attention she needed so she got it elsewhere. After our divorce, I moved into a new condo in Irvine and took a new roommate, too. Her name's Dawn, only 26 years old."

Shortly the sleek jet leveled out at their cruise altitude of 41,000 feet. Marie brought the two men their drinks from the bar just behind the pilot's compartment. As she handed them their Irish crystal glasses, she pronounced in the best manner of a stewardess, "Gentlemen, the co-pilot Cindy, informs me our estimated time of arrival at New Orleans Lakefront Airport will be 6:30 pm. We have a 100 knot tail wind!"

"Great!" replied Richards. "We should be at the Marriott Hotel by 7 pm. Lakefront's a lot closer to the city than New Orleans' International Airport.

Marie added, "I have some other good news! New Orleans is in the middle of the Carnival season leading up to Mardi Gras next Tuesday. We should have fun looking at the crowds in their outrageous costumes in the French Quarter tonight!"

Ford interjected, "Sounds great. Let's have dinner at Gallotoire's tonight. We can mix with the Carnival crowds before and after dinner."

Marie replied, "Yes, sir. I'll have the co-pilot phone ahead and make dinner reservations for five at Gallotoire's at 8 pm"

Grinning, Richards said, "That's fine! My mouth is watering for New Orleans food!"

The quintet met in the lobby of the new Orleans Marriott at 7:30 pm. They walked out the hotel entrance on Canal Street, strolled the short distance to Bourbon Street, and were immediately engulfed by the Carnival throng. They marveled at every conceivable costume -- clowns, goddesses, nymphs, men dressed as women, topless women, and a few bottomless men. There was a strong holiday spirit with lots of singing plus small musical bands of costumed groups playing raucous music.

Jim Atkins remarked, "Doc, it's too bad we can't be here for Mardi Gras. If you think this is wild, you should see this street next Tuesday! There'll be public sex acts taking place wherever you look. Really crazy!"

"I get the idea! Here's the street Gallotoire's on. Let's hurry. It's almost eight."

The group entered Gallotoire's in the French Quarter, decorated to remind them of French manners and customs from the exploration days in Louisiana. The menu was extensive and they finally agreed to have French onion soup, fish with a rich, pink sauce, and fried mushrooms and onions. After the main course, in the French fashion, they enjoyed a green salad with sliced avocados and delicately flavored wine-olive oil dressing. They topped off their meal with Kahlua coffee.

Back at the hotel, Cindy and Marie stayed in Richard's room where they had a warm and wonderful reprise of the night before.

Chapter 5

Michoud

Richards and Ford met in the lobby of the New Orleans Marriott at 8 am. Ford greeted Richards brightly, "Good morning, Don. Are you ready to go to Michoud?"

"Good morning, Gus! Here comes Jim with our rental car now. Jim and the girls will take a taxi out to Lakefront Airport and meet us there this afternoon."

Atkins handed Richards the car keys and whispered with a leer, "How were Cindy and Marie last night, Don?"

"They were fabulous, really skilled in their special arts." Richards answered. Then in a more normal tone he continued, "Jim, plan on a 4 pm departure for Washington. We should be back from Michaud by then."

Ford added, with a sparkle in his eye, "Yes, Don, that sounds about right. I called my secretary this morning and she'll make reservations for three rooms at the Capitol Quality Inn."

"Good. Let's head for Michoud."

Richards and Ford strode out of the lobby with their small carry-on suitcases and briefcases. They put their bags in the trunk and drove off for Michoud, north of New Orleans. This was the facility where the large liquid fuel tanks were fabricated. Each tank carried some two million liters of liquid hydrogen and liquid oxygen. These tanks were strapped to the underneath side of a space shuttle at the launch pad and provided the fuel for the launch booster during the first few minutes of flight from the ground into space. After the first boost phase, these fuel tanks were jettisoned and dropped into the ocean and were not recovered. The next phase of boost used two solid propellant rockets which pushed the huge shuttle into orbit. These second rockets had parachutes so they could be recovered and reused. NASA was very sensitive about the safety of the external tanks and the solid propellant rocket engines since the loss of Challenger on the 28th of January 1986. Challenger exploded during boost, some 75 seconds after lift off from Cape Canaveral. Although the post accident investigation could never be completely certain as to what happened, the final report of the investigation stated there was streak of flame from the solid rocket engine – due to a defect – which had ignited the remaining explosive mixture of hydrogen and oxygen in the big tank causing an explosion at 52,000 feet. All seven crew members were lost in that tragic accident. That caused NASA to perform exhaustive testing and investigations.

Richard and Ford had to fight their way through the heavy morning traffic of New Orleans before they arrived at the NASA facility at Michoud about ten minutes to nine. They showed their NASA picture badges to the guard at the entrance gate and were waved into the grounds. They headed for the big headquarters building easily identified by the huge American flag flying outside. Richards pulled into a space marked 'Reserved for Visiting NASA Executives" and parked the car. They retrieved their briefcases and strode into the lobby and onto the elevator, which carried them swiftly to the third floor conference room.

Jack Kelly, Director of the Shuttle External Tanks section, met them at the door and greeted them happily, "We worked all night and we think we've found the problem. There's a small leak due to a defective weld on tank 193. It doesn't appear there is any design defect. Just a random failure in a weld joint. We have a briefing prepared for you."

In one voice, Richards and Ford chorused, "That sounds good."

Ford added warily, "We'd like to see your evidence first before agreeing with your diagnosis."

Jack Kelly called to the projectionist, "Roll 'em, Charlie!"

Kelly went through a 45 minute briefing summarizing the problem of the leak discovered in tank 193, the tests run, the investigation to look for design deficiencies, and the conclusions.

Kelly summarized, "According to our procedures, we have to inspect each and every weld made by the welder whose defective weld was found. That means we have to inspect the welds on all six thanks that are currently in inventory – tanks 193 through 198 – because he worked on all of them!"

Richards interrupted, "But we only need two tanks for next two launches – Atlantis at Canaveral and Discoverer at

Vandenberg. Can't you just inspect the tanks to be used on those two launches?"

Gus Ford answered, "Unfortunately, Don, we can't do that. We have to inspect all six, since we may discover some pattern that indicates a broader problem. This procedure was established after the Challenger accident and we can't by-pass it."

Richards asked with concern showing in his voice, "Jack, I have two questions: first, which two tanks are scheduled for the next launch? And second, how long will it take to inspect all six tanks?"

"To answer the first question, we have tank 194 scheduled for Atlantis at Canaveral and Tank 193 for Discovery at Vandenberg. The answer to your second question is, it will take about two days per tank or twelve days before we can inspect all the welds. We have to use special x-ray inspection equipment to inspect each weld thoroughly."

Richards calculated mentally and they said, "That means the earliest we could launch Atlantis would be the eleventh of March. Right?"

Kelly's answer disappointed Richards, "No, there's another problem. We have to transport the tank to Canaveral by barge. That takes about two days. Then the tanks have to be filled at least three days before launch to make sure they reach thermal equilibrium. That would add five days. The earliest the launch from Canaveral could be made is the 16th of March.

Richards continued probing for a solution, "Why can't we ship tanks 193 and 194 as soon as they're inspected? Then they'll be there in time for an earlier launch?"

"Dr. Richards, the only way we could do that would be to get a procedural exception – Form 287 - signed off by Dr. Adams, the NASA Chief Engineer."

Richards turned to Ford and asked bluntly, "Gus, would you initial the Form 287 asking for the exception?"

Ford coughed nervously and said hesitantly, "Well, Don, that's quite a responsibility to take on. What if something went wrong? That would be the end of my career."

Richards said bluntly, "If we don't rescue those fourteen people stranded in space, you're not going to have a career either! Remember the pressure is building in Washington!"

"OK, Don. I'll initial the Form 287." He turned to Jack Kelly and ordered him, "Prepare the Form 287. I want you to ship tank 193 to Vandenberg as soon as you finish inspecting it. Then ship tank 194 to Canaveral when it has been inspected. We're meeting with Dr. Adams in Washington tomorrow morning. I want to be able to hand him the exception form for him to sign. You be sure the Form 287 is ready for us to take when we leave here this afternoon!"

"OK, sir. I'll have the 287 ready for you by 1:30 this afternoon." Kelly turned to his deputy, Bert Lehr, saying, "Bert, you heard the discussion. Get Form 287 prepared! Give a thorough explanation of why we're requesting the exception: Columbia stranded at the Space Station, need for rescue mission as soon as possible, etcetera!"

"OK, Boss, I understand. Don't worry. The 287 will be ready for you by 1:30 with all the rationale for the exception included."

Richards worked out the schedule mentally: 'Tank 193 testing finished 1 March. Ship to Vandenberg through the Panama Canal. Ten days. That's 11 March. Fill tank with liquid hydrogen and oxygen. Three days, that's 14 March. Two days for count down. That means a 16 March launch for Discovery from Vandenberg, at the earliest.'

He went through the same mental figuring and concluded Atlantis could be launched from Canaveral in Florida on the 11th of March. He shared his mental calculations with the others, "Gentlemen, I figure we can launch Atlantis from the Cape a week from Tuesday, which is the eleventh of March, and then, if necessary, we can launch Discovery from Vandenberg on the 16th of March as a back up. Do you agree, Gus?"

Ford checked the dates mentally and responded, "Yup, that sounds good."

Richards pushed for a decision, "Then, can we commit to those dates at NASA Headquarters tomorrow? That is, if Dr. Adams will sign the 287 form?"

"Yes, if he'll sign, I'll commit to those launch dates!"

"Good!" Richards thought to himself, *the way to get bureaucrats to make a decision is to demonstrate the negative results that will fall on their shoulders if they don't make the decision. Dr. Adams will sign Form 287 because if he doesn't, the rescue launch will be delayed. With the President's Science Advisor in the act, Adams doesn't want any unnecessary delays. There's a lot of pressure from the White House on him and on the NASA Administrator to rescue those people lost in space.*

Richards, Ford, and Kelly broke for a long lunch in the NASA executive dining room. They returned to the conference room shortly before 1:30 and Bert Lehr already had the Form 287 all typed in quintuplicate, ready to take to Washington, DC. Ford ceremoniously wrote his initials in the place that said, "Authorized signature" so that Dr. Adams would know he supported the exception. Richards and Ford each took a hard copy of Jack Kelly's briefing about the external tank problem to put in their briefcases. They took a copy for Dr. Adams as well. They were smiling as they left for the New Orleans Lakefront Airport.

Chapter 6

Washington DC

Richards and Ford arrived back at the flight line at Lakefront Airport just before 3 pm after fighting the extra heavy New Orleans traffic caused by the pre-Mardi Gras celebrations. They found Atkins and the two girls in the executive pilot's lounge watching a movie on TV. Richards told Jim, "We're back a bit early. Let's leave for Washington DC as soon as I turn in the Hertz car."

"Doc, we thought you might be back early. I've already filed our flight plan for Washington National to make sure we get our landing slot. Don't worry about the car. I'll give the line boy a tip to turn it in for you. Just climb aboard."

Richards responded in a friendly tone, "See, Gus, why we keep Jim here? He's super efficient!" He turned to Atkins, "Great, Jim. Here are the car keys."

Cindy bubbled, "I'm looking forward to a night in Washington, DC."

Ford interjected lightly, "The first item there will be dinner at Fort McNair tonight. Dutch, of course. This is their Officer's Club special night – all the lobster you can eat for two dollars! Afterwards they have a dance band."

Cindy added, "The evening sounds fabulous, even if it is Dutch."

Fifteen minutes later they were airborne on their way to Washington National Airport. Shortly after take-off, Richards used the intercom to talk to Atkins in the cockpit. "Jim, when do we get to Washington, DC?"

"Doc, that's the good news. There's a deep low pressure area over Kansas City this afternoon. It's making horrible weather for them but we're going to go like banshees. Our tail wind at our cruise flight level of four-five-oh (or 45,000 feet) will be 150 knots. Our estimated time to National is one hour and fifty minutes. It usually takes two and a half hours. That'll put us there at 5:50. We lose an hour because of the time change, you know."

Ford called over the intercom, "In that case, Jim, have Cindy call ahead and make reservations at the Fort McNair Officer's Club for 7:30. That should give us plenty of time to check in to the Quality Inn."

The quintet arrived at the venerable Fort McNair Officer's Club in Richards' Hertz rental car just before 7:30. Atkins was driving and he let the other four out at the club entrance and then parked the car.

As they were walking to the elegant dining room, Richards thought to himself, *It's a nice 'perk' for US Government executives to be permitted to use the military officer's clubs. You can't beat the service or the price. The food's good, too. This elaborate dinner for five including drinks and champagne will be less than $20. At a public restaurant in Washington, the bill would be at least $250. We wouldn't get 'all the lobster you can eat' either!*

After gorging them selves on Maine lobster and dancing to the live band, the quintet returned to the Quality Inn. Richards agreed to meet Ford in the lobby at 8:30 the next morning before following the two girls into the elevator.

Their tenth floor corner room overlooked the brightly lighted capitol dome. However, they did not spend any time admiring the view. The three ran for the shower, dropping their clothing every which way. Taking turns drying each other off, splashing on cologne and perfume, the trio headed for the king sized waterbed, a Quality Inn feature. They found the undulations of the mattress added to their pleasure. Totally spent, the three fell into a satisfied deep sleep.

Chapter 7

NASA Headquarters

In the morning, Richards asked Jim Atkins to wait at the National Airport to fly Ford and the girls back to Houston in the Lear-Gates jet after their NASA Headquarters meetings. Richards, himself, would fly back on the United Airlines non-stop to Los Angeles. Richards had already said goodbye to the girls, who were sleeping late this morning.

Richards and Ford climbed in their rented Hertz car and Richards drove the short distance, about a mile, from the Quality Inn to NASA Headquarters, which itself was about a half mile down Constitution Avenue from the capitol building.

When they reached the sprawling, six-story NASA Headquarters building, Richards drove into the underground parking lot and parked in a space marked "Reserved for Visiting NASA Executives". The two picked up their briefcases and headed for the elevator. On the sixth floor, they exited the elevator and walked down the hall to the capitol end of the building where they checked with Dr. Adam's secretary and found their meeting was to be held in the NASA Administrator's conference room, adjacent to his office. The secretary asked Richards and Ford to go straight to the conference room. Then she added, "The Administrator is meeting with the President's Science Advisor. They both will be in shortly, and then you may begin your briefing, Dr. Richards."

Richards and Ford thanked the secretary for the information and went into the conference room to get their view graphs and papers ready for the briefing. They were met at the door by Dr. Bill Adams, Chief Engineer of NASA, who reported directly to the Administrator. Dr. Adams spent a great deal of his time on space operations matters so he knew Richards and Ford quite well.

He greeted them with a hearty, "Good to see you, Gus and Don. I hope you have a good solution. Because if you don't we're all going to be in hot water with the White House. Dr. Davidson's meeting with the Administrator right now!"

Richards replied, "Bill, I think we have everything worked out, but, to keep on schedule, you're going to have to sign a Form 287. We're asking for an exception to procedure. We want to ship the external tanks for Atlantis and Discovery before all six tanks have been inspected."

Adams answered with an air of alarm in his voice, "Don, we're treading on touchy ground there. Those procedures were set up after the Challenger accident in 1986. We have to have a damn good reason to take exception. What happens to your schedule if I don't sign?"

Gus Ford broke in, "Bill, that would add about two weeks to Atlantis' launch date. In other words, from 11 March to 26 March."

"That doesn't sound like too bad a date. I just hate to stick my neck out on something as sensitive as the external tank. Remember the pain we went through when we lost Challenger! My predecessor lost his job as a result of that one!"

Richards pursued Adams doggedly, "Bill, my briefing gives a launch date of 11 March for Atlantis. Are you saying you want me to change and say 26 March? That's what it means if you don't sign the Form 287."

"Yes, I guess that's what I'm asking you to do. But, give me the form. I'll take it and keep it anyway. Did you initial it, Gus?"

"Yes, I did, Bill. I support the exception."

"Well, let's hear the briefing – with the later launch dates. That's the way I want it! Don, you can start just as soon as the Administrator and the President's Science Advisor get here. Do you need to change the dates on the charts?"

"No, I didn't have the launch dates written down. I just planned to give the dates verbally."

"Good! Now let's go on inside where the others are waiting."

At that moment the Administrator and the Science Advisor strode into the room. Everyone in the room stood until the Administrator was seated at the head of the conference table, facing the projection screen. The Science Advisor sat on his right hand side. The Administrator nodded recognition of Richards and announced stiffly, "Dr. Richards, you may begin your briefing now."

Richards gave the briefing he had presented in Houston augmented by the details on the external tank problem using charts borrowed from NASA Michoud. He finished by saying, "And, Gentlemen, the planed launch date for the rescue of the stranded crew by Atlantis is Wednesday the 26th of March. The back up launch date is – "

At that moment the President's Science Advisor, red in the face, almost yelled, "Are you telling me, Dr. Richards, that it takes the United States of America a full month to rescue the Columbia crew after the loss in space?"

"Well, yes, Dr. Davidson. That's the way it works out with all of the constraints tied in with the tank problem."

Davidson turned to the Administrator and yelled, his face growing almost purple with rage, "The President will have your balls, Mr. Administrator! You might as well turn in your resignation now. He'll ask for it when I tell him that date!"

Bill Adams rose from his chair and said, soothingly, "Just a minute, Dr. Davidson. Please calm down. NASA has a solution that will advance the launch date to 11 March, a week from Tuesday."

"Well, that's a lot better. We can live with that date. What's your solution?"

"Before the meeting, I asked Gus Ford here to prepare a Form 287. That's a NASA procedures exception form that allows him to authorize the external tanks to be shipped to Canaveral before all the tanks are inspected. That will allow us to meet the earlier launch date."

Davidson turned to Richards and frowned, "Dr. Richards, that's such a logical solution! Why didn't you think of that?"

With a great show of calm, Richards answered, "Sir, we rely upon the expertise of NASA to solve schedule problems like that."

Richards noticed that Adams gave him a grateful but sheepish smile. Then Adams spoke up, "Dr. Davidson, just for the record, would you please sign here where it says 'Authorized by'? It has already been initialed by Mr. Ford. That way you'll get full credit for granting the exception. These procedures we're bypassing were established after the Challenger loss."

"Yes, I remember the Challenger tragedy. I was just finishing my PhD in physics at Caltech that January in 1986. Yes, of course, I'll sign. Give me the form."

Davidson signed with a flourish. Adams carefully avoided initialing the form.

Then Adams said, with authority in his voice, "Dr. Richards, you have the launch date for the rescue. Please prepare the detailed implementations plan and report back to Houston on Monday."

"OK. That makes for a short week end."

The meeting broke up. The Administrator and the Science Advisor were all smiles. Richards heard Davidson say to the Administrator as they were leaving, "The President will be happy to hear about your thorough and timely rescue plan."

As Richards and Ford were leaving the conference room, Adams asked them to join him in his office. As soon as they were inside, Adams closed his door and said apologetically, "Don, thanks for saving my butt in there. That meeting would have been a monumental disaster if you hadn't given me that Form 287. I hope you didn't mind NASA taking credit for the suggestion."

"No, not at all, Bill. You and Gus just remember you *owe me one* at next year's Space Station funding negotiations."

"Yeah, we may allow UAC 5% profit instead of beating you down to 4%."

"You're all heart! You know Universal gets 12% profit on its commercial aircraft business."

"I know, but when you do work for NASA you're doing service for your nation."

"I know, but the stock owners have a hard time understanding our low profits, when it depresses the stock price."

Adams laughed heartily and said, "Such is the disadvantage of our capitalist society!"

Richards called his deputy, Tom Rubin, and asked him to set up a meeting with the crisis team at 9 am Saturday to prepare the rescue implementation plan based upon an 11 March launch date. He explained he had to present the implementation plan to NASA on Monday.

Richards and Ford left NASA Headquarters and headed for National Airport where Richards dropped Ford off at the executive aircraft terminal, within sight of the Lear-Gates jet parked on the ramp. Atkins, Marie and Cindy were waiting in the executive pilot's lounge there. Richards shook hands with Ford and wished him goodbye until Monday. He gave Cindy and Marie each a hug and kiss and whispered to each, 'Until next time'. He told Atkins that he would be in Houston with the implementation plan on Monday.

Then Richards drove alone to Dulles Airport to catch the afternoon non-stop United Airlines flight to Los Angeles. When he called Dawn from Dulles to give her his flight number and arrival time, he promised to take her out to dinner to make up for being gone all week. He passed up dinner and the movie on the trip and instead took a nap to catch up on lost sleep and to re-adjust back to West Coast time.

Richards' flight arrived at the Los Angeles International Airport on time at 7:30 pm. As he left the aircraft, he saw Dawn's bright, shining face waiting for him in the crowd that thronged the passenger exit. He threaded his way through the congestion to where Dawn was standing, he hugged and kissed her and exclaimed, "I really missed you, Darling. Where do you want to go for dinner?"

Dawn cried ecstatically, "You did remember! I thought you would stuff yourself on the steak in first class and weasel out on your promise!"

Laughing, Richards answered, "Of course not! A promise is a promise. How about Chez Cary's in Orange?"

"Oh, wonderful. You know I love Chez Cary's. Let's go. The car is in the lot just across the street."

Richards and Dawn had a sumptuous dinner of steak and lobster with champagne at Chez Cary's. The bill came to well over $100 for the two, and that went on his company credit card. The notation on the back of the dinner receipt said "Dinner with Gus Ford."

When Richards climbed into bed that night he found Dawn's warmth and loving caresses renewed his interest in love making. They fell asleep with their arms wrapped around each other.

Chapter 8

Detailing the Rescue Plan

Richards convened a meeting of the Space Station crisis team at the Universal Aircraft Corporation at 9 am Saturday to work on the details of the plan to rescue the shuttle stranded in space. Video links with NASA Houston and with the orbiting Space Station were connected as the meeting began. Gus Ford and his staff were shown on the Houston video screen. General Jack Robbins and Dr. Barbara Rosen were smiling from the Space Station video screen.

Richards opened the meeting, "Ladies and Gentlemen, yesterday Gus Ford and I met in Washington DC with the top NASA Headquarters officials and with the President's Science Advisor. It was agreed the Atlantis would be launched from Cape Canaveral on Tuesday, March 11. Discovery will serve as the back up and will be ready for launch from Vandenberg five days later, Sunday, March 16. These launch dates required an officially signed Form 287. This exception form permits the external tanks to be shipped to the launch sites as soon as the welds on these two tanks have been inspected and repaired if necessary."

Robbins, on the Space Station screen, interrupted, "Don, what would the launch date have been if the Form 287 hadn't been signed?"

"We saved about two weeks by using the exception form. Otherwise, we would have had to wait until *all* the fabricated tanks had each been tested."

Robbins commented, "Good, that is a more comfortable date for us up here in the Space Station. We were hoping you could launch Atlantis soon!"

Richards continued with his introductory remarks, trying to bring everyone up-to-speed, "The purpose of the meeting today is to work out the detailed rescue implementation plan. I have to take it to NASA Houston Sunday night for a Monday morning meeting there. NASA will review the plan and sign off the approval."

Richards and the various members of the crisis team worked the rest of the day trying to coordinate all the efforts the team members had made during the time Richards had been dashing around the country. They interacted with the key people at NASA Houston and on the Space Station to finish roughing out the plan. Finally, about 5:30 pm Richards called an end-of-the-day meeting with the whole team where they all reviewed the details thoroughly. Richards declared, "I think we've got an excellent workable plan now. Congratulations for the good work! Those souls lost in space are lucky to have a professional team like you supporting them."

Richards turned to the video screens which linked up with NASA Houston and the Space Station orbiting above. He addressed this global-spatial audience in his authoritative baritone voice, " Gus and the team in Houston, General Robbins, Colonel Johnson and Barbara up there in the Space Station: We've just reviewed the detailed rescue plan draft. The crisis team members here at Universal Aircraft will spend tomorrow putting the plan into briefing format. I'll come down to Houston Sunday night and will present the plan – with the blessing of Gus, I hope – to everyone early Monday morning. The bottom line is that everything is clear for a rescue launch from Canaveral on the 11th. The back up launch from Vandenberg is planned for the 16th. The President is in the act, and his Science Advisor, John Davidson, is following our plan closely and reporting daily to the President."

Dr. Rosen broke in and asked, "Don, who comes down and who stays? There won't be room for all fourteen souls to come back on the Atlantis."

"Barbara, I'm glad you brought up that question. I would like to ask that you commanders up there, General Robbins, Colonel Johnson and Dr. Rosen, meet among yourselves and recommend the return crew and the details of the docking and tethering."

General Robbins responded in an authoritative tone, "Thank you, Dr. Richards, for allowing us to have a part in the rescue plan. I hereby delegate Dr. Rosen and Colonel Johnson to work out the Space Station part of the plan. We will transmit our recommendations to you at NASA Houston during the Monday morning meeting."

Richards replied, "Thanks, General Robbins. I appreciate your help. You picked two good people to work up the plan. They can explain your part of the plan directly to Washington during our video teleconference."

With this interchange, the meeting broke up and everyone returned to their respective tasks.

The Space Shuttle was one of the most complex machines ever built by man – until the Space Station was built. The shuttle design was started in the late 1960's when microelectronics were just beginning. As a result, the shuttle technology was primitive compared to that of the new Space Station. The designers tried to design the Space Shuttle to act as a work horse to carry people and material into space, and yet be as safe as a commercial airliner. Just like an airliner, it had no means for the passengers or crew to bail out. In order to achieve a required level of safety and reliability with the relatively old technology, NASA and its industrial team members used redundancy. In simple terms, this meant that elements were replicated, repeated, so if one or two failed, then the remaining elements could perform the mission safely. In most cases, quadruple redundancy was used. For example, there were four (quad) redundant digital computers for the basic software. The four computers used quad redundant sensors (accelerometers, rate gyros, etc.)

Then someone began to worry about the software. What if the software had some obscure fault that was never found during testing? In that case, the software would lock-up and the shuttle couldn't be controlled and would be lost. To solve this potential hazard, a fifth digital computer with a second version of software developed by an independent team was employed.

However, in certain areas, due to carefully considered design compromises, only triple redundant elements were used. Theoretically, with triple redundant elements, the function of the element would be retained even if two of the three elements failed. The hydraulic power elements – the large electric motor driven hydraulic pumps which provided control to the aerodynamic surfaces – were triple redundant. Even through two of the power elements failed, the shuttle should have been able to re-enter Earth's atmosphere from orbit and land safely. After the space shuttle began flying, strong cross winds and shear winds were discovered high in the Earth's atmosphere. It was also discovered that the shuttle hydraulics needed power from at least two power units to assure a safe passage through these high atmospheric levels during re-entry. When two of these units failed as the shuttle began its journey home that precipitated the current emergency on the Space Station. Columbia became *lost in space.*

Dr. Barbara Rosen and Colonel Billie Joe Johnson met in her medium sized deputy commander's cabin to discuss the details of actions and decisions that had to be made on the Space Station in anticipation of Atlantis's rescue on 11 March.

Barbara Rosen had enjoyed a brilliant academic career. She had graduated first in her high school class in Richmond, California. Although she had offers to go to Caltech and MIT for her undergraduate engineering degree, she chose to go to the University of California at Berkeley. That way she could continue her sexual relationships with her three boy friends from Richmond High who also went on to Berkeley. She used sex as an escape from the rigors of her engineering studies during her undergraduate and graduate school studies. By the time she received her PhD at Berkeley in 1982, she had experienced a great many men.

She was an accomplished pilot with an Air Transport Rating and was a member of the 99's, the woman pilot's organization. She won the Powder Puff Derby several times, using the prize money to finance her PhD classes.

Barbara became an astronaut after graduation and was appointed as a co-commander of the Space Shuttle. When NASA asked for astronaut volunteers to man the Space Station in 1986, she immediately volunteered and was selected as deputy commander serving under Commander General Jack Robbins. She was more qualified then Robbins (and he grew to learn this) but the NASA Space Program was still a male dominated club. So she had to be satisfied with playing second fiddle. Robbins' knowledge of Barbara's extreme capabilities was the reason he gave her the tough assignments, like coming up with their part of the rescue plan.

Barbara had not lost her appetite for variety in sexual encounters after joining the astronaut's corps. She had slept with most of the astronauts. Barbara did her most creative thinking after having finished a sexual. It relaxed her body and her mind. She had been very busy since arriving at her Space Station post three months ago, working many 15 to 18 hour shifts, getting the new Space Station initially operational. She had definitely neglected her sex life and as a result, her carnal hunger was growing. Billie Joe was the object of her desire at this moment.

Billie Joe Johnson was an old fashioned astronaut (a pilot with many hours, rather than a scientist or engineer like many of the later astronauts). He had been a major in the US Air Force during Vietnam, flying attack missions over North Vietnam in his F-4 with all those new terminally homing missiles and other electronic gadgets the engineers were always jamming into his overworked fighter craft. He learned how to use them quickly and effectively. He earned the Distinguished Flying Cross for his more than 100 combat missions in 'Nam. He was cited for his expertise in using all those electronic gadgets.

After the Vietnam War ended, Billie Joe became disgusted with the military brass. He felt their constraints had prevented him and his flying buddies from winning the war. As a result of his dissatisfaction, he applied to NASA to become an astronaut, and was accepted. He quickly assumed the role as a commander of the Space Shuttle. He had already flown some ten orbital missions when Columbia failed in orbit. He was a veteran 47 year old astronaut and one of the best in the business. He had been in space on this mission for only eight days, but he was already feeling passionate. Since his divorce three years ago he had been friendly with the young space bunnies who hung around Cape Canaveral and Vandenberg hoping to have 'fun' with real astronauts. Billie Joe had frequently complied with their hopes. He felt a strong physical attraction to Barbara Rosen. He was eager to bury his head in her 42 inch bosom and to find out more about her.

Barbara Rosen started the planning meeting with Billie Joe Johnson by locking the door to her private cabin and turning off the video monitor and intercom. She informed the communications duty officer that she and Colonel Johnson were not to be disturbed for four hours while they worked on the urgent assignment from General Robbins.

She turned to Billie Joe and said, in her authoritative voice as deputy commander, "Let's make love. I can't think clearly until after I've had some fun and games."

"Hooray, Barbara, I thought you would never ask!" he responded as he began pulling off his light weight uniform.

The Space Station consisted of several cylindrical modules which were intended to increase in number as the Space Station evolved over the next decade or so. Currently there were two Habitation Modules, two Laboratory Modules, a Service Module for garbage, toilet waste and expendable storage, a Guidance and Control/Communications Module which acted as a command and control center, and a Docking Module which permitted docking of the Space Shuttle for re-supply missions.

Barbara's cabin was in the Habitation Module farthest from the command center. During the early Space Station design stages, the design engineers had thought about possibly providing artificial gravity by rotating the entire structure, but this idea was dropped when it was discovered the procedure would add a prohibitive amount of weight to the structure. As a result, the Space Station crew and all other objects inside the Station were weightless. This posed a particularly difficult challenge to any potential lovers.

The designers of the Space Station solved one problem – how to keep clothing from floating around the cabin – by providing Velcro bands on all items of clothing plus Velcro clothes hangers. Barbara and Billie Joe were utilizing these Velcro devices as they stripped off their clothes. Otherwise, there would have been underwear, pants, and shirts floating all over the cabin!

Barbara looked at Billie Joe's limp member and said with a laugh, "Billie Joe, your flag's at half mast. I'm going to have to fix that!"

She pushed off the wall opposite to Billie Joe and headed for the member, slowly, like a floating arrow. She missed her mark by a foot, but grabbed it with her extended right hand as she floated by. This caused the two to begin rotating slowly near the center of the cabin. Barbara used Billie Joe's member as a handle and pulled herself closer. Billie Joe maneuvered until he got ahold of one of Barbara's ample breasts. As they moved closer together, they began rotating more rapidly. Both were oblivious to the rotation until they drifted into a corner. Then both reached out to the walls to stop the circling. Billie Joe held them steady by grabbing Barbara's slacks which were connected to the wall by one of the Velcro fasteners. Billie Joe grabbed two of the Velcro fasteners while Barbara managed to brace her body against his by pushing against the wall. After some experimentation, they learned to coordinate their movements in spite of their weightless condition.

As they were floating around the cabin locked in a close embrace, relaxed from their lovemaking, Barbara stated, "Now, that's a lot better. I can think clearly again. Let's get our rescue plan finalized. We can use the computer terminal in the corner to work out the details. By using the graphics capability we can generate the view graphs for tomorrow's meeting with NASA Houston."

Billie Joe looked at her in a questioning way, and then said laughingly, "Doctor Rosen, you're amazing! You're the first woman I ever made love to that wanted to play with a computer terminal after finishing! Usually they want to go to sleep!"

Barbara replied lightly, "Well, this is the first time you were ever lost in space with a sex crazed woman. One that's got to figure out how to get you back down to Earth. Let's get going with the plan."

"OK, Deputy Commander! I hope you're as good at planning as you are at loving!"

"Don't worry! I am!"

The two slithered into their clothes and plunged into their planning task. They reviewed the crew members and decided who would stay and who would return. They devised a time sequence for every action that had to be taken on the Space Station during the rescue. They used a computer program to assign tasks to individual crew members. Three hours after they began the meeting, the plan was complete. It was thorough, professional, and documented in video view graphs that could be transmitted to NASA Houston for the Monday morning meeting.

Barbara called the communications officer. "Joe, you can take the DO NOT DISTURB sign off my quarters now. Colonel

Johnson and I have finished the plan. Inform General Robbins that we are ready to brief him."

"OK, Commander. I'll let the General know. He just called a few minutes ago and said you and the colonel should come to his quarters when your briefing was ready."

Barbara and Billie Joe proceeded to General Robbins' cabin. Barbara stated, "General Robbins, we have a sound, workable plan. If you'll turn on your computer terminal and ask for RESCUEPLN, I'll go through our briefing."

The General turned on his terminal and keyed in the briefing name. The briefing charts were displayed in brilliant colors. Barbara used the voice command mode to tell the computer when to switch to the next briefing chart. At the end, General Robbins smiled and said, "You two do good work! I couldn't have come up with a better plan if I had done it myself!"

Barbara thought to herself with a smirk, *Yes, I know, Robbie. That's why I'm your deputy*, but she said graciously, "Why, thank you, General, but Billie Joe here should get most of the credit. He provided the proper environment for our creative interlude."

General Robbins thought to himself, *This is the most relaxed Barbara has been since we arrived in space. Those two must have had a good roll in the hay!*

Chapter 9

Sunday 2nd March 1992

Richards spent a quiet Sunday with Dawn at their Irvine condominium taking a much needed rest and sunning by the swimming pool. He had been going almost continuously since the beginning of the Space Station crisis a week ago. Dawn rode along as Richards drove to the Universal plant at 3 pm to pick up his briefing charts for the Monday morning meeting at NASA Houston. He was scheduled for the 4 pm Pan Am flight from John Wayne Orange County Airport to Hobby Houston.

Richards drove his sleek, white Dotson sports car through the guard gate where he and Dawn showed their picture badges to the UAC guard who greeted him with a cheery, "Good afternoon, Dr. Richards." Richards parked in front of the lobby and Dawn went with him up to the Space Station conference room. He was met there by Tom Rubin and few other members of the crisis team. Tom quickly flipped through the set of view graphs, projecting them onto the big conference room screen.

Richards commented appreciatively to Tom, "This looks like a good briefing for the rescue plan, Tom. You and the crisis team did a great job! I have to run now or I'll miss my 4 o'clock flight!"

As Richards rose and got ready to leave, Tom interrupted him, "Don, you better take these ten hard copies of the view graphs to give to the NASA people. You know how they've always got to have copies of everything we tell them."

"Thanks, Tom. You think of everything!"

Dawn and Don left quickly and hurried through the big UAC lobby to their car parked just outside. Don drove out the guard gate, managed to merge into the traffic on MacArthur Boulevard and headed north toward the new Orange County airline terminal. He parked in the lot and Dawn went with him into the terminal to see him off.

His flight was called just as they entered the building. Before he went out to board the waiting DC-9, Richards turned and grabbed Dawn and kissed her passionately. He broke away saying, "Darling, the flap is almost over for awhile. We've got the rescue plan all worked out. I'll be back from Houston tomorrow night. Then we can relax for a week until time for the Atlantis launch a week from Tuesday. It's scheduled to go in the early morning of the 11th. I'll take you out to dinner when I get back Monday. I should be on the Pan Am flight from Houston that gets here at 7:30."

OK, Don, Darling. I'll pick you up here tomorrow night. Let's go to EL Torrito's for dinner. I love their good Mexican food!"

"It's a deal! See you then."

Richards rushed out of the terminal and walked through the new jet way to the aircraft. The stewardess showed him to his first class window seat and served him a glass of champagne. He unbuttoned his shirt collar, loosened his tie, took off his shoes and leaned way back in his first class seat. He was completely relaxed by the time the DC-9 became airborne, headed non-stop to Houston.

Jim Atkins met Richards at Hobby Airport with the UAC helicopter. Marie and Cindy were waiting in the back seat. Jim greeted Richards, "Hi, Doc! I thought you'd like a little companionship again this evening. Climb in. The girls say they're ready and waiting!"

Richards laughed, "Jim, I don't know what I'd do without you. You're a hell of a pilot and you really know how to pick the girls!"

Richards clambered into his place in the back seat between Cindy and Marie and greeted each with a passionate kiss.

Cindy said huskily, "Don, we've really missed you."

"I can hardly wait. Jim, get this machine fired up!"

Soon the helicopter sat down at the NASA Houston flight line. Jim drove Richards and the two girls to the nearby Quality Inn using the UAC station wagon waiting on the ramp. As they climbed out of the car, Jim handed Richard the keys to his suite, saying, "Doc, you're already checked into your room. Just go on up. I'll pick you up at 7:30 for your 8 am meeting at NASA."

"So long, Jim. See you at 7:30. Thanks for everything – especially for Cindy and Marie!"

"Only the best for our UAC executives, Doc!"

Richards, Cindy and Marie met Jim in the Quality Inn lobby just after 7:30 Monday morning. Jim dropped the girls off at the NASA building where they worked and then took Richards to the big headquarters building housing the Space Station control center. After making arrangements for Jim to fly him to catch his 6 pm Pan Am flight to Orange County, Richards went up to the conference room.

The room was packed with NASA employees. There were at least 75 people jamming every inch of available space. Richards was always amazed at how many people came to this type of meeting. It was as though they sensed the excitement of the rescue and had come as spectators. Very few in the room would contribute meaningfully to the rescue mission. But they would all receive their NASA salaries while attending the meeting.

Richards glanced up at the multiple TV screens showing the far flung participants in this meeting. Dr. Bill Adams and Dr. John Davidson were on the NASA Headquarters screen. Dr. Barbara Rosen and General Robbins were on the Space Station screen. Tom Rubin and the crisis team were on the screen linked to UAC in California.

Richards strode to the head of the long conference table and was greeted by Gus Ford, "Don, give me your view graphs and I'll give them to the projectionist behind the screen. Get started. Everyone is waiting for your briefing."

"OK, Gus. Here are the view graphs and also ten hard copies. The plan looks good."

He began the briefing, "Lady and Gentlemen, I think we have a feasible rescue plan. Atlantis is scheduled for the rescue launch on Tuesday 11 March from Canaveral. Discovery is scheduled for a back-up launch from Vandenberg on 16 March. I will present the complete plan, except for one part. The details of what is being planned at the Space Station will be presented by Dr. Barbara Rosen. Are you ready with your presentation, Barbara?"

"I sure am, Don. Billie Joe and I prepared the briefing Sunday. General Robbins has approved our part of the rescue plan."

"Great, Barbara. You can give your part right after I finish. My briefing takes just under an hour."

Richards proceeded to lay out the detailed rescue implementation plan. There were a few questions, which he answered crisply. Then the NASA Headquarters video screen responded, "Don, this is John Davidson, the President's Science Advisor. Your plan looks good to me. You have the green light from here. I plan to summarize it to the President later this morning."

"Thanks, John. We just hope everything goes smoothly. OK, Barbara. Let's hear your part of the plan."

Barbara Rosen went through the rescue plan she and Billie Joe had prepared in the seclusion of her cabin. She outlined just how they expected to tether the disabled Columbia while Atlantis was docked. She went through a step by step procedure of the activities on the Space Station from the time of the Atlantis' launch from Canaveral until it departed from the Station for the re-entry into Earth's atmosphere.

At the end of the presentations, the NASA Headquarters chief engineer, Dr. Bill Adams, spoke up in his authoritative voice, "Lady and Gentlemen, the NASA Administrator has authorized me to approve the plan as presented. Let's move out!"

The conference room crowd drifted back to their individual work areas.

Gus Ford motioned for Richards to come over to one side away from the multitude of attendees. Gus asked with concern in his voice, "Don, what do you really think the chances are for a successful rescue?"

Richards reflected carefully and responded slowly, "Well, Gus. I think we're doing everything we can to assure a successful rescue. But remember, these Space Shuttles are tired old birds. They're almost twenty years old now. We have a lot of redundancy in them, but there are still a lot of things that could wear out or break down."

Gus Ford answered, quietly, "Let's just keep our fingers crossed and hope everything goes smoothly. We're running out of assets."

Chapter 10

Launch of Atlantis

Hurrying off the DC-9 at the John Wayne Airport, Richards scanned the waiting crowd just outside the gate. Almost immediately he picked out the face he was searching for. He rushed over to Dawn, kissed her and said excitedly, "Hello, Darling! It's good to be home. I can stay a while now."

"How was your trip to NASA?"

"We got the rescue plan approved and moving. The action is in NASA's hands now."

"Good. Let's go to El Torrito's. I made dinner reservations for 8 pm hoping you'd arrive on time."

"Great. I'm starved for Mexican food and a big Marguerita."

Richards spent a great deal of time during the next week following up on the actions required by the rescue plan. He confirmed that external tank 194 was shipped by barge to Canaveral on time. So the launch date of 11 March looked good. Later, he checked and found that external tank 193 was also shipped on time to the second launch site at Vandenberg in California, so the back up launch date of 16 March was also good. The launch preparations at Canaveral and Vandenberg progressed nicely. Everything looked green for a successful rescue of the stranded astronauts.

Richards joined the UAC crisis team in the UAC control center at 2 am PST Tuesday 11 March 1992. The launch was scheduled for 6 am EST, only an hour away since Canaveral time was three hours later. The count down was progressing smoothly. There was a short hold to check a red light that came on in the main engine warning system. The technicians investigated, concluded it was a minor switching logic error, and the count down continued. Richards talked with Barbara Rosen up on the Space Station, Gus Ford at NASA Houston, and Bill Adams at NASA

Headquarters in Washington. All were anxiously waiting for the launch. Richards and the UAC crisis team were also in contact with the Canaveral launch control center. Everything looked good. Everybody was tense, but pleased with the smooth count down.

At 2:59 am Canaveral announced a planned one minute hold. A minute later, the launch controller announced, "Ten seconds to ignition, 9, 8, 7, 6, 5, 4, 3, 2, 1." He yelled, "We have ignition and lift-off!"

Cries of exhilaration emanated from the various TV monitors and from the UAC crisis team members.

Richards couldn't take his eyes off the TV monitor from Canaveral. The screen was filled by vibrant orange flames and clouds of grey smoke as the liquid propellant boosters of the Space Shuttle roared into action. The huge space ship accelerated into the brilliant blue Florida sky. The launch and boost sequence went smoothly. Seventy five seconds after ignition, the shuttle reached 100,000 feet over the Atlantic Ocean. The liquid propellant tanks fell away and the solid propellant booster engines were ejected and floated down by parachute for recovery and reuse. The main liquid propellant engine provided the final impulse to push the shuttle into an Earth orbit matching the orbit of the Space Station.

Everything was going well with Atlantis' rescue mission. The Space Station crew had anchored Columbia using the tether cable to free up the docking port. Barbara Rosen announced the Atlantis was in sight and only two kilometers away.

The shuttle used the liquid propellant main engine for the trimming maneuvers while in orbit in order to rendezvous with the Space Station. The main engine was also used to retrofire (reduce orbital energy) for the re-entry into the Earth's atmosphere before landing.

Just before Atlantis issued the final impulse from the main engine to begin docking with the Space Station, the commander of Atlantis, Colonel Richard Rogers, reported in a seemingly calm voice, "Mission Control, we seem to have a problem here with the main engine. We've got the same warning light that came on just before launch. I've commanded a main engine impulse for docking and nothing happened. Can you look at the telemeter data and tell me what's wrong?"

"Roger, Atlantis, this is Mission Control. The main engine specialist is now looking at the telemeter data. He should have an answer in three minutes."

"OK, Mission Control. We are stuck here until we can fire the main engine. We can use the reaction jets to maneuver a little, but not two kilometers!"

"Roger, Atlantis, Mission Control reads you. Just stand by for the problem assessment."

The Atlantis carried only a short crew of three to provide more crew space for returning the astronauts now stranded on the Space Station. The tension among the rescue team in the UAC control center grew. Richards looked around the room at the people watching the various TV monitors. The expressions on their faces and in their wide opened eyes showed their growing concern.

Finally, after a seeming eternity, Mission Control came back on the air, "Atlantis, this is Mission Control. Dick, I'm afraid we have some bad news. The telemeter data shows there has been some major damage to the main engine control. Probably an explosion caused by a leak in the liquid oxygen/hydrogen fuel lines. At any rate, your main engine is not operative. Suggest a physical inspection when you get docked to the Space Station."

"Hell, Mission Control! I know it's not operative. We can maneuver closer to the Space Station using our reaction jets, but it'll take a long time."

Barbara Rosen came on the communication net, "Welcome to the neighborhood, Colonel Rogers! Look, Dick, if you can use your reaction jets to get within a kilometer of us, we can send two crew members wearing EVA suits and back packs to pick up your tether cable – you did bring a tether, didn't you?"

"Affirmative, Barbara. We have our tether aboard. I estimate we'll close to one kilometer in about 100,000 seconds. We can increment our velocity about .01 meter per second. That's about 27 minutes."

"Good, Dick. We'll get two of the fellows into their space suits ready to come to meet you. Open the cargo hatch so they can get the tether cable. They'll bring the cable back to the docking module. Then we'll reel you in just like a great, big fish!"

"Sounds great, Barbara. Let's do it!"

Colonel Rogers commanded his navigator to use the Shuttle computers like a calculator to compute the attitude angle and time for firing the reaction jets to close in towards the Space Station. The computations took five minutes. The closing maneuver began. Atlantis crept slowly toward the Space Station.

Meanwhile on the Space Station, two astronauts suited up in the bulky Extra Vehicular Activity (EVA) suits and exited through the pressurized locks in the docking module into the vastness of empty space surrounding the Space Station. Fortunately, it was light for the next 45 minutes so the rescue could occur with the sun shining brightly on Atlantis.

The astronauts maneuvered slowly towards Atlantis using the reaction jets built into their EVA suits. The Earth shuttle crept slowly towards them. Finally they reached each other. The Atlantis crew had opened the huge cargo bay doors and one of the crew, also dressed in an EVA suit, floated waiting in the cargo bay with the free end of the cable in his hand. The other end was firmly attached to Atlantis. The two Space Station astronauts maneuvered themselves into the cargo bay and clumsily shook hands with the Atlantis crew member. They could communicate with each other by using their built-in radio transceivers.

The two Space Station astronauts took the tether cable and started maneuvering back towards their 'home'. The Atlantis crew member reeled out the tether cable as the EVA men worked their way back to the Space Station. It took about an hour and fifteen minutes for them to get their end of the cable all the way to the station where they ran the cable through a pressure lock and attached it to a motorized winch on board the pressurized Space Station.

Barbara Rosen then communicated with Colonel Rogers, "Dick, we've got you all connected to the winch now. Ready to be reeled in?"

"Yep, Barbara. Take it slowly. I've got to maneuver this big mother with the reaction jets to keep the tension on the cable so we don't get tangled."

"OK. We'll reel you in about .02 meters per second. Is that about right?"

"Yeah, that's fine. Figure that'll take about fourteen minutes to get to the docking port."

The reel-in process began and thirty minutes later the Atlantis crew was safely inside the pressurized Space Station enjoying a cup of hot coffee with Barbara Rosen and General Robbins in the officer's mess room.

Meanwhile the two EVA astronauts went through the docking port onto Atlantis and removed the inspection plates to assess the damage to Atlantis' main engines. They reported back an hour later to General Robbins, "General, we inspected the main engine. It appears there was an explosion, Sir. All the main engine controls were badly damaged. Looks like a major repair job is needed before Atlantis can head back toward Earth. Probably take three months after parts and a specialist arrive up here."

Barbara Rosen broke in, "General, we're really up a creek without a paddle now. Seventeen people stranded up here. The new supplies added to what we had before mean we have expendables through August now. I'm sure glad Don Richards insisted the Atlantis carry up three more months of expendables!"

General Robbins formally announced over the communication network to all the interested parties, "This is the Space Station Commander, General Robbins speaking. My crew has just assessed the Atlantis' main engine damage. It's beyond repair here without more parts and a specialist. Better get Discovery launched on the 16th without problems!"

Chapter 11

Back-up Rescue Mission

By the time Atlantis was docked to the Space Station, it was 9 pm California time. Richards was still at the plant. He telephoned his secretary, "June, I'm sorry to bother you at home, but I've got to ask for some help. I'm sure you heard, Atlantis has failed in orbit. I just got a call from Dr. Adams at NASA Headquarters. He wants to review the catch-back launch plans for Discovery first thing in the morning Washington time. That means we have to start at 5 am California time! Would you please call Tom Rubin and the other crisis team members and ask them to be in the main conference room for the 5 am meeting?"

June answered sympathetically, "Oh, Dr. Richards, you've sure had your share of problems recently. Of course, I'll call them. I have their home phone numbers here in my emergency phone book. Don't worry! It sounds like you'll probably have to go to Houston tomorrow after your meeting here. Do you want me to make reservations for you?"

"Thanks, June. You think of everything. Yes, get me a seat on the 11 am Pan Am flight to Houston Hobby. I'll be through with the meeting by then."

"OK, Dr. Richards, and I'll call Jim Atkins to meet you in the company chopper on arrival. You should be getting there at 3 pm., right?"

"Right. Do call Jim. I'll see you in the morning. Thanks again."

Richards strode into the Space Station conference room at 5 am. Tom Rubin and the rest of the crisis team were already seated around the big conference table drinking black coffee and eating donuts that someone had brought in from Winchell's. The TV monitors were on with the video links established with NASA Headquarters in Washington, NASA Houston, and the Space Station orbiting high above.

Richards could tell everyone was tense because two of the available shuttles were stranded in orbit with seventeen people jammed into the Space Station. He began the meeting, "General Robbins, how's everyone up there on the Space Farm?"

"Don, we're all in good shape here, but it's getting a bit crowded. We've already transferred the new expendables you sent up on Atlantis. Now we've got food and fuel to last through August."

"Good, Jack. That takes away some of the worry, doesn't it?"

"Yeah, it sure does, but we're really looking forward to the visit by Discovery on the 16th. Does that launch still look good?"

Richards replied, "I'll let Gus Ford down at Houston answer that one, Jack. How does it look, Gus?"

Gus answered confidently, "Still looks good for a launch on the 16th. I just checked with Vandenberg launch control. They received word that the barge with tank 193 is just off Ensenada heading north. Should be at Vandenberg by sundown tomorrow. That'll keep Discovery's launch on schedule."

Jack Davidson, the President's Science Advisor, interrupted from the NASA Headquarters monitor, "As you might expect, the President is quite upset by the latest Space failure. He's really concerned that the Russians will make a big propaganda campaign out of the US's problems in space."

Richards replied with a sharp edge to his voice, "Dr. Davidson, you should remind the President that even though the Russians launched their Salyut Space Station MIR in 1986, our Space Station is bigger and has newer technology."

"I know, Don. But in these propaganda campaigns the facts don't count. It's what each side can get the media to say that counts. We have to worry about the public relations aspect of this problem."

Richards answered curtly, "Well, John, right now we've got to get our back-up rescue plan detailed. Otherwise, we'll have a real problem, not a public relations problem."

Gus Ford broke into the interchange, "Don, we'd better get on with the meeting. What does the rescue plan look like now?"

Richards took out some handwritten notes he had made and replied calmly and authoritatively, "OK, Lady and Gentlemen. Here's the way it looks to me. There are seventeen souls up on the

Space Station now. We had planned to have a permanent crew of ten remain on the station – that is, when we had three functioning shuttles. Now we're going to have to reduce to a skeleton crew of four to assure that our remaining shuttle can provide adequate re-supply services. That means we'll have to eliminate the six laboratory personnel manning the lab modules until we get some more shuttles in service."

Dr. Davidson interrupted with an agitated voice, "You can't do that! The reason for having the Space Station is for science experiments. If you eliminate the laboratory personnel you eliminate the science!"

Richards replied calmly, "John, I'm afraid we don't have any choice except to reduce to a skeleton crew. And you don't give our astronauts enough credit. They all have enough scientific background to keep the priority experiments going."

Barbara Rosen boomed in from the Space Station video monitor, "You bet your boots, John! Richards is right! We astronauts and even commanders can keep the experiments going. Even with just a skeleton crew."

Davidson, noticeably relieved, said, "Well, good. We're in enough trouble now. We don't want to give the Russians another thing to criticize us for: that we've eliminated science from the Space Station. They've already accused us of using the Space Station for military purposes instead of science."

Barbara added, "John, you should be able to get the White House PR staff to counter that kind of criticism. The Russians know as well as I do what we are doing in our space experiments. Remember, we invited Dr. Chekhov, head of the Russian Shuttle program, to spend a week going through all the Space Station modules before we launched them a couple of years ago. He knows!"

Davidson replied defensively, "Yeah, Barbara, but the Russians are better at propaganda than we are."

"That's hard to believe when I see all the non-sense coming out of Washington!"

Richards interrupted the bickering between Barbara Rosen and John Davidson with a curt, "Let's get back to the real problems at hand – namely, how are we going to get all but the skeleton crew off the station?"

Richards answered his own question by outlining the modified rescue plan, "By leaving four on the station, we've got to ferry thirteen people back. By stripping the shuttle launch crew to the bare minimum – three – it will take three round trips to get the thirteen back if we schedule five people back from space on the first mission and four back on the next two. That will load the shuttle up to near its comfortable capacity on each mission."

General Robbins broke in with a comment and an order, " Don, Barbara and Billie Joe worked out the crew return schedules when we thought we had two functioning shuttles. Now they'll have to re-work the schedule. Barbara and Billie Joe, we need your revised plan within three hours!"

Richards responded, "Jack, that's good. We would like to incorporate your schedule into our overall revised rescue pan. The timing is good."

Gus Ford interjected himself into the discussion, "Don, your rescue plan outline sounds fine. How about putting a little meat on the bones and then high tailing it down here to Houston? I think you should stay over for the launch on Sunday."

Richards replied, "Gus, you've just read my mind! OK, I'll be on the 11 am non-stop to Hobby. Jim is picking me up in the chopper at 3 pm. Should be in your office by 3:30. I'll have my revised plan briefing ready by them."

Richards turned to his chief engineer, Tom Rubin, and said pointedly, "I will have the briefing by then, right?"

"Right, Boss! The charts will be ready, don't worry."

Richards turned back to video, "The meeting's over, Gus. I'll see you in Houston this afternoon. General Robbins, Dr. Adams, we'll keep you informed and fill in the details early tomorrow. Video fax Barbara's charts as soon as they're ready, General."

"OK, Don. We'll transmit the charts as soon as they're done. See you later," replied Robbins.

Bill Adams added, "Don, you see how important your progress is to the folks here in Washington. You heard Dr. Davidson about the President's concern. Good luck with the planning and so long."

Richards and the UAC crisis team started working on the revised rescue plan, updating the outline presented earlier. Thanks to the multi-user word processor connected to the crisis team members' video consoles, the multicolored view graphs detailing the rescue plan were finished by 10 am. Richards had plenty of time to catch the 11 am flight to Houston.

As usual, Jim Atkins had Cindy and Marie with him in the UAC helicopter when he met Richard's flight . Richards took his seat between his lascivious playmates for the short flight to NASA Houston. When they arrived at the flight line, Atkins parked the chopper while everyone else loaded into the company station wagon. Jim dropped Richards off at the headquarters building for his 3:30 meeting with Gus Ford. Jim and the two girls took Richard' small carry-on bag to the nearby Quality Inn to check into his suite. Marie and Cindy would be waiting for Richards after he finished at NASA.

Richards spent the next hour and a half briefing the NASA Houston team in person and the NASA Washington and Space Station personnel by video link. The NASA officials approved the revised plan, including Barbara and Billie Joe's part.

When Richard arrived at his suite in the Quality Inn he found Cindy and Marie in bed watching x-rated movies on TV. He quickly showered and climbed into bed between them. He asked, "Do you two mind if we don't go out to dinner? I'm too tired to eat dinner anyway."

Cindy turned and looked at Richards. Her face broke into a big grin showing her beautiful white teeth contrasting with her dark-skinned face, "Don, Marie and I don't mind missing dinner at all. Besides, if we get hungry later, there's plenty for us all to eat right here in the room's refrigerator bar!"

The trio spent the next hour satisfying their appetites with love making, not food.

Richards spent the next three days at NASA Houston following the details of the preparations for the launch of Discovery from Vandenberg Air Force Base, California.

Everything was proceeding on schedule. The enormous external tank number 193 arrived on time. The defective welds in tank 193 had been repaired before it was put on its barge in the Mississippi River at Michoud and sent on its long voyage through the Panama Canal. The three day count down continued through

Thursday, Friday, and Saturday heading for the scheduled launch at 6 am PST on Sunday, March 16, 1992.

At 5 am Houston time, or 3 am California time, Richards joined Gus Ford and the Mission Control crew in the cavernous NASA Houston control center.   The tension was electric. Everyone realized that Discovery was the last functioning shuttle in the asset inventory.   Columbia and Atlantis were both stranded in space.   The original shuttle, Enterprise, had long since been retired to the Smithsonian Museum in Washington, DC, and, like all the other exhibits there, was no longer operational.

The revised rescue plan required three round trip missions to take necessary repair parts to the floating shuttles and to bring back the thirteen astronauts scheduled for return.   The four remaining skeleton crew members on the Space Station would work on the preliminary steps for fixing the two disabled shuttles in orbit.   The repairs would take about a year because of the complexity of the failed elements.   Meanwhile, Discovery would have to re-supply the Space Station every couple of months as the expendables needed replenishing.

The count down for Discovery continued smoothly.   Even the usual California coastal clouds stayed out to sea.   There were no holds except for the normal scheduled ones.   One minute before launch the Mission Controller announced as usual, "We are entering a scheduled 60 second hold.   When we resume counting it will be 10 seconds to ignition."

To Richards and the others waiting for the launch, the 60 second hold seemed like an eternity.   Finally the Mission Controller announced routinely, "We are resuming the count down: ten, nine, eight, seven, six, five four, three – Oh my God! What happened?"

There was an enormous explosion with fire and pieces of the shuttle spewing into the blue California sky.   Everyone watching was horrified.   Discovery was no more.   The three astronauts on board were vaporized!

Chapter 12

Flight to Washington DC

Most people watching the Discovery launch were numbed by the tragedy. Richards recognized action had to be taken. Alternatives had to be considered. Decisions had to be made. Immediately!

He remembered there was one more US Shuttle on Earth – the original Enterprise which had been donated by NASA to the Smithsonian Museum in Washington, DC, many years ago. He realized it was the last American asset that could be used for the rescue. There were many unknowns though. Would the Smithsonian give it back? How long would it take to refurbish it and get it ready for launch? These questions had to be answered and quickly. Or else they would have to ask for help from the Europeans or the Russians, who both had their versions of the Space Shuttle in early stages of operation.

Richards voiced his thoughts to the shocked and dumbfounded audience on the video monitors, "Ladies and Gentlemen, we've got to come up with a recovery plan quickly. As I see it, there are only three options:

1. Refurbish the Enterprise at the Smithsonian.
2. Ask the Europeans to launch their shuttle, or
3. Ask the Russians to rescue our astronauts with their shuttle."

Bill Adams, from the NASA Headquarters video screen, shot back with unusual decisiveness, "Don, get your ass in that jet of yours and fly from Huston to Washington now. We'll go look at the Enterprise in the museum and check out that alternative pronto! If it looks GO there, then you can check with the folks in Downey and see how long it would take them to get Enterprise ready to launch."

Dr. Davidson broke in, "I like that idea best. I'll tell you now the President wouldn't be happy if we had to ask foreigners for help, especially the Russians! It would be a big embarrassment to his administration."

Barbara yelled over the video link, "To hell with his administration's embarrassment! Let's come up with a rational plan to get us down from here. Ask the devil for help if we have to!"

General Robbins responded in a calm voice, "Yes, I agree with Barbara. We have to consider all three options in an objective fashion. Don, I suggest you task your crisis team to start looking at all three options in parallel."

Gus Ford interrupted, "General Robbins, I agree, but we'll start today with the Enterprise option. The other two will take longer to investigate."

Richards replied in his authoritative baritone voice, "You're right, Jack. We'll study all three options in parallel. But we can have an answer about Enterprise by Tuesday. I would guess that it'll take at least two weeks to tie down answers on the European and Russian options. Bill, I'll leave for Washington National as soon as Jim Atkins can get the Lear-Gates fired up. Figure on an arrival time at 12 noon, about two and a half hours from now."

"OK, Don. I'll meet you at the National Airport executive aircraft terminal at 12 noon. See you then."

Richards called Jim Atkins at the NASA pilot's lounge on the base intercom, "Jim, this is Don Richards. We've got to fly to Washington National. Can you file for an immediate departure? I'll be right there. Gus Ford will drive me over."

"Sure, Doc. I just saw the big explosion on TV. Terrible to lose those three astronauts. I knew them all personally. I figured you'd be going somewhere. One Uniform Alpha is ready when you are!"

Richards turned to Gus Ford, "Will you drive me over to the flight line? You're welcome to come along on the flight, too."

"Yep, Don, I'll drive you. But nope, I better not go." The two started walking toward the elevator. "With the explosion of Discovery, there'll be another big witch hunt! Just like after Challenger blew up in '86. You know how the bureaucracy is. Someone will have to be fired for Discovery blowing up. I want to make sure it's not me. Remember, I initialed the Form 287."

Richards replied, "Yeah, I know about the bureaucracy, Gus. Remember, I used to be a part of it. By the way, I noticed Bill Adams didn't sign or initial the 287. He had John Davidson sign it."

"I noticed the same thing. Bill learned about such things after the Challenger accident. They fired his boss and threatened to fire him, but he somehow escaped. Don't be surprised if the president fires John Davidson when he finds out he signed the 287."

"That is really wild! Here is this guy who has been driving us crazy always reminding us that the information released to the press about our troubles with the shuttles must not reflect badly on the President's administration, and HE may get fired!"

Taking the elevator down to the lobby, the pair hurried out the front door and climbed into Ford's car parked in front. Ford drove as fast as he dared toward the NASA flight line, just a few minutes away. On the way he asked anxiously, "Don, you're going to have to take the lead in studying the three rescue options you outlined. I'll give you whatever support I can and so will Bill Adams. But we're going to be up to our eyeballs in the Discovery investigation."

Richards reflected on Ford's words for a moment, then responded quietly, "Don't worry, Gus. I'll carry the ball. I want to save those seventeen people lost in space! Nobody can help the Discovery crew now. They're gone forever. It's too bad the 'system' spends so much time agonizing over failures. We need to solve the real problem: how to get the Space Station crew home!"

Ford pulled up to the gate at the NASA Houston flight line and both men flashed their picture badges to the NASA guard on duty, who waved them onto the flight ramp. Jim Atkins was standing next to the boarding stairs of the trim, gleaming, white Lear-Gates jet parked near the hanger. He was flanked by Cindy on his right and Marie on his left. Ford drove right up to the jet and parked next to the stairs. He grinned as he said to Richards who was getting out of the right hand seat, "Don, looks like you've got excellent company again for your trip to Washington. I'll set up a meeting at the shuttle integration contractor's plant in Downey, California, next Tuesday for you, me, and Dr. Adams. Seymour Bloomberg's our contact there. He's the shuttle program director. Not very busy any more."

"Great, Gus. That's a big help. Don't let the investigation get you down., Remember, the President's Science Advisor insisted on the Form 287."

"Yeah, I know. That may save my ass! So long, and good luck!"

"OK, Gus. I'll keep you informed. So long."

Richards strode up to the stairway to the jet and stated brusquely, "Let's get it rolling, Jim. Climb aboard, girls, or you may get left behind."

Cindy laughed, "We can't let that happen, Don. I can tell you're up tight over the Discovery accident. You need some loving tonight to make you relax."

Richards grinned and replied, "Cindy, you're probably right. You and Marie are just the pair that can make me relax, too. But first, we've got to get to Washington."

Climbing up the stairs, Richards asked Atkins, "Jim, how about me being co-pilot today instead of Cindy? I have a Commercial License too, you know."

"Yeah, I remember the old Bonanza you used to fly all over. Too bad you had to sell it when you got divorced."

"I miss ole Two Two Seven Eight Zero, but that's what happens when you split up. I couldn't support an airplane, an ex-wife, and a new live-in girl friend."

Cindy said, pouting, "Why, Don! First, you take away my job as co-pilot. Then I find out you have a fulltime girl friend. You white folk sure do discriminate against us black folk. Haven't you heard about the affirmative action laws?"

Richards laughed, patted Cindy on the behind, and stated lightly, "Don't worry, Cindy. I'll give you lots of affirmative action in the ole Washington Quality Inn tonight. Marie, too. I'll show you both I believe in equality for females, black or white!"

Everyone laughed uproariously at this interchange. Jim Atkins slipped into the pilot's seat and Richards adjusted the seat belt and shoulder harness on the co-pilot's side.

Jim said, "Doc, while I'm firing up the engines, you call up the flight plan on the area navigation console. The ID code is 10. And then call clearance delivery for our IFR clearance. I've already filed the flight plan and checked the weather. It's called bravo today."

Richards replied in his best professional pilot tone, "Yes, sir, Captain! Wilco!" He flipped on the flight computer and the navcom radios, tuned the number one communication transceiver to 119.75, the clearance delivery frequency, and spoke into the mike, "Clearance delivery, this is One Uniform Alpha. Requesting clearance for flight plan ten to Washington National."

"Roger, One Uniform Alpha. You're cleared from NASA Houston to Washington National via flight plan route. Contact departure control on 133.25 on reaching one thousand feet. Your initial altitude will be five thousand feet."

"Roger, clearance delivery. Clearance accepted by our flight computer. So long."

Richards turned to Jim and asked, "You ready to taxi now?"

"Yep. Contact ground control and let's roll."

Richard switched to 121.55 and said, "NASA Houston ground, this is One Uniform Alpha, with clearance and weather bravo. Ready to taxi."

"Roger, One Uniform Alpha, you are cleared to runway two one left. Contact the tower on 124.35 when you're ready to take off."

"Roger, NASA ground, will do."

Gently pushing forward on the throttles, Atkins taxied the jet up to the active runway and nodded to Richards that he was ready to take off.

Richards switched to the comm set on 124.35 and said, NASA Houston tower, One Uniform Alpha, ready to roll."

"One Uniform Alpha is cleared for take off. After reaching five hundred feet, turn right to a heading of two four zero degrees. You are now cleared to your cruise flight level of four one zero."

"Roger, NASA tower. We're rolling now."

The sleek jet leapt off the ground after a short ground roll and the indicated airspeed accelerated to 150 knots. They turned right to the assigned heading and Richards switched to their departure control frequency after passing 1000 feet, saying, "Departure control, this is One Uniform Alpha, passing through one thousand feet, with you."

"Roger, One Uniform Alpha. Switch to transponder code 1310 and squawk for positive identification."

"Roger, departure."

Richards looked at the video monitor of the area navigation computer that showed him their route of flight, the aircraft's true course, ground speed and current wind; everything they needed to fly effortlessly to Washington National. Atkins had switched on the autopilot which was coupled to the area navigation computer which issued guidance commands. Richards turned to Atkins who was leaning back in his seat with his hands behind his head, "Jim, you've got everything on this bird! It sure takes the work out of flying."

"Yeah, Doc, you electronic wizards have made it a lot easier and safer for us ole pilots. Not like the good ole days back in the sixties when I first started flying. Then we thought VOR was great!"

After reaching their assigned cruise altitude of 41,000 feet, there was little work to do in the cockpit. The airborne data link sent position reports down to the air traffic control center periodically. The ground data link sent traffic and weather information to Atkins and Richards which was displayed on the video monitor. Richards took advantage of the lull in the work load to call Tom Rubin on the airborne telephone system installed on the Lear-Gates jet. Richards dialed the three digit airborne access code and then the 1-714 area code for Orange County and finally the seven digits of the UAC control center phone. His secretary answered and Richards told her, "Hi, June! I didn't expect to find you in the control center on Sunday morning."

"I came down to watch the launch, Dr. Richards. The explosion was horrible. We're all shaken up here."

"Yes, June, it was terrible. Now, we've got to come up with a way to rescue the people left up on the Space Station. May I speak to Tom Rubin, please?"

Rubin came on the phone, "Where are you, Don? I understood you were flying to Washington this morning to look at the Enterprise."

"Yes, I am. I'm calling you from the company jet. We're at 41,000 feet over Tennessee right now. Tom, you probably heard General Robbins ask us to work on all three options in parallel.

"Yep, I heard. I think you came up with the only three alternatives there are, considering that the US is fresh out of operational shuttle assets!"

"Right, Tom. What I would like you and the crisis team to do is to start the ball rolling on the European and Russian options while I'm pursuing the Enterprise option. We should know by Tuesday if refurbishing the old Enterprise is feasible."

"OK, Don. Where should we start?"

"I want you to do two things: first, contact the program managers for the European and Russian space shuttles. I met them both at last year's International Symposium on Manned Space Exploration in Vienna. Dr. Jacques Dubois at Aerospatiale in Toulouse is in charge of the European shuttle. Professor Dr. Nikolai Chekhov is the program director for the Russian shuttle. He's headquartered in Moscow at the Russian Space Institute headquarters. June has their telephone numbers."

Rubin interrupted, "How should I approach them? It could be sensitive. I heard what President Williamson's Science Advisor said about foreign help."

"Yes, Tom, extremely sensitive. Just emphasize that this is an unofficial contact. That you are just soliciting information to develop rescue options in case the US decides to ask them officially for help. In other words, one engineer to another!"

"OK. That sounds good. What was the second thing?"

"Second, try to collect as much technical information as possible on the European and Russian shuttles from our files and from the various computerized technical library services that we subscribe to. Assess the technical problems of using those shuttles, like:

What interface modules will be needed to allow them to dock at our Space Station?

How many rescued crew members can they carry?

How soon can they be launched?

And so forth."

"OK, Don. We'll start working on the options. Good luck with the Enterprise. When can we get together?"

"Plan on a meeting in the conference room first thing Wednesday morning. I should be through finding out about the Enterprise option by then."

"OK. So long, Don."

"So long, Tom."

Richards turned to Atkins, "Jim, this air to ground phone sure makes a busy executive's life easier."

Atkins looked at Richards, "I don't know about that, Doc. Before we got the phone, you executives could relax when we took off. Now you've got that phone growing out of your ear just like you were in your office."

"You may be right, Jim!"

An hour and a half later, the Lear-Gates jet touched down on the runway at National Airport. Atkins turned off the runway onto the high speed taxiway and pulled up to the executive aircraft terminal. Dr. Bill Adams was standing on the ramp in the bright March noonday sun, waving to them.

Cindy quickly opened the stair door of the jet and Richards rushed out to greet Adams with a cheery, "Hi, Bill! We had a quick flight. Sorry to be here on such a somber occasion."

"Welcome back to Washington, Don. I just got off the phone with John Davidson. He said President Williamson is really upset over the Discovery explosion. He wants a briefing on the rescue options as soon as possible. I guess that really puts you in the hot seat, Don. You've got to get an options briefing together real quick."

Richards looked Adams straight in the eye and said calmly but firmly, "Bill, you handle the Washington scene. I'll come up with the options. But it's going to take time. I don't see how we can present a briefing covering the options before a week from Tuesday at the earliest."

"Well, Don. I'll do my best to hold off the screaming hordes until then. But that's a last ditch date! With President Williamson in the act, the pressure is really escalating!"

"Bill, we'll be working around the clock. I'll commit now to a briefing, and our recommendations on which option to follow, on Tuesday the 25th of March."

"OK, Don. That'll have to do. I've got a meeting set up with the Smithsonian Director at 12:30. He's made arrangements for us to climb all over Enterprise to see what it has and what's missing."

"That'll bring back old memories. Remember, Enterprise first flew during my watch while I was still with NASA Houston."

"Yes, I remember, Don. You were my toughest competitor for the top shuttle job. You won and I lost. After I missed out on that job, I applied for a transfer to NASA Headquarters. Been here ever since."

Richards said in his best professional tone, "Bill, enough of this reminiscing. Let's get over to the museum and Enterprise."

He then turned to Atkins, "Jim, you pick up our rental car and take the girls over to the Quality Inn and get us checked in. I'll ride with Bill to the Smithsonian. And plan on a 7 am departure Monday morning for Orange County. You might as well bring One Uniform Alpha to California for a while. We're going to be flying a lot the next week or so."

"OK, Doc. That's what the ole girl's for – flying fast! And don't worry, I'll take care of Cindy and Marie 'til you get to the motel!"

"I'll bet you will! See you this evening. We'll all go to dinner at the Flagship."

Chapter 13

Smithsonian Enterprise

Richards and Adams climbed into Adams' car and headed away from the National Airport executive terminal at the north end of the field. They came out onto the parkway and crossed the 14th Street Bridge into Washington, DC. They passed by the Treasury Building, turned right onto Constitution Avenue, and proceeded toward the capitol building. They quickly covered the short distance to the big, white Smithsonian Aerospace Museum on their left. They were lucky to find a parking space just across the street. The two entered and turned left, where Adams showed his NASA badge to the guard and told him they had an appointment with the museum director, Dr. Jonathan. The guard pointed the two toward the director's office in the restricted area of the museum.

The pair walked down a long hall to the office and entered the reception area. His door was open and he saw the two visitors approaching. The white haired old man hobbled out and greeted them, "Hello, I'm Dr. Jonathan. You must be Doctors Adams and Richards. I'm terribly distressed by what happened to Discovery this morning. I watched on TV. What a catastrophe! Do you really think you can use Enterprise after all these years sitting in the museum?"

Richards looked the director in the eye and said firmly, "Dr. Jonathan, that's exactly what Doctor Adams and I are here to investigate. You may remember, Sir, that I met you back in the seventies when NASA delivered the Enterprise to the Smithsonian. I was with NASA Houston, then."

"You do look familiar, Dr. Richards, but a bit older. I guess we've all aged a bit since then. Well anyway, the Smithsonian won't be too happy about giving up Enterprise. It's a real crowd pleaser here in the museum. But I guess it's in the national interest to permit it to be used again after all these years."

Richards responded in a friendly tone, "The Smithsonian won't be giving up Enterprise. Let's just say it'll be loaning it back to NASA for a while, that is if we determine it can be readied for flight in time to rescue our astronauts stranded on the Space Station."

"That's well put, Dr. Richards. It will be easier to get the Smithsonian Board of Directors to approve a loan of Enterprise back to NASA rather than giving it back."

"Dr. Jonathan, President Williamson will probably make that decision, not the Smithsonian Board."

"Yes, the President of the United States does have extraordinary powers, the Executive Order, when he chooses to use it. Well, let's get on with your physical examination of Enterprise. My administrative assistant, Ms. Nancee Browne, will take you to the Enterprise. I'll ring her now."

Ms. Browne, a beautiful African American girl about 27 years old, walked briskly into the office a few moments later. The director introduced her, "Ms. Nancee Browne. Doctors Adams and Richards. Nancee, these are the two gentlemen from NASA I told you about. Please give them our total support while they examine Enterprise."

She addressed them in a friendly, helpful tone, "Gentlemen, if you'll follow me please, I'll take you to the Enterprise. I've arranged for two of our maintenance men to remove the access plates so you can climb inside and get a good look at the machinery."

As they were leaving the director's office, Richards asked, "Ms. Browne, do you have an inventory of just what machinery is installed in the Enterprise?"

"Dr. Richards, I anticipated your question when Dr. Jonathan asked me to show you Enterprise this morning. I dug up all the original paperwork pertaining to the gift of the Enterprise to the Smithsonian. I'm sorry but the only description on the paperwork is 'one space shuttle, Enterprise, weight 395,000 pounds.'"

"I was afraid of that! Well, I guess Dr. Adams and I will have to go through and make a manual inventory of the equipment left aboard. It's been a long time since I was involved in the details of the shuttle, but I still remember what subsystems and equipment it had."

Dr. Adams piped up, "Don, I've got a good memory for the equipment details, too. Between the two of us we should do a pretty thorough job of inventorying the installed equipment and subsystems."

Nancee added helpfully, "Gentlemen, you won't have to do the inventory manually. Here's a little electronic gadget that'll automate your job. It's a hand held inventory terminal, just like the inventory clerks use in the supermarkets. You can enter the data using the little keyboard and it goes into the memory. Later we can plug it into a telephone modem connected to our computer and you'll have a print out before you leave."

Walking back down the hall, Richards exclaimed, "Thank God for the wonders of microelectronics. That should be a great help. Nancee, I hope you can stay with us and help with our inventory process since you seem to understand how the gadget works."

"Don't worry, Dr. Jonathan has assigned me full time to help you until you're finished."

The trio reached the elevator. Nancee said to Adams and Richards in her efficient manner, "Gentlemen, we'll take the elevator down to the ground floor where Enterprise is resting. We had originally wanted to suspend Enterprise from the ceiling like the 'Spirit of St. Louis' but the enormous weight ruled that out. Besides, the museum visitors love to go through the cockpit and crew quarters. It makes them feel like astronauts."

The elevator carried them down to the first floor and they walked the short distance to the large space vehicle exhibition. The display featured the early space capsules – Mercury, Gemini, and Apollo but it was dominated by the huge Enterprise.

Approaching the space shuttle they found Nancee had arranged to have a DO NOT ENTER chain barrier around Enterprise to keep the museum visitors out while Richards and Adams were examining the relic. Richards gazed up and remarked wistfully, "Bill, looking at this old bird really brings back fond memories, doesn't it?"

"It sure does, Don. I still remember the big review team my predecessor assembled to make sure Enterprise was ready for the first flight. There were over a hundred people on that review team!"

Richards responded brightly, "I remember that review team well. I think NASA called it the Preflight Audit Team. I was in charge of the Guidance, Navigation, and Control, or GN&C, subteam."

"I remember. And I was in charge of the Thermal Protection System, or TPS, subteam. We found some real problems with those heat protection tiles. They kept falling off!"

"Yeah, your 'fixes' of the TPS tiles delayed the first flight by almost six months. Meanwhile, my GN&C subteam found a problem with the yaw control system. We had to make some changes in the flight software. But adjusting your tile problems gave us plenty of time. No one was really aware of our GN&C problems until we had already corrected them."

Nancee broke in and exclaimed with awe in her voice, "Wow! You two are famous space veterans, aren't you? This is really exciting to be able to help important men like you. It's this kind of assignment that makes my job here at the Smithsonian so rewarding!"

Richards laughed. "We do have a lot of experience, Nancee, but we old timers have a tendency to reminisce when we should be working. Bill, I have the following suggestion. Let's go through the old bird subsystem by subsystem. Let's start with the GN&C system, then the TPS system, and then on through the other subsystems. How does that sound?"

Adams reflected for a moment and then answered enthusiastically, "Don, you were always well organized. That's probably why you beat me out for the top shuttle job at NASA Houston. That sounds like a good approach.."

The pager on Nancee's belt suddenly buzzed. She excused herself and answered the paging telephone. She returned in a moment and announced, "Dr. Adams, someone's on the phone. I explained to him you were really busy on an important task. He almost bit off my head and insisted on interrupting!"

"OK, Nancee. I better answer it. It may be my boss."

Adams hurried off to the phone. He returned in a few minutes and announced to Richards and Nancee, "Oh, damn! The Discovery witch hunt has already started! That was my boss, the NASA Administrator. He said he just got a call from John Davidson. President Williamson has set up a Presidential Investigation Commission to find out who's responsible for the Discovery explosion and the other shuttle failures. I've got to get over to the headquarters building and meet with the administrator to see how we're going to interface with the President's Commission. Don, I guess you're on your own now. I won't be able to go with you to Downey next week either."

Richards replied disgustedly, "What a mess! Just when we need the most experienced people, like you, Bill, to define the options to rescue our people lost in space you get tied up in this witch hunt!"

Adams answered, "Don, don't anguish over this. That's the way Washington and the bureaucracy is now. You remember NASA when it was pioneering in the development of space vehicles and carrying out the exploration of the universe. Now, NASA spends most of its time protecting itself against its critics, most of whom are in the Administration or Congress!"

Nancee, who had overheard the interchange, interrupted soothingly, "Yes, that's right, Dr. Richards. But I'll still be here to help. You just tell me what to do and I'll enter the inventory data into the terminal for you. We can do it."

Richards answered with growing confidence, "OK, Bill, Nancee and I will go on without you. It'll probably take longer now. Hope I can finish by late tomorrow afternoon since I have that meeting in Downey, California, Tuesday morning."

"Don, call me at home tonight and let me know how it's going." Adams handed Don a card with his home phone number. "Don't call before midnight, though. I'll be with the Administrator until quite late."

"So long, and good luck with the witch hunt!"

Richards and Nancee spent the next hours going through the Enterprise and entering data listing what equipments were left in the Shuttle and what was missing."

Finally, about 7 pm, Richard sighed, "Nancee, let's call it a day and start again early Monday morning. With the progress we made today, we should finish by noon tomorrow."

They were standing alone in the Enterprise cockpit. Everyone else had gone. Nancee touched Richards tenderly on the side of his face and said slowly, "Dr. Richards, you look like you need something to take your mind off your problems. Why don't you spend tonight at my apartment? I'm a really good cook. And I can make you feel really relaxed."

Richards thought to himself, *Atkins did say he could take care of Cindy and Marie this evening. They probably won't miss me at all.* Then he said, "Nancee, please call me Don. That's a really thoughtful idea. Yes, I'll be glad to accept your offer. But first, I've got to call my pilot and tell him of my plans."

"Wonderful, Don. I'm looking forward to a night with a famous man like you. You can use the phone on the wall over there to call your pilot. Just dial the access code 9117 to get an outside line."

Richards phoned the Quality Inn and reached his suite. Jim Atkins answered the phone. Don heard giggles in the background. He asked, "Jim, is that you? You sound like you've been running."

"Yeah, Doc. This is ole Jim all right but I haven't been running. I've been busy all afternoon. Cindy and Marie are a wild pair. How in the hell can you keep up with them? When are you coming back for dinner?"

"They are great, aren't they? Jim, that's what I called you about. I won't be coming back for dinner – er – I've got other plans for this evening. Can you keep our friends happy without me?"

"Well, Doc. I've kept them busy all afternoon. I guess after a couple dozen oysters and some lobster for dinner, I can keep them satisfied tonight. What happened? You found some good entertainment?" The leer showed in Atkins' voice.

"Jim your mind's always in a hole! But, yes, I did, and I'll be staying at her apartment. I've got some more work to do at the Smithsonian in the morning. Get One Uniform Alpha ready to depart at noon tomorrow. We'll stop in Houston to pick up Gus Ford and then fly on to John Wayne."

"OK, Doc. The plane will be all set to leave at noon. And don't worry about Cindy and Marie. I'll tell them you had to 'work' all night. Hope you like the new chick!"

"Thanks, Jim. See you at the flight line about noon tomorrow."

Chapter 14

Enterprise Option

Nancee and Richards left the darkened Smithsonian and Nancee used her plastic encoded pass to open the video monitored security door to the parking garage under the building. The pair walked to Nancee's car, a white Fiat Panda. She opened the doors and they both climbed in, with Richards on the passenger side. Her car was the only one in the cavernous garage. Nancee skillfully maneuvered through the light Sunday evening Washington traffic, passing by the White House on her way to Georgia Avenue.

As they passed the President's residence office, Richards thought to himself, *President Williamson is probably back from his week end retreat at Camp David by now. His Presidential Commission to investigate the Discovery disaster and the other shuttle failures will start tomorrow morning with organizational meetings in the old Executive Building Annex of the White House. The Commission's 'Witch Hunt' will start in earnest on Tuesday. The investigation will completely saturate the time of the NASA executives I need to help me organize the rescue of the stranded astronauts. These NASA leaders will be forced to give first priority to their efforts to protect themselves in this 'Who shot Cock Robin' drama that will unfold over the next several weeks and months. Such is the politics of disaster in the US! I'll have to take the initiative to get the rescue organized and underway*, Richards concluded.

Nancee interrupted his thoughts, Don, what is your choice for dinner? Steak or chicken? I have both in the freezer."

"What a wonderful choice. I'll take the chicken. I probably eat too much steak, what with all my travels. My doctor says it raises my uric acid level too high and I'll end up with gout. By the way, where are we headed?"

"I live in an apartment house in Silver Spring near the metro station. During the week I take the metro rather than driving. The

Washington work day traffic is terrible. We'll take the metro in the morning. It's a lot faster than driving!"

Nancee continued heading out Georgia Avenue, a long artery leading from Washington, DC, to the Maryland suburbs, where so many of the Government employees lived. They passed a formerly elegant part of Washington which had been converted into the expanding, run down, Black ghetto of the DC area.

Nancee and Richards reached her high rise apartment house just before 8 pm. She parked her Fiat in the underground garage and they took the elevator to her elegantly furnished apartment on the tenth floor. Richards was carrying a small carry-on bag that doubled as a briefcase for his papers. Nancee put it in the master bedroom which featured a large circular water bed with a mirror on the ceiling. Richards looked at the mirrored ceiling questioningly.

Nancee caught the look and laughed, "You're wondering about the mirror, aren't you?"

"Yes. I've never seen a bedroom like this, except in the luxury hotels in Las Vegas."

"I'll have to admit, Don, I got the idea from staying at the Las Vegas Dunes on my vacation a few years back. As soon as I got my next raise, I had the ceiling mirror installed. I get a real kick out of watching what goes on in here. You'll see later. But now for our food. Let me get our dinner started. Get into something more comfortable."

Richards quickly changed into the sports shirt and running pants he always carried on trips and returned to the living room. He found Nancee had changed into a short, see-through nightgown. She had turned on the Hi Fi which was playing good disco music; it was hooked up to an electronic colored light display.

She said, "Let's dance, Don. I want to feel your body."

Richards answered, "I'd love to dance, but I thought you were cooking dinner?"

Don't worry about dinner. My programmed electronic food console is taking care of everything. I push a few buttons to select the menu and ten minutes later the salad will be served. Then the chicken cacciatore will be served along with champagne. Finally our dessert of fresh strawberries on cheese cake will be placed on the table. All done with automation and my cooking/serving robot. It even clears the table and washes the dishes."

"Wow! I'm impressed. It must have cost a fortune for all that automation."

"Nope, didn't cost a cent. I arranged for General Robotics Corporation to put a display in the Smithsonian. This installation was a gift from the vice president of marketing."

"One of the fringe benefits of being a Washington bureaucrat, right?"

"Right! Now. Let's dance!"

Nancee's athletic body leapt into action in resonance with the music. Her undulating creamy brown figure gleamed in the disco lights that varied with the intensity and frequency of the music. Richards got into synchronism with her movements and felt his member grow as he watched his partner move sensuously to the music. Their dance interlude was interrupted by the synthetic voice of the electronic robot in the cultured accent of an English butler, "Ms. Browne, your salad course is now served. I am serving avocado and lettuce salad with honey-mustard dressing. Will you and your guest please be seated?"

Nancy and Richards stopped their dancing and complied with the robot butler's request. The Hi Fi switched from the disco music and began playing the Hungarian Fantasy by Franz Liszt for piano and orchestra. The pair greatly enjoyed their three course dinner served properly by the robotic servant.

After dinner, Nancee and Richards retired to the bedroom and climbed into the round, undulating waterbed. The Hi Fi switched to soft, smooth music with a quiet but strong beat, to enhance the mood for love making. Richards watched the erotic image of Nancee's creamy brown body in contrast with his pale white skin on the ceiling. Soon they were completely relaxed.

Richards glanced at the glowing, red digits of Nancee's bedside clock and realized it was midnight. He had promised to call Bill Adams. Richards asked, "Mind if I use your phone now?"

"Of course not. After that session you can use anything I've got, Darling!"

Richards dialed Adams at his home. Adams answered and Richards greeted him, "Hi, Bill. Don, here. Hope I didn't wake you."

"Hell, no, Don. I just got back from my meeting with the NASA Administrator. President Williamson has decided to place one of the Deputy Defense Secretaries from Jimmy Carter's administration as Head of the Commission. He's the one that thought NASA should report to the Pentagon rather than be autonomous! Not exactly an objective guy! We spent all evening strategizing on how to counter the attack this bastard will mount! Anyway, how did your assessment of Enterprise go?"

"So far it doesn't look too good. Looks like NASA pretty well stripped Enterprise before they shipped it to the museum. A lot of subsystems and equipment will have to be replaced before she can be made fly-worthy again."

"Did you finish your inventory?"

"Not quite. It'll take another couple of hours in the morning to finish. I should have the inventory print out by 11 am. All the computers are gone and guess what?"

"What else is missing?"

"All three hydraulic power units. That's the subsystem that failed on Columbia. Lots of other big expensive things are gone, too."

"The computers wouldn't be a big problem by themselves, but the lead time on the hydraulic power unit is at least six months. The original vendor hasn't made one since the early 80's."

"I'll report that at the meeting at the shuttle integration contractor's plant in Downey on Tuesday morning. Gus and I are meeting with Sy Bloomberg, the Program Manager."

"Don, you should go to the meeting in Downey, but don't be surprised if Gus Ford can't make it. He may be involved with the Presidential Commission. Remember, he initialed the Form 287!"

"I remember! Good night, Bill. I'll keep you informed!"

"OK, do that. Good night, Don."

The next morning, Nancee and Richards took the metro back to the Smithsonian. Richards completed his equipment inventory of the Enterprise by 10:30 with the efficient, professional help of Nancee. She made the inventory computer print out for him while he phoned Atkins to say he'd be at the airport early. Catching the metro, Richards arrived at the Washington National Airport just after 11 am.

Jim, Cindy and Marie were waiting for him in the executive pilot's lounge. Richards strode in and said to Atkins, "Let's head for Houston." Turning to Cindy, he announced, "You can have the co-pilot's job back. I'm bushed! Inventorying the Enterprise was hard work!"

Jim replied, "OK, Doc. I've already filed the flight plan. They gave us a long departure window today, from 11:15 to 12:15. Let's fire up One Uniform Alpha right now. Maybe we'll get our clearance without having to wait very long."

The group hurried out to the waiting jet and climbed aboard. Jim and Cindy took the pilot and co-pilot seats in the cockpit. Richards and Marie chose the face to face seats on the left side of the main cabin. Richards heard over the cabin speaker, "One Uniform Alpha is cleared to Houston via flight plan route, squawk 1305, contact departure on 132.15 after reaching one thousand feet – "

Richard fell into a deep sleep. He woke up some two and a half hours later when he heard over the cabin speaker, "This is NASA Houston tower. One Uniform Alpha cleared to land, runway two one, wind one eight at two three zero degrees with gusts to two five knots."

"Roger, Houston. One Uniform Alpha."

Richards picked up the intercom mike next to his passenger seat and called the cockpit, "Hey, Jim! I forgot to call Gus Ford and tell him to meet us. He's going to fly to California with us for the meeting in Downey tomorrow."

"No, he ain't, Doc! I called him while you was snoozing. He says he's *up to his ass in alligators*: the Discovery investigation commission! He can't go. He's got to get ready for the witch hunt that starts Wednesday morning. He says keep him informed by video link. And good luck!"

"That's too bad. Guess we'll let Cindy and Marie out and continue to John Wayne."

"Roger, Doc. It'll take about twenty minutes to refuel here. I've already filed an IFR flight plan to John Wayne Airport. It'll take about two hours and twenty minutes from wheels up."

"Good. I'll fly shot gun the rest of the way since you're losing your beautiful co-pilot here."

Jim laughed, "Yep, you're a lot uglier than Cindy, Doc. But you're all I got now."

Two hours and forty five minutes later One Uniform Alpha pulled up to the ramp on the Universal Aircraft flight line at John Wayne Airport, Orange County, California. Dawn was waiting on the ramp, waving happily. It was 3:30 pm, Monday the seventeenth of March, less than forty eight hours after the tragic explosion of Discovery. There were more people involved in the Presidential investigation commission than there were working on the rescue operations trying to get the stranded crew members down from the Space Station.

As Richards left the sleek jet, he turned to Jim and said crisply, Jim, keep One Uniform Alpha ready to go. But tomorrow I need you to fly me in the company chopper to Downey. See you at 7:30 am. Thanks for the flight."

"Roger, Doc. See you in the morning."

Richards rushed down the stairs of the Lear-Gates, grabbed Dawn waiting there, gave her a big hug and a kiss, "Dawn, Darling, I've got to stop by the office for a minute and see Tom Rubin before I can go home. I've got to check on the European and Russian rescue options."

Dawn was a step ahead of him, "Tom's waiting for you in the pilot's lounge. He rode to the flight line with me. He knows you're probably worn out and want to go home early."

"Great. In that case, I'll talk to him there. I'll be quick."

"I hope so. I've really missed you. I can hardly wait to get you home. You haven't been home much lately, you know."

"I'll make up for that tonight, Darling."

Richards rushed into the pilot's lounge and greeted Tom Rubin, "Hi, Tom, Were you able to get anything done on the European and Russian options?"

"Yes, we got a good start. I was able to get in touch with Dr. Dubois in Toulouse and with Professor Dr. Chekhov in Moscow. They both gave their sincere regrets for the Discovery accident. They both pledged to help in any way possible. Dr. Chekhov said he would have to get his government's approval, of course, and that his formal support would require a government to government request. Dr. Dubois said the same thing in fewer words."

"That sounds like good news, Tom! How about technical data on the European and Russian shuttles?"

Our computerized library services spewed out several thousand pages on each shuttle. I've got the crisis team working up a briefing covering each option. They should be ready to brief you Wednesday morning."

"That timing is good, Tom. I'm meeting with Sy Bloomberg over at Downey tomorrow. Let's plan an 8 am meeting Wednesday to review the three rescue options. Be sure and plug in NASA Houston, NASA Headquarters, and the Space Station folks on the video net."

"OK, Don. Will do. See you Wednesday morning."

"See you Wednesday, Tom. I'm going home now. I 'm beat!"

Chapter 15

Downey California Meeting

Richards and Dawn drove up to the UAC flight line just before 7:30 am Tuesday morning. Jim was already in the helicopter waiting and he started up the rotors as the sports car came in sight. Dawn kissed Richards goodbye and left for her job at UAC. He walked briskly to the chopper, ducked as he walked under the whirling blades, and climbed into the right front seat next to Jim, who called out, "Good morning, Doc. Off to Downey!"

"Good morning, Jim. Let's go."

Jim clicked on the mike, called the tower and got permission to depart. They lifted off, crossed the active runways at midfield and turned west-north-west to head for the big space shuttle plant in Downey. They were flying at one thousand feet along one of the low altitude helicopter routes that crisscrossed the Los Angeles basin. To the left Richards admired the blue Pacific Ocean, sparkling in the bright mid-March California sun. Beyond the beach, the blue mountains of Catalina Island, some 25 nautical miles away, were beckoning visitors from the mainland. A few minutes later, just south of the green Whittier hills, they crossed under the approach path to Los Angeles International Airport. Looking east, Richards watched a continuous stream of big jet airliners bringing the early morning rush of travelers to LAX. He knew the chopper was about seven minutes away from the Downey plant, which had been built during World War II by Consolidated-Vultee to build fighter planes used in that war. The plant had long since been transformed into a huge space development and production facility, first for the Apollo capsule and later for the Space Shuttle.

Richards used the air-to-ground telephone in the helicopter to phone Sy Bloomberg at the Downey plant. It was just before 8 am and Sy answered the phone himself, "Sy Bloomberg here."

"Sy, this is Don Richards from UAC. I'll be landing on your helicopter pad in about six minutes."

"Good, Don. The pad's on the roof just above my office. I'll walk up and meet you there with your visitor's badge. My secretary's not in yet."

"Thanks, Sy. See you then."

The shuttle integration plant was in Richards' field of view now. A few moments later the helicopter landed on the roof top helipad. Richards asked Atkins to return for him at 3 pm. Sy Bloomberg rushed out of the waiting room to greet Richards as he came out of the chopper. Richards strode over to Sy, shook hands and said, "Thanks for meeting me, Sy. I spent Sunday and Monday crawling over the old Enterprise."

"Glad to help, Don. That was quite a shock about Discovery. The President's 'boarding party' arrives here Thursday. They're stopping at Houston on the way here."

"I know, Sy. Gus Ford of Houston was planning to come with me today but had to stay to get ready for the Commission's arrival."

Bloomberg said in a positive tone, "Don, let's get down to the shuttle conference room. I've got my technical team assembled there to meet you."

On the way, Sy commented, "Our shuttle organization is down to a skeleton crew of only a thousand people – engineers, logistics staff, clerical staff, maintenance people – everyone! In the old days we had over twenty thousand people here working on the shuttle."

"Sy, I spent a lot of time here at Downey during the development of the shuttle. I was at NASA Houston then."

"Yes, I remember. I was a young engineer working on the flight software in those days. I never met you then. You always met with the *wheels*, not the lowly engineers like I was."

"Sy, I spent my time working on the problems that looked like they might cause a delay in the date scheduled for the first flight of the shuttle. The flight software was never a schedule threat. Some other problems always loomed up and took my attention. Right now my problem is how to rescue the crew members stranded on the Space Station!"

The pair reached the shuttle conference room. It was packed with people. The possibility of refurbishing the space shuttle Enterprise was the first new activity for the aging space shuttle team in several years. The staff was excited over the prospect of this new work. At the same time, however, everyone on the Downey shuttle team was anticipating that the Discovery Accident Investigation Commission was about to descend upon them. Many of them still remembered the travail they went through in 1986 from the Challenger Investigation Committee. They expected the Discovery's commission to be even more acrimonious and disruptive than the Challenger's commission had been.

The large group grew quiet as Bloomberg lead Richards to the front of the conference room. Bloomberg opened the meeting by addressing the audience in a slow, but clearly authoritative voice, "Ladies and Gentlemen, this is Dr. Don Richards from our big competitor over in Irvine, Universal Aircraft. Dr. Richards is vice president of the Space Station section. You remember the big contract we lost! Anyway, Don is here, with the blessing of NASA, to investigate the feasibility of refurbishing the old Enterprise, now in the Smithsonian Museum in Washington in order to rescue our astronauts stranded on the Space Station. As you all know, with Columbia and Atlantis stuck in space and with Discovery now gone, Enterprise is the last US shuttle left on Earth. It's too bad the US Government spent all the funds on Star Wars instead of building a few more shuttles. Then we wouldn't be in this mess!

Richards interrupted, "Sy, that's a little unfair. The Government was worried about the Russian threat of a first nuclear strike using the big ICBM fleet they built up during the 70's and early 80's. The Government also thought the Strategic Defense Initiative would help develop American technology. They didn't realize focusing so many resources on SDI would dilute the US commercial technological developments and reduce the US to third in commercial technology products, behind Japan and the European Economic Community."

Sy responded sadly, "I know the Government had good intentions – the road to hell is paved with good intentions! But enough of the politics of technology. Let's get back to the crisis at hand. I've got the video links set up with the major shuttle sub-contractors."

Richards scanned the wall of the conference room where there were ten video screens, each displaying the smiling face of a shuttle equipment program manager who was attending the meeting by video link.

"I have requested each sub-contractor to provide us, over the shuttle information data link, their best schedule for providing the equipments and subsystems you found were missing during your inventory of Enterprise.

Richards interrupted Bloomberg again, "Sy, here is the inventory list printed out."

Bloomberg took the list and handed it to an assistant who placed it in front of a video camera. Bloomberg then continued with his introductory remarks, "Now, you all have the list on your video screens. Don, the shuttle team will do its best to give you our best schedule for refurbishing the Enterprise and readying it for launch. I must be honest with you though – it's going to be a big job. We believe the long pole in the tent will be the amount of time needed before the missing subsystems can be delivered. Remember, some of this equipment hasn't been built for over ten years. No one has kept an assembly line waiting over a decade for an order! OK, Don, you can have the floor now."

Richards stood before the conference room packed with more than a hundred attendees. There were another hundred members of the audience via the video link to the shuttle subcontractors. Richards addressed this large group, speaking slowly for emphasis, "Ladies and Gentlemen, thank you for attending this meeting. The US space programs is at a crucial cross roads. We have seventeen American astronauts lost in space along with two space shuttles stranded up there. As you know, we lost Discovery Sunday. We've only got three options to rescue these astronauts: refurbish and launch Enterprise; ask the Europeans to launch their shuttle; or have the Russians rescue the Americans with their shuttle. I might add, President Williamson wants an American solution. He doesn't want to ask foreigners to help. As program manager of the Space Station, I feel responsible to objectively consider all options – that includes the US option using Enterprise plus the two foreign options. I need your help in investigating the feasibility of using Enterprise. I hope you can have an answer for me soon."

Bloomberg stood and addressed the audience, "Everyone has heard Dr. Richards. I want a schedule for the launch of Enterprise complete with a detailed pert chart no later than Friday. That means a lot of uncompensated overtime for everyone."

Bloomberg sat down next to Richards and said quietly to him, so no one else could hear, "Don, I'm going to give you an unofficial assessment before you go today. What time do you have to leave?"

"I've got the helicopter picking me up at 3 this afternoon."

Bloomberg stood again and spoke to the audience, "I've asked my deputy to provide a briefing detailing all the things we believe must be done to refurbish and launch Enterprise. It's a briefing we prepared for NASA about a year ago. It was a theoretical exercise for NASA's budget planning purposes and we didn't actually assess what items of equipment were still on Enterprise. We just assumed a hollow hull and listed the equipment needed. It's not a close fit but at least it's in the ball park. The briefing is quite long. It takes at least a couple of hours."

Sy turned to his deputy, "Larry, let's get started."

Richards listened to the detailed briefing that droned on for over two hours. It provided a lot of information about what needed to be done, but didn't answer the key question – *when could it be finished?"*

When the briefing finally ended, Bloomberg invited Richards to lunch in the shuttle plant's executive dining room. They were served an exquisite repast by a waiter in a tuxedo. They started with a fresh spinach salad with hot bacon dressing followed by a main course of charcoal broiled filet mignon with Bordelaise sauce. They were served three separate French wines with the courses. Dessert was a festive flaming cherries jubilee followed by Kahlua coffee. This lunch was one of the 'perks' of the aerospace executives. The cost was incorporated into the negotiated G&A rate reimbursement paid to the company by the US Government. The banquet was free to the executives. Aerospace companies were not permitted by law to *entertain* government employees or members of the military. Richards recognized a NASA Houston manager at a nearby table. A three star general from the USAF Space Division in El Segundo sat at another table. The executive dining room was not considered 'entertainment' according to the US Government accounting rules. Besides, there was a box at the door for the Government employee or military officer to pay for his lunch if he had a twinge of conscience. Richards noticed the three star general slip a one dollar bill into the box as he left the dining room..

After the long lunch, Richards returned to the shuttle conference room with Bloomberg where the Enterprise refurbishment assessment team was busily working, trying to determine how soon the Enterprise could be launched. Bloomberg excused himself and Richards watched him walk around the room, stopping to chat with various team members, to look at charts they had prepared, to talk with various program managers on the video links, etc. Meanwhile, Richards reviewed the hard copy of the briefing that had been presented to him earlier.

The clock ticked on to twenty minutes to three, when the helicopter was scheduled to pick him up. Richards was beginning to feel a little left out of the activities going on in small groups around the conference room, when Bloomberg approached him apologetically and explained, "Sorry to leave you sitting there alone, Don, but I wanted to get a personal feeling for how the assessment is going."

Richards asked anxiously, "And, how does it look?"

Sy looked straight into Richards' eyes and said quietly, so no one else could overhear, "Look, Don, I'm going to be straight with you. What I'm going to tell you is un-official. I've got to get approval from our senior management before I can give you our official answer. As one program manager to another, there's not a chance in hell we can refurbish and launch Enterprise before next January, nine months from now. It will take eight and a half months to get the hydraulic power units alone! Sorry, Don! You're going to have to select one of the foreign options!"

Chapter 16

European Option

Richards strode into the Space Station conference room just before 8 am on Wednesday, 19 March 1992. Tom Rubin and the crisis team were assembled waiting to start the meeting.

Tom rushed up and blurted, "Don, I hear that Downey can't get Enterprise ready before next January. Is that what you discovered?"

"Well, Tom, that's unofficial. We're supposed to get Downey's official position Friday. But yes, that's how it looks. How did you hear?"

"I've got a good spy from Downey. She's Sy Bloomberg's secretary and my live-in girl friend. She called me late yesterday afternoon and gave me the date Bloomberg put in a memo to his boss."

"You do have a good information source. I'm afraid we're going to have to choose one of the foreign options since the American option is out. Which looks best, the European or the Russian option?"

"I'd rather not say until after you've heard our briefings covering the two foreign options. I'd like to hear what you think after you've seen all the data."

Richards looked at Tom questioningly, then broke into a laugh, "OK, Tom, Let's have the briefings. Hope you're not becoming a yes man, though."

"Don't worry, Don. I'm not. I wrote you a memo with my recommendation. It's in this sealed envelope. Here!" Tom held out the envelope and added, "I just didn't want to influence you before you had heard all the facts. After all, you're going to have to stand up in Washington next week and tell all those big shots what we ought to do!"

They were interrupted by the ring of the conference room phone. A secretary answered it and put the caller on hold while she walked over to Richards, "Dr. Richards, the phone is for you. I tried to tell him you were very busy but he claims to be the President's Science Advisor, a Doctor Davidson – "

"OK, Donna, I'll take the call." He put the receiver to his ear, "John, I told you I would come to Washington and give our recommendations on what rescue option – "

Davidson interrupted with a quaver in his voice, "Please, Don. That's not what I called about! William Wiley, the Chairman of President Williamson's Discovery Commission just found out I signed the Form 287. He wants the President to fire me! He says the explosion would never have happened if we hadn't taken – I'm quoting him now – all those short cuts and exceptions!"

Suddenly Richards felt a deep sympathy for John Davidson. Before this call, he had felt Davidson was smug and over-confident. But now he understood that if Davidson was fired for signing the Form 287, his career was finished, forever!"

"Look, John. You did the right thing in signing that Form 287. I fully supported the exception. In fact, I originally suggested it as a way to launch Atlantis and Discovery earlier."

"Did you really, Don? I feel better already. Can you help me?"

"Damn right, John, I'll help. I'll call Bill Wiley and tell him who really pushed the Form 287. If anyone should be fired, it's me. Give me his phone number and I'll call him right away."

Davidson supplied the phone number and added, "But you can't reach Mr. Wiley until after 5 pm Houston time. He's flying to NASA Houston to meet with Gus Ford. He found out Gus had initialed the Form 287. He's convinced he's uncovered the reason for Discovery's explosion: short cuts and exceptions!"

"OK, John. Try not to worry. I'll call Wiley in Houston. That's 3 pm California time. See you next Tuesday in Washington."

"OK, if I haven't been fired by then!"

"Don't worry, John. You're not going to be fired. I repeat, you did the right thing!"

"Thanks, Don. I feel a lot better already."

Richards returned to his meeting to review the two foreign options. He was given a comprehensive two hour presentation. At the end, it was apparent to him the Russian option carried the fewest risks and had definite advantages. The Russian shuttle design was more mature than the European shuttle. The Russian shuttle used older technology but it was designed in the staid, conservative fashion the Russians had made a hallmark in their space program. It was somewhat bigger than the European shuttle and therefore could carry more crew members. That might reduce the number of rescue missions needed to bring back all the astronauts.

Richards turned to Rubin, "Tom, I've come to my conclusion already as to which option to select. I believe we should go with the Russian option. Now, what did you recommend?"

Tom broke into a wide grain, "Open the envelope and read my memo!"

Richards tore open the envelope and read the title: 'Rationale for Recommending the Russian Option'. He scanned the one page memo and saw Tom had emphasized most of the same points Richards had noted from the briefing.

Richards glanced up, smiled at Tom, "I guess we're in agreement. The Russian option is it! But, we need to go into a lot more detail on the rationale. Your one page memo won't be enough to convince the folks in Washington. I need a one hour briefing. It's got to be good and crisp!"

Ruben stopped him and said quietly, "Don, there's one more US option we should present."

"And what's that?"

"We could use the USAF satellite launcher to boost repair kits up to the Space Station to fix Atlantis and Columbia in space."

"Tom, that's good creative thinking! You've come up with another logical American option. I'll tell you now though, it suffers from the same problem as refurbishing the Enterprise."

Tom looked surprised, "What's that?"

"The components to go into the repair kits will take too long to make. They're mostly the same components that Enterprise needs. We better include the option in our briefing though. Otherwise some smart ass in the audience will say, 'Why didn't you think of this?'

Richards' secretary buzzed him in his office and said, "Dr. Richards, I've got Mr. William Wiley on the phone."

Richards picked up his phone, "Mr. Wiley, this is Don Richards out at Universal Aircraft in California."

Wiley replied with a condescending air, "I tried to explain to your secretary that I'm very busy, but she insisted you had some very important information about the Discovery tragedy."

"Yes, I do, Mr. Wiley. I understand you have identified as a problem the Exception Form 287 which was executed to permit the early launch of Atlantis and Discovery."

"Right, Dr. Richards. I'm convinced the short cuts and exceptions allowed by that Form 287 contributed directly to the tragic explosion of Discovery. I believe in personal accountability! I'm going to recommend to President Williamson that he fire the people responsible for executing that form."

"In that case, you'll have to have him fire me. I'm responsible for having the Form 287 signed."

"But, you work for a private company. He can't fire you. Besides, John Davidson and Gus Ford signed the form. They're civil servants. He can fire them!"

"Mr. Wiley, aren't you interested in why the Form 287 was executed in the first place? I thought you were charged with conducting an objective investigation into what caused the Discovery explosion."

"Of course I'm interested and, of course, my commission is going to be objective in their findings and recommendations. Do you have some information we haven't considered yet?"

"Mr. Wiley, I can give you a perspective that perhaps you don't have. I'm responsible for devising and carrying out a rescue plan for the seventeen Americans stranded up on the Space Station. They have a limited supply of food, fuel, and oxygen up there. If we don't get a rescue mission up there they are all going to die in space, in front of the whole world, just like the Discovery explosion!"

Wiley interrupted Richards and said in a sarcastic tome, "Yes, yes, Dr. Richards. I know all about the people stranded up on the Space Station. My commission is charged by the President to find out why the Atlantis and Columbia failed in space, too! But, what has the Form 287 got to do with that?"

Richards responded coolly and logically, "Everything, Mr. Wiley. We saved two weeks in launching the Atlantis by executing the Form 287. Atlantis failed in space, but nevertheless it carried enough expendables up to guarantee survival of those Americans until the end of August. Without those additional supplies, the Space Station would have run out of oxygen in May. There's not an icicle's chance in Hades that we can get any kind of rescue operation up there by that date. The early launch of Atlantis saved those people. Are you sure you want to ask the President to fire the people who signed the Form 287 and made the survival of those people in space possible?"

There was a long silence at the other end of the line. Wiley finally responded in a halting voice, "Dr. Richards, when you put it that way, I can see the Form 287 in a different light now. Maybe I was a little over-enthusiastic on that point. Remember, I've only had this job for three days. You've been thinking about this problem for a long time."

Richards replied in a demanding voice, "Mr. Wiley, are you going to drop your request to have Davidson and Ford fired?"

"Er – er – why, yes, Dr. Richards. I am going to drop that request, at least for the time being. You've presented me with information I didn't have. Thank you."

Richards, feeling like he had won a major point, continued to press on with his attack, "And, Mr. Wiley, one other point – I hope your commission doesn't disrupt the time of key NASA people like Bill Adams and Gus Ford. We need them to help devise a successful rescue plan to save those seventeen stranded astronauts. You wouldn't want the media to get the idea you're interfering with the rescue plans, would you?"

"Of course not, Dr. Richards. Don't worry, I have your message."

"Nice talking to you, Mr. Wiley. Goodbye."

"Goodbye, Dr. Richards, and thank you for the additional information!"

Richards and the crisis team established an around the clock schedule to develop the three rescue options in detail. The advantages and disadvantages of each option were laid out in comparison charts. The final output of this extensive effort would be a two hour briefing that Richards would present to NASA Houston on Monday. A one hour version would be prepared for

NASA Headquarters personnel in Washington. In addition, Richards planned to pick out a fifteen minute executive summary of the briefing. He had in mind that John Davidson could use the executive summary to brief President Williamson on the options, if need be.

Richards was in the Space Station conference room with the crisis team reviewing the first draft of the two hour briefing when his secretary came in and slipped him a note.

He read, 'Dr. Richards, Mr. Moore wants to see you in his office right away. (signed) June.'

Richards turned to Tom Rubin and whispered, "The boss wants to see me right away. When the president calls, I have to jump. I'll be back as soon as possible. Continue with the review."

"OK, Don. Good luck! Hope you're not in trouble with the old man!"

"Me, too!"

Richards left the darkened conference room as the view graphs were being projected on the screen in the front of the room. When they reached the hall outside, June said with a concerned note in her voice, "I explained to Mr. Moore's secretary, Janice, that you were busy reviewing the rescue options briefing for NASA. She said Mr. Moore was really upset about something and that you better come up right away."

Richards responded calmly, "June, I think I know what he wants. Bill Wiley probably called him and asked him to fire me."

"You mean the Mr. Wiley you had me call for you in Houston Wednesday?"

"Yes. That's him."

"Why in the world would he want to get you fired, Dr. Richards?"

"Simple. He's vindictive! He didn't like my pointing out his stupidity."

June knew her boss well enough not to press him any further and she simply said, "Good luck, Dr. Richards. Call if I can help with anything."

"Don't worry, June. I'm not going to be fired."

Richards took the elevator to the top floor where the president of Universal Aircraft's huge executive office suite was located. His office staff included three secretaries (all looked like

Hollywood starlets) and three administrative assistants. His office overlooked the magnificent panorama of Newport Harbor and its multimillion dollar homes and boats, with the blue Pacific beyond.

David Moore was the chief operating officer of the vast empire of Universal Aircraft Corporation, responsible for sales of five-billion dollars per year and some fifty thousand employees. He and Richards were very close. Moore had convinced Richards to leave NASA and join UAC back in the early 80's. His belief that Richards was a winner was confirmed when Richards won the multi-billion dollar contract for the Space Station for UAC. This one contract contributed about 20% of UAC's gross sales per year. And, although it only contributed 8% of UAC's operating profits, it paid for 40% of the corporate G&A expenses and 35% of the overhead. Richards was truly an executive star of UAC, a team member that Moore could always count on. So it is with some trepidation and sadness that he had called Richards on the carpet this morning. William Wiley had called Moore a few minutes earlier, quite agitatedly, and had said that Moore had better fire Richards or else UAC would lose its Space Station contract. A chief operating officer, Moore knew UAC couldn't survive a cancellation of the Space Station contract. No matter how much he liked Richards, the survival of UAC was more important than his friendship with Richards or Richards' job.

Richards strode into Moore's office and said, smiling broadly, "What's up, Dave? I understand you want to see me right away."

Moore rose from his desk chair with a grim expression on his face and walked around to where Richards was standing in front of his desk.. Putting his hand on Richards' shoulder, he said sadly, "Don, it looks like I'm going to have to fire you."

Richards laughed lightly, "I see you got a phone call from Bill Wiley."

Moore looked surprised, "Right. How did you know?"

"And, he said if you didn't fire me, UAC would lose the Space Station contract. Right?"

"Why, yes. But how in the world did you know?"

Richards looked sternly at Moore and said authoritatively, "I didn't know, Dave. But I do know how ass holes like Wiley operate. He's a know-nothing phony but he knows how to use fear, how to take advantage of the power of a Presidential appointment."

With alarm growing in his voice, Moore asked, "What do you mean, *fear*?"

"Dave, I guess I should have told you. I talked to Wiley Wednesday afternoon just after he got to Houston on his witch hunt. He was going to have Dr. Davidson, the President's Science Advisor, and Gus Ford of NASA Houston both fired."

Moore interrupted to ask, "But, why, Don?"

"Because Davidson and Ford initialed the Form 287. This is the exception form that allowed us to launch Atlantis two weeks sooner than without the form."

"That sounds like it was a good idea to me. We were all really worried about the survival of the Space Station crew with their expendables running out and all."

"Right. I told Wiley he shouldn't have Davidson and Ford fired and that he should have me kicked out instead because I was the one who had insisted that the Form 287 be signed to permit the earlier launch."

"I guess he took your advice. Don, we can't afford to lose that contract."

Richards said soothingly, "Of course, we can't. But if you do fire me, this victory will allow Wiley to run roughshod over all of NASA, keeping the key employees busy answering his questions. They won't have time to concentrate on the rescue activities and that will seriously interfere with our rescue efforts. The astronauts will be lost in space. Then you really will lose the Space Station contract!"

A determined look came over Moore's face and he stated defiantly, "You're absolutely right! Let's fight this bastard. You have an idea how we can do it?"

"Simple. Let's bring forth the facts of why Discovery really blew up on the launch pad. It wasn't because of the Form 287. You can be sure of that!"

Moore questioned, "And how do we do that?"

"I don't know yet, but give me a little time. I'll get the facts. That is, if you don't fire me!"

Moore laughed, "Don't worry, Don. I'm not going to do that. I'll have to admit, Wiley panicked me with his phone call. But you brought me back to reality."

Richards stated confidently, "Well, Boss, if you'll excuse me now, I've got two urgent matters to attend to. Figure out how to rescue the astronauts and find out what happened to Discovery!"

"Good luck, Don. I'm, behind you all the way!"

Chapter 17

Discovery

Richards returned to his seat next to Tom Rubin in the darkened conference room and whispered in Tom's ear, ""How's the briefing going?"

Tom whispered back, "A little rough in spots, but it looks pretty good. We'll spend all day tomorrow, Saturday, cleaning up the charts so they'll be ready for you to take Sunday. But, what did the boss want?"

Richard chuckled softly and answered quietly, "He wanted to fire me, but I talked him out of it."

In a loud voice, startling the other people in the room, Tom exclaimed, "He what?"

Richards put his finger to his lips, "Shhh – Don't worry. It's OK. I just have to find out what made Discovery explode!"

"Oh! Is that all! You and the other hundred people on the President's Commission!"

After the last chart had been flashed on the screen, Richards asked for the room lights to be turned on. He stood up and addressed the crisis team, "I'm pleased with what I've seen of the rescue options briefing. I know we've got a little polishing work to do but the briefing is sound and logical. I have a list of notes Tom and I made about the charts that we think need changing. Since this is Friday, let's get these charts cleaned up today. I think you all should have the weekend off."

A cheer went up in the room. One of the engineers in the back stood up, " Don't worry, Dr. Richards. We'll have these changes into the graphics department before the cocktail hour! On behalf of the rest of the team, thanks for the week end. My wife was threatening to move out since I'm never home any more."

Another team member chimed in, "Amen! I think we've got the options really tied down now. Good luck with your briefings in Houston and Washington, Doc!"

The meeting broke up and Richards hurried back to his office. His secretary called to him as he walked in, "Oh, good. I'm glad you're back. Dr. Davidson is on the phone from Washington."

"Thanks. June, and while I'm talking to him, would you try to locate Jack Kelly down at NASA Michoud? I need to talk to him."

"That's a coincidence. He just phoned a few minutes ago. He was very mysterious. He said he needed to talk to you. He asked for your home phone number and said he would call you at 7 pm California time tonight. He said not to call him at NASA."

"Strange. Well, I'll wait for his call tonight. Better not keep Dr. Davidson waiting any longer."

Richards spoke into the phone in a friendly manner, "Sorry to keep you waiting, John. What's up?"

"I've got some good news! I don't know what you did but it must have worked."

A little puzzled, Richards asked, "What do you mean? What good news?"

"I'm not going to get fired. Bill Wiley called about an hour ago and said, quote, *Dr. Davidson, I'm not going to ask the President to fire you for signing the Form 287. I've found the real culprit!* unquote. Boy, am I relieved! I could just see my career ending!"

Richards laughed, "I know who the 'culprit' is. It's me. Wiley called Dave Moore, the president of UAC, and asked him to fire me."

Dismayed, Davidson blurted out, "Oh, no, Don. I feel responsible since I asked you to help."

"Don't worry, John. I'm not going to be fired. But I've got to find out what happened to Discovery. Pronto!"

"How are you going to do that? That's what Wiley's big Commission is supposed to find out."

"I don't really know yet. But, I'm highly motivated to get the facts quickly. Otherwise, Wiley and his Commission will get in the way of our rescue efforts. I don't want all those American astronauts to die in space because of a bungling Presidential Commission!"

"Don, you shouldn't be so critical. There are some good men and women on that Commission."

"I know, but Wiley's not one of them!"

"But he has a good reputation."

"Yeah. For jumping to conclusions. His approach may work in the Pentagon, but not when seventeen lives are in jeopardy."

"Anyway, Don, thanks for your help. Sorry it made Wiley turn on you. See you in Washington next week with the rescue options."

That same evening, while Richards and Dawn were watching the evening news on their TV, their phone rang. Dawn started to answer it but Richards stopped her, "I'll answer it. I know who it is."

He hurried into his study to get away from the blare of the TV and picked up his phone extension there, "Jack, why all the mystery? I wanted to talk to you in your office today."

"Don, I'm calling you from a pay phone. Wiley's got all the key NASA people's phones tapped. I didn't want to talk from my office. I know what happened to Discovery. I don't want that bastard, Wiley, to get credit for finding out. All he's done so far is to muddy the water."

"Yes, I know, Jack. He called my boss today and tried to get me fired for getting the Form 287 executed."

"That jerk! He obviously didn't succeed or I wouldn't have been able to get your phone number from your secretary earlier today. Anyway, the Form 287 didn't have anything to do with the explosion."

"You're right, he couldn't get me fired. But, what did cause the explosion? And how are you so sure?"

Slowly and carefully, Jack Kelly explained, "First, I spent all day yesterday examining the micro-photographs of the explosion. It was the external fuel tank that exploded. The photos show clearly that it ruptured and they also show where it ruptured. It was NOT at one of the welds. It separated in the middle of the upper extruded section – the one that carries a lot of the load of the pressurized tank."

Richards interrupted, "That sounds like defective material – the metal used to make the tank – not a defective weld."

"Exactly! The metal had to be defective to rupture where it did. So next I dug up the inspection report out of our files for the material used in that section of the tank. The metal came from a

Japanese steel company that makes the material under a stringent NASA spec."

Richards asked, "Why is a Japanese steel manufacturer used on the American Space Shuttle?"

Kelly responded, "The answer to that is easy. The Japanese steel making technology is so far advanced compared to ours that they are the only ones who could meet NASA's specifications!"

Richards pursued his question, "But, how are you sure the metal was defective? What proof do you have?"

"I have the proof signed in blood!"

"What do you mean?"

Kelly answered slowly and sadly, "There was another casualty of Discovery. One in Tokyo."

"Jack, how could someone in Tokyo be killed by the Discovery explosion?"

"Don, be patient and let me finish."

"I'm sorry, Jack. Go ahead. It's just that I'm really emotionally involved with the Discovery!"

Kelly continued, "So was the Japanese inspector who signed the inspection report verifying that the tank metal met all the NASA specs! I called the plant in Tokyo and asked to speak to the inspector, a fellow named Yoguigushi. I met him during a routine inspection tour late last year. We called him Yogi."

Richards interrupted, "What did Yogi have to say?"

"I didn't talk to Yogi. He's dead! Committed suicide – Hari Kari! But he left a last note, signed in blood so to speak. His supervisor sent me a copy of the note and a translation over the telefax."

"Go on, go on," Richards urged.

"Don, his supervisor said, 'I'll probably be fired when the company lawyers find out I sent you this information. They'll be worried about a lawsuit. But I believe it is the honorable Japanese way to send you this note. After all, Yogi took his own life!"

"Jack, the note. What did it say?"

"I'm sorry. I'm still thinking about poor Yogi. Here. I've got the note with me. I'll read it to you. It is addressed to the chairman of the steel company, a father figure for Yogi:

Dear Mr. Chairman,
I'm sorry. I committed a dishonorable act. I certified that the metal shipped for tank 193 used in the Discovery's external tank met all of NASA's specs. It didn't. It was defective. It was much too low in tensile strength. My intentions were honorable. I was trying to meet our quota goals set by the plant manager. I shouldn't have relaxed our high Japanese standards. Please forgive me. I ask that my family and ancestors forgive me. I ask the crew of Discovery to forgive me. I ask that Buddha forgives me.
I now commit my last honorable act. I take my life now. Goodbye.
(signed) Matsu Yoguigushi

Richards was silent for a moment as he reflected over this further Discovery-related tragedy. He then said solemnly, "Jack, I want you to summarize what you just told me in a 'memo-to-file'. Then fly to Washington Monday morning and hand carry a copy of your memo and a copy of Yogi's suicide letter to John Davidson. He's the President's Science Advisor. His office is in the White House Annex.

Kelly asked cautiously, "But, can we trust him? Won't he just give it to Wiley?"

"Don't worry about that. He won't give it to Wiley. He hates Wiley. He'll give it to the President. He's got good access to President Williamson. I'll call Davidson and explain what you've just told me. I have his home phone number. That won't be bugged!"

Chapter 18

Rescue Option Recommendation

Richards looked at his watch set on Houston time: 9 am Monday 24 March. He adjusted the area navigation mode switch to read out the estimated arrival time for NASA Houston. The numbers told him they would arrive in 45 minutes. He turned to Jim Atkins in the pilot seat, "Jim, we've got a 140 knot tail wind. We're really moving. Our ground speed's 690 knots. Looks like we'll arrive in plenty of time for my 10 am meeting."

"Yep, Doc. We've got the jet stream pushing us along real good today."

His two day weekend away from the pressures of the rescue decisions had left Richards feeling refreshed, relaxed and ready to go. The view graphs in his briefcase in the back seat were ready to review with Gus Ford and the NASA Houston team. At 4 am this morning, before leaving for the flight line at John Wayne Airport, Richards had phoned John Davidson at home in Washington and had explained that Jack Kelly would be bringing him a memo and Yogi's suicide letter today at his office. Davidson had been relieved that the mystery of the Discovery explosion had been solved so quickly. He had assured Richards that he would get the word to the President right away. He also said he would make sure Kelly got the credit for solving the case, -- not Wiley!"

One hundred nautical miles out from the NASA Houston field, Richards called air traffic control on the VHF radio and requested a profile descent for landing at NASA Houston. His request was granted. Twelve minutes later he switched to the NASA tower frequency, "NASA tower, One Uniform Alpha with you at eight nautical miles, three thousand feet. Request landing."

Immediately, the answer came back, "Roger, One Uniform Alpha is cleared for a straight in approach, runway eight, wind one one zero at twelve knots. Cleared to land."

Gus Ford was standing there waving them a welcome at the NASA ramp as Atkins pulled up. Richards started to leave the cockpit, then said, "Jim, plan on a 3 pm departure for Washington National. Gus Ford will be coming along."

"OK, Doc. See you then. One Uniform Alpha will be ready when you are!"

Richards grabbed his briefcase, opened the door, let down the stairs and rushed over to Ford, "Hi, Gus. Got the briefing all ready. Let's get going!"

"Great, Don. We're ready to hear your presentation. We had Wiley here all weekend with this inquisition. Funny thing, though, about 9 am today he left the meeting room to answer a phone call. He came back – his face was ashen – and said the meeting was all over. He had to get back to Washington right away. Didn't say why. Maybe there was a death in his family."

Richards smiled knowingly, "No, Gus, it wasn't a death in his family. It was probably a call from the White House."

"What do you know that I don't know?"

I'll tell you on the way to the conference room. We better not keep the audience waiting."

On the short drive to the NASA Houston headquarters building, Richards explained his Friday evening phone call from Jack Kelly about the reason for the Discovery explosion. Then he described his phone call with John Davidson earlier that morning. He finished the story as Gus turned off the car.

Ford smiled happily, "Maybe that will finish off Wiley's witch hunt. Now we can get on with the rescue plan!"

Richards replied confidently, "Gus, by the end of today, I think Wiley will be finished, period. He made a powerful enemy by threatening to have Davidson fired. The tables are turned now. Davidson has the ammunition to get Wiley fired. He was in that mood when I talked to him this morning."

The conference room was packed. It seemed everyone wanted to hear what the rescue options were and what Richards was going to recommend in his two hour briefing.

The video links to the Space Station and to NASA Headquarters were not connected. Ford wanted to be sure he approved the options before they were recommended to NASA

Headquarters.   After the meeting in Washington tomorrow and after the selection of the rescue option, the Space Station crew would be informed.

Richards went through the two American options, the shuttle from the Smithsonian and the US Air Force booster, and explained neither one was feasible because the time period to obtain the necessary equipment was too long.   He then presented and compared the European and the Russian options.

In conclusion, he stated, "As you can see from the details presented, both the European and Russian options appear to be feasible. Either one can rescue our stranded astronauts. However, the Russian Shuttle has been in operation longer and can carry back more of the stranded crew per rescue mission.   For that reason, we are recommending the Russian option be selected."

Someone in the back of the room stood up and asked, "Dr. Richards, who has to approve the option selected?"

Ford rose from his seat, "I'll try to answer that question. First, we here at NASA Houston have to give preliminary approval of the selected option. I am willing to endorse the Russian option as being the best. Next, Dr. Richards will present his briefing to NASA Headquarters.   Bill Adams and, probably, the NASA Administrator, will have to re-approve the option. Finally, since the Space Station rescue is of such great National concern, John Davidson, the President's Science Advisor will have to endorse the option selected. Then I think the information we have just heard will be presented to President Williamson and he will probably have the final say."

Richards and Ford walked up to the NASA Houston flight line at 2:30 pm. They found Jim Atkins in the pilot's lounge watching TV with Cindy and Marie. Atkins exclaimed, "Hi, Doc. You're a bit early. The flight plan's filed anyway, though. Lookee who's goin' along – your playmates!"

Richards laughed, "Glad you two are here! We are a bit early, Jim. Let's head for 'puzzle town'. Cindy, you can be co-pilot this time. I'm going to relax."

The quintet quickly boarded the waiting Lear-Gates jet. Atkins and Cindy took the pilot and co-pilot seats. Richards, Ford, and Marie buckled themselves into seats in the main cabin. Soon they were airborne, climbing rapidly to their ATC assigned cruise altitude of flight level 430 (43 thousand feet), headed for Washington, DC. Some thirty minutes later, as they reached their cruise altitude and leveled off, Marie asked for their drink orders. Richards ordered a double Tanqueray on the rocks and Ford wanted Jack Daniel's Green Label with ice and a little water. Finishing his gin quickly, Richards retired to the wide back seat, pulled the curtains and fell fast asleep, exhausted from the early morning start and from presenting the extremely detailed two hour briefing.

Richards woke up when he felt the jet descending for its approach to Washington National Airport. He was surprised to find Marie curled up sleeping next to him. He kissed her awake, "We'll be landing soon. Let's go to our seats."

Marie responded sleepily, "Wow! I went out like a light. I had one split of champagne after I served you and Mr. Ford your drinks. I came back to cuddle next to you and that's the last thing I remember."

Richards joked, "If that's the effect champagne has on you, don't drink any more tonight. I want you awake later!"

Marie grinned and winked at him.

They moved to two seats on the left side of the aircraft, facing each other. They fastened their seat belts as Richards turned to Ford, "Gus, we'll be landing soon. Where shall we have dinner tonight?"

"Let's go to the Andrews Air Force Base officer's club. This is their special steak bar-b-que night. All the steak you can eat for $2.50.

"That sounds great. Now for a harder question. How do you think the briefing will go tomorrow?"

Gus looked Richards in the eyes, "Don, I go along with your recommendation to use the Russian Shuttle for the rescue. The real question is: will the President buy the Russian option?"

Their rental car was waiting for them when they landed at Washington National. The three men and two women loaded their light baggage into the car and headed for the Capitol Quality Inn. Richards and the two girls took a suite on the tenth floor overlooking the Capitol Building. Atkins and Ford were assigned single rooms on the same floor.   As they passed Ford's room, Richards said, "It's now a quarter past six, Washington time. Let's rendezvous in the lobby at 7:15 to leave for dinner."

"That sounds good.   I'll call the officer's club and make dinner reservations for 8 pm for five people.   They have dancing on Mondays after the bar-b-que."

"See you then."

The quintet spent a pleasurable evening dining and dancing. Cindy and Marie took turns dancing with all three men so no one felt left out.   When they returned to the Quality Inn, Richards, Cindy and Marie had an enjoyable and passionate period of fun and games in bed.   The trio fell asleep fully satisfied from the three-way love making.

Chapter 19

NASA Selection

Richards and Ford arrived at the NASA headquarters building on Constitution Avenue at 7:30 am. Richards parked the rental car in the basement in a spot reserved for Visiting NASA Executives. They rode the elevator to the sixth floor and walked eastward down the hall toward the Administrator's office complex. Adams had left a message at their hotel for Richard and Ford to meet him at 7:30 in his office before the final briefing began at 8:30.

They found Adams sipping a cup of coffee and eating a donut for breakfast.

Adams greeted the two and offered each a cup of coffee from the coffee maker located clandestinely in a cupboard in his office. NASA executives were supposed to use the coffee machines in the halls or else the cafeteria down in the basement.

Adams gave them the latest Washington rumor – President Williamson had dismissed William Wiley as Chairman of the Discovery Accident Investigation Commission. The rumor had it that his deputy, Dr. Jane Skidmore, had been asked to wrap-up the Commission's work and to publish the final report within ten days. Furthermore, the Commission was not to interfere with the rescue plans for the astronauts stranded on the Space Station. Specifically, the Commission was to avoid bothering the senior NASA management involved in the rescue plan and to write up their final report using information already at hand.

Adams explained, "If the rumor is true, this will be the shortest lived Presidential Commission in history. I did nothing but meet with members of Wiley's Commission all last week, continuing until 11 am yesterday. Then, all of a sudden, their leader got a call during the meeting, and ten minutes later, they were all gone."

Richards queried, "Bill, do you think the rumor is true?"

"Well, the NASA Administrator got a call from John Davidson late yesterday afternoon. One of the secretaries overheard the conversation on the Administrator's squawk box. It's pretty sure!"

Ford added, "Well, it's a rumor until the dismissal is reported publicly."

Richards laughed, "I think the rumor's true, Bill. And I know why."

Richards then told Adams how he learned about Yogi's suicide note from Jack Kelly of NASA Michoud. He also told about his 4 am Monday morning phone call to John Davidson.

Adams commented, "Boy, you and Jack Kelly do good work! Congratulations! That guy Wiley was a real pain in the ass. I really hope the rumor's true and that he's gone!"

Continuing Adams stated, "Enough of this rumor mill! What option do you recommend, and why?"

Richards spent the next few minutes summarizing what he was going to present in his 8:30 briefing and finished by saying, "So you see, Bill, it looks like asking the Russians to use their shuttle is the best option."

Adams nodded his head in agreement, "It's too bad the American option didn't prove feasible. That's what the Administrator and the President wanted. Anyway, it's just after 8 am here and just after 4 pm in Moscow. I think we should call Professor Dr. Chekhov in Moscow and warn him we will probably be asking for their help."

Richards replied, "I think that's a good idea, Bill. Tom Rubin called him last week so he knows we are considering the Russian option. Be sure to emphasize the call is unofficial though. Remember, you're in the government. Rubin isn't."

"That's a good point, Don. We wouldn't want him to think this was an official call. We need to get our option recommendation approved first!"

Adams buzzed his secretary and asked her to get Dr. Chekhov on the phone.

Lois immediately answered, "OK, Dr. Adams. I'll dial him right way. I know the number's in our phone book."

A few moments later they were connected with Dr. Chekhov on the speaker-phone so everyone could hear.

"Dr. Chekhov, this is Bill Adams at NASA Headquarters. Good afternoon, sir."

"And good morning to you, Dr. Adams, it sounds like you are speaking in a cave." He laughed and added, "You must have the CIA recording our conversation."

Adams laughed and replied, "No, no, nothing like that. I just have you on our speaker-phone here. I'm with Dr. Richards, the Space Station program manager, and Gus Ford, from NASA Houston."

Chekhov greeted them, "Good morning, Dr. Richards and Mr. Ford. I remember meeting both of you in Vienna last year at the International Space Symposium. Also, Mr. Rubin from your organization called me last week, Dr. Richards."

Adams responded, "Dr. Chekhov, I want to emphasize this is an un-official call."

Chekhov said in a friendly, understanding tone, "Yes, yes, I understand. Just one engineer to another, right?" He chuckled loudly.

"That's right, Dr. Chekhov. One engineer to another."

"And, what can I do for my colleagues in America this beautiful Spring day?"

Richards broke in, "Dr. Chekhov, I am about to brief the NASA Administrator and recommend that we formally request your government's aid in rescuing our stranded astronauts, using the Russian Space Shuttle."

Dr. Chekhov replied soothingly, "Well, Dr. Richards and Dr. Adams, all I can say is that if such a request is made, I will recommend that my government respond affirmatively. You must understand, though, in today's Russia all decisions are made collectively. My individual opinion means very little."

Richards added, "Dr. Chekhov, you are much too modest. I am sure your opinion would carry a great deal of weight with the Russian collective leadership."

"Oh, no, no. But, nevertheless, I predict that the decision would be favorable. After all, if the tables were turned, we would hope you would give us the same assistance. Yes?"

Adams responded, "Why, yes, Dr. Chekhov. I'm sure the US Government would agree to help rescue your astronauts if they were stranded and we had the resources to respond." Dr. Chekhov laughed, "Let us all hope our governments are as reasonable as we engineers are! Gentlemen, there's little more I can tell you until a formal request comes from the US Government to the Russian Government, through proper channels, of course. Good morning!"

Adams said, "Good afternoon, Dr. Chekhov, and thank you for your informal comments. Believe me, they will be most helpful. Goodbye." And he hung up.

Adams continued, "C'mon, Don, it's almost 8:30. We have to head for the Administrator's conference room. He's anxious to hear your option recommendation. Please let me tell him about our phone call to Dr. Chekhov, after your briefing."

Richards nodded in reply.

The three men left Adams' office and walked across the foyer to the NASA Administrator's conference room. As they walked in, Adams turned to his secretary who was waiting just outside the room, "Lois, please tell the Administrator's secretary we are ready to present him the briefing as soon as he is available."

"Yes, Dr. Adams. I will."

A few minutes later, the Administrator strode into the conference room. The several deputy administrators rose as he entered and remained standing until he was seated. He turned to Adams, who was standing at the end of the long conference table, "Bill, you may commence with the rescue option briefing now."

Adams introduced Richards by saying, "Mr. Administrator, Gentlemen and Lady (there was one lady deputy administrator), most of you have met Dr. Richards who will present the three rescue options and will recommend one option. Let me say, I've reviewed Dr. Richards' most thorough briefing. He and his crisis team at Universal Aircraft out in Irvine, California, have put a lot of good work into this briefing. I heartily endorse Dr. Richards' recommendation. Please begin."

Richards moved over to the speaker's podium in front of the huge, back-projected screen. His title chart was showing: SPACE STATION RESCUE OPTIONS.

He began, "Lady and Gentlemen. UAC and NASA have defined three rescue options: the Enterprise option and the European Shuttle and Russian Shuttle options. Dr. Adams and I personally climbed through the Enterprise over at the Smithsonian to assess the inventory of equipment, and what is missing. The shuttle integration contractor in Downey contacted all the shuttle contractors to obtain delivery schedules for Enterprise's missing equipment. We even considered using the US Air Force satellite launching system to send up repair kits to the Space Station to repair Atlantis and Columbia in orbit as an alternative to using Enterprise. We analyzed more than five thousand pages of documentation about the European and Russian shuttles during our study of these two options. In short, UAC and NAA have done their homework in arriving at our recommendations for the rescue option.

Richards then presented his briefing explaining each rescue operation in detail. He concluded, "Unfortunately, neither of the US options will result in a rescue before the expendables on the Space Station are exhausted, the end of next August. So we are left with one of the two foreign options: rescue by the European or by the Russian shuttle. Our study shows the latter is the best with the least risk. We recommend the Russian option be approved."

Adams stood up and added, "Mr. Administrator, NASA Houston and my office endorse the recommendation for the Russian option. Just before our meeting, Sir, I took the initiative of calling Dr. Chekhov, the Russian Shuttle director. Dr. Chekhov assured me he would recommend to his government's leadership that the Russian's aid in this rescue by using their shuttle. He believes that a request by the US Government – through the proper channels – would be acted upon favorably by the Russian Government."

The Administrator reflected for a moment and then asked a question, "Dr. Richards, would you be able to live with the European option? I know that President Williamson will find it very distasteful to ask the Russians for help. He is always sensitive about the attacks from the conservative political community about cooperating too much with the Russians."

Richards got a questioning look on his face, thought for a few seconds, and then responded, "Well, yes, Sir. We could live with the European option, but we feel it raises the risks. The European shuttle is less mature than the Russian one. They have had some difficulty with meeting their scheduled launch dates. If we don't rescue these astronauts before the end of August, then they're lost! I believe the Russian option is more prudent – politics aside!"

The Administrator responded, "Before I give you my response, there is an announcement I would like to make. My secretary informs me there are some wild rumors floating around about the President's Discovery Accident Commission and the Commission chairman, Mr. William Wiley, who is a dear friend of mine. Let me just say these rumors are false. The President has not fired Mr. Wiley. Mr. Wiley submitted his resignation this morning for personal reasons. His deputy, Dr. Jane Skidmore, will take over as chairman. Since our Mr. Jack Kelly of NASA Michoud solved the mystery of why Discovery exploded on the launch pad, the President has asked Dr. Skidmore to wrap up the Commission's work and publish the final report by April fourth. The report will consist mainly of a memo written by Mr. Kelly which details the reason for the explosion, plus a few other administrative matters. I hope my announcement puts these vile rumors to rest."

Adams replied, "Thank you, sir. My staff wondered why the Commission staff left our meeting so abruptly yesterday morning. Your announcement explains it clearly."

The Administrator cleared his throat and stated, "Dr. Richards, Dr. Adams, I endorse your recommendations that we select the Russian option – with the following reservation. Before I give my endorsement formally, I request that you brief Dr. John Davidson, the President's Science Advisor. If Dr. Davidson concurs with the recommendation, after informing the President, then I will formally endorse your recommendation. You may expect my written response in the form of a NASA directive by Thursday afternoon. I know time is of the essence in this crisis!"

Richard thought to himself, 'The NASA Administrator is the perfect bureaucrat. He recognizes the Russian option recommendation is politically sensitive. He doesn't want to go on record, officially, of endorsing a position that the President may reject. He will wait until he gets feedback on the President's response from Davidson before he commits himself in writing. That's the bureaucratically safe way!'

Richards responded, "Thank you, Mr. Administrator. We will not take any further action until we receive your directive on Thursday."

Chapter 20

President Selects the Option

Shortly before 2 pm, Richards, Adams, and Ford walked up to the security entrance of the White House Annex and submitted to the elaborate security procedures which were required before they could be admitted.

They were escorted upstairs to Dr. Davidson's office by his pretty young secretary. She lead them to his office at the end of the hall and said, "You may go right in. Dr. Davidson is ready for you now."

Richards was pleased to see Davidson looked relaxed today. He seemed to be over the panic he had been in when he called Richards last week afraid of being fired for signing the Form 287. It was clear Davidson really enjoyed the prestige of being the President's Science Advisor. He greeted the trio with a big smile, "Welcome to the White House, Gentlemen. I understand you have selected the rescue option."

Richards responded diplomatically, "No, John. We are recommending an option. You get to select the actual option."

Davidson pointed out his office window which overlooked the White House garden, "Wrong, Don. The gentleman sitting over there in the Oval Office will select the option. He has become personally involved in this Discovery accident and in the astronaut's rescue."

Richards asked, "What do you mean, 'personally involved', John?"

"Well, when I gave him Jack Kelly's memo and Yogi's suicide letter, he read them, turned red in the face, called Wiley down in Houston, and fired him on the spot!"

Adams came back with surprise, "But, we were told that Wiley resigned for personal reasons!"

"Bill, that's the official story, but, believe me, he was fired! I heard it with my own ears

Richards questioned, "But why do you think the President fired Wiley? After all, he picked him in the first place."

"Richardson responded, "The President decided he had made an error in appointing Wiley when the truth of why Discovery exploded came to light in Kelly's memo."

Richards stated grimly, "John, the Wiley affair is behind us now, thank God. Let's move forward with finalizing the plan for rescuing the astronauts. We need you to endorse the option and to get the President to concur with that recommended option. The NASA Administrator will issue a directive authorizing the recommended option, after he hears the President doesn't object."

Davidson laughed and replied lightly, "I see! The Administrator is playing the old Washington game: *don't take a firm position until you're sure it won't be controversial!* Let's hear your briefing, Don."

Richards handed the executive summary of the rescue option briefing to Gus Ford who projected the first chart onto the screen in the corner of Davidson's large office, using the projector on the conference table.

Richards went through his presentation in a clear, firm manner, emphasizing the key factors for each of the three options. He concluded, "And, for the reasons given, we recommend the Russian option."

Davidson responded thoughtfully, "I have followed your logic and rationale, Don. I agree completely with your conclusions and I agree with the Russian option. The earliest I can see the President is tomorrow – Wednesday afternoon."

Richards smiled, "John, thanks. I would appreciate a call when you know if the President agrees."

"OK, I'll call you as soon as I have the word. I'll also call the NASA Administrator and tell him."

Adams interrupted, "John, I'd like to have you call me before you call the Administrator, so I'll know."

"OK, Bill, will do! Thank you, Gentlemen. I have to go to a security council meeting in the White House now. Thanks for the briefing."

The trio shook hands with Davidson and left.

Richards dropped Adams off at NASA Headquarters and he and Gus went on to the Washington National Airport executive aircraft terminal where they found Atkins and the two girls watching TV in the pilot's lounge. Richards told Atkins, "You fly Gus back to Houston in One Uniform Alpha. I'm going to fly commercial back to LAX from Dulles Airport. It's just 3:30 so I can still catch one of the late afternoon non-stops."

Atkins answered helpfully, "OK, Doc. Cindy and Marie'll help me fly him home. Will you be needing the jet next week?"

"Probably not. I may be flying to Russia – if the President approves our rescue plan."

Cindy broke in, "That sounds exciting, Don. Don't make love to any of those beautiful Russian girls."

Marie remarked, "Yeah. Our security briefings say the good looking Russian girls who try to take American visitors to bed are always KGB agents."

Richards laughed, "I doubt that, but anyway, you two have worn me out. It'll take weeks to recover."

Richards kissed the girls goodbye, shook hands with Ford and Atkins, and drove off toward Dulles, just in front of the afternoon mass exodus from Washington.

At Dulles, he turned in the rental car, headed for the TWA counter, presented his credit card for a first class seat on the 5:30 pm non-stop flight to Los Angeles International Airport. He went down the escalator to the TWA Ambassador Lounge, checked in, got his boarding pass, and settled down in one of the comfortable lounge chairs to watch TV and sip a double Tanqueray on the rocks. Remembering Dawn, he picked up the telephone on the table at his elbow and reached her at her UAC extension, "Dawn, Darling. I'm arriving at 7:30 on TWA flight 843. Pick me up at LAX and we can go to dinner at the Balboa Bay Club this evening."

"Oh, great, Don. I love their shrimp and hors d'oeuvres buffet. I hope you'll be home for a while now that your big briefing is over."

"I'm afraid not! I'll probably be going to Moscow next week."

"You'll what? Tell me all about it over a bottle of Corbel's Brut Champagne this evening. Goodbye, Darling. I love you."

"I love you, too!"

Exercising great willpower, Richards passed up the fantastic repast in TWA First Class. When he discovered he had seen the in-flight movie twice before on other trips, he leaned way back on the super soft, reclining seat and soon sank into a deep sleep. The tranquility brought his body back into synch with California time. He woke up to see the glittering lights of the Hollywood Hills on his right and realized they were on final approach into Los Angeles, lined up to land on runway 24 left, one of the two parallel runways north of the passenger terminals. A few minutes later he strode off the plane through the jet-way tunnel and into the waiting arms of his roommate, Dawn.

Less than a half hour later, Richards turned off the Pacific Coast Highway into the circular driveway of the plush Balboa Bay Club. They gave their car to the doorman to park and walked through the front doors of the club. In the dining room they were shown their table next to the window overlooking the lights sparkling in the blue-black waters of exclusive Newport Harbor. They had an expansive view of huge, expensive white yachts tied to the docks outside the dining room. Richards pointed out the sleek Formula 40 catamaran owned by his friend, Randy Lyle, on an end-tie because it was too wide to fit in the space between the regular docks. Randy, a former Olympic sailing champion, won first place in the European Formula 40 Regatta Series last year. The Formula 40 Series was referred to as the Grand Prix of Yacht Racing. These races were all held near the shore where the spectators lined the cliff tops to watch the huge 40 foot long multihulls hitting over thirty knots on the reaching legs of the race courses. Randy would be shipping his boat by 747 to France for the 1992 multi-coque regatta at Brest, France, next week, hoping for a repeat win this year.

The waiter appeared with menus. Richards ordered a magnum of Corbel Champagne, Extra Brut, Dawn's favorite! He told the waiter, "We'll be going to the hors d'oeuvres bar after you bring the champagne. We'll order dinner later."

The waiter replied, "Thank you, Sir. I'll bring your champagne right away."

After their elaborate feast of hors d'oeuvres, Richards ordered Shrimp Canlis, a dish made famous by the Canlis Restaurant in Honolulu. The shrimp, in a lemon-butter sauce with vermouth, was prepared by the waiter in a flaming pan at tableside. They finished their evening repast with a fantastic dish of fresh strawberries covered with thick, sweet, sour cream, also prepared flambé on a tableside brazier.

When the pair arrived at their hillside condominium in the Irvine Hills, they immediately headed for the hot shower. As Richards and Dawn got into bed, he turned out the lights and turned on the Hi Fi, which played a beautiful flute and guitar duet, the Sonatina by Tedesco. As the dulcet sounds floated through the bedroom, Richards opened the motorized drapes and gazed for a moment at the carpet of lights spreading out below the wall of glass. He felt Dawn's warm body next to his. He turned and massaged her nude body. A few moments later, they both burst into a climax of love and then melted into a deeply, relaxing sleep.

The ringing of the telephone jarred Richards awake. He looked at his watch – 5:30 am, Wednesday morning, 26 March 1992. Dawn also woke up. She asked sleepily, "Who in the world is calling at this ungodly hour?"

Richards didn't answer but picked up the phone and said hoarsely, "This is Don Richards here."

The voice at the other end of the line said, "Good morning, Don. I tried to reach you until after midnight your time last night, but you weren't in."

Richards asked groggily, "Who is it?"

The voice replied, "Oh, I'm sorry. This is John Davidson. I've got a message for you from the President."

Richards became awake immediately, "What's up, John. I thought you weren't going to meet with the President until Wednesday afternoon."

"I thought so, too, but he caught me after the Security Council meeting yesterday afternoon and asked which rescue option NASA was recommending. When I said the Russian option, he hit the ceiling, and said, 'There's no way I'm going to ask Russia to rescue American astronauts with their shuttle! If I did that, the conservative block in the Senate and House would get together and my legislative agenda for the year would be down the drain! You tell those clowns over in NASA to get their act together and get Enterprise fixed up to rescue the astronauts. If they really can't do that, then use the European shuttle. The Russian Shuttle is out! That's final, John!' And he rushed out of the room, leaving me standing there with my mouth hanging open."

Richards replied sympathetically with a little laugh in his voice, "Well, look, John. Thanks for trying, but you know as well as I do that the Enterprise is out. There's just no way to get it re-outfitted and launched before the end of August when the expendables run out."

"Yes, Don. You convinced me of that. Then you better move out with the European option. Is that a problem?"

"No, John. That's the second best option, but we can live with it. It's the only feasible option considering the President has ruled out the Russian alternative. I'll call Dr. Dubois in Toulouse today and try to set up a meeting to discuss the rescue plans next week. I'll also call Dr. Chekhov, unofficially of course, and explain this development to him"

"OK, Don. I'll inform the NASA Administrator and make sure President Williamson knows there's no hope for using Enterprise."

Chapter 21

European Option

When Richards arrived at his office he found a telex waiting on the machine:

ATT: DR. RICHARDS, VICE PRESIDENT
SPACE STATION PROGRAM DIRECTOR
UNIVERSAL AIRCRAFT CORPORATION
IRVINE, CALIFORNIA

YOU ARE HEREBY AUTHORIZED AND DIRECTED TO
PURSUE THE EUROPEAN RESCUE OPTION PER
DIRECTIVE ISSUED THIS DATE BY THE NASA
ADMINISTRATOR. YOU MAY CONTACT DR.
JACQUES DUBOIS, PROGRAM DIRECTOR OF THE
EUROPEAN SHUTTLE, TOULOUSE, FRANCE, C/O
AEROSPATIALE. DR. DUBOIS HAS BEEN OFFICIALLY
ADVISED BY THE US GOVERNMENT THAT HE IS
REQUESTED TO NEGOTIATE A RESCUE LAUNCH
DATE WITH YOU.

BEST REGARDS,
GUS FORD, MANNED SPACE PROGRAM OFFICE
NASA HOUSTON

Richards looked at his watch – it said 7:30 am – and he switched it to Paris standard time. He remembered that Europe would switch to daylight saving time this next weekend and then there would be ten hours time difference between California and France instead of the nine hours difference now. So it was 4:30 pm in Toulouse. If he called immediately, he should be able to catch Dr. Dubois before he left for the day. Since his secretary was not in at this early hour, Richards picked up the phone himself, dialed the international access code, the country code for France, the area code for Toulouse, and then the seven digit number that rang in Dubois' office.

Dubois himself answered, "Bon soir. Il y a Docteur Dubois ici."

Richards responded, "Dr. Dubois, my French is a little shaky. This is Don Richards at Universal Aircraft in California."

"Ah, yes, Dr. Richards. I received a telex from the NASA Administrator about an hour ago. It advised you are authorized to negotiate a launch date for the European Shuttle to rescue the astronauts on the US Space Station. So I was expecting to hear from you. But not this soon. You Americans don't waste time, do you?"

"Well, Dr. Dubois, sometimes I think we Americans should learn to enjoy life like you Europeans and quit rushing around so much. But with this Space Station crisis and the explosion of Discovery, I don't have much control over my life style any more!"

"Why, yes, Dr. Richards, I understand the pressure you're under. You have had an unbelievable chain of failures in your shuttlecraft. The probability that all these catastrophes would happen must be infinitesimal. Anyway, you are welcome to come to Toulouse to discuss a launch date for a rescue by the European Shuttle. I must get approval from the European Space Council before I can commit, but under the circumstances, I expect a favorable decision."

"Good, Dr. Dubois. Would a meeting Monday morning be OK?"

"Why, yes, it would. You Americans do move quickly! What time would you arrive in Toulouse?"

"I haven't made my reservations yet, but I expect to leave from Paris Sunday morning for Toulouse."

"Oh, fine, Dr. Richards. There's an Air France flight that leaves Le Bourget Airport at 10:30 am and arrives at Toulouse at noon. I'll call now and reserve a seat for you. Aerospatiale always keeps five seats on that flight. You can have one of them. Otherwise it may be full. I'll meet you at the airport. You will be Aerospatiale's guest at the Toulouse Grand Hotel."

"Great, Dr. Dubois. See you at noon Sunday at the Toulouse Airport. Au revoir."

"Au revoir."

Just as he finished his phone call at 8 am, June walked into the office. Richards buzzed her on the intercom, "June, I'm going to Toulouse, France. Make a reservation for me on the non-stop Pan Am flight from Los Angeles to Paris tomorrow. I'll spend two nights in Paris adjusting to the jet lag."

June laughed and interrupted Richards' flow of instructions, "Just a minute, Dr. Richards, until I get my note pad. You caught me off balance. From what I understood when you left for Houston earlier this week, I thought you'd be going to Moscow, not Toulouse."

Richards laughed in return, "Sorry to surprise you so early in the morning. President Williamson decided we should get the Europeans to help, not the Russians. As a result, I've got to go to Toulouse to meet with the European Space Shuttle Program Manager, Dr. Dubois."

"OK, I'm up to speed now. And where do you want to stay in Paris?"

Put me up at the George Cinq. Dr. Dubois is making reservations on the 10:30 am Air France flight from Le Bourget to Toulouse Sunday morning. He's also making my hotel reservations in Toulouse."

"Fine, Dr. Richards, I'll have your tickets and money for you before the end of the day. Is two thousand dollars enough cash?"

"Well, Paris is expensive but two thousand ought to be enough."

Richards spent the rest of the day in meetings with the crisis team preparing the documentation he would need for his meeting with the European Space Shuttle team in Toulouse. By the end of the day, he had his briefcase packed with all the papers he would need. June delivered his airline tickets and trip cash about 4 pm. He decided to leave early to get packed. He called Dawn and the two slipped away from work together.

The next morning, Richards caught the corporate helicopter from the helipad on top of the UAC headquarters building at 10 am for his noon Pan Am flight to Paris. The helicopter landed on the tarmac next to the plane Richards would be taking. He climbed the stairs into the Pan Am terminal and continued on into the Pan Am

Clipper Club. The receptionist gave him his boarding pass for the 747, seat 6B, an aisle seat near the front with a good view of the movie screen. He had time for two Bloody Marys before it was time to board the Clipper for Paris.

When he reached his seat, one of the most beautiful women he had ever seen was sitting in the window seat next to his aisle seat. She had blonde hair, cut in a short style, brilliant blue eyes above exquisite high cheek bones, long slender legs, large breasts, and was about 26 years old. She was dressed in Parisian high fashion clothing. As he took the seat next to her, she looked up, smiled happily, showing her beautiful white teeth and said captivatingly with a soft French accent, "Oh, I am so lucky. I was so afraid my seat partner would be a fat oaf like the one I had coming from Paris. You are so handsome. My name is Brigitte Michon. I live in Paris."

Flattered by the greeting from this beautiful creature, Richards responded, "My name is Dr. Don Richards, Ms Michon."

"Please call me Brigitte. May I call you Don? Doctor Richards is so – formal."

Yes, of course, Brigitte."

She shook his hand and gave it a tender squeeze before letting go.

Richards felt a warm twinge through his loins at the touch of her soft warm hand.

A short time later the stewardess poured Richards and Brigitte each a glass of Mumms Champagne while the tourist class passengers were filing into the rear of the huge 747 Clipper. Richards raised his glass and toasted, "To a smooth flight to the beautiful city of Paris!"

Brigitte laughed, "Let's change the toast a little – to a beautiful evening in Paris! I hope you can be my guest for dinner at Lasseres' Friday evening. That is, if you are unengaged?"

Richards answered enthusiastically, "I have no plans for Paris other than to relax for two nights and adjust to the time change."

Brigitte clapped her hands in happiness, "Then, plan on relaxing with me. I can show you what Paris is really like, Don."

"That would be enchanting. I would love your company, Brigitte."

They clinked their glasses together to toast their planned relaxation in Paris.

Shortly Richards felt the pushback from the jet way and soon they were taxiing to the active runway, 24 right, for take off. The enormous jet turned onto the runway and the captain pushed the four throttles forward. Richards felt himself pushed into the back of the seat by the take off acceleration. Thirty seconds later, the Clipper leapt into the air, climbed steeply over the blue Pacific before turning northward to the great circle route from Los Angeles to Paris. It was a beautiful clear day in wind swept Los Angeles with more than a hundred miles visibility. Richards could see the tall skyscrapers of the center of the city to the east, with the majestic snow capped Sierra Madre mountains further east.

Richards and Brigitte engaged in a captivating conversation. They talked of art, music, recent literature, world events, and finally, of restaurants, food and night clubs in Paris. The time passed quickly and soon they were served a fantastic dinner featuring chateaubriand served from a cart wheeled down the aisle. The fresh spinach salad was accompanied by a piquant moutard sauce. For dessert they had huge sundaes with lots of chocolate sauce and mounds of chantilly (whipped cream). They finished their repast with brandy coffee au lait.

By that time, they were over the Arctic wastelands of Northern Canada. They watched the sun dipping below the horizon adding a reddish tinge to the desolate snow fields below. Shortly afterwards, they watched an in-flight movie about the colonization of Mars by a combined team of American astronauts and Russian cosmonauts. Watching, Richards thought to himself, *The director who made this film did a good job on the technical aspects of such a colonization mission. The space vehicles were realistic extrapolations of those now being used. But there has to be a change in the mentality of the American and Russian leaders before such a mission can really take place. Perhaps such a change in outlook would have resulted if the Russian rescue option had been approved.*

When the film ended, Richards turned to Brigitte and vocalized the thoughts coursing through his mind, "Do you think the Americans and Russians could ever agree to such a cooperative venture as the colonization of Mars?"

Brigitte looked into Richards' brown eyes with her deep blue ones, "Don, we Europeans think quite differently about the Russians than you Americans do. Russia is a part of Europe. There is a continuum of culture from Western Europe through Eastern Europe to Russia. There is continuity of railroads and highways from the East to the West. We experience a commonality in classical music, ballet, and opera with the Russians. We recognize their form of government is different from the Western parliamentary democracies but we Europeans don't have the same phobia that communism is a horrible evil that you Americans do…"

Richards interrupted Brigitte's comments and said defensively, "Maybe so, but none of the Western European countries has a communist prime minister!"

Brigitte replied calmly, "No, Don, that's true. But we do have legally recognized communist parties in many of the Western European countries who elect representatives to parliament: France, Italy, Spain, and Portugal, for example. Even Switzerland, the permanent bastion of capitalism with their banking laws that protect capitalists' funds through secrecy, has a small but active communist party. In the US, the communist party is illegal. I understand your defense workers can't have a security clearance and be a communist. That if they are found to actually be members of the communist party, they would go to jail."

Richards thought a few moments about Brigitte's comments and responded with a wry smile, "Maybe we Americans are not as broad minded and objective as we think we are. But let's turn to lighter matters."

Brigitte smiled back, "Don, you sound as if you have a broader outlook and better understanding of the world than most Americans that I've met in the past."

Richards responded lightly, "It's probably because my job gives me a global view of the world."

"And what is your job?"

"Space explorer!"

Brigitte laughed at his answer and then looked at her watch, "Don, it's almost 4 am Paris time. If I don't get some sleep, I won't be very good company for you tomorrow evening, -- only I guess it's really this evening!"

"I can't imagine your not being good company, but sleeping is a good idea."

They extended and reclined their sleeper seats until they were almost in a double bed. Brigitte covered them both with a blanket. She fell asleep curled up next to Richards with his arms around her.

When they woke up the sun was shining brightly low on the horizon as they were now heading south east on the great circle route to Paris, about an hour and a half until landing.

Chapter 22

Jet Lag Adjustment

Richards and Brigitte slept until 10 Saturday morning. While they were enjoying continental breakfast in their room, Brigitte suggested, "Why don't you check out of the hotel and spend tonight at my apartment? I'll prepare an early diner tonight and we can go to the opera. Do you like opera?"

"I love opera. That sounds like a wonderful plan. Where do we get the tickets?"

"The easiest way is to get them from the concierge in the hotel, but we'll get better seats if we take the metro to the opera house and buy the tickets there."

Richards was enthusiastic, "I like that idea. That gives us a chance to walk through the city. Since you paid for dinner last night, I haven't had a chance to exchange my dollars for francs. Are the banks open on Saturday? The hotels always give a lousy exchange rate."

"In France, some banks are closed on Saturday and open Monday, while others are closed on Monday and open on Saturday. There is a bank open on Saturdays across from the opera house."

They quickly packed and Richards checked out of the hotel, paying with his credit card. He and Brigitte put their bags in her car in the hotel garage, then walked to the nearest metro stop. The sparkling clean subway carried them to the opera house stop within ten short minutes. They stopped at the bank and Richards exchanged his two thousand dollars for French francs, receiving over 18,800 of them. He studied the colorful images of famous French people on the bills and Brigitte pointed out the same person's portrait could be seen if he held the bill up to the light. Also he noticed the bills for the larger denominations were bigger than those for smaller amounts.

He and Brigitte walked across the street to the white and shining classical columns of the Paris Opera House where the posters announced 'Die Frau Ohne Schatten' (The Woman without a Shadow) by Richard Strauss was playing. Richards commented, "I've never seen this opera. Do you know the story?"

"Yes, it is a magnificent opera. I first saw it at the Opernhaus in Zürich. It's a complex story with really beautiful music. The heroine is the Empress, a supernatural being, who has no shadow, which is a symbol of her infertility and inhumanity. She is happy as the wife of the Emperor who captured her as a white gazelle. A messenger from the King of Spirits tells her that if she doesn't find a shadow within three days, she must return to the World of Spirits and the Emperor will be changed to stone. The rest of the story tells how she finds her shadow and rescues the Emperor who has been turned to stone. The final scene features the voices of unborn children who will now have life in the future because she gained fertility along with her shadow."

It was an unusually warm day for late March, and Richards and Brigitte enjoyed their early Spring stroll along the boulevards of Paris, enjoying the museums, the shops, the magnificent monuments, and the weather. They stopped for a light lunch in a sidewalk café and watched the parade of pedestrians pass in review. The spectrum of dress was amazing: girls in tight form-fitting jeans; girls in the latest Parisian fashions; men with long, straggly hair and filthy clothes; dapper businessmen in dark grey suits and ties. They saw everything!

About 4 pm, Brigitte suggested, "Let's go back to the hotel for my car. We'll go together to the supermarket and buy fresh food for the feast I'll prepare for you tonight."

Richards surprised her by saying with a laugh, "You bought dinner last night. Tonight I will prepare the dinner. I'm a pretty good chef. You may make the salad if you like."

There was a market near Brigitte's apartment. Richards was surprised by the variety of food and the freshness of the vegetables and fruit in this typical French supermarket which was much smaller than a regular American supermarket. One surprise was the UHT milk: milk prepared by ultra high temperature pasteurization which allowed it to stay fresh in a cardboard container for several months without refrigeration. This was a European advance in food packaging not used in the US. They wandered through the store and picked out chicken breasts, artichokes, lettuce, tomatoes, avocados, and green beans.   He bought an inexpensive champagne that Brigitte recommended. They went to the boulangerie across the street and bought two half kilogram loaves of bread. Richards paid for all the food. It came to 110 francs, just over $12.

Richards and Brigitte worked together in the kitchen of her smartly furnished apartment to prepare the gourmet feast which turned out even better than the restaurant dinner the night before and at a small fraction of the cost. They set the table with linen, crystal, silver, and glowing white candles. They began with a mixed green salad with avocado, champignon, tomato, and lettuce, plus a piquant French dressing mixed by Richards. The main course was baked chicken breasts and rice with béarnaise sauce and asparagus spears. On a separate dish were boiled artichokes with a mustard-mayonnaise sauce. They enjoyed the bottle of champagne served in flaring crystal glasses. The pièce de résistance was a specialty of Richards' – chocolate fondue bubbling in a pot at the table. The huge fresh strawberries were dipped into the thick chocolate mixture by each diner and eaten immediately.

Loading all the dishes and pans into Brigitte's automatic dishwasher, they headed for the opera house. Their $75 seats were front row center, so close to the stage they really felt enveloped by the music and the singers. It was a magnificent performance. The enthusiastic audience brought the cast back five times for curtain calls.

Brigitte and Richards returned to her apartment where their love making was even more satisfying than the night before. Afterward, they both fell into a deep sleep, completely satiated with food, sex, and culture. A perfect end to a perfect Parisian evening.

The next morning, Brigitte drove Richards to Le Bourget Airport to catch his 10:30 flight to Toulouse. She let him out in front of the terminal. They kissed goodbye wistfully. As they exchanged 'au revoirs', Richards thought, *What a divine woman. Too bad I'll never see her again* Brigitte smiled gaily, waved goodbye, and drove away.

Richards proceeded through the boarding formalities for his Toulouse flight. He fell asleep shortly after take off. He woke up when the plane was descending for its landing in Toulouse in southern France. Out his window, he admired the beautiful, deep-green fields surrounding the city. To the south the majestic, snow capped Pyrenees Mountains separated France and Spain. Sixty miles south of Toulouse, nestled in these mountains, was the tiny country of Andorra, one of the few tax free havens of the world.

Richards was one of the first to exit the plane, carrying his small carry-on bag and briefcase. He quickly passed through passport control, went through the green 'Nothing to Declare' gate at customs, and spotted a smiling face holding up a large, white card that said, "Dr. Richards.' Standing next to the man with the card was a strikingly beautiful woman. She was dressed in tight, black pants and a lacey, black blouse that showed off her ample bosom. Her long, black hair fell below her waist. Richards assumed she must be Dr. Dubois's wife. He strode up to the pair, "I'm Dr. Richards. You must be Dr. and Mrs. Dubois."

The young woman looked up at Richards with her beautiful brown eyes, which were outlined with luminescent blue eye shadow, and laughed, "Dr. Richards, you are half right. This is Dr. Dubois on your left, but I am Juanita González Ramón."

Dubois interrupted the awkward exchange, "I'm sorry, Dr. Richards. I should have told you that Professora Dr. González would be here this week. Dr. González is director of the European shuttle computer software and lives in Malaga, Spain, where she also serves as Professora of Infomatica at El Ejido in Malaga."

Richards regained his composure at this 'faux pas' and responded in a friendly tome, "I am pleased to meet you, Dr. González. Is your husband with you in Toulouse?"

He received the response he was hoping for, "I'm afraid I'm much too busy with my profession to have found a husband yet. I'm here on a week long business trip to present the latest update of the European shuttle software to the Shuttle Technical Management Council."

As the trio began walking toward the airport exit, Dr. Dubois interjected, "Dr. Richards, you will be meeting the other three members of the council tomorrow. The others are Dr. Enrique Rodriguez, Dr. Heinz Zinn, and Professor Dr. Tom Shepherd. I've set up a 9:30 am meeting. The Council will be responsible for setting a launch date for the rescue of your American astronauts."

Dr. Gonzalez added, "Meanwhile, we are taking you to the Grand Hotel in Toulouse. Here's your room key. You're all checked in, courtesy of the European space shuttle program office. I'm staying in the same hotel, in the room next to yours."

Richards smiled secretly to himself.

By now they were entering the parking lot, across the street from the airline terminal. Dubois waved toward his car, "That's my blue Peugeot over in the third row. I hope you can have dinner with Dr. González and me this evening. The other council members will be arriving tomorrow on early morning flights – Dr. Rodriguez from Madrid, Dr. Zinn from Munchen, and Professor Dr. Shepherd from London. We'll have a reception in your honor tomorrow evening with the complete council present."

"That sounds wonderful, Dr. Dubois."

Dubois interrupted him, "Please, don't be so formal. Call me Jacques."

Dr. Gonzalez added with a smile, "And call me Juanita."

Of course, Richards immediately responded, "And please call me Don, Jacques and Juanita."

The Toulouse Airport was just west of the city, fairly close to the center. Dubois drove into the city on Avenue de Grand Bretagne, turned an easy left onto Avenue de Lombez, and crossed the Garonne River on Pont Neuf Metz. He turned left on Langedoc, proceeded north to Rue de Matabiau, heading toward the rail station, the Gare Matabiau. The Grand Hotel was a short distance from the train station on Boulevard de Minimes.

Dubois parked in front of the hotel and the trio went into the lobby, rode the elevator to the fifth floor and walked down the hall to Richards' room. Dr. Gonzalez unlocked her adjacent room, saying, "Don, if you'll open your connecting door, I'll join you two in your room after I freshen up a bit."

"OK, hasta luego."

The two men went into Richards' room and Richards put his bag away quickly, saying, "Would you like something from the refrigerator, Jacques?"

"Why, thank you, Don. I'll have a Campari and soda, please."

Richards fixed Dubois' drink first, then poured himself a gin and tonic, and opened the door connecting to Juanita's room. Juanita soon joined the two men, wearing a bright turquoise dress that set off her coloring beautifully, plus white leather boots. She was stunning.   Richards was taken aback by her beauty, but recovered and asked graciously, "Juanita, what would you like to drink?"

"Thank you, Don. I'll have a split of champagne, please."

While Richards was pouring, she said, "Tell me, how soon do the astronauts have to be rescued?   I mean, how long will their expendables hold out?"

Richards smiled, "Thank God we sent another three months worth of expendables when we launched Atlantis.   With the seventeen people now in the Space Station, we have enough to last through August."

Dubois interjected, "Of course, I can't commit to a launch date without consulting with the rest of the council, but we should be able to launch a rescue mission before the end of August."

Richards replied, "I certainly hope so. The earlier the better, in case there are problems."

Dubois stated confidently, "We don't expect any problems, Don. You know we use our Ariane rocket to boost our shuttle into space. We're launching an Ariane with all the latest changes this week – in fact, day after tomorrow, Tuesday. We will have even more confidence in a rescue date after that launch."

Richards responded, "I'm glad to hear that."

Dubois continued, "I'm sorry but I'm going to have to leave you now.   I have some family obligations to attend to this afternoon. However, I'll return to take you and Juanita to dinner at 8 pm.   Being the Sabbath, most restaurants are closed, but the dining room here in the hotel is excellent. I'm sure Juanita can show you the sights of Toulouse. She knows the city well."

Juanita added with a laugh, "In Malaga, everyone walks along the Paseo del Parque on Sunday afternoon, enjoying the sun and looking at the other people. In Toulouse, we can do the same thing - stroll down the street in the center of the city, looking at the shops and the other strollers."

Richards smiled happily, "Juanita, I would love to stroll the streets of Malaga or Toulouse with you. Let's go!"

Having finished their drinks, they took the elevator down to the lobby.   Richards and Juanita wished Dubois au revoir and watched him drive off.

Richards and Juanita spent a pleasant Sunday afternoon strolling up and down the streets and alongside the river and canals of the city. It was a relaxing experience for Richards, who was accustomed to the hustle and bustle of American life. At home or on trips to other American cities, he never had time to walk and enjoy the sights of the cities. In Europe, walking the streets of the center of a city was a major pastime. Toulouse was no exception. It was a beautiful old French city. The people appeared to be more friendly than the people in Paris. Richards noticed people here tried to understand his poor French. In Paris, so it seemed, no one would try to understand a foreigner speaking French if it was not perfect. Richards found Juanita a pleasant companion who spoke good French and good English. He enjoyed her company very much.

Richards and Juanita met Dubois in the hotel dining room shortly after 8 pm for a relaxed dinner. Richards was impressed with the quality of the food and service. He enjoyed the conversations with Doctors Dubois and González. The subjects were wide ranging, from world politics to art to music. They avoided talking business. At the end of the dinner as the three were enjoying the after dinner coffee and liquor, Dubois said, "Let's plan on meeting in the conference room near my office at 9:30 in the morning. Juanita can drive you to Aerospatiale in her rental car. The other members of the council will have arrived by then."

Richards replied, "That sounds like a good schedule. Thank you for the excellent dinner, Jacques. I can see why the French are world renowned for their cuisine. The food and conversation and company were all fantastic."

Dubois continued, "Thank you, Don. I enjoyed the company, too. I must leave now. Au revoir."

Richards and Juanita chorused, "Au revoir."

Walking down the empty hall on the way up to their rooms, Juanita stopped and faced Don, "I hope you don't think I'm being too forward, but I find you very attractive physically."

Richards looked into Juanita's eyes, smiled, kissed her lightly, and whispered, "Please leave your connecting door open. I find you physically attractive, too!"

Juanita smiled. She unlocked her room and went in, closing the door behind her. Richards walked the few steps to his room next door, unlocked it and walked in. The connecting doors were still open from the afternoon visit with Jacques. He immediately went through the connecting door into Juanita's room, took her in his arms, and kissed her again, this time very passionately. She responded with a deep passion that showed her desire for him.

She whispered in his ear, "Let me take a shower. I'll join you in my bed – soon!"

Richards tenderly kissed her again and quickly returned to his room to undress and shower.

Shortly the pair met in Juanita's bed. They melted in a tangle of embraces and fell asleep entwined in a tight embrace.

Chapter 23

European Launch Date

The next morning, Richards and Juanita enjoyed a continental breakfast served in her room before going down to the lobby. The doorman retrieved her rental car and they drove a few kilometers along the Canal Lateral a la Garonne and arrived at the huge Aerospatiale plant that headquartered the European Space Shuttle program. They reached the large space shuttle conference room just after 9:30 am. The other members of the technical committee of the European Space Council had assembled and were waiting to meet with Richards to discuss a rescue launch date.

Dubois introduced Richards to the other members of the council in turn. The first council member was Dr. Enrique Rodriguez Manuelo, a Spaniard of medium height and build, with black hair and a rather bushy moustache. Dubois said, "Dr. Richards, please meet Dr. Rodriguez. Enrique is deputy program director and is with Iber Avion Spacio in Madrid."

The two shook hands and exchanged greetings. Richards commented, I've already met your colleague, Dr. Gonzalez."

Rodriguez smiled, "Yes, Juanita is very skilled at making the software work properly. Not to downplay your American shuttle software, but the European shuttle software provides ten times as many functions as the American shuttle has. Also, the software is more sophisticated. It uses a fault tolerant concept conceived by Professora Gonzalez working with our colleague, Professor Shepherd."

The second council member was Professor Dr. Tom Shepherd, a rather large man with a red face and reddish hair who spoke with a sometimes difficult to understand English accent. "And, Don, this is Professor Shepherd, who is director of trajectories for the European Space Shuttle. Tom is with the Cranfield Institute of Technology in Milton Keynes, England. He will be a key factor in defining the orbital path to properly rendezvous with the American Space Station during the rescue."

Richards shook hands with Professor Shepherd and said, jokingly, "Pleased to meet you, Professor Shepherd. You're the only member of the council who doesn't speak American."

Shepherd laughed heartily, "Yes, I'm afraid my colleagues learned the wrong dialect when they learned English!"

Everyone laughed at this joke between the two native English speaking members of the group.

The last council member was Heinz Zinn, a very slender man in his early 40's with sparse blonde hair and deep blue eyes. He was deputy director of the European shuttle. Dubois introduced him, "And, Don, this is Dr. Heinz Zinn from Munchen in the Bavarian part of West Germany. Heinz, who heads up our shuttle systems engineering discipline, will define the exact way our shuttle will connect with the Space Station."

Richards responded, "Pleased to meet you, Dr. Zinn. We will have to work out a docking adaptor to permit your shuttle and our Space Station to mate."

Zinn laughed, "Dr. Richards, that should be a simple task. We have already designed our docking adapter to be the same as the American shuttle docking adapter. We anticipated we might want to dock with your Space Station when we designed our shuttle."

"Good! That solves a major interface problem."

After the lengthy introductions and interchanges, Dubois announced with authority, "Lady and Gentlemen, I believe we should start our formal meeting. I'm sure these mission interface details will be covered during our discussions."

He turned to Juanita, "Dr. Gonzalez, I don't want to appear to be a male chauvinist, but may I impose upon you to take notes for the minutes of our meeting? You're the best organized of the council members."

Professor Shepherd interrupted with a laugh, "Jacques, I doubt that Juanita is better organized than I am, but I'll concede her the task of preparing the minutes."

The other two male members of the council chorused happily, "Yes, we vote for Juanita, too."

Juanita looked a little irritated, "I think you all three are male chauvinist pigs! But I'll take notes and write up the minutes anyway." Then she laughed, "At least the minutes will be correct then!"

Dubois nodded and smiled, "Well, with that weighty issue resolved, let's get on with the meeting. We have another issue to resolve. When can we launch a rescue mission?"

He turned to Richards, "Don, could you give the council a summary of the current situation on the Space Station and your requirements for the rescue mission?"

"Jacques, I've prepared a view graph briefing that should answer most of the questions the council may have. And don't hesitate to interrupt and ask questions, please!"

Shepherd added jovially, "Don't worry, Don. This council is not shy about asking embarrassing questions. I'm going to start by asking one. That is, I will, if our director will allow me, while you are getting your view graphs ready."

Dubois nodded his assent and Richards said, "OK, what's your question, Tom?"

Shepherd was obviously relishing his role as 'Devil's advocate'. His eyes narrowed, "Can you tell me, Don, just how in the bloody hell could your three space shuttles have failures – three in a row? First, Columbia with two hydraulic power units that failed, then Atlantis with the main engine controls gone, and then the final tragedy of Discoverer blowing up on the launch pad? I understood that the failure rate for the shuttle is 10^{-9} per hour. That means the probability of three shuttles failing is 10^{-27}."

Then Shepherd exploded in a loud voice, "Why, that's the same bloody probability that the universe will blow up tomorrow, for God's sake!"

Richards answered calmly, "Tom, I agree the probability is pretty low, but there's one factor you forgot to include in your probability calculations."

"And just what factor is that?"

"The human factor, Tom. The human factor! Remember, these shuttles are almost twenty years old, and tens of thousands of people are involved in maintaining, refurbishing, and launching them. If someone in the human chain makes a mistake, puts in the wrong part, or the material used is deficient, then your probability calculations are all wrong."

Shepherd mumbled condescendingly, "Don, my probability computations are mathematically and logically sound. What do you mean?"

"Tom, a good example is the Discovery accident. We've attributed it to a human error, or human frailty, if you wish."

He then told the story of the use of the deficient metal in the external tank and the suicide of Yogi. Shepherd reflected a moment, got an understanding look on his face, and commented, "Yeah, I guess you're right, Don. My probability computations can't take into account that kind of factor. But how about the other two shuttle failures?"

"We don't have the answer completely tied down yet. But there's a human factor on the Columbia we do know about."

"And what's that?"

"A design compromise was made when the shuttle was originally designed, Tom. We decided to use triple redundancy instead of quadruple redundancy in the hydraulic power units. It was an easy compromise to make because the units were so big and expensive. Anyway, we figured we could get by if two units failed. Later, we discovered that re-entry is not possible with only one hydraulic power unit working. The cross winds encountered during re-entry would cause the shuttle to lose control and burn up."

"Touché! My calculations didn't include stupid design decisions either!"

Dubois interrupted this interchange, "Don, your view graphs are ready to project now. Perhaps you should start your briefing. It sounds like this philosophical discussion between you and Professor Shepherd could go on for a long time."

Richards laughed, "You're right, Jacques. It could go on for a very long time."

Then Richards began his briefing, "We have seventeen astronauts stranded in space now. We plan to leave a skeleton crew of four aboard the Space Station, so thirteen have to be rescued. We estimate this will require three rescue missions with the crew carrying capacity of your shuttle."

Shepherd interrupted and agreed, "Yes, Don. That's right. Three rescue missions will do it. We send a crew of five and bring back four, four, and five. The last mission with five will be a bit crowded, but we can do it. We could crowd in more passengers by reducing the crew size, I suppose."

Richards continued, "Good. Another key point: We have expendables to last through August. We feel that the first rescue mission should be scheduled at least thirty days before the expendables run out. We also feel the first rescue mission should carry up another three months of expendables, just in case!"

Dubois interjected, "Don, carrying the three months expendables is no problem, but a launch date by the first of August – that could be a real problem. It depends on how our launch goes tomorrow. If it goes smoothly and our latest software and hardware changes look good, we may be able to make that date. Otherwise, it looks very tight!"

Richards answered, "Perhaps we should work out a rescue schedule assuming your launch is going to confirm your changes are OK. I will stay over until Wednesday, after your Tuesday launch. Then we can adjust the launch date, if need be."

Dubois smiled and replied, "I can see why UAC selected you as program director for the Space Station. You keep a clear and logical perspective on the whole problem at all times instead of getting mired down in the details. Yes, your schedule makes sense. Doesn't it, Council Members?"

He turned and surveyed the other four council members. They each nodded in agreement to Richard's plan.

Richards went on with his briefing and, at the end, said, "So you see, Lady and Gentlemen, we're up the proverbial creek without a paddle. We need your help to get back."

Jacques responded, "Don, the council needs some time to decide on a launch date. We have to see if we can commit to the 1 August rescue launch that you feel is necessary. If you will excuse us for thirty minutes, we need to caucus in my office. Then we'll return with a firm commitment, contingent on the results of tomorrow's launch, of course."

Richards answered, "That sounds fair to me. I have a novel in my brief case. I'll read that while you have your caucus."

Jacques looked at his watch, "It's 11 am now – we'll return before 12. Then we'll adjourn for lunch."

The five council members filed out, leaving Richards alone in the conference room. He took out his novel and started reading it.

The council filed back into the conference room at 12:15. Richards noticed Zinn, Rodriguez, and Shepherd had grim looks on their faces. Juanita and Dubois were smiling. Dubois announced, " Don, it was a tough caucus. Some of our council members wanted to set a date of 30 August. But Juanita presented an impassioned rationale as to why we should agree to an earlier date. She prevailed. We will commit to a one August launch date."

Shepherd added, scowling, "That is, if everything goes well with the launch tomorrow!"

Dubois agreed, "Yes, of course, if the launch goes well. Now, let's retire to the Executive Dining Room for lunch."

Richards was invited to a special reception at the Toulouse City Hall on Monday evening, hosted by the Space Council. A number of the top management of Aerospatiale and city dignitaries, including the mayor of Toulouse, attended the reception. They were served champagne and the varietal wines of the region. In addition, there was a continuous stream of waiters circulating among the guests offering an array of delicious hors d'oeuvres. The mayor gave a short speech in French. Richards, with his limited understanding of the French language, only partially understood what the mayor said:

"We of Toulouse are proud to have Aerospatiale as part of our city's community of companies. We are proud of our city's role in the European Space Shuttle. We are also proud that the European Space Shuttle will rescue the American astronauts lost in space. In recognition of the friendship of Toulouse, as representative of the European Community, we wish to present Dr. Richards the key to our city. Please come forward, Sir."

Richards didn't understand the last part of the speech. Juanita nudged him and whispered in his sear, "Don, you are supposed to go forward. The mayor is going to present you with a key to the city."

Richards looked embarrassed, smiled, and walked forward to where the mayor was standing.

The mayor placed the bronze key, hung from an elaborate blue ribbon like an Olympic medal, around Richards' neck, kissed him on both cheeks, and announced in French, "Welcome to Toulouse, Dr. Richards. The city is yours to enjoy."

Richards shook hands with the mayor and addressed the audience in English, "I am flattered by this recognition by the beautiful city of Toulouse. On behalf of all Americans, we thank our European friends for your willingness to use your shuttle to rescue our stranded astronauts. I will treasure this key and have already enjoyed your city immensely. Thank you, Mr. Mayor."

The French audience applauded, as most of them spoke and understood several non-mother tongue languages.

When Richards and the council members returned to the hotel, Richards was treated to another elaborate dinner paid for by Dr. Dubois. Just before they separated after dinner, Juanita whispered in Richards' ear, "My door will be open. Please come back again."

He whispered back, "Don't worry, I'll be there."

As the whole group was leaving the dining room, Dubois said, "Don, you are invited to our launch control room tomorrow morning for the Ariane launch. Be there by 7 am."

"OK. See you then. And thanks for the dinner. It was great."

The next morning was Tuesday, the first of April. Richards and Juanita rose early in order to be at the launch control center at Aerospatiale on time. They left too early to have breakfast in the room, but Juanita assured Richards there would be coffee, Danish rolls, and orange juice in the launch center.

They were in the launch center well before 7 am. The count down was in progress and they arrived during a technical hold. The launch control spokesman estimated the launch would be just after 7:30 am local time. Multiple video screens around the room displayed the big rocket with its dummy payload to emulate the European shuttle sitting on its pad from several points of view. Richards and Juanita were standing together drinking coffee and munching Danish rolls when the launch controller announced the hold was over and the count down was continuing from minus five minutes. The time seemed to those watching the video screens to go very slowly. Finally the controller counted down the last five seconds – "5, 4, 3, 2, 1" and then yelled, "We have lift off! Everything is in the green!"

A cheer went up in the launch room. Dubois walked over to Richards and said, "Don, it looks like the one August rescue launch is OK!"

Richards replied, "Great, Jacques. Congratulations on a successful launch!"

At that instant there was an enormous flash on the screen. An anguished moan rose in the control center. Ariane had exploded in flight, 93 seconds after lift off.

Dubois's face turned ashen. He stood silently as others in the room asked each other questions like, "What happened?", "What do we do now?", etc.

Finally Dubois turned to Richards and said in a very low voice, almost a whisper, "Sorry, Don. We can't meet your first of August rescue launch. It doesn't look good at all."

Richards asked grimly, "When can you launch?"

"Don, I can't answer your question now. I suggest you return to your hotel. You better start considering any other options you have. I'll meet with the council. We'll call you as soon as we have an answer."

Juanita said plaintively, "I'm really sorry, Don. That's a blow to us as well as you. Here are the keys to my rental car. You can drive it back. I have to stay for the council meeting, of course."

Richards took the keys and responded mechanically, "Thanks, Juanita. See you later."

Richards returned to the hotel alone. There was nothing for him to do except wait for the council's report.

Chapter 24

What Happened to Ariane

Richards was watching the evening news on television when he heard Juanita walk slowly into her room. He hurried through the connecting door, "Buenas tardes, Juanita. Como se va"

She looked up glumly, then rushed over, put her arms around Richards, "We spent all day trying to figure out what went wrong with the launch. Tom Shepherd claimed it must have been the software!" She broke down and sobbed, tears pouring down her face.

Richards held her tightly, comforted her, and asked, "What evidence is there that the software caused the explosion?"

"None! That's what is so infuriating about the accusation. All he could say was *I have computed the probabilities of what could have caused the explosion and mathematically it looks like the software.* Oh, that man can be so overbearing and cocksure of everything!"

Richards replied soothingly, "Yes, even when he's wrong.. Juanita, don't worry. You don't need mathematical proof. What you need is physical evidence of what happened. I know! I just went through the explosion of Discovery. I believe Professor Shepherd may be guilty of jumping to conclusions."

Juanita regained her composure and responded defiantly, "I think so, too. I spent hundreds of hours validating the software loaded into the computers for this flight. I'm sure the software was OK. Besides, the fault tolerant algorithm we incorporated would protect the software against faults not detected in our validation tests."

"Didn't Tom Shepherd collaborate with you on the fault tolerant algorithms?"

"Yes, but he claims we *must not have implemented the algorithm correctly!*"

Suddenly Richards had an idea. He grabbed Juanita, "Where does Aerospatiale get the metal for those external tanks used on Ariane?"

Juanita, surprised by the question, searched her memory and responded after a delay, "Don, that's out of my field, but I do remember a briefing when they said the specialty steel came from a steel company in Japan."

"Juanita, I may be jumping to conclusions, too, but I'll bet that, if the material inspection report is examined, the Japanese inspector was named Yogi!"

Juanita looked even more confused, "Who's Yogi?"

"Do you remember my story yesterday about the reason for the Discovery explosion?"

"Yes. Oh, you mean the Japanese inspector, Yogi, who committed suicide for allowing defective material to be passed as OK. The defective metal that was used on the Discovery external tank —Yes, now I see what you mean!"

"Well, at least it's a possibility that should be looked into."

Juanita replied with a knowing gleam in her eye, "I agree. In fact, I'm going to call Dr. Dubois at his home now and explain the theory."

She strode over to the telephone, dialed Dubois' home number and spent several minutes talking to him in French. Richards could only understand a few words here and there, but enough to understand she was explaining Richards' theory of what might have caused the explosion. Hanging up the phone, Juanita said excitedly, "Jacques thought your theory might prove true. He knew our European shuttle uses the same Japanese steel company for our external tanks as the American shuttle. That's the reason we selected the Japanese company. Jacques is heading for the plant right now to meet with the Ariane production manager and review the material inspection reports."

"Jacques certainly doesn't waste any time, does he?"

"No, he's a very effective program director. He asked if you could get some information for him. It's quite urgent."

"What does he want?"

"He would like you to get the data and batch numbers of the metal used in the shuttle external tank that exploded. Can you do that?"

Richards checked his watch – 8:15 pm. He mentally computed it was six hours earlier at NASA Michoud in New Orleans. "Yes, I'll call Jack Kelly at NASA Michoud now. He should be able to give me that information."

Richards checked his personal phone book and dialed direct to Kelly's office at Michoud. After a seemingly interminable dialing time punctuated with clicking noises, Kelly's phone finally started ringing. He answered, "Kelly here."

Richards explained, "Jack, this is Don Richards over in Toulouse."

"Too bad about Ariane. I just heard about their launch failure when I came into the office this morning. Sounds like it might be the external tank. They use the same Japanese steel vendor as we do, you know."

"Yes, Jack. I just found that out. Can you find some information for me? It's really urgent!"

"What do you want?"

"What was the fabrication date and manufacturing lot number of the metal used in the Discovery tank – tank 193?"

Kelly answered calmly and efficiently, "That's easy. I've got the papers right here on my desk. I was using them as exhibits in my expanded report I'm writing for headquarters. Just a moment."

Richards heard Kelly rustling through papers on his desk..

"Here it is, right here. The date of fabrication was 7 December 1991. That's ironic, isn't it? The fiftieth anniversary of Pearl Harbor Day. The batch number was 17132."

"Thanks, Jack. That's exactly what I needed. I'll call you back if I have any questions."

"OK, Don. I'll be in the office all day. And you have my home number. Feel free to call me there if you have to. Sounds like Yogi may have done in the Ariane, too! Well, check it out."

"So long. Thanks a lot."

Richards handed Juanita a note with the numbers written on it. "Here's the information you asked for."

"You Americans are amazing. I ask you for some obscure information, you make one phone call, and five minutes later you have the answer! I'll have to admit we Europeans couldn't have obtained the information so quickly."

Richards laughed, "This was an exceptional case, Juanita. It just so happened I called the man who was writing up the Discovery accident report and he had the information on his desk. Otherwise I'd still be waiting."

Juanita waited about 20 minutes to make sure Dubois had reached his office at Aerospatiale. She called his number and he answered. She gave him the information. After a short conversation in French, she hung up and turned to Richards, "Jacques was astounded I had the information so soon. He said the Ariane production manager was going through the files and might find the inspections report in a couple of hours."

Richards said sympathetically, You've had a hard day, Juanita. How would you like me to take you out to dinner?"

"That's very nice of you, Don. But really, I would rather just have dinner served in the room and then go to bed early – with you. I'm exhausted and we have a 7 am meeting again in the morning."

"That sounds fine to me. I really want you again, Juanita – more than dinner. By the way, am I supposed to be at the meeting at 7 am also?"

"No, Don. Jacques wants the council to meet alone for a couple of hours. Then you're invited to come to the meeting at 10 am."

"That time is fine. I hope to get a launch date commitment by then, considering your unfortunate explosion."

Richards and Juanita enjoyed a relaxed dinner in her room with a bottle of champagne to finish it off. They retired to her bed and renewed their passionate love making, trying to forget the terrible explosion of Ariane that morning.

The next day Richards slept late. When he woke up just before 9, he found a note from Juanita:

Thanks for a wonderful night. Here are the keys to my rental car. See you in the space shuttle conference room at 10.
Con amor, Juanita

Richards arrived on time at the conference room. The space council members looked glum. Dubois greeted Richards, "Thanks for the information I asked for last night. Unfortunately, we found out our shuttle tank and your shuttle tank came from the same defective batch of material made on 7 December 1991."

Richards replied, "Glad to help. At least it appears you have the reason Ariane exploded."

Professor Shepherd interrupted, "Yes, it appears with a probability of 99.997% that it was the defective material in the tank."

He turned to Juanita and said somewhat sheepishly, "And, Juanita, I guess I was wrong about it being a software error. You must have implemented the algorithm correctly after all. I apologize for the accusation."

Juanita replied graciously, "Don't worry, Tom. I know you were just trying to find a reason for the explosion. I knew it couldn't have been the software. Our validation tests were quite thorough."

Richards spoke next, "Jacques, I'm glad the reason for the explosion has been established. That takes a lot of uncertainty out of the situation, doesn't it?"

"Yes. It does, Don. But it doesn't really help the date for a rescue attempt."

"I know. What is the council's verdict on the earliest launch date now?"

Dubois shook his head, "It doesn't look good at all. The earliest we can launch now is the middle of October."

Richards sucked in his breath. He replied, being very careful to keep his voice calm, "But the expendables on the Space Station will be gone by then. Isn't there some way you can accelerate the date?"

"I'm afraid not. Our review revealed that all the launcher tanks we have in inventory used the defective Japanese metal. We'll have to make all new tanks. Trying to launch with the tanks on hand is not a risk we are willing to take. We did an updated PERT (Program Evaluation Review Transaction) chart showing all the steps that must be taken before another launch. Really, the middle of October is the earliest possible date. Even that date assumes nothing will go wrong."

Tom Shepherd interrupted, "Sorry, Don. We really looked at every possible short cut. There just isn't any bloody way we can speed things up. We don't want you Americans to have to rely on the Russians any more than your President does. But it looks like they are your only hope. That is, unless you can get the shuttle that's in the Smithsonian, the Enterprise, refurbished."

"Tom, we looked into that option already. The earliest we could launch Enterprise is early next year. That's way too late. I'm afraid the Russian option is the only one left. I guess I better go call my boss and give him the bad news. Then I'll have to catch a flight back to Paris and try to get home right away."

Shepherd broke in with his booming voice, "Aw, what the bloody hell, Don. Relax! You Americans rush around too much. You can't call America now. Everyone's asleep there. Spend one more night here with us. We'll all go out and get drunk. You can't get home any earlier leaving this afternoon anyway. You've already missed the non-stop flights from Paris to the US. The next one's at noon tomorrow. You can make it easy catching the 8 am flight from Toulouse to Paris."

Richards looked at his watch and then at Tom. He smiled, "OK, Tom. You're right. I might as well stay over and enjoy your company here."

Shepherd added with a hearty laugh, "Yes, you might as well get to know us better. With the luck you've had so far, the Russian Shuttle may fail in orbit, too. Then you'll need us in October after all."

Everyone laughed at Shepherd's outlandish contention. Then Richards looked Shepherd in the eye, smiled and said, "Now I suppose you'll compute the probability of that happening. Right?"

Shepherd responded, "Oh, hell, that's easy. It's about one in three with the jinx you've got!"

Richards answered, "I certainly hope that computation is wrong!"

Dubois interrupted this repartee between Richards and Shepherd, "Don, we have about forty-five minutes before lunch. Would you like to take a tour of our shuttle integration area? At least you can see first hand what our shuttle looks like."

"I'd like that very much."

That evening Richards had dinner and drinks with the whole space council. They all got somewhat inebriated trying to forget the frustrations of the day. And later Richards spent one more night in Juanita's bed. They got up early Thursday morning and Juanita drove him to the airport for the 8 am flight. He kissed her goodbye, "I would like to visit you in Malaga someday."

She replied wistfully, "I hope so, Don. I really hope you find a reason to visit Malaga. Soon!"

Richards arrived at Charles de Gaulle Airport just after 9:30 am. He took the longish walk to the Pan Am terminal, went up on the escalator, and walked through passport control to the Clipper Club. After signing in, he was given his boarding pass by the pretty attendant on duty. He found a seat, ordered a Bloody Mary from the young lady handling the club's bar, and started to read the latest *International Herald Tribune*. Looking up, he caught sight of Brigitte sitting across the room from him.

Picking up his drink, he walked over to her, "Fancy meeting you here. And where are you going today?"

Brigitte looked up in surprise and her face broke into a beautiful smile, "Why, I'm going to Los Angeles today. Here's my boarding pass."

He compared his seat with hers and exclaimed happily, "Guess what, we're seat partners again."

Brigitte stood up, grabbed Richards and kissed him passionately. She whispered, "I'm so glad to see you again."

Brigitte asked, as Richards sat down next to her, "How was your trip to Toulouse?"

"Not so good, Brigitte. I went there to arrange for the European Space Shuttle to rescue the American astronauts stranded in space. Their launcher blew up and the rescue can't be made now."

"So what will you do now? You can't just leave the cosmonauts – I mean, astronauts in space."

"That's right. We'll have to ask the Russians to rescue them with their shuttle."

"When do you expect to ask them?"

Richards looked at Brigitte quizzically, "You seem very interested in all this. If I didn't know better, I would suspect you of being a KGB agent!" Then he laughed.

Brigitte laughed lightly, "Of course I am. Can't you tell? 'Femme fatale' and all!"

Richards replied, "Now seriously, what do you do? I guess I never found that out."

Brigitte smiled, "That's right. You were too busy with other things. I really work for an import/export company. It causes me to do a lot of traveling."

"What's the company's name?"

Michon Import-Export Corporation. Our main office is in Paris, but I'm establishing a new office in Moscow. I'll be going to Moscow shortly after returning to Paris from Los Angeles. That's why I was interested in your comments about Russia."

"But Michon is your last name. Does your father own the company?"

"No, Don. I'm afraid my father is dead. Actually I own the company outright. The company only has five other employees."

"And what does your company do?"

Now Brigitte laughed and said, "You seem very interested in all this. If I didn't know better, I would suspect you of being a CIA agent!"

"Touché!"

"Well, anyway, Don. We ship a lot of microcomputers to Russia and other high technology items. They seem to have a voracious appetite for all kinds of technology items."

"But, don't you have trouble shipping that kind of thing to Russia? Isn't it difficult to get export licenses. I know it would be in the US."

"Not really, Don. The Europeans see Russia as a legitimate trading partner. No, I don't have any particular trouble with export licenses. Everything we ship is benign. I mean, no munitions or anything like that."

"Brigitte, you're an amazing woman. Beautiful, sexy, and a good business woman. I may be going to Russia soon myself."

"Who will decide whether you go?"

"Actually, President Williamson has to decide that it's OK to ask the Russians to rescue the astronauts."

"Do you think he will?"

"Yes. He really has no choice now!"

Brigitte gave a sexy laugh, "Well, if you go to Russia, maybe I'll see you there. If you'll excuse me for a moment, Don, I have to make a phone call before we get on the plane."

"OK, but hurry back. I miss you already!"

Richards had no way of knowing it, but the Soviet Premier Michail Gorbachev will learn that the American President will ask him to use the Russian Shuttle to rescue the American astronauts before the President himself knows.

When Brigitte returned from the phone call, she said, with a sad look on her face, "Don, I'm sorry. That was my business associate in California. I won't be going to Los Angeles with you after all. He asked me to cancel my visit."

She bent down, kissed Richards passionately, and whispered, "I hope to see you in Moscow. I'll be staying at the Metropole Hotel from the thirteenth to the twenty-first of April. Call me there if you come to Moscow. Goodbye, Darling!"

Richards replied, "I'll miss having you as my seat partner on this flight. I promise to call you if I come during that time. Goodbye!"

After Brigitte left, he looked at his watch. It was 11:30 am Paris time. He thought to himself, *It's 1:30 in the morning in LA. Everyone's asleep now. Guess Brigitte had to wake up her business associate in California.'*

Just then the Clipper Room hostess came over to where Richards was sitting and said, "Dr. Richards, you better go out to the boarding area now. Your flight will be ready to board soon. Remember, you have to go through the security inspection first. The line may be long."

Richards looked up, "Thank you, Miss. I'll leave right now. I enjoyed the Clipper Club hospitality as usual."

"You're always welcome here, Dr. Richards. Have a nice flight to Los Angeles."

Richards' Pan Am flight arrived at the Los Angeles Bradley International Terminal just before 4 pm. He quickly cleared passport control and customs. He was delighted to see Dawn's happy, smiling face in the crowd as he left the customs area. He kissed her, "Darling! I'm so glad to be home again!"

Chapter 25

What Do We Do Now?

Richards got to his office at 7:30 Friday morning. He had phoned his secretary from the airport the day before to ask her to set up a 9 am meeting with Mr. David Moore, president of Universal Aircraft. In response to her question about the subject of the meeting, he had replied, 'What option now?' On his desk he found a note from June confirming his 9 am meeting. He began reading the mail stacked in his URGENT box. He had long since given up trying to read the ROUTINE mail. He just put it in a big drawer in his desk marked 'Un-read mail'. Just before 8 his phone rang. He answered himself since June was not there yet.

It was Gus Ford saying, "Don, I saw the Ariane explosion on TV Tuesday. What's the latest launch date for the European shuttle?"

"Gus, I'm afraid we're out of luck on the European shuttle. They're going to have to re-fabricate all their existing booster fuel tanks. They all have Yogi's defective metal."

With tension showing in his voice, Ford interrupted, "But, when can they launch?"

That's the bad news, Gus. The earliest launch date is the middle of October."

"But that's too late. The expendables will be gone."

"Exactly! We're going to have to ask the Russians to help, but we're hampered since President Williamson has said 'No' to that option!"

There was a silence on the other end of the line while Ford absorbed the impact of the situation. After a few moments he asked haltingly, "What are you going to do, Don?"

"There's only one thing I can do. I'm meeting with someone in an hour who can point out to the President that we have no option except a Russian rescue, someone who can get the President to back down from his negative position."

"Who's that? John Davidson?"

"No. We'll need Davidson's support of our position, but right now we need someone with some political muscle."

Who do you have in mind?"

"The president of Universal Aircraft, Dave Moore."

"Why do you think he has the political clout, Don?" He's just the president of an aircraft company."

"Yes, but he was chairman of the political action committee called the Aerospace President's Group. They raised over ten million dollars for President Williamson's election campaign. That kind of money talks."

"I see your point, Don. I sure hope your plan works. Now to what I called you about. I need to ask you to do two things: first, we need to set up a 10 am meeting, your time, over the video link to Houston, Washington, and the Space Station. General Robbins is really upset that he doesn't know what's going on. Bill Adams at headquarters is getting pressured by the NASA Administrator and by Dr. Davidson."

Richards interrupted, "That's a good idea, having a video link meeting. I thought we had a solution until the Ariane booster explosion. Then, by the time I had the European's launch date, it was too late to inform anybody."

"Yes, I understand, Don. The meeting will clear the air on that point. Second, I would like you to meet with me and Adams in Washington Monday morning. Adams has invited Dr. Davidson to come to the meeting as well."

"That's good, Gus. I hope by then Mr. Moore will have cleared the air by calling President Williamson. It would help if Davidson would support our position that a Russian rescue is our only option now."

"I agree. See you on the video link in a couple of hours. Good luck with your meeting with Mr. Moore. I certainly hope he can convince the President of the value of the Russian option. I agree, we don't have any other choice now. So long."

"So long, Gus. See you at 12 noon your time."

June hurried into Richards' office, "I just got a phone call from Mr. Moore's secretary. She said he wants to see you right away, that he can't wait until nine."

Richards answered calmly, "OK, June. I'll go right up. While I'm gone, please set up a meeting of the crisis team in the big conference room at 10 am. Also, ask Tom to set up the video links with Houston, Washington, and the Space Station. Then set me up to leave on the United non-stop to Washington Sunday morning. Leave the return open. Put me up at the Capitol Quality Inn."

June said anxiously, "Dr. Richards, I hope I got all that. You better hurry. Mr. Moore's secretary sounded like it was urgent."

"OK, June. Call her and tell her I'm on my way."

Richards walked into Moore's large outer office just after 8:15 am. His secretary, Janice, said agitatedly, "Go right in, Dr. Richards. I better warn you. He's a little upset."

"OK, Janice. Thanks."

Richard's hurried into Moore's huge office that had floor to ceiling windows facing in three directions: north toward the Santa Ana Mountains, east toward the verdant Irvine Hills, and south toward the blue Newport Harbor and the calm Pacific beyond. Moore was just over six feet tall and a former USC football guard. He received his BS in Engineering and MS in Business Administration from USC. He greeted Richards in his booming baritone voice in a threatening tone, "What the hell is going on here, Don? I just got a call from the president of Aerospatiale. He told me they can't launch a rescue mission before the 15th of October. That's too damn late! Why didn't you call me and tell me all this? Why do I have to find out from Aerospatiale?"

Richards strode over to Moore's disk, looked him straight in the eye, "Calm down, Dave. You'll have a heart attack. Look, I've been riding on airplanes and attending meetings in Toulouse continuously for the last week. It's a politically sensitive situation that I didn't want to discuss on the phone. Yesterday afternoon I set up a meeting with you for this morning after flying for thirteen hours from Toulouse. Now, do you want to hear the details of the situation or do you want to bitch about the poor communication?"

Moore knew Richards was his most valuable executive and the only one who could solve the rescue problems. He regained his composure, and said, somewhat apologetically, "I'm sorry, Don. I just don't like surprises. You know that!"

"Yes, I know, Don. But right now we're in between a rock and a hard place. You're going to have to call President Williamson to resolve our dilemma!"

"What do you mean exactly? I'm not with you."

Richards continued calmly, "Look, Dave, we're getting the cart before the horse. Let's back up a bit and have the meeting I asked for in the first place. You must understand exactly what is going on, if you're going to call the President!"

"I certainly agree. Give me the story."

Richards recounted the details from his trip to Toulouse. He explained he had been given a commitment for a 1 August rescue launch which would have been OK, but that the explosion of Ariane had delayed that commitment to the 15th of October, which was too late because the expendables would be gone by the end of August. He finished his summary, "Dave, the only viable option left is to ask the Russians to rescue our astronauts using their Space Shuttle. We've already contacted their program director, Dr. Chekhov, and he has indicated the mission could be arranged through the 'proper government-to-government channels'. At this point, that probably means President Williamson calling Premier Gorbachev."

Moore interrupted, "Then why don't we just inform NASA that we go with the Russian option and get on with it?"

"Dave I'm afraid it's not that simple. NASA originally recommended the Russian option. The President rejected it vehemently and insisted the NASA Administrator issue a directive for the European option. He's put himself in a box."

"Well, what can I do, Don? It's obvious the Russian option is the only way to go."

"Exactly. Just call the President and explain that to him!"

"But why can't NASA do that, for Christ's sake?"

Richards looked at his boss and smiled, "I used to be a bureaucrat. I know how they think. Since the President rejected their recommendation before, they are afraid to confront him again, unless they are sure he will say 'yes'."

"In other words, if I call the President and explain the facts to him, unofficially, then when NASA makes their recommendation, this time he will buy it. Is that about right?"

"Exactly. Remember, you were chairman of a political action committee that raised a lot of money for the President's election. That will make a difference when you call."

"I believe you're right, Don. I'll call him now."

"Thanks, Boss. I really need the help. Assuming you get a positive response, I'll 'leak' this to the NASA chief engineer when I meet with him Monday. He'll tell the NASA Administrator, who'll then have the self confidence to recommend the Russian option again."

"OK, Don. Sorry about my outburst when you first came in."

"That's OK, Dave. We're all under a lot of pressure. We've got seventeen lives up there on the Station depending upon us to do the right thing."

"I'll let you know how my call with the President goes as soon as I can."

Chapter 26

Soviet Option Revisited

Dave Moore's secretary, buzzed him, "Mr. Moore, I have the President's personal secretary on the phone. She says the President is ready to speak to you."

"OK, Janice. Thanks." Moore switched to the flashing button on his phone, "Hello, this is Dave Moore out in California."

"Good morning, Mr. Moore. This is Mary Jane, the President's secretary. I explained to the President you were the same Mr. Moore who was the chairman of that aerospace group that contributed so much money to his campaign. He said, "I'm always glad to talk to supporters!' Mr. Moore, if you'll hold for just a moment, I'll tell the President you're on the line."

After a long wait, there was click on the line and the very familiar voice of the President of the United States came on the line, saying, "Dave, it's really great to hear from one of my supporters. That ten million your committee contributed to my campaign is what pushed us over the top. Thanks again for your help. What can I do for you?"

"Mr. President, I'm also the president of Universal Aircraft. We're responsible for the Space Station, you know."

"Yes, Dave. That's a dreadful situation up there with our seventeen astronauts stranded. I'm sure glad the Europeans are going to rescue them with their shuttle. I'm just glad we didn't have to ask the Russians for help. That would have politically embarrassing consequences for me, you know. The conservatives would have jumped on that and wrecked my legislative program."

"Well, Mr. President, that's what I called you about. As a result of the Ariane explosion this week, the Europeans aren't going to be able to launch a rescue mission in time after all!"

"Oh, that's too bad. I guess we'll have to get the old Enterprise fixed up after all then."

"No, Mr. President. The Enterprise can't be fixed up in time either. I'm afraid the only viable option we have left now is the Russian option: use the Russian space shuttle for the rescue."

There was a silence at the other end of the phone. Then the President responded, "That's terrible. This is going to be awfully embarrassing for me. Are you sure there's not some other way, Dave?"

"I'm afraid not, Mr. President. I've just reviewed the situation with our vice president, Dr. Richards, who is director of the Space Station Program. He and his team of experts have looked at every possibility and that's the only way left to save the astronauts."

"I respect your opinion. You must be right. Does my Science Advisor have the details on this situation?"

"Dr. Richards is meeting with Dr. Davidson Monday morning."

"Well, I want to hear from Dr. Davidson and I want the NASA Administrator to concur. Do you think they will endorse your recommendation, Dave?"

"Yes, Mr. President. I believe they will."

"Then, I guess I'll have to call Premier Gorbachev and ask for their help. I need to get the National Security Council to agree to this course of action first through. Thanks for the call. Always good to hear from my supporters. Goodbye."

"Goodbye, Mr. President."

Richards arrived in the Space Station conference room just before 10 am. The video images of Barbara Rosen and General Robbins from the Space Station were on one screen, Gus Ford and his team in Houston were on another, and a third screen showed Dr. Adams and a few of the associate administrators at NASA Headquarters. Tom Rubin and the crisis team were already gathered around the huge conference table. The atmosphere was tense. Everyone was waiting to hear Richards' status report about his trip to Toulouse and his plan for the rescue option.

As Richards walked into view on the UAC conference room TV camera, General Robbins spoke up brusquely, "Don, this is Jack Robbins up here at the Station. What the hell is going on? We haven't heard from you in a week. I heard a rumor the European option is kaput. Is that true?"

"Yes, I'm afraid it is. The explosion of the Ariane launcher was the final blow to the European rescue plan."

Robbins became agitated, "Why can't they just use one of their other launchers? I understand they have two more."

Richards explained the problem with defective metal in the fuel tanks that was discovered after the Ariane explosion. He summarized, "Jack and Barbara, I know that you and the rest of the crew up there are concerned about this latest mishap, and rightly so. But let me assure you we are doing everything possible to get the Russian rescue option approved."

Barbara Rosen exclaimed, "What in hell do you mean 'approved'? We seventeen are sitting up here with our life sustaining expendables disappearing day by day and you're talking about 'approval'! My God! Just get on with asking the Russians to get their damn shuttle up here!"

Just as Richards was about to respond to Barbara's outburst, his secretary, June, tapped him on the shoulder, "Dr. Richards, Mr. Moore's on the phone. I told him you were conducting a big video link meeting, but he insisted on interrupting."

Richards turned to his global audience, "You'll have to excuse me for a moment while I take a phone call that may answer Barbara's question."

Richards strode out of TV camera range to take the phone call. Moore explained the gist of the phone conversation he had just had with President Williamson. He summarized, "The President will call the Russian Premier to ask for the rescue mission, but he wants his Science Advisor and the NASA Administrator to endorse the position as the only viable option. He also wants his National Security Council to support the Russian option. He's still worried about the conservative block torpedoing his legislative program if he asks the Soviets for help."

Richards responded angrily, "To hell with his legislative program. If he lets our astronauts perish, he'll be impeached."

It was Moore's turn to sooth Richards, "Now calm down, Don. Don't worry. The President will call Gorbachev. He just wants to protect his ass. That's politics!"

"Touché, Dave. I understand. Thanks for the info. I better get back to the meeting. There are seventeen agitated people up in space that I'm trying to calm down. OK if I mention your call with the President?"

"Yes, I guess it's OK. Just be careful what you say."

"Good. That'll help. I'll be careful."

Richards walked back to his original position in front of the TV camera and said authoritatively, "Lady and Gentlemen, I have an announcement to make. I just heard that the President is willing to call the Russian Premier to ask him to use the Russian shuttle for the rescue."

Barbara Rosen called out from her screen, "Now, that's a lot better! Enough of that bureaucratic "approval' business!"

Richards smiled at Barbara's comment and nodded, "However, the President wants an endorsement from the NASA Administrator and his Science Advisor."

Bill Adams broke in from his TV screen, "Don, don't worry. The Administrator will endorse the position. I'll get with him right after this meeting. I'm ready to leave my badge on his desk if he says 'No'."

Richards was impressed with Adams' unusual dedication to principles, and replied, "Bill, we need Dr. Davidson's endorsement as well."

"Davidson is out of town for the whole week end. But you and I have an appointment with him in the White House at 9 am Monday. I'm sure he will endorse our position."

General Robbins broke in at this point, using a conciliatory tone, "Don, Bill, Gus Ford, and the rest of you – Barbara, the rest of the Station crew and I thank you for your professional support to get us out of this mess. I for one appreciate the awkward position that President Williamson is in, having to ask the Russians for help in the rescue. You may not remember, but when he was in the Senate, he was one of the 'hawks' who insisted upon denying the export of advanced US technology to the Soviet Union. It's like having to eat crow to admit the Russians have been able to develop the advanced technology needed to save all of us Americans up here."

Richards replied, "Thanks for that insight. It helps to understand the background for the political decisions we were discussing earlier. Let me present a few view graph charts

Universal Aircraft has prepared to summarize the Russian option based on what we know now."

Richards went through a short briefing and summarized, "We will be sure that the Russian shuttle brings at least three months expendables on the first rescue mission. This will build up our margin of safety in case of another mishap, God forbid!"

Gus Ford added, "The three months of expendables are a damn good idea. That would move our date for the exhaustion of expendables to within the launch window of the European shuttle."

Richards agreed, "Exactly, Gus. Then we would again have a viable European option if we should need it."

General Robbins interjected, "Thanks, Don, for the information. It really helps reduce our anxiety up here on the Station."

Barbara added, "Yes, thanks, Don. It'll be good to see some new faces up here. I hope the Russian commander is good looking."

Everyone laughed at this completely irrelevant comment and Richards closed the meeting, "I will go to Russia just as soon as possible, probably within a week. I'll keep you all informed on our progress. Thanks. So long."

The rest of the global audience signed off and the video screens went blank.

Chapter 27

White House Decision

For the first time in two weeks Richards was home for the weekend. He took advantage of the short weekend (he would fly to Washington Sunday morning) to spend a relaxed Saturday with Dawn. They both wanted to do something really different from their logical, scientific, high pressure job activities so they decided to drive to the Farmers' Market in west Los Angeles. They wandered through the food stalls at lunch time trying to choose among the huge variety of exotic dishes: Mexican food, Jewish delicatessen with pastrami sandwiches, Texas bar-b-cued sandwiches, Italian spaghetti, Indonesian shashlik, Indian curry, hamburgers, hot dogs, ice cream, soft drinks, fresh fruit juices squeezed on the spot, bakeries with lemon meringue pies and German cakes, and myriad more.

With a great deal of vacillating they finally decided pick their favorites and then split each portion so each was able to have some of everything. They chose Mexican enchiladas, Texas bar-b-cued pork ribs, honeydew melon juice, a slice of Boston creme pie, a chocolate sundae, and a Coke and a Dr. Pepper to drink. They found an empty wooden picnic style table for their weird combination of food and thoroughly enjoyed everything.

After lunch, they wandered through the multitude of gift shops. Dawn and Richards each picked out a tee shirt with rather vulgar sayings on the back. Dawn's said, 'Ask my father if you want to bed me." Richards' said, 'I love boobs.'

Next they drove down Wilshire Boulevard to the Los Angeles Museum of Art, next door to the La Brea Tar Pits. They parked on a side street off Wilshire and walked along the paths through the Tar Pits, looking at the many reconstructed carcasses of the animals which were found by scientists in these ancient, natural animal traps. They continued on to the art museum and spent several hours wandering through the extensive galleries. One special exhibit this day was a set of treasures of King Tut on loan from the Egyptian National Museum in Cairo. Richards had viewed these treasures in their home museum during a business trip, but Dawn had never seen them before. Richards commented, "These items look better in Los Angeles than they did in the Cairo Museum."

"Why?" asked Dawn.

"The Cairo Museum was not air-conditioned like this one. They just open the roof louvers to improve the circulation of local desert air. As a result, the dust settles on the exhibits. Never-the-less, it's a fantastic museum."

Dawn replied wistfully, "Oh, Don. You are so lucky. You've traveled all over the world. I wish I could see all the things you've seen."

Don laughed, "Well, I'm a bit older than you so I've had time to do more traveling. But I'm going to take you to Japan now."

Dawn teased, "You are getting a bit ancient, all right, but how are we going to Japan?"

"Actually, we will just go to Little Tokyo right here in downtown Los Angeles. I'm taking you to the Horikawa's restaurant where I'll feed you sukiyaki. It's supposed to arouse you sexually."

"Silly. I don't need any more arousing with you gone so much. I'm already ready. But sukiyaki at Horikawa's sounds fantastic!"

Richards and Dawn had an authentic Japanese dinner cooked right at their table by the kimono clad waitress, complete with hot sake and a delicious green tea ice cream dessert. Afterwards they took the freeways home to their Irvine Hills condominium.

Once there they took a warm shower together. Then they turned on the Hi Fi in their bedroom and danced nude as the soft moonlight filtered in through the large floor to ceiling glass doors. Soon they lost interest in dancing. They tumbled into bed for an interlude of love making which erased the pangs of being away from each other for too long.

Sunday morning Dawn drove Richards to the Los Angeles International Airport to catch the 9 o'clock United non-stop to Washington Dulles Airport.

After a typical first class flight in the big DC-10, Richards arrived at Dulles. He boarded the transporter for his ride from the aircraft, parked out on the ramp, to the huge Dulles terminal building. He was one of the first to exit from the bus into the terminal. He was amazed to see Marie and Cindy waiting to meet him. He rushed up to them, kissed each one in turn, and asked, "What are you doing here? And how did you know what flight I was on?"

Cindy answered the first question, as they began walking toward the airport exit, "We're here on special assignment helping Dr. Adams prepare a report on the Discovery accident. Gus Ford recommended us for the job."

Marie piped in, "Yeah, thanks to you we have met some big NASA wheels and they learned our capabilities."

Cindy added, "And we knew you were coming today because Dr. Adams mentioned he was meeting with you tomorrow morning."

Marie interrupted, "We knew you would take one of the non-stops from LAX to Dulles, so we just came out and met each one. You were on the third one."

Cindy added, "We didn't mind waiting, though. We saw a lot of interesting people getting off planes. Some really good looking fellows travel on those flights."

Marie added, "But, we're saving ourselves for you, Don."

Richards laughed, "Thanks a lot girls. You're quite a pair. Good to see you both. Where are you staying?"

Cindy answered, "Where else but the good old Capitol Quality Inn."

Marie chimed in, "NASA gets a special rate there, you know."

Richards replied, "Yes, I know. Remember, I used to be with NASA, too."

Cindy giggled, "But, this trip you're going to get an even better rate – free! You can stay with us. Why waste money for another room?"

Richards smiled, "Good question. You talked me into it, you smooth talking angel, you!"

By now the trio were walking out of the Dulles terminal. Cindy pointed, "Right over here's our rental car. Marie's driving. You and I will sit in the back seat and smooch!"

Richards looked at the sign, "But, that's the Diplomatic Parking Lot. How in the world did you get to park here?"

Cindy laughed, "The parking lot attendant is black. We drove up. I rolled down the window and said to him, *Brother, we black diplomats have to stick together, right?* He said, *Right on, Sister. Go right on in.* I slipped him a fin. You white folk jes' don' understand the benefits of being black!"

Richards and the two girls laughed uproariously as they climbed into the car.

As they neared the exit of the Diplomatic Parking Lot, Cindy said to Marie, "Stop for a minute! I want to tease my friend!"

Cindy rolled down the window and said to the attendant, "Brother, lookee here. I just kidnapped the South African Ambassador!" She held her index finger as a mock gun to Richards' head. Richards joined in the charade and held up his hands. The parking lot attendant laughed, "Sister, you have my permission to do him in!"

They all laughed and the trio headed off toward Washington, happy that Cindy had been able to arrange the special privilege of parking in the very convenient Diplomatic Parking Lot.

Marie drove down the George Washington Parkway. By the time they crossed the 14th Street Bridge heading toward the Quality Inn, Richards made the suggestion, "Girls, why don't we go up to the room, order dinner served in the room, watch dirty movies on TV and then make love?"

Cindy rolled her eyes, "And not even go out dancing or nothing?"

"Right!"

Cindy and Marie chorused, "That's a great idea!"

Richards and the two girls fell asleep in the big king sized bed just after midnight, with their hunger satisfied and their passions spent.

The next morning was Monday, 7 April 1992. Cindy and Marie dropped Richards off at the White House Annex just before nine for his meeting with Drs. Adams and Davidson. The two girls continued on to NASA Headquarters for their special assignment. After clearing the extensive security procedures, Richards was escorted to Davidson's office. Adams was waiting for him in Davidson's outer reception area. Davidson's secretary informed

Richards and Adams that Dr. Davidson would be with them in about ten minutes.

Richards took advantage of the wait by asking Adams, "And what did the NASA Administrator say when you asked him to support the Russian option, Bill?"

"Well, at first he wasn't enthusiastic at all. He called it a career limiting position."

"Then what?"

"Don, I explained I had it from a reliable source that the President was willing to call the Russian leader and ask him to launch a rescue mission for our astronauts, but the President wanted NASA's endorsement first. The Administrator's whole attitude changed and he said, *In that case, Bill, I'll call Davidson first thing Monday morning and tell him I endorse the Russian option.*"

Richards smiled happily, "It looks like we have the bureaucracy moving in the right direction, Bill."

"Now, we have to convince Davidson."

"Right."

A few minutes later, Davidson's secretary announced, "Gentlemen, you may go right in now. Dr. Davidson is off the phone."

As the pair walked into the big office, Davidson rose to greet them, "Bill, that was the NASA Administrator. He tells me the European option is dead. That you're recommending the Russian option again. What the devil happened?"

Richards replied seriously, "John, as you know, I was in Toulouse last week. I had a commitment from the European Space Council for a 1 August rescue launch date, contingent upon a successful Ariane booster test. Then, as you must have seen on TV, the Ariane booster exploded shortly after launch."

Davidson interrupted, "Why can't they just use one of their other boosters?"

Richards thought to himself, *These questions sound like a broken record.* Then he replied, "John, remember Yogi? The culprit of the Discovery tank metal?"

"Yes, of course! How could I forget! – You mean they used some of Yogi's metal, too?"

"Yep, in *all* their other booster tanks, too. So there's no way they can launch before mid October. We're stuck with the Russians."

Davidson paused a moment for the impact of Richards' statement to sink into his consciousness. Then he responded slowly, "I guess we have no choice. I'll give my endorsement of the Russian option to the President. Hope he doesn't go through the ceiling like last time."

Richards said soothingly, "Don't worry, John. I had my boss call the President last Friday and explain the facts of life about the Russian option. The President said he would be willing to call Gorbachev and ask for the rescue mission, but he wanted the endorsements from you and from the NASA Administrator first."

Davidson added, "I'm surprised he wouldn't pass that one by the NSC before calling Gorbachev."

Richards smiled, "John, you know the President well. He gave that caveat as well."

Adams responded with a serious tone, "I had a note from the President's personal secretary, Mary Jane, that I should call the President this morning after my meeting with you, Don. I wonder how he knew I was meeting you."

"My boss told him."

"Oh, is that it. – Now, if you two will excuse me for a moment, I'll call the President and give him my endorsement and also tell him the NASA Administrator endorsed the Russian option."

Adams and Richards rose to leave but Davidson motioned them to stay. He added, "It's OK. You can stay. Maybe you never heard anybody talk to the President before."

Both men spoke simultaneously, "No, I haven't!"

Davidson dialed the President's secretary, "Mary Jane, this is John Davidson."

"Oh, yes, Dr. Davidson. The President is having a short discussion with the National Security Advisor. It should break up soon. Please hold. He wants to talk to you about the Space Station matter."

"OK, Mary Jane." Then Davidson switched on his speaker phone, turned to his two visitors, "You spend a lot of time on hold when telephoning the President."

A few minutes later, Mary Jane came back on the line, "Dr. Davidson, the President is ready to speak to you now. I'll put you right through."

Several seconds later, the familiar voice of the President was heard on the speaker, "John, are you there?"

"Yes, Mr. President. I just met with Dr. Adams from NASA Headquarters and Dr. Richards from Universal Aircraft about the rescue of our astronauts."

"Yes, John, and what is your recommendation?"

"Mr. President, I endorse the Russian option. It's the only way to save the astronauts now."

"And what about NASA? Do they agree?"

"Yes, Sir, Mr. President, the NASA Administrator called me this morning and said he endorsed the Soviet option."

"Well, fine, John. I just told the NSC Chairman to set up an emergency meeting of the whole NSC at 9 tomorrow morning. Please be there, John. Thank you. Goodbye."

Richards commented, "That didn't take long, did it?"

"No, it never does. The President's a decisive man. I think we'll have the green light tomorrow or Wednesday at the latest. Don, can you stay over until the decision is made?"

"Of course, John. I'm anxious to get this matter resolved."

Davidson turned to Adams, "Bill, as soon as I get this decision on the Russian option, I want to meet with you, Dr. Richards, and the NASA Administrator. Here in the White House. I'll call your office just as soon as I have the word."

Richards interrupted, "John, I would like to get authorization to go to Moscow to meet with Professor Dr. Chekhov just as soon as we get the green light. There are a lot of details to work out."

"OK, Don. I'll make sure the NSC blesses your trip. I should have the approval for your trip when we next get together."

Richards answered, "John, I really appreciate your help in this."

Davidson turned slowly, looked into Richards' eyes intently, "Don, remember, you saved my ass recently. I have a long memory."

Richards and Adams shook hands with Davidson, said goodbye, and left the White House Annex.

Chapter 28

Security Council Concurs

President Williamson arrived at the National Security Council meeting room promptly at 9 Tuesday morning. The security council members rose as the President entered. He strode to his chair at the head of the oblong table and took his seat. The NSC members then took their seats.

The President began the meeting, "Gentlemen, I called an emergency meeting of the council to inform you that we are going to have to ask the Soviet Union to use their space shuttle to rescue our astronauts up on the Space Station. I want your concurrence in this decision. I have asked Dr. John Davidson, who is familiar with the details of the situation, to present a short summary of why this decision is necessary. John – ."

Davidson walked to the podium in the front of the room, Gentlemen, I have a short briefing on the Space Station crisis and a review of the options that have been considered. I believe you will agree, after I show you this information, that the Russian option is the only viable option left after the unfortunate explosion of the European shuttle launch rocket last week."

He used Richards' viewgraphs and covered the essential details of the crisis and the rationale for requesting the rescue mission from the Russians. He ended, "So you see, we have no choice except to ask the Soviets to rescue our astronauts with their shuttle."

The Chairman of the Security Council stood and said, in a pompous tone, "Mr. President, the Science Advisor has presented an excellent summary of the technical aspects of the situation. However, he has not considered the security aspects of such a request. A Russian rescue will necessarily divulge important secret information to the Russians. Such a breach of national security could be much more damaging than the loss of seventeen lives."

The Chairman of the Joint Chiefs of Staff added in his brusque military manner, the four stars of his uniform gleaming under the lights of the chandelier, "Yes, Mr. President. I agree with the Security Chairman. Sometimes it is better to sacrifice the lives of a few to save the lives of many. This simple military principle has been demonstrated time and time again over a long period of history."

The President turned red in the face and retorted angrily, looking first at the Security Advisor and then at the four star general, "Are you telling me, Gentlemen, that you recommend we let the seventeen astronauts perish, under the glare of television, in view of the whole world, because you don't believe my government can protect our secrets during a Russian rescue?"

The Chairman of the Security Council, sensing he had touched on an open nerve, retreated hastily, and said somewhat sheepishly, "Why, of course not, Mr. President. I was merely emphasizing that our national security interests must be considered as well as the technical aspects of the rescue."

The President glared at the Chairman of the Joint Chiefs of Staff, "And what did you mean, if I may ask, General?"

The JCS Chairman cleared his throat, looked flustered, "Well, of course, I didn't mean to just let them die up there. What I meant was, if the Soviets are going to attack the US – "

The Secretary of State stood and almost shouted, interrupting the General, "Who in the world said anything about the Russians attacking the US? They're too busy reorganizing their country after the collapse of the Soviet Union. And don't call them Soviets – they're Russians! The President is merely suggesting we ask the Russians to engage in a humane rescue of seventeen brave American astronauts – at least one of whom, may I remind you, the commander of the Space Station, General Robbins, has shown his valor in time of war. You're not going to sacrifice General Robbins, are you?"

The President, perceptibly calmed now, rose from his seat, "Gentlemen, please! This discussion has been enlightening. The points raised by our Security Council Chairman and our JCS Chairman are valid concerns. He paused, then, "Are there any more comments regarding the rescue of our astronauts by the Russians?"

The President scanned the room. No one said anything. The Security Council members looked grim. The President then requested, "In that case, I would like to ask that you formally approve my calling Premier Gorbachev and requesting a Russian rescue with their shuttle."

The Chairman of the Security Council asked, "Mr. President, you know the Russians as well as I do. There will undoubtedly be a 'price' for the rescue. Are you asking our endorsement of any conditions the Russians may place on the US in return for the rescue mission?"

The President responded, "No, Mr. Chairman. I am only asking that you endorse my calling him. Obviously I would want the NSC's counsel on any such conditions that might be imposed as a requisite for providing the rescue. Will you poll the members please?"

The President sat down and the Chairman of the National Security Council rose and said, "Gentlemen, you heard the President's request. All those in favor, raise your hand."

All the hands were raised.

Chapter 29

Soviet Accords

The Security Council Chairman turned to the President, "Mr. President, it's unanimous. The NSC endorses your call to Mr. Gorbachev. Do you wish me to have the call placed now, over the 'hot-line'?"

"Yes, if you can be sure we can reach him now. The President checked the time, "It's 9:22 here. Then it must be 5:22 in the afternoon in Moscow, eight hours later. Will he be in his office?"

"Mr. President, I called Moscow this morning and spoke to the Russian Ambassador to Washington who was in Moscow. I said you might be calling the Premier this morning between 9 or 10 our time. He said he would advise the Premier. The Ambassador called back just before our meeting started and said Mr. Gorbachev would be in his office until 1800 Moscow time today. Then, Mr. President, the Ambassador asked a curious question. He said. *Will the President be asking Mr. Gorbachev to rescue the astronauts with our shuttle?*"

"Yes, that is curious. And what did you say?"

"I replied, *Only the President knows the purpose of the call.*"

"It's almost as though they knew I was going to call before we knew!"

"Well, Mr. President, the Russians watch western TV, too. They probably suspected the Ariane explosion wiped out our European option."

The National Security Council Chairman and the Russian translator joined the President in the Oval Office for the phone call to the Soviet Premier. The NSC Chairman dialed the secret code number that connected the President's red, hot-line phone with the Premier's red, hot-line phone. This was a procedure worked out almost two decades earlier when the agreement to establish a hot-line was made during a thaw in relations between the two super powers. The translator then gave the oral code in Russian as a further confirmation that it was indeed the US President calling. The Russian translator gave the Russian's oral code in English as the NSC Chairman listened for confirmation of the code that the Russian Premier was at the other end of the line. The NSC Chairman flipped a switch on the phone that connected the phone receiver to a speaker in the room. He turned to the President, "Mr. President, in accordance with mutually agreed security procedures, I have confirmed that you are connected with Premier Gorbachev."

The President spoke into the speaker box connected to the red phone, "Good afternoon, Mr. Premier. Thank you for taking my call so quickly. I have a request to make of you."

There was a short pause as the President's translator repeated his statement in Russian. Shortly the Premier's translator said in perfect American-type English, "Good morning to you, Mr. President. And what may I do for you this beautiful Spring day?"

"Premier Gorbachev, I would like to get straight to the point. We need your help to rescue the seventeen American astronauts stranded in space. We need you to launch your shuttle to save these men and women, as a humanitarian gesture."

After a short translation delay, the Premier replied, "President Williamson, I must be brutally frank with you. Our two countries have not been on the best of relations in recent years. As you know, we were never able to reach a disarmament accord with either of your two predecessors, even though I personally made numerous reasonable disarmament proposals. They were all rejected. Furthermore, your predecessors started this 'Star Wars' program that has further destabilized the strategic balance we had achieved in the early 80's. Your Star Wars program has forced Russia to spend enormous sums on defense to keep matters in balance. We had hoped to spend our resources on improving the standard of living of our people rather than on this mad arms race. Nevertheless, Mr. President, Russia says 'yes' to your request. Anticipating that you might make this request, I put the question before the Politburo. They unanimously approved that Russia would grant this humanitarian rescue mission, if asked. But, as you know, we have collective leadership in our country and they requested we have agreement on three issues which I will define shortly."

There was a long delay due to translation and the President paused briefly as he formulated his reply, "Premier Gorbachev, please remember I have been in office less than four months now. Renewing the disarmament negotiations is high on my agenda. Our country would like to reduce the enormous amount of expenditures for armaments also and use the resources to improve the standard of living of our population at the bottom end of the economic spectrum. As for our Strategic Defense Initiative, -- or Star Wars as you call it – when I was a Senator, I opposed the program. During my Presidential campaign, one of my platform planks was to review this program with the view of canceling it, provided it doesn't damage the security of our nation. Regarding making agreements on the three issues your Politburo requested, I must point out we also have collective leadership, of a different form, but nevertheless, our Congress is a body that gives 'advice and consent' for Presidential actions. I am willing to consider your three issues on which you desire agreement. But, obviously, I can't agree during our telephone conversation."

There was another long translation pause. Then the Russian Premier responded, "I am encouraged by your positive reply, Mr. President. I must say your predecessors talked a lot about disarmament, but never did anything about arriving at a meaningful agreement. My government became convinced the administrations of your predecessors were using the Geneva Disarmament Negotiations as a stalling tactic while they implemented their strategy of achieving military superiority vis a vis the Russian forces. For example, I was personally bitterly disappointed when the US administration and their NATO allies rejected my proposal to demilitarize Europe, both East and West from the Atlantic to the Ural Mountains. Previously your government had used the argument that they had to maintain US troops and intermediate range ballistic missiles such as Pershing II and the Cruise Missiles to counter the 'superior conventional forces' of the Warsaw Pact countries in Europe. If my demilitarization proposal had been accepted, this argument would have been eliminated. As far as Star Wars was concerned, that was the final straw. Your government spent vast sums on research for Star Wars because it was claimed 'research' didn't violate the

'Anti Ballistic Missile Treaty' between our two countries. Now we believe you are beginning to deploy the Star Wars Element, which is a clear violation of the Anti Ballistic Missile Treaty."

Following a translation pause, the President responded, "Premier Gorbachev, I am impressed with your in-depth knowledge of disarmament issues. Your twelve years in leadership in the USSR and Russia have given you a long view depth and grasp of issues which is difficult for an American President to achieve, because of his shorter tenure of office. But let me remind you, I was a US Senator for twenty years before I became President. I also have the historical view that you have, even though from a different vantage point. I would appreciate it if you would list the three issues on which your government is asking for agreement."

After a short pause, the Premier said, "Thank you for your complimentary statements, President Williamson. I understand clearly that the President of the US has the Congress for advice and consent, but I also understand the enormous personal power the US President has – independent of Congress – by virtue of the 'Presidential Decree'. I'm afraid this unique tool of power is more absolute than any power that I have as Premier of Russia and Leader of the Communist Party. I am sure you understand this tool, also. I do expect agreement in principle on these issues *before* the rescue launch. Here are the three issues:

FIRST: We want the Geneva Disarmament Conference to be reconvened and we want a meaningful disarmament agreement in principle before the rescue launch. Our rationale for this first accord is that both sides have proposals which were presented previously. If both sides are reasonable, we should be able to consummate an agreement within 90 days. We believe we are reasonable and we hope your side will be now.

SECOND: We want agreement that you will stop the deployment of the destabilizing Star Wars system. Our rationale for the second accord is that if, in fact, agreement is achieved on the first accord, there is no conceivable need for your Star Wars program.

THIRD: We want your government to cancel your restrictive export regulations that prevent a free interchange of technology between our two countries. Our rationale for the third accord is that the very restrictive export regulations your country imposed during the mid 1980's caused us to independently develop our own advanced technology. At this time we believe it would be mutually beneficial to remove the irrational trade barriers set up during your predecessors' regimes, especially those applying to advanced technology."

"May I have your response?" Gorbachev concluded.

During the translation delay, the National Security Council Chairman Dr. Barnes, whispered to the President, "Don't forget. We know about Russia's super secret 'Invisible Bomber' program. That's the huge program they initiated in response to President Reagan's SDI program. If it does what the CIA claims it does, it makes the Star Wars obsolete. The Russians will just deliver their thermonuclear warheads with the Invisible Bomber instead of ICBM's. Their Invisible Bomber employs much more advanced technology than our Stealth Bomber. The Premier was probably referring to some of this new technology when he referred to their independently developed technology. They have also made some fantastic advances in micro-electronic technology. After all, they were able to buy the same lithographic machines for making the sub micron chips from Lichtenstein that we purchased for our VHSIC (Very High Speed Integrated Circuit) program. *Aviation Week* magazine had some pictures of their chips recently that show they are a generation ahead of us."

"Good points, Dr. Barnes. I think I should use your points in my response. Do you agree?"

"Yes, but I would advise against revealing that we know about the Invisible Bomber. It would reveal our intelligence sources."

"I don't subscribe to that theory that we shouldn't reveal what our Intelligence Community has found out about our adversary, when we can use it to our own advantage."

"That's your prerogative, Mr. President."

The President said into the red phone, "Premier Gorbachev, before I respond to your three proposed accords, I want to make sure I understand your position. You stated earlier that you will use the Russian shuttle for a rescue mission. Do I understand now that we must agree to these three accords before you launch the mission? In other words, if we do not agree, you will permit those seventeen people to die in space? Is that right?

The Russian Premier responded, "As far as the seventeen lives are concerned, your highways kill twice that number of people each hour. I see by my watch that seventeen people have perished on your highways while we have been talking. Why don't you divert those enormous defense expenditures to devising means of saving the lives of all those people? But no, of course we will not allow those seventeen people on your Space Station to perish. However, there could be technical difficulties that develop that might delay our launch until the expendables on your Space Station run out, I understand, at the end of August."

After the President heard the translation of the Premier's deft handling of that question, he realized he had a very clever and tough adversary. He further realized no one could ever prove the technical difficulties were not real, considering all the space mishaps that had occurred so far. He took a deep breath and said, "I will respond now to each of your three proposed accords:
      FIRST: With regard to the Geneva Disarmament Conference, I agree we can arrive at some meaningful agreements within ninety days. But specifically, with respect to your earlier suggestion of demilitarizing from the Atlantic to the Urals, remember that France and Great Britain, who are sovereign governments, have nuclear weapons. I can't force them to agree to the demilitarization, even with my power of Presidential Decree. An agreement on that suggestion would require a four party negotiation (the US, Russia, France, and Great Britain) which I am sure would take longer than 90 days.
      SECOND: With respect to canceling the deployment of the Strategic Defense Initiative, I realize there is some precedence for a new President canceling the deployment of a major weapon system (President Carter cancelled the B-1 bomber shortly after his election) but I'm not willing to do that. I'll tell you why. We have conclusive proof you have developed the Invisible Bomber. I

would not even consider dropping SDI unless you agreed to drop the Invisible Bomber, and we would insist that we have on-site inspection to assure you eliminate all these horrible machines of destruction.

THIRD: With respect to revising our export regulations to permit free Interchange of technology, I would be willing to negotiate such an agreement if, we can couple this agreement with the FIRST and SECOND accords, and you agree to release your advanced secret technology to the US."

After a long delay which indicated the Russian Premier was discussing these responses with his advisors in the room with him, he finally responded, "Mr. President, you are a lot tougher than I expected you would be, based on your election campaign rhetoric. I must admit you surprised me very much with your knowledge of our Invisible Bomber program. Both our KGB and GRU had assured me your CIA knew nothing of this program. Intelligence is obviously not a perfect art, even though our respective Intelligence Communities would lead us to believe so. Now, let me respond to your responses:

FIRST: I concur that agreement on any issue such as demilitarization of Europe which involves third sovereign nations of both Eastern and Western Europe could not be concluded within the ninety days. However, I believe the meaningful agreement we can conclude in ninety days can lead naturally to the demilitarization of Europe, if we each encourage our allies to enter into serious negotiations. In other words, our agreement would set the example for this broader accord.

SECOND: I would be willing to couple the cancellation of our Invisible Bomber with the cancellation of your Star Wars program with the proviso that we have on-site inspections to see that you complied. Since our KGB and GRU inform me you have elements of the Star Wars system operating now on your Space Station, operated by the people you are asking us to rescue, then we would ask, as a part of this on-site inspection program, that we have a permanent crew member as observer on your Space Station.

THIRD: Of course I would agree to releasing our advanced technology, including the Invisible Bomber technology and new generation of micro electronics, in a high technology interchange accord.

"I believe that concludes my comments. If we can agree in principle today on these matters, I will authorize our Professor Dr. Chekhov to meet with your American delegate to develop the details of the rescue mission as soon as possible."

After a translation delay, the President whispered to Dr. Barnes, "You have heard the complete interchange. Do you think we can get the NSC to endorse agreement in principle on these three accords?"

"Mr. President, there will be a lot of grumbling from some of the hawkish members, but yes, I believe the NSC will endorse these accords, in principle."

The President responded, "Yes, Mr. Gorbachev. I agree in principle to these three accords. Furthermore, I believe we should document our verbal agreements so that our Geneva negotiators have guidance for their detailed negotiations following the broad principles you and I have established today."

After a short delay, the Premier responded, "Your decisive and reasonable attitude is a welcome change from your predecessors', President Williamson. I truly hope this rescue mission, and these three accords, will greatly improve the relations between our super power nations. I'm sure the citizens of the Earth would welcome a relaxation of tensions. With respect to the documentation of the 'Accords in Principle', I hereby authorize our Washington Ambassador to negotiate the language. He's a member of the Politburo, you know. He was here during our discussions and has heard our agreements."

The President closed out the discussion of accords, "Thank you, Premier Gorbachev. I hereby authorize my Security Council Chairman, Dr. Barnes, to negotiate the language with your delegate, the Ambassador. He was also here during the discussion. Perhaps they can meet as soon as the Ambassador returns to Washington."

"Thank you, President Williamson. The Ambassador will return to Washington tomorrow. He will be ready to meet with your Security Council Chairman on Thursday."

The President continued, "Now, with regard to the details of the rescue mission discussions, our American delegate to meet with your Professor Dr. Chekhov is Dr. Richards. He's program manager of the Space Station for Universal Aircraft. That's how our free enterprise system works here in America, Mr. Premier."

After another short translation delay, the Premier responded, "Our delegate, Dr. Chekhov, is authorized to meet with your delegate as soon as they are able to arrange a mutually agreed time. Our delegate in the rescue mission discussions, Professor Dr. Chekhov, is Director of the Russian Shuttle Program at the Russian Space Institute. That's how our system of rewarding outstanding people works here in Russia, Mr. President."

"Touche, and goodbye, Mr. Premier."

"Goodbye, Mr. President."

Chapter 30

Russian Trip Authorized

Richards had spent all day in his room at the Quality Inn, reading and watching TV, while waiting for word on his next White House meeting with Dr. Davidson. Finally, just before 3 pm, Davidson called him.

After exchanging hellos, Davidson announced happily, "Don, the meeting is all set in my office at 9 in the morning. I've already called the NASA Administrator. He will be there and will bring Dr. Adams along. I'll give you the details tomorrow, but your trip to Moscow is authorized. Go ahead and have your office make your reservations. You are to meet with Professor Dr. Chekhov. He is authorized to negotiate the details of the rescue mission!"

"That's great news, John! I think I'll leave Friday. That'll give me the weekend to adjust to the time change. See you in the morning at 9. Goodbye."

As he hung up, Richards remembered Brigitte has said she would be staying at the Metropole Hotel in Moscow beginning about the 12th of April, the day he was scheduled to arrive. He thought to himself, *What a great coincidence!* He looked at his watch, saw it was almost noon in California. He dialed his office number, hoping to catch June before she left for lunch. He was lucky. She answered the phone.

"Dr. Richards' office. June speaking."

Richards replied happily, "I'm glad I caught you before your lunch. I've got something for you to do."

"Oh, it's good to hear from you. I've got a whole deskful of messages for you. Do you want me to read them to you?"

"No, thanks, June, not unless there are any I need to take care of right now. I need you to make reservations for me to go to Moscow."

"Oh, how exciting! When do you want to leave?"

"Get me on the 9 am Friday TWA flight to New York. I believe I can connect with a Pan Am or Aeroflot non-stop leaving for Moscow in the late afternoon. Leave the return open."

"Just a moment, Dr. Richards. I'll check the Airline Guide here on my desk." Richards heard her flip through the pages and finally she said, "Yes, here it is, Dr. Richards. The Pan Am flight leaves too early. It's not a legal connection. But the Aeroflot non-stop to Moscow leaves an hour and a half after your TWA flight arrives. I'll put you on that. It arrives in Moscow at 11:30 Saturday morning."

"That's great, June. Book me first class and request an aisle seat. Also, put me up in the Metropole Hotel in Moscow. It's lucky you took care of getting me that three month visitor's visa."

"Yes. I'll get your tickets and trip cash. Will $3000 be enough?"

"That's fine, June. See you in the office Thursday morning. Please call Dawn and tell her my travel plans. Ask her to pick me up at the American Airlines terminal at LAX tomorrow. I'm on the non-stop that comes in at 7:45 pm."

"OK, Dr. Richards. Don't worry. I'll take care of everything. Goodbye."

"Goodbye."

Just as Richards hung up, Cindy and Marie returned to the room. He greeted both with a kiss and asked, "What are you two doing back so early?"

Cindy answered, "We finished the report today. Dr. Adams was really happy with our work."

Marie added, "Yes, we want you to take us out to celebrate the finishing of the Discovery accident report. You can't get away with dinner in the room tonight."

Richards responded, "Well, I've got something to celebrate, too. My trip to Moscow to arrange for the rescue launch was approved. Let's go to the Flagship Restaurant down on the Potomac River and celebrate both events. I'm buying!"

Cindy joked, "Of curse you are. Our room and other services ought to be good for a big dinner out. We want champagne, too."

Marie added, "Yes, and some of that great soft shelled crab with all the trimmings."

The trio showered and dressed for their festive night out in Washington. After watching the afternoon news on TV, they left for the Flagship in the girls' rental car. They enjoyed a delightful seafood dinner featuring the famous soft shelled crabs from the Chesapeake Bay as the main course. Whey they got back to the Quality Inn, they engaged in another night of amour d'trois.

Richards was dropped off at the White House Annex the next morning, Wednesday, just before nine. The two girls, finished with their special assignment at NASA Headquarters, drove on to National Airport, where they dropped off their rental car and caught their 10 am flight back to Houston.

Richards patiently went through the thorough security procedure for visitors to the White House Annex and then was escorted to Dr. Davidson's office reception area. Adams and the NASA Administrator came in a few minutes later and Lois, Davidson's secretary, lead the trio into the large office and directed them to sit around the conference table where they were joined a few minutes later by Dr. Davidson.

Davidson opened the meeting, "Yesterday, the President approved and the NSC endorsed the Russian Rescue Option for saving the stranded astronauts. Afterwards, the President called the Russian Premier to formally request the rescue mission using the Russian space shuttle. Professor Dr. Chekhov was designated by the Russian government to be our point of contact for arranging the details of the rescue. Dr. Richards, here, is authorized to visit Dr. Chekhov in Moscow next week."

The NASA Administrator spoke up authoritatively, "But, Dr. Davidson, Dr. Richards is from a private company. This should be a government to government negotiation. I insist that a NASA executive make this trip to Moscow."

Davidson faced the Administrator, "The President specifically named Dr. Richards to be the US point of contact. I believe the President did this because it was the president of Richards' company, David Moore, who originally telephoned the President to inform him the Russian option was the only viable option."

The Administrator answered huffily, "Well, OK, but I insist that Gus Ford from NASA Houston accompany Dr. Richards on the trip to Moscow."

Davidson replied, "Mr. Administrator, I have no objection to that arrangement so long as you instruct Mr. Ford that Dr. Richards is head of the delegation."

The Administrator replied haughtily, "Well, it still seems a bit unusual, but I will so inform Mr. Ford."

Dr. Davidson replied, "Gentlemen, if there is no further discussion of the decision, I would like you all to be party to a call to Professor Dr. Chekhov. The President asked me to call him directly to set up the meeting with Dr. Richards next week."

Davidson turned to Richards, "Don, I suggested to you yesterday that you make arrangements to be in Moscow next week. When do you leave?"

"John, I arrive in Moscow on the non-stop Aeroflot flight from New York at 11:30 this coming Saturday morning. I'm staying at the Metropole Hotel."

The NASA Administrator then turned to Adams, "Bill, make sure Gus Ford has reservations for the same Aeroflot flight and hotel as Dr. Richards."

"OK. I'll call Gus as soon as the meeting breaks up."

Davidson buzzed his secretary, "Lois, please get Dr. Chekhov on the phone." He turned to the other men, "We have already notified Dr. Chekhov's office we would be calling to make sure he didn't leave early today. It's 5:15 pm in Moscow now. I'll put him on the speaker phone as soon as we're connected."

A few moments later Lois buzzed Davidson, "Dr. Chekhov is on the line now."

Davidson flipped the switch on the speaker phone, "Good afternoon, Professor Dr. Chekhov. This is Dr. Davidson, President Williamson's Science Advisor."

Chekhov's voice came through the speaker, sounding as though he were in a cave, in perfect American dialect English, "And good morning to you, Dr. Davidson. I heard from our Premier's office that someone from your government might be calling to discuss our rescue of the American cosmonauts."

"Yes, Dr. Chekhov, and I have with me the NASA Administrator and his chief engineer, Dr. Adams, together with Dr. Richards. We have you on the speaker phone in my office."

"My, you Americans do go in for gadgets, don't you? Hello, Gentlemen. Dr. Gorlovka is here with me on an extension phone. I understand from the Premier's office that Dr. Richards is authorized to visit me to work out the details of the rescue mission using the Russian space shuttle."

"That's right, Dr. Chekhov. And good afternoon to you, Dr. Gorlovka. Dr. Richards and Mr. Ford of NASA will be arriving in Moscow on Saturday morning at 11:30 on the Aeroflot flight from New York."

"That will be fine. My deputy, Dr. Linda Gorlovka and I will meet Dr. Richards and Mr. Ford at the Moscow Airport. I assume our visitors are staying at the Metropole Hotel. We will have theater tickets for them. Opera Saturday night and the Bolshoi Ballet Sunday night. We will start our meetings at nine Monday morning."

"I must say, Dr. Chekhov, you think of everything. Is there anything else you wanted to say? Dr. Richards is motioning he would like to ask you something."

"No, Dr. Davidson. I believe I have covered all the essential points."

Richards came on the line, "Professor Dr. Chekhov and Dr. Gorlovka, this is Dr. Richards. I met you both at the reception of the International Space Symposium in Vienna."

Dr. Gorlovka answered, "Why, yes. I do remember you, Dr. Richards. You were the handsome American who gave the paper on the *Deployment of the US Space Station*."

Dr. Chekhov laughed, "Dr. Richards, to be frank, I don't remember what you looked like. I met so many Westerners at that reception. But Lina has an eye for handsome men. She can help identify you when you get off the airplane Saturday. Did you have a question?"

Richards replied, "Dr. Gorlovka, I'm flattered by your comment. And Dr. Chekhov, rather than a question, I have more of a comment on a problem I foresee that must be solved."

Dr. Chekhov asked, "And what is that?"

"We will need to fabricate an adapter so your space shuttle can interface with our Space Station docking module."

"Good point, Dr. Richards. I'll make sure we have an expert in our meeting Monday morning to address that problem. Since we worked out the linking of the American Apollo and the Soviet Soyuz, I'm sure we can work out this interface as well."

"I'm sure we can, Dr. Chekhov. I will bring a briefing along to show you the essential facts needed for the rescue mission."

Davidson signed off, "Thank you, Professor Dr. Chekhov and Dr. Gorlovka. That is all we had here. Goodbye."

Chekhov replied, "Goodbye, Gentlemen. Lina and I will see you at the airport on Saturday, Dr. Richards.

Richards reached the Dulles Airport just after 4 pm and immediately headed for the American Airlines' Admirals Club downstairs from the main boarding area. The beautiful receptionist at the entrance greeted him, "Good afternoon, Dr. Richards. And where would you like to sit in first class, window or aisle? I remember you always take no smoking."

"I usually take an aisle, but today, I would like a window seat. I'm going to stare out the window at our beautiful country today while I sip my Tanqueray."

"Here's your boarding card, Dr. Richards, seat 6A with a good view of the movie screen."

"Thank you. That's great."

Richards walked into the lounge, found a seat in front of the TV, and ordered a Tanqueray on the rocks. He phoned Dawn on the credit card phone on the table at his elbow. She answered on the extension in the Universal Aircraft computer room where she worked. Richards said, "Dawn, this is Don. I'm at Dulles. Did you get my message?"

Dawn answered with joy in her voice, "Yes. I'll meet you at the American terminal at 7:30. June tells me you will be going to Moscow Friday morning. I don't get you very long this week, do I?"

Richards laughed, "No, I'm on the move again. But think of the quality, not the duration. Anyway, I'll take you to dinner tonight on the way home. How about El Torrito's in Huntington Beach?"

"I love their Mexican food and Margueritas. See you at 7:30, Darling. I love you."

Richards walked out of the Admirals Club at 5:20, took the escalator up to the departure level, proceeded through the security check point to Gate 4, and climbed onto the transporter for the ride out to the waiting DC-10. He boarded through the first class entrance near the nose and found his seat. The plane was not full and the seat next to him was empty. Shortly after he sat down, the pretty blonde stewardess poured him a glass of champagne and handed him a menu.

He handed the menu back, "Miss, I won't be having dinner this evening. I promised my girl friend I would take her out to dinner after she picks me up in LA."

She replied, "Well, at least you can watch the movie. Here's the program."

Richards scanned it, "I saw that on the flight coming out Sunday."

She laughed, "We can't give you much service today. I suppose you're a teetotaler, too?"

He laughed back, "No, not yet anyway. Just keep feeding me Tanquerays on the rocks. Then I'll stay happy and think you are giving me wonderful service."

"You're easy to please. Enjoy your flight, Sir."

Soon the big DC-10 was airborne and climbed rapidly to its cruise altitude of 41,000 feet for the five hour flight to Los Angeles. It was one of those rare days when the whole continent was dominated by a big high pressure system over Kansas. The weather was crystal clear with over a hundred miles visibility. Richards stared out the window and enjoyed the beauty of his vast country, the United States of American. His mind wandered as he flew along. He though about the bizarre chain of events that had lead up to his impending trip to Russia. Watching the terrain unfolding below him, he wondered if the Russian landscape was as beautiful from an airliner as America. Next week he would find out.

He woke up from his short end-of-the-trip nap to hear the Captain announce their approach for landing at Los Angeles. He looked out the window. The city lights were gleaming below him. There was still a little light left in the western sky. Los Angeles

Airport was covered by the usual spring low clouds from the moist marine layer drifting in from the chilly Pacific Ocean. Sometimes these clouds were low enough and thick enough to close down the airport, but not today. Following the blinking, guiding approach lights, the pilot set the huge plane down smoothly on the runway and soon pulled up to the jet-way.

Richards was first off the aircraft with his carry-on bag. He hurried through the jet-way and found Dawn's happy, shining, face greeting him as rushed into her warm, wide-spread, waiting arms.

Forty minutes later, Richards took the Bolsa Chica turn-off from the San Diego Freeway, turned his car onto Golden West and almost immediately turned left into the El Torrito Restaurant. He and Dawn were escorted to a table in the central patio. Richards ordered two Margueritas while they studied their menus. Richards scanned the beautiful restaurant and remarked to Dawn, "You know, Dawn, this restaurant is a near replica of the Shrimp Bucket Restaurant in Mazatlan, Mexico. There is a major difference, though."

Dawn quizzed him, "What is the difference between El Torrito's and the Shrimp Bucket?"'

Richards laughed, "The Shrimp Bucket was the official race headquarters for the Los Angeles to Mazatlan Yacht Race sponsored by the Los Angeles Yacht Club. I crewed on the race twenty years ago this year. Anyway, the Shrimp Bucket had hotel rooms upstairs. El Torrito's has only tables."

Dawn laughed, "Don, you are really ancient! I was only five years old then!" Then she exclaimed wistfully, "Oh, Don. You are so lucky to have been almost everywhere, except Russia. And now you're going to go there!"

They were distracted by the arrival of the waiter. They ordered Fajitas, meat barbecued at the table, with a variety of piquant sauces in which to dip the meat pieces before eating. They were served a crisp green salad with avocado dressing. For dessert they had Kahlua mousse, a chocolate mousse made with Kahlua liqueur.

They drove to their Irvine Hills condo and spent a beautiful night making love, with the bitter-sweet realization they only had tonight and tomorrow night before Richards left for Russia.

Chapter 31

Russian Trip

Richards and Dawn walked onto the UAC heliport on the roof of the headquarters building at 8 am, Friday 11 April, 1992. She had come with him up to the roof to wish him goodbye. He threw his small carry-on bag and briefcase into the back seat of the waiting helicopter, wrapped his arms around Dawn and kissed her tenderly, and climbed in beside his luggage. He was the only passenger. The pilot greeted him and started the take-off procedure immediately. The helicopter leapt off the pad and headed across the middle of the active runway, number19, at the Orange County airport. Peering out the window, Richards studied the line up of passenger jets, all scheduled for 8 am departures from John Wayne Airport. The helicopter followed the Orange County coast line north-easterly towards Palos Verdes. A short time later they turned more northerly, paralleling the jam-packed San Diego Freeway, heading towards the Los Angeles Airport. Thirty minutes after departing the UAC heliport, the chopper touched down near the terminal where Richards' big TWA 747 was waiting to take him and another 450 passengers to New York. The helicopter pilot had called a special VHF frequency to alert the security guards of Richards' arrival. He was allowed to go in through the crew entrance and continue into the passenger terminal near the parked plane. He went up the stairs to the TWA Ambassador Lounge and immediately was given his first class boarding pass for the non-stop flight to New York. He would be joined in New York by Gus Ford from NASA Houston and the two of them planned to take the same Aeroflot flight to Moscow.

Richards had time to have a Bloody Mary while he read the *Wall Street Journal* to check the value of his stocks and bonds. He noticed his index option spread was doing nicely. He thought to himself, *I should make $10,000 from that spread this month. And since the spread is in Dawn's name, I don't have to share the profits with my ex-wife.*

It was time to board his flight. Walking down to his boarding gate, he thought to himself, *I'll be leaving the world of the free press today, where I can get all the news in objective form. I'll be going into the world of the state managed press where the news is limited and biased by the government. I think I'll look for an English language version of Pravda and compare it with the newspaper I just read to see for myself the difference.'*

Richards walked on board the big TWA jet and settled into his luxurious first class seat. Soon they were airborne and he was enjoying his filet mignon brunch with champagne, followed by an R-rated movie he hadn't seen before. He woke from a short nap when the captain announced they were descending for a landing at Kennedy Airport. Richards looked out his window and picked out the huge airport ahead. Soon they were on the ground and he was off the plane. He had no trouble fining Gus Ford waiting for him. They hurried to the airport bus that carried them to the Aeroflot terminal, where they had to line up in a long queue to get their boarding passed for their flight to Moscow. When they finally reached the ticket agent, Richards asked for two seats together, but there were not two adjacent seats available. Richards complained they had requested two seats together when they made the reservation. The attractive blonde ticket agent apologized profusely, but insisted she could do nothing about the situation at that time.

The line at the counter had been so long and so slow that by the time Richards and Ford had their boarding passes, it was already time to board their flight. After passing through a thorough security search, they went into the waiting room for boarding. Richards noticed the Russian passengers banded together in the crowded room. They seemed happy and anxious to board the aircraft to take them back to their homeland. He couldn't find anyone trying to escape and stay in the 'capitalist paradise' called New York City.

He thought to himself, *From everything I read in the US newspapers, I would expect almost all Russian citizens to be trying to escape to freedom in the US. I wonder why so many are returning. It is probably because the communist government is holding their families hostage so they have to return.*

Shortly, Ford and Richards climbed aboard the wide-bodied Ilushin jet. Their seats were on opposite sides of the first class section. Richards was pleasantly surprised to find his seat partner was Brigitte. She rose, kissed Richards, "What a surprise, Don, that we ended up on the same Moscow flight! What a coincidence!"

Richards smiled happily, "What a wonderful coincidence! I was going to try to find you at the Metropole. That's where I'm staying. Instead I find you seated next to me!"

A short time later their aircraft pushed back and taxied to the long line of evening departures from Kennedy. After the usual -- for Kennedy Airport -- wait of almost an hour, they were airborne and headed along the great circle route from New York to Moscow. This was the first Russian aircraft Richards had ever ridden. He remarked to Brigitte, "I'm amazed at how well built and luxurious this Ilushin jet appears. It compares favorably with the DC-10, L1011, and Air-Bus wide body jets."

As the beautiful stewardess served the pair champagne, he added, "And the service is just as good, too!"

Brigitte smiled, "You know, Don, Russia isn't exactly a backward country, technologically. After all, the Ilushin wide body is a more recent design than the others you mentioned."

Richards laughed, "I'm always surprised to see anything good from Russia. All I read in our newspapers and news magazines is how in-efficient the Russian economy is and how backward their products are compared with those of the western world."

Brigitte smiled again, "I've been to Russia before. They have their problems like every other country in the world. But I think you are going to be pleasantly surprised at what you see. Most Americans are during their first trip to Russia."

Richards leaned back, sipped his champagne, "Let's just enjoy the flight, Brigitte. I don't think I'm going to be able to reconcile the differences between communism and capitalism this trip!"

Brigitte put down her champagne, looked into Richards' eyes, and said seriously, "Don, from what you told me in Paris about your trip to Russia, that you were going to arrange for the Russians to rescue the American astronauts, I believe that you may do a great deal to reconcile the differences!"

Richards smiled, "Don't look so serious, Brigitte. At least, I hope I can arrange a successful rescue. That's enough for one trip."

About an hour later, they were served an elaborate gourmet dinner. It was one of the best meals Richards had enjoyed on any flight. After dinner, they were entertained by a beautiful video rendition of Wagner's 'Tristan und Isolde' opera performed by the Moscow Opera Company. This was followed by an exquisite presentation of Tchaikovsky's 'Swan Lake' by the Bolshoi Ballet Troupe.

After the entertainment, Richards escorted Brigitte over to meet Gus Ford. They exchanged greetings and Ford exclaimed, "Don, how do you luck out and get such a beautiful seat partner?"

Richards looked at Ford's seat partner – a tall, fat man, sound asleep, "Gus, I'm just lucky. Brigitte was also my seat partner last month on the flight from Los Angeles to Paris. So you see we're 'old friends'."

Brigitte interrupted, "Oh, you two are so complimentary. You make me feel so good. Mr. Ford, I hope to see you in Moscow. I'm going back to my seat and get some sleep now."

Richards added, "That's a good idea, Brigitte. See you in Moscow, Gus."

The two returned to their assigned location. Richards removed the arm rest between their two seas and Brigitte covered them with a blanket. They curled up together and fell asleep.

When Richards woke up he checked his watch, which had been set to Moscow time, and found it was just before 10 am. The sun was shining low in the southern sky. They were approaching the long, fjord coast of Norway. Richards saw the northern city of Tronheim to the left. The stewardess came by and offered them breakfast. Brigitte also woke up and both sleepily agreed to the idea of breakfast.

As the pair finished their elaborate morning meal of orange juice, fresh fruit, ham and eggs, croissants, Danish rolls and coffee, Richards looked out the window and noticed they were leaving the east coast of Norway at Hudlksvall and flying over the Gulf of Bothnia. A short time later they intercepted the southern coast of Finland at Turku and then passed over the Gulf of Finland just south of the capitol city of Helsinki. Richards noticed the Russian city of Tallinn in the Russian Republic of Estonia, out of the right side of the plane. This was the port city where the USSR held the Olympic Yachting games. Richards remembered that in 1986 the American yachtsman, Ted Turner, who also owned the TV chain CNN, organized the Olympic-type Friendship Regatta between the Russians and American yachtsmen in Tallinn, since neither country attended the other's Olympic Games in 1980 and 1984 because of petulant leaders.

Less than an hour later, the big Ilushin jet landed at Sheremetyevo Airport in Moscow, just before the scheduled 11:30 am arrival time. As they were taxiing up to the terminal jet-way, Richards explained to Brigitte, "Mr. Ford and I are being met by an official delegation from the Russian Space Institute. Since we will be riding with them to our hotel, I will see you there later."

Brigitte smiled, "That's fine, Don. One of my business associates is meeting me and I will ride to the hotel with him. Also, I have a lot of luggage to pick up. I'll leave you here so I won't get mixed up with your welcoming delegation."

"Fine, Brigitte. I'll call you from my room."

Brigitte reached over, kissed Richards, and whispered, "I'm looking forward to spending the night with you tonight. I really missed you."

Richards and Ford exited the plane and its jet-way. Almost immediately they found the smiling faces of Professor Dr. Chekhov and Dr. Lina Gorlovka. They rushed up to the Americans and greeted each other warmly. Then Chekhov whispered, "Come with us. We will simplify all the formalities of entering our country."

Ford walked with Chekhov, and Richards, struck by the Slavic beauty of Lina Gorlovka, walked next to her, chatting happily in English. Lina spoke the perfect American idiom. They were led to a Russian official who quickly stamped their passports and waved them out of his office without examining their luggage. They were the first passengers from the flight to reach the outer doors of the terminal. The other passengers were still waiting in long, slow passport control and customs inspection lines.

As they exited the terminal, Chekhov directed them to get in a black Chaika limousine with a chauffer. Richards and Lina settled on the back seat. Chekhov and Ford sat in two backward facing but comfortable seats. Chekhov acted as their tour guide, proudly pointing out the various sights of interest as they drove into the huge city of Moscow from the airport to the north.

The roads were crowded with private automobiles packed with families driving out of the city for a day in the country. Richards remarked, "I'm surprised at the number of private cars I see on the highways. I thought it was very difficult for Russian citizens to purchase an automobile."

Lina laughed, "It sounds like you have been reading the western 'free press'. I'm always astounded at the misconceptions I read about my country, its government and my people in the western newspapers when I travel abroad. It's true, Dr. Richards, we had to wait up to a year or more for a new car in the early 80's, but Premier Gorbachev greatly expanded the production capacity of our automobile factories such as the Volga factory in the province of Kuibishev. He insisted we apply the technology of robotics to increase production. It worked. Now, cars are available when you want one."

Richards replied, "Dr. Gorlovka, please call me Don. But, aren't the cars in Russia terribly expensive?"

Lina laughed again. "OK, Don, but you must call me Lina. Yes, cars are very expensive for the ordinary worker who makes about 4000 rubles a year. It costs about 2000 rubles for a car, six months salary."

Richards tried to satisfy his curiosity, "How about other living costs here? Are they very high? How much is an apartment, for example?"

Lina answered, "A typical family of three in Moscow spends about 400 rubles per month for all living costs including car operating expenses. An apartment costs between 6 and 50 rubles a month. If it is close to a metro stop it's 50 rubles. If it's a long walk, it's six rubles."

Richards was amazed, "That sounds very cheap for an apartment. But the living costs of 4800 rubles a year is expensive if the family income is only 4000 rubles."

Lina replies, "But in Moscow virtually all the wives work as well as their husbands. So the family income is 8000 rubles, leaving 3200 rubles a year for saving and occasional luxuries like a chalet in the country. I understand the typical savings account of a Russian citizen is much higher than that of the typical American citizen."

Richards asked, surprised, "You mean you have banks in Russia? I thought that was a capitalistic form of enterprise."

Lina laughs, "You do have a distorted view of my country. Of course, we have banks. Where else would we keep our money? In an old shoe? We get paid interest on our savings, too."

Richards laughed at himself, "Thanks for the short course in Russian economics. It looks like I'm going to have to re-learn what I thought I knew about your country."

Chekhov interrupted, "Enough of this economics lesson, Dr. Richards. We're now entering the city of Moscow. I want to show you some of our war monuments."

Chapter 32

Moscow Diversions

The Chaika limousine carrying Richards and Ford with their Russian hosts, Drs. Chekhov and Gorlovka, headed down the broad avenues of Moscow where there was orderly but not heavy traffic flowing smoothly. Dr. Chekhov motioned the driver to pull over to a large monument. Chekhov explained, "This is a memorial to the Soviet soldiers killed in the Great War. You know, more than twenty million Soviets were killed by the Nazi invaders, almost ten percent of our population."

Lina added, "Each Russian city in the zone of the Nazi invaders has a memorial to the soldiers and civilians killed. In one small village west of here, the Nazis killed everyone in the city. They herded all the people into a wooden building, locked the doors, and then set fire to it. One father returned to the village after the Nazis left, found the carnage, and his dying son among the bodies. The war memorial in that village is a statue of the man crying, holding out the dead body of his young son. We call our hero villages or cities 'Red Star Cities'."

Chekhov added, with tears welling up in his eyes, "We Russians don't want another war – ever! That's why we have built up our defenses, to prevent another carnage in Mother Russia, like the Great War. We have no interest in taking over Western Europe. We cannot understand why your American newspapers and government leaders incessantly claim that we do."

Richards was touched by this outpouring of emotions about the distant World War II. Richards was quite young during World War II but remembered the war years vividly. He could still remember going to the local movie theater in his home town and seeing propaganda films depicting the 'evil Soviet Bear' invading Finland and followed by the collection cans being passed around for money to help the Finns. Then, only a few weeks later, after the Nazi invasion of Russia, he could remember the propaganda movies showing the Soviets as 'our brave allies' with the collection cans being passed around for relief money to send to the Russians. He remembered many hundreds of thousands of American servicemen lost their lives in the war, but not ten percent of the US population!

He responded to Chekhov's comment, "I never realized such a huge section of your population was annihilated by the Nazis. I'm pretty sure not many Americans understand the trauma you underwent here in Russia. However, I do believe, Dr. Chekhov, that you are being unfair to say that *American newspapers and leaders incessantly accuse Russia of wanting to take over Western Europe.*"

Chekhov turned and looked straight into Richards' eyes with a grim look on his face, "Dr. Richards, please! I travel to the west frequently in my role as a member of the Russian Space Council. I make a point of reading the US newspapers any time I take a trip abroad, usually the *International Herald Tribune* in Western Europe or the *New York Times* or the *Washington Post* in the US. I am always appalled at the negative image of Russia portrayed by your papers. We are always accused of threatening world peace, when we are only attending to our defense and national interests around the world, just as the US attends to its defense and national interests around the world."

Richards smiled and said, diplomatically, "Dr. Chekhov, you may be right that our newspapers over-react, but I don't think we can reconcile the differences between our two countries today. However, it is refreshing to hear your view point."

Gus Ford chimed in, "Doctors Chekhov and Gorlovka, the beauty of Moscow and the pretty girls I see walking along the sidewalks have already made a positive impact on my image of your country. Perhaps we believe your country is a threat to world peace because of your enormous build-up of both conventional and nuclear armaments. That fact is frightening to westerners."

Lina interrupted, "It sounds like we are presenting the plenary arguments for the Geneva Disarmament negotiations. But, we in my country, still don't understand why your leaders rejected Premier Gorbachev's proposal for demilitarization of Europe from the Atlantic to the Urals. How could this proposal be a threat to world peace?"

Richards tried again to diplomatically close out this Soviet-American impasse, before it affected the personal relationships involved, "Lady and Gentlemen, let me suggest that the Geneva negotiations would be the proper place to air these arguments, not in Moscow and not by us. For my own part, I came to Moscow with an open mind. I intend to observe your country and your people, and draw my own conclusions. But, please, today, let us enjoy your pleasant country and beautiful capitol city, without political arguments."

Chekhov turned to Richards, held up his hands in mock surrender, laughed, and said, "Dr. Richards is right. Let's just relax and enjoy this ride to the hotel as friends and colleagues, not as members of two opposing armed camps."

Lina smiled in agreement, "Yes, Dr. Chekhov, that's a good idea."

The limousine continued its journey to the Metropole Hotel with Chekhov still acting as tour guide, pointing out the various sights of Moscow to his American guests. The politically sensitive comments were dropped and his explanations of the sights were factual and interesting to Richards and Ford. When they pulled up to the hotel entrance, Lina pulled out two envelopes, "Dr. Richards, -- Don, here are your theater tickets, three for each night. I am sorry I won't be able to accompany you to the opera tonight. Originally I intended to, but I have family obligations tonight. I'm staying at my mother's home tonight. But I will accompany you to the Bolshoi Sunday and will stay in the Metropole Hotel until I return to Novosibirsk later this week. See you Sunday evening."

Chekhov added, "Our first business meeting is at 9 am Monday. See you then. Dr. Gorlovka will escort you both to my office from the hotel."

Richards responded, "Thank you very much for the tickets. It is most thoughtful. How do we find the Moscow Opera House?"

Lina smiled, "If you are brave, you can take the metro. There's an entrance inside the hotel. You get off in five stops. If you are like most rich American, you can have the doorman call a taxi. He will write out the destination in Russian for the driver."

Richards boasted, "I'm adventurous. We'll try the metro. Thanks again, Doctors Chekhov and Gorlovka. See you Sunday, Lina. Have a nice visit with your mother and family."

Ford echoed, "Thanks for everything and goodbye."

Richards and Ford walked into the lobby and up to the registration desk. They handed their passports to the clerk. The clerk gave them a broad smile, "Americans! Welcome to Russia and to the Moscow Metropole. Just a moment. I'll check your reservations." His speech was accented but easily understandable.

He keyed their names into the computer terminal at the desk and a few seconds later, their registration slip and security card were printed out. The clerk asked them to sign the registration slip and then gave them their cards, "Let me explain the security card. Use the card to enter your room instead of a key. It won't work for any other room. Just insert it and it will open the special security door to your room. Also, if you have any room or restaurant charges, use your card to register the charges. Memorize your room number – it's not on your card. That way if your card is lost or stolen, it can't be used to gain entrance to your room."

Richards responded, "That's a very sophisticated system. I suppose it's connected to your hotel computer so the bills are automatically accumulated to the room."

"Of course, Sir. You are computer knowledgeable. Dr. Richards, your room number is 2015 and Mr. Ford, your room number is 1515. I see you do not need help with your bags. The elevator is to your left. Have a pleasant stay, Gentlemen."

The two headed for the elevator and Richards said, on the way up, "Gus, I'm going to take a two hour nap. I'll call you about 3 to see if you would like to take a stroll around Moscow. Maybe we can learn to use the metro."

"Sounds good, Don. When you call me, I'll let you know how I feel. I'm going to take a nap, too. This time difference is numbing."

Richards had no trouble using the security card to get into his room. He was pleasantly surprised at its luxury. It had a large double bed, a couch, table, and comfortable lounge chairs. There was a large color TV in a corner of the room. The bathroom was complete with tub, shower, toilet, bidet, and a sink set in the counter. There was also a refrigerator that opened with his security card.

Curious as to what was on Russian TV, Richards found a Saturday copy of *Pravda in English* in his room. He turned to the last page and under PROGRAMS found a section called TELEVISION which said 'First Program' through 'Fourth Program' that he interpreted to mean channels. Scanning the list, he found a good variety of entertainment, educational, and news programs. Feeling like listening to a symphony orchestra, he tuned in the Second Program which was just starting 'A. P. Borodin's Symphony number 2, Hero of the Russian Epic, played by the Grand Symphony Orchestra of Radio-Television.'   It was a brilliant rendition of the symphony. The video had good color. The audio was of good quality. Richards left it playing while he took his nap.

He woke up just after 2:30. He realized he hadn't contacted Brigitte since he arrived and remembering he had an extra opera ticket she could use., he called the hotel operator to ring her room. He spelled Brigitte's last name to the operator and she responded, "I'm sorry, Sir. There's no B. Michon, but we have a B. Michov. Shall I try that room number?"

"Yes, try, please."

Richards recognize Brigitte's sleepy voice saying, "Hello."

"This is Don. I wasn't sure it would be you, Brigitte. The hotel operator had your last name spelled wrong."

Brigitte replied happily, "Oh, Don, it's you. I was taking a short nap, but I wanted to get up soon anyway. When I'm in Russia I use a slavakized version of my name, Michov." She spoke 'Michov' with a very Russian pronunciation.

Richard laughed, "You are a real Russophile!"

Brigitte answered, "My family originated in Russia, Don. I also speak Russian, you know. When can we get together?"

"Just as soon as I get dressed. What room are you in?"

Brigitte replied, "Room 2017, but don't bother to get dressed. I'll come to your room now."

"That'll be easy! You're right next door! Just open your side of the interconnecting door and I'll do the same." The hanging up clicks were simultaneous.

Richards rushed to his side of the connecting door and there was Brigitte, without a stitch on, her beautiful blonde hair and blue eyes setting off her wide, warm, welcoming smile.

Richards, also nude, embraced her warm body close to his. They moved slowly to his bed and watched the closing strains of Borodin's symphony. Richards switched off the TV and two became entangled in a passionate love session.. Their later relaxation was interrupted by the jangle of the telephone. Richards glanced at his watch – it showed 3:30 – and picked up the phone.

"This is Gus, I thought you were going to call at three."

"Sorry, Gus. I fell asleep and you just woke me up. Let's plan on our stroll at 4 instead of 3. I'll call you when I'm ready to go down, OK?"

"OK. See you about four then."

Richards turned to Brigitte, "How would you like to show two Americans around Moscow this afternoon? And then go to the opera with us this evening?"

Brigitte's face lit up, "Oh, Don, you know I'd love to. You do remember we went to the opera in Paris, don't you? Of course you do! It'll take me twenty minutes to get dressed for our walk."

"I better get dressed, too. Let's eat out before the opera. Maybe you know a typical Russian restaurant?"

"Yes, I know just the place. It's near the opera house, too. See you in a few minutes."

Richards and Brigitte met Ford in the hotel lobby just after 4 pm. Richards introduced his companion, "Brigitte will be our Moscow guide this afternoon since she has been here many times and she speaks Russian. And she will go to the opera with us, using the extra ticket.

Ford smiled, "It's wonderful to have such a beautiful guide. I was worrying this stubborn guy here was going to get us lost – he was insisting we go to the opera on the metro. Now, where should we go first?"

Brigitte answered, "Since it's your first visit to Moscow, first things first! Let's visit Lenin Square and the Kremlin. That's a nice two hour visit. We should get to the restaurant by six since it takes almost two hours for a Russian dinner."

The men chorused, "Sounds great!"

"Let me give you your first lesson on how to use the metro. We can get there by going down the stairs over there."

They enjoyed the still chilly, but sunny weather in Moscow this mid-April Saturday. The Americans were amazed at the grandeur of the Kremlin and the monuments in Lenin Square. They found it cost only a few kopeks to ride the metro, just like the old five cent New York subway of long ago!

At 6 at the restaurant, after some heated and persistent arguing by Brigitte in Russian, they were seated in a few minutes. The waiter almost immediately brought out an elaborate tray of appetizers including hard sausage, white mushrooms in a pickled sauce, cold red salmon, smoked sturgeon, and black caviar flown from the Caspian Sea. Brigitte told them the appetizer array was called 'zakuski'. The men decided to let Brigitte choose the rest of the sumptuous Russian dinner.

The opera was an excellent performance of "Boris Gudonov' and after returning to the hotel, Richards and Brigitte had a reprise of their afternoon lovemaking.

The next morning, Brigitte told Richards her business would take her to Kiev in the Ukraine that afternoon. She would be checking out of the hotel early to catch a 10 am flight. Richards held her close, kissed her goodbye, and told her truthfully he hoped he would see her again. It never occurred to him that she was a KGB agent who had played a key role in helping get the positive decision by the Politburo for the Russian rescue of the American astronauts.

Chapter 33

Moscow Meeting

Richards and Ford spent their Sunday riding the Moscow metro to a few places recommended by the hotel clerk. They walked along the Moscow River and generally enjoyed the sunny but chilly day, mingling with the Muscovites. Back in the hotel lobby just after 5 pm, Richards decided to read the Sunday issue of *Pravda in English* and mentally compared it with US newspapers. He found *Pravda* covered world events in a reasonably thorough fashion. He found, of course, that the news was slanted to the Russian viewpoint, just like US newspapers were slanted to the American viewpoint. He found more articles 'pleading' for disarmament and world peace than in the typical US newspaper. He attributed those articles to the 'propaganda of false peace' that the US administrations had accused the Russians of over the last several years.

He looked up from reading a rather boring article extolling the joys of being a taxi driver in Moscow and caught sight of Dr. Lina Gorlovka coming into the lobby carrying a small bag. She was wearing a short white leather coat with a fur collar, tight black slacks, and white boots with high heels. Her light brown hair was loose and streaming down her back, almost to her waist. Richards was suddenly taken by her overpowering Slavic beauty and sparkling brown eyes. As he stood up to greet her, she saw him. She rushed over to him, put down her bag, hugged and kissed him on each cheek in the European fashion of greeting good friends.

"Don, what a pleasant surprise to find you so soon. When I told my mother I had two American visitors waiting at the hotel, she insisted I pick you up and bring you home for dinner before the ballet."

Richards answered happily, "What a wonderful treat. I would love to visit your mother's home. Gus Ford is up in his room, but I'm sure he will appreciate the invitation also."

"This will give you a chance to see a typical Russian apartment, nothing fancy, but comfortable and homey. But first, I need to check into the hotel and put my bag away. Would you like to come up to my room while I do that?"

"I'd love to, Lina. Also, Gus and I thoroughly enjoyed the performance of Boris Gudonov last night. The Moscow Opera Company is fantastic."

Lina checked in, obtained her security card, and the two walked to the elevator where Lina pushed the button for the twentieth floor.

Richards remarked, "Oh, you're on the same floor as I am. What's your room number?"

"Room 2017. What's yours?"

"What a coincidence! I'm in room 2015. Right next door to you. In fact, there is a connecting door."

Lina laughed, "Oh, how convenient. We can open the door and begin discussing business early!"

Richards stopped at his door, "Lina, I'll stop and pick up the ballet tickets and a coat. I'll call Gus Ford and have him meet us in the lobby. Knock on the door when you're ready to leave."

"That's fine, Don."

They used their security cards to open their respective rooms. Richards phoned Ford to tell him about the dinner invitation. Gus was delighted to be able to visit a Moscow family. Just as Richards put the phone down, he heard a knock on the interconnecting door. He opened it and found Lina standing there. She had taken her coat off and now her ample breasts pressed against her tight, black sweater. Again, Richards was overcome by her beauty. He took her in his arms and kissed her on the lips.

Startled, Lina started to pull away and then moved closer to Richards. She grasped him tightly with her slim arms and returned his kiss passionately.

Richards whispered hoarsely, "I wish we had time right now. Please sleep in my room tonight!"

She looked up into his eyes and nodded, "I can see now we didn't need two rooms. The State is going to waste money on an unused room tonight."

"It's not a very big expense anyway."

Lina laughed, "Not compared with what they're going to spend rescuing your astronauts!"

"That's right! Come on, let's leave for your mother's right now or we'll never get out of this room. I've got the tickets and Gus is waiting in the lobby."

Lina put on her coat again and picked up her hand bag, "You're so right. Let's go!"

The trio arrived at Lina's mother's apartment twenty minutes later on the efficient Moscow metro. The apartment entrance was close to the metro so the rent must have been about 50 rubles, or about $70 a month.

They rode the elevator to the 20th floor, walked down the hall and rang the doorbell. Lina's mother was a very handsome and trim woman in her early sixties. She hugged Richards and Ford in turn, smiled and said something in Russian. Lisa translated, "Mother says you are just like her two sons. And you are welcome to her home."

Richards replied, "Thank you, Mrs. Gorlovka. We are happy to be in your home and feel like we belong to your family."

When Lina translated his comment, her mother smiled happily and gave Richards another hug. She said something in Russian. Lina blushed deeply at her mother's comment.

Richards asked, "What did your mother say?"

Lina hesitated, then translated, "She said she wished you were her son-in-law. She said the two of us would make beautiful babies together."

Richards laughed and said in a light tone, "She's probably right."

Richards and Ford were pleasantly surprised at the comfort and at the beautiful and tasteful furnishings of the apartment. There was a lovely view from the lace curtained windows of Moscow and of the wide river winding through the city. They enjoyed two hours of warm, family hospitality and good hearty Russian food cooked from fresh vegetables and fresh chicken purchased the day before in the markets of Moscow. During the course of the dinner, Richards asked Lina, "Do you think your mother would be offended if I asked her a question about the lines in the markets?"

"You means the queues? Of course not."

Richards phrased his question, "Mrs. Gorlovka, forgive me for asking, but we are always reading in our newspapers about the long queues in your markets to buy food. Is that a problem for you?"

Lina translated and her mother replied and Lina re-translated, "Why heavens no! It's no problem at all. We women who do the shopping for our families know when the fresh fruit and vegetables arrive at the market. We always want to be first to get the freshest. As a result, we all crowd there at the same time and that causes the queues."

"But I understood the queues were caused by shortages."

"No. We can buy anything we want that is in season. If we really want to avoid the queues we could go there three hours after the fresh produce arrived. Then there are no queues, but the things are not fresh then."

Richards laughed, "In our markets, we never worry about freshness. We just buy frozen or canned foods. We're usually too busy working to prepare fresh fruits and vegetables."

Mrs. Gorlovka looked aghast, "My dear boy! You must move to Russia. I don't think your life style is healthy. We can buy frozen and canned foods, too, if we want to, but we think fresh food is healthier."

Richards added diplomatically, "Thank you for the offer, Mrs. Gorlovka. You have such a beautiful daughter that it is a tempting thought. But I'm afraid my 'teshcha' (mother-in-law) would make me fat with her healthful foods."

Everyone laughed heartily at Richards' joke. Lina looked at her watch, "I'm afraid we are going to have to break up this family gathering and leave for the Bolshoi now or else we'll be late."

As they left, Richards kissed Mrs. Gorlovka on both cheeks and said warmly, "Thank you, mother, for the dinner. You made me feel part of your family."

When Lina translated his comment, her mother grabbed Richards with tears welling up in her eyes, hugged and kissed him again.

The trio took the metro to the Bolshoi, and enjoyed a fantastic performance of Swan Lake. They returned to the hotel just after 11. When Lina and Richards were alone in his room, Lina remarked, "I hope my mother didn't embarrass you with talk of becoming a member of the family and making babies with me."

Richards took her in his arms and kissed her softly, "Your mother has good ideas. No, I'm not embarrassed. I noticed you blushed a deep red though."

Lina looked deeply into Richards' eyes, "Yes, I was embarrassed, but not because I didn't like my mother's idea. Oh, I just know it's not possible anyway."

Richards kissed Lina again, feeling a strange attraction he hadn't felt for a woman since he met his first wife during college. "Stranger things have happened!"

Richards and Lina spent a tender evening of love making. When Lina fell deeply asleep in Richards' arms, he allowed his eyes to travel thoughtfully over her lovely face and body and he recalled her mother's remark about what beautiful babies they would make together. That night he dreamed of what it would be like to live in Russia with the beautiful Lina.

The next morning, Richards, Ford, and Dr. Gorlovka took the metro to the big Russian government building housing the Russian Space Institute headquarters in Moscow. The Russian Space Shuttle Program and its director, Professor Dr. Nikolai Ivanovich Chekhov, had an elaborate complex of offices in the imposing building. Unlike many Soviet government buildings, the name of the Space Institute and its modernistic logo were emblazoned boldly on the front of the building. Over the years, the Russians had learned how to play the game of world publicity for their space program, using the western media, TV and newspapers, as well as the Russian media, to tell of their expanding space exploitation. They learned from NASA of the benefits of image building to display their space missions on international TV in real time. Their unmanned probe to Mars in 1989 was a real TV spectacular. Showing for the first time to the whole world concrete proof that there was at one time life on Mars, the probe had found and displayed a fossil in the strata. No doubt that it was a fossil, confirmed by chemical analyses telemetered back to Earth. This evidence of life on another planet had greatly increased the world's awareness of the Russian space exploration program.

The Russians had a much more modest space station, called 'MIR', which had cosmonauts in orbit continuously since 1986. The original crew members, Leonidas Kizim and Vladimir Soloviov, had been awarded the Red Star Medal for their space station pioneering. The importance of MIR was dwarfed by the new US Space Station with its much larger structure and larger crew compartment. Also its architecture permitted an evolution and expansion so that by the year 2000, the US Space Station would have a crew of almost 100 aboard.

Lina escorted Richards and Ford into Chekhov's large corner office overlooking a big park. The deciduous trees were beginning to develop green leaves. Spring came late in Moscow.

Lina said to Chekhov, "Nikolai Ivanovich, here are our American visitors ready to begin our discussions."

Chekhov turned to Richards and Ford, grinned, and said expansively, "Welcome to my humble office. Please be seated." He directed them to an open area which included a large couch, coffee table, and four plush arm chairs. Just as they seated themselves, his secretary brought in a carafe of coffee on a large tray with a beautiful array of chocolate confections.

Richards opened the discussions, "Professor Dr. Chekhov, first, let me thank you for the hospitality you and your colleague, Dr. Gorlovka, have shown me and my colleague, Mr. Ford. We enjoyed the opera and ballet very much. It was a real pleasure to enjoy the high culture of Moscow and its beautiful sights."

Chekhov smiled broadly, "I am so glad you and Mr. Ford have enjoyed your visit so far. I hope you will see more of our city and our country before you leave. Now, here are the agendas for your meetings here in Moscow."

Chekhov handed Richards and Ford each a copy of the program in English while he and Lina each had a copy in Russian Cyrillic letters.

Richards scanned the program quickly, "I see the program covers only two days. Except for the first topic, the Docking Module Adapter, it appears the topics are general in nature: the Russian space program, the space shuttle program, etc. I had hoped to get into more detail – "

Chekhov interrupted, "Why, yes, of course you will get more detail. As I said, this is the agenda for the Moscow portion of your visit. On Wednesday morning, you and Mr. Ford will fly to Novosibirsk with Dr. Gorlovka to visit our Space Institute there. You will get into the 'nitty-gritty' details thhere. Dr. Gorlovka has prepared an agenda for that portion of your trip.

Lina handed Richards and Ford a more elaborate and detailed agenda for their meeting in Novosibirsk. Richards quickly looked it over and noticed it was packed with detailed technical discussions for Wednesday afternoon through Friday afternoon. It covered all the technical topics he had expected to see, such as launch data, trajectory matching, docking, return entry, etc. Richards smiled, "Very good. This covers everything we need."

Chekhov added, "You see, Dr. Richards, the Space Institute here in Moscow is like your NASA Headquarters in Washington. We just establish broad policy guidelines and allocate the funds. Novosibirsk is like your NASA Houston. There they manage the details of the program. And of course, we have Baikonur where our actual space launch facilities are found, like your NASA Kennedy site."

Lina went on, "Dr. Richards, when you phoned from Washington last Wednesday, you mentioned the Docking Module Adapter that would let our space shuttle dock to your Space Station."

Richards nodded, "Yes, I didn't want to over-emphasize that detail, but it is quite necessary."

Lina continued, "Yes, of course. You may remember Dr. Chekhov made the comment, 'Well, if we did it on the Soyuz-Apollo, we can do it again'."

Dr. Chekhov beamed at this reference to his comment.

Richards said, "Yes, I remember. A good point."

"I thought it was a good point as well. So I checked into who worked out the Soyuz-Apollo docking module. I found out that on the Soviet side it was Yuli Litvinov who has since retired. Nevertheless, Yuli is waiting outside in Dr. Chekhov's reception office. We should have him in here for the first agenda discussions."

Dr. Chekhov buzzed his secretary and told her to send Litvinov in. Chekhov rose to greet his old friend with a hug and a kiss on each cheek. He held Litvinov with both arms outstretched,

"Yuli Ilyich, retirement has done wonders for you. You have lost 15 kilos and have a great suntan. You look twenty years younger."

"Yes, Nikolai Ivanovich, I have lost 18 kilos. I spend two hours sunning on the Black Sea beach every day and run five kilometers each day. I feel like I did when I ran cross country at Moscow University 40 years ago. But I'm glad to come back to work, for a while, on our space shuttle."

Chekhov turned to Richards and Ford, "Forgive us for reminiscing but I haven't seen Comrade Litvinov since he took early retirement and returned to his hometown of Wilkowo in the Ukraine on the Black Sea coast. He was our chief systems engineer on the Soviet space shuttle. Yuli Ilyich, meet Dr. Richards and Mr. Ford from America."

Yuli strode over and shook hands with the men, kissed Lina on both cheeks, and continued, "I have been to America. I spent six months in Downey, California, working on the Soyuz-Apollo mission. My contact there was Buck Woods. We designed the docking mechanism to link the Soyuz and Apollo capsules together. I guess that is why I'm here. I sure wish we had old Bucky helping on this docking module design."

Ford broke in, "I remember ol' Bucky. I worked on Apollo, too. Bucky retired a few years back. I believe he stayed in California. At a retirement community in Orange County called Leisure World."

Yuli replied, "I can't imagine Bucky in leisure. He always worked so hard. Any chance of getting him to help?"

Richards chimed in, "Of course. I'll call him today and see if he's interested. He probably will be when he finds you're working on the project, Yuli. It makes a lot of sense."

Yuli replied, "That would be great. I'm sure we can get the docking adapter designed and built in not much more than a month. That won't hold up the rescue, will it?"

"No, Yuli, that would be good. We hope the launch can be made about the first of July. That's two and a half months from now."

"Plenty of time."

Dr. Chekhov interrupted, "Now, Dr. Richards, we haven't committed to a launch date yet. And remember, Comrade Litvinov's comments are strictly unofficial."

Richards laughed, "Yes, of course I realize that. We're just two engineers discussing 'parameters'. I understand any agreement has to be blessed by a higher authority. Remember, Dr. Chekhov, we have a complex bureaucracy in the US just like you have in Russia. Both Mr. Ford and I are accustomed to 'working within the system'!"

Chekhov replied, "Good, then let's get started officially discussing the first agenda item."

The meeting continued going over the details of the docking mechanism. Richards provided Litvinov with drawings of the opening the docking adapter had to fit. He also had diagrams of the power and vacuum connections that were necessary.

The remainder of the next two days were spent listening to informal briefings covering the Russian space program and shuttle program as listed on the agendas. The briefings were general in nature, as Richards had suspected they would be. He realized at the end of Tuesday, that he would have to wait until he got to Novosibirsk before he could get the depth of detail he really needed. However, the boring briefings were relieved by two more nights of passionate love with Lina in the Metropole Hotel.

The black Chaika limousine picked up Dr. Gorlovka, Richards and Ford at 5 am Wednesday for their 6 am flight from Moscow to Novosibirsk. It was still dark when their airliner lifted off the runway at Sheremetyevo Airport. Since Novosibirsk, some 1500 nautical miles away, was almost due east of Moscow, they flew into the rising sun and soon it became light. The weather was exceptionally clear and they could see for many miles in all directions. Richards and Lina shared a pair of seats, with Ford across the aisle from them. Lina asked Richards to take the window seat for the two hour and forty five minute flight, so he could look down at the beautiful country she was so proud of. They were scheduled to arrive just before 11 am.

The first large city they found, on the left side, was Gorky, a city of over a million people, alongside the wide Volga River. Richards remembered Gorky as the city where the dissident Soviet Physicist, Andrei Sakharov and his wife, Elena Bonner, were sent for internal exile. As the plane rushed over the ground, Richards noticed the land east of Moscow was quite flat except for a ridge of low mountains bordering the Volga as it wound its way south to the Black Sea. The land was criss-crossed by a network of rivers whose valleys provided some fertile agricultural fields.

The next large city they passed over, also on the left side of the aircraft, was Perm, which also had a population of over a million people. It sat near a large reservoir-like lake fed by the confluence of the Kama and Klova Rivers. Just beyond Perm, they flew over the famous Ural Mountains, a narrow ridge running north and south across Russia along the 60 degree longitude line. The peaks were low close to their flight path with one 2443 foot (746 meter) peak. The highest snow capped peak in the Urals, 4889 feet or 1493 meters, towered some 120 nautical miles to the north.

Just east of the Urals they saw another city of more than a million on the right hand side of the plane – Sverdlovsk. East of the Urals began the flat tundra of Siberia, which was also crossed by many number of rivers and tributaries. The largest river they flew over was the Irytsch which flowed through the city of Omsk.

Richards told Lina, "Your country is really beautiful. It reminds me of flying over the US, similar, yet quite different."

Lina answered, "Don, we all live in the same biosphere. I hope no one decides to ruin it. By nuclear war, I mean!"

"Yes, Lina, that's what I thought you meant. Maybe this mission will make that possibility more remote."

"I hope so!"

Thirty minutes later they landed at the Siberian city of Novosibirsk, the space-science capitol of Russia, on the Ob River on the flat land of Siberia, but to the east and south there was gently rising terrain, finally leading to some high mountain peaks along the Russian-Mongolian border.

The trio was met at the airport by another black Chaika limousine belonging to the Russian Space Institute. Their first meeting was scheduled for 1 pm, which gave time for Richards and Ford to sign in at their hotel and then have lunch in the institute's executive dining room.

Chapter 34

Novosibirsk Space Institute

Dr. Lina Gorlovka escorted Richards and Ford to the big conference room at the Novosibirsk Space Institute. The room was filled with members of the Russian shuttle team. The top program management personnel were all there, led by Dr. Gorlovka, deputy program manager, and Colonel Georgi Andrejevich Gusev, cosmonaut and commander of the rescue shuttle. The key technical people were there as well, led by Yuli Litvinov, the acting chief engineer for the rescue project, brought back temporarily from retirement for this special assignment. There were TV monitors on the wall similar to those in the UAC conference room, back in California. The launch control team from Baikonur, where the shuttle would be launched, were on one video screen. Professor Dr. Chekhov in the Moscow Headquarters of the Space Institute was on the other screen.

Lina lead both men to the head of the table and introduced Richards to the live and video audience as the director of the US space program and 'special envoy' of President Williamson. She explained that he and Ford, of NASA Houston, were here to arrange for the Russian shuttle rescue of the stranded American astronauts on the Space Station. Lina said to the TV screen showing Dr. Chekhov, "Do you have anything to add at this time, Professor Dr. Chekhov?"

Dr. Chekhov cleared his throat and then spoke authoritatively to his far flung audience, "Comrades, I wish to inform you that the mission to rescue the stranded Americans has been approved by the highest levels of the Russian government. Premier Gorbachev himself wanted me to ask you, the Russian Space Shuttle Program personnel and support workers, to provide your fullest support to this important effort. He said, and I quote: *I am sure that our Russian space technology and our dedicated space workers and Comrades will be successful in this humanitarian rescue mission of the stranded American cosmonauts.*

"And for my own part, Comrades, the Russian space shuttle program office assigned 'Red Priority One', the highest priority, to this rescue mission. Let Lenin be proud of your efforts!"

A loud burst of applause filled the room. Richards felt the strong sense of dedication of the Russian personnel for a successful mission.

Lina said at the end of her boss's speech, "Thank you, Comrade Professor Chekhov, for your inspirational introduction. Now, Comrades, Dr. Richards has an hour long briefing during which he will present a summary of the situation on the American Space Station and the requirements for the rescue mission."

Richards strode to the podium in front of the room, near the huge back lighted screen on which his view graphs would be projected. He began his formal presentation, first, by pushing the button to signal the projectionist to project the first view graph, and second, by speaking into the microphone provided on the podium, "Ladies and Gentlemen – er, I mean – Comrades."

There was laughter from the audience.

"We have seventeen people stranded on the Space Station with expendables to last through August. We should plan on the first launch no later than the first of August. Furthermore, we should carry another three months worth of expendables, in case your shuttle should be disabled in orbit."

There was more laughter, and Colonel Gusev, the Russian shuttle commander, interrupted, saying seriously, "Dr. Richards, of course we don't think that will happen, but as a prudent commander, I support your contention to carry three months expendables on the first launch."

Richards felt the consensus develop in the room since the space personnel present had the highest regard for Colonel Gusev, one of the Hero Cosmonauts of Russia. Richards continued, "The next key point is that I computed, based on the sketchy information I had before I came here, that, to bring the stranded astronauts back, assuming a crew of three on the Russian shuttle, will take three rescue launches. We would like to carry additional expendables aloft during each rescue launch."

Gusev interrupted again, "Our Russian shuttle is larger than your American shuttle, Dr. Richards. We can bring back everyone in two launches. Besides, aren't you going to leave at least a skeleton crew aboard to keep the Space Station 'alive'?"

Richards smiled, "Yes, of course, Colonel Gusev. That means we only have to bring back thirteen people, six and seven in two launches."

Richards then continued with the details of his briefing, presenting the orbital parameters, the details of the two stranded shuttles tethered to the Station, etc. At the end he summarized, "So you can see we have a lot of details to discuss during my two and a half days here. One is the docking module adapter that will let your shuttle dock to our Station."

Richards turned to Yuri Litvinov, "Comrade Litvinov, I received word from my office that they have located Bucky Woods and he has agreed to come out of retirements for a few months to work with you on the rescue mission. He sends his regards."

Litvinov smiled broadly, "With Comrade Bucky working on the project, I am sure we will be successful!"

The people in the conference room spent the rest of the afternoon preparing a list of action items to discuss during the next two days while Richards and Ford were still at Novosibirsk. At the end of the day, Richards had a short, private meeting with Lina to summarize what needed to be done. As they finished, Lina said, "Don, please stay in my apartment during your visit here. I've arranged for Yuli Litvinov to entertain Gus Ford so he won't miss us. I would like to cook dinner for you tonight."

Pleasantly surprised, Richards responded enthusiastically, "Thank you, Lina, I would love that. But I need to pick up my bag at the hotel."

Lina laughed, "I had already assumed you would say 'yes' to my proposition. So I had the limousine driver return to the hotel and get your bag. It's in the trunk of the car now. He also told the hotel you wouldn't need your room after all. Think of it. We will save the state three nights hotel bill. They will save 30 rubles a week."

Richards laughed, ""What a schemer! And what if I had said no?"

"Don, I know you well enough by now to know that you would never say 'no'!"

Richards and Lina left the Space Institute in the Chaika limousine which was hers because of her position as deputy program director of the Space Institute. She was one of the highest ranking managers in Novosibirsk. On the way home, she asked the driver to stop at a farmers' market, outdoors in the brisk Siberian air. The last traces of snow were still on the ground. Spring was struggling to replace the frigid winter. As they pulled up to the market, Lina said to Don, "Come with me. You may want to see a typical farmers' market."

Walking from the limousine to the sprawling market area, Lina explained, "This is a market where the local farmers sell their produce grown on private plots of land. There is almost everything here: all kinds of fresh vegetables, fruit, chickens, eggs and meat. We'll buy what we need for the next few nights dinners."

Richards was quite surprised, "I didn't realize your farmers had private lands. And I didn't think you had private markets. Aren't all the farms collectivized in Russia?"

Lina laughed, "You Americans don't understand Russia very well. Of course there are the huge state owned farms which are collectivized and run by large state companies. They are very much like your large American multi-national corporation-owned farms, such as those in the California San Joaquin Valley. But our government permits farmers to also have private plots and to sell what they grow."

Lina moved from stall to stall in the market, picking the best and freshest vegetables she could find. She bought a fresh chicken, and had the farmer clean and cut it up for her. She bought a dozen eggs. She spent a total of 2.60 rubles or a little over three and a half dollars at the official exchange rate. They returned to the limousine with four plastic bags full of things and Richards remarked, "I'm amazed at how cheap things are."

Lina replied, "Don, that's why I like to shop in the market. Remember, Russia is part of Europe. All of the European countries have markets like this. When I travel to France or Holland or Switzerland, for example, I go to look at their markets, just to compare. Our markets are just as good, and cheaper!"

Richards responded, "I never thought of Russia as being a part of Europe. In our newspapers, we read about the Europeans and then, as a separate group, the 'communists to the east'!"

Lina answered, "That is a strange point of view. True, we have a more advanced form of government than the western European governments – at least, we think so – but the highways, the trains, the mores and customs: they all continue beyond the hypothetical east-west line. We think of Czechoslovakia as being west."

"Our newspapers and leaders refer to the line separating the east and west as the 'Iron Curtain'."

A sad look came over Lina's face, "What unfriendly rhetoric, or hyperbole! Come on, get in the car. Let's go home where we can forget about east-west politics and have dinner."

Richards and Lina had a nice, quiet evening in her comfortable one bedroom apartment in a high rise building in the southern section of Novosibirsk. Her apartment faced south, with views of the large lake-reservoir fed by the Ob River as well as the rolling terrain to the south east. She and Richards prepared dinner together. They had a green salad, baked chicken, and boiled artichokes with Lina's special mustard/mayonnaise. After dinner they watched a movie and then a symphony on the color television set.

Richards admired Lina's thirty-five year old body as they climbed beneath the warm down comforter on Lina's bed. As on previous nights together, they enjoyed each other's bodies and then fell into a deep sleep.

In the following days, Richards and Ford continued the technical meetings with the Russian personnel, sometimes working together and sometimes separated into smaller sub groups. They made good progress on the plans for the rescue mission.

On Friday, the last afternoon of their visit, the complete group reassembled for the summary meeting. The video monitors were again connected with Moscow and Baikonur. Dr. Lina Gorlovka began the meeting, "Dr. Richards, we in the shuttle program office have carefully reviewed all the steps required for the first rescue launch and Professor Dr. Chekhov has approved the eighth of August as a launch date. Can you live with that date?"

Richards reflected a moment, "Yes, it's eight days later than we would have liked, but we can live with it. Does that include the design and fabrications of the docking module adapter?"

Yuli Litvinov answered this question, "Yes, Dr. Richards, it does. But the plan assumes that I will meet with Bucky Woods at your plant in California a week from next Monday to complete the final detailed planning for the adapter. Is that date satisfactory?"

"Yes, that's fine. I will make sure Bucky is there. We will provide all the support you need to do your planning there."

Litvinov added, "One more thing. After our planning session I think Bucky should return to Novosibirsk for a month to perform the detailed design and fabrication. Is that OK?"

Richards replied, "I see no problem with that arrangement. It sounds like a good idea."

Lina went on, "Dr. Richards, we further believe you should return for a mid-term program review meeting here in Novosibirsk the end of June. You should bring Mr. Woods with you at that time, assuming he will have returned to America by then."

"Dr. Gorlovka, that sounds like a good plan. I do hope to visit Baikonur at that time."

Lina answered slowly, "We usually do not permit foreigners to visit our Baikonur launch facility, Dr. Richards."

Chekhov interrupted on the TV screen, "Don't worry, Dr. Richards. That can be arranged. Dr. Gorlovka, I will issue a directive from Headquarters here in Moscow authorizing Dr. Richards and Mr. Woods to visit the launch site during his visit the end of June."

Lina formally closed the meeting. She turned to Richards, "I would like a private meeting with you in my office."

Once there, Lina said, "First, the business matter: I think you and Mr. Ford should return home by flying on our new Russian mach 5 supersonic transport. You will get home in Los Angeles before you leave Novosibirsk."

"That sounds great! Can you really arrange it?"

"It's already arranged. Here are the tickets for you and Mr. Ford, compliments of the Russian government. The flight leaves at 8 am tomorrow morning. Now, let's go home. I want you for this last night in Novosibirsk!"

The Chaika limousine with US and Russian flags flying side by side on the front fenders, picked up Lina and Richards at her apartment Saturday morning at 7 am. Gus Ford was waiting for them inside the limousine.   The official status of the Chaika allowed it to drive at high speed through the very light early morning traffic and they reached the airport at 7:20.   Lina was met at the entrance by a special Russian security man who escorted the trio very quickly through the passport and customs formalities. Soon they were in the VIP lounge waiting to board the supersonic transport parked out on the ramp.

After the crash of the original Soviet supersonic transport during the Paris Air Show back in 1985, the Russians initiated a high priority re-development program to upgrade their SST by adding the advantages of the latest supersonic aircraft technology. They used their own technology as well as technology developed by NASA which was published openly in magazines like *Aviation Week* and available to the Russians. The ecology movement in the US had doomed the American supersonic transport development. As a result, the Russians leap-frogged the obsolete Concorde SST technology and developed a mach 5 aircraft that cruised at an altitude of 150,000 feet.   At this height, the shockwave hitting the ground was greatly attenuated, permitting the large aircraft to fly at supersonic speed above populated land areas, something the Concorde could not do because of the shock wave noise problem. The US still had not granted landing rights to the Russian SST, but Japan allowed the huge jet to land at Tokyo.   At mach 5, five times the speed of sound, the big jet took 55 minutes to fly the 3080 nautical miles from Novosibirsk to Tokyo.

The hostess in the VIP lounge gave Richards and Ford their boarding passes to Tokyo.   She told them they would arrive in Tokyo at 12:55 pm Tokyo time and that they were booked on the Northwest Orient Airlines flight 002 non-stop from Tokyo to Los Angeles. The flight would arrive at 7 am Saturday morning. Since they would cross the International Date Line between Tokyo and Los Angeles, they would arrive in Los Angeles one hour before they would leave Novosibirsk, local times considered.

Richards kissed Lina goodbye, "Thank you for everything, especially the SST tickets. This is going to be a real experience in speed."

Lina replied, "You are welcome. Our country believes the mach 5 SST is the wave of the future. It flies so high the sky is dark and you can see stars, even though it is light on the ground. It is almost like riding in a space ship, a fifth the speed of the orbiting shuttle!"

Gus Ford added, "I'm truly looking forward to the experience. I can hardly wait to tell my friend, Larry Terry at NASA Langley, about the flight. He developed the basic aerodynamics in the Langley supersonic wind tunnel that this Russian SST uses!"

Richards and Ford boarded the sleek, space ship-looking SST aircraft. Richards climbed into the window seat and Ford settled next to him in an aisle seat. The plane taxied to the take off end of the active runway 24. The wind indicator alongside the runway said there was a 20 knot west wind blowing almost straight toward them. The captain applied power to the four huge bi-phase engines. The engines acted as turbo-fan engines during the take off and landing. They switched to the second phase, ramjets, after the aircraft accelerated to mach 2, about three minutes after take off. Richards and Ford felt the acceleration pushing them back into their seats. They were truly impressed by the outstanding performance of the fantastic plane. The futuristic aircraft climbed very steeply and reached its cruise altitude of 150 thousand feet five minutes later.

Ten minutes later they were over the northern tip of the 300 mile long Os Baikal Lake in the autonomous Russian republic of Burjaskaja. Richards computed the aircraft was going almost a nautical mile a second, 560 nautical miles every ten minutes! The sensation of speed was astonishing. Ten minutes later they passed just north of the northern-most Chinese province of Daxinganling that jutted into Russia at a latitude of 54 degrees north.

Nine minutes later they passed over the large Russian Asiatic city of Charborovsk, on the large Amur River. Here the aircraft turned south towards Tokyo. A few minutes later they left Russia and passed over the Sea of Japan. Fifteen minutes later they were on the ground in Tokyo. A 3080 nautical mile flight, farther than Los Angeles to New York, in fifty five minutes!

An hour later they were aboard the big Northwest Orient 747, heading for Los Angeles. They arrived in Los Angeles at seven Saturday morning, the same day they took off.

Chapter 35

Space Station

Barbara Rosen woke up and looked at her watch, set on California time. It was 7:30 in the morning, Monday 21 April. She looked over at Colonel Richard Rogers, the commander of Atlantis, one of the stranded shuttles tethered to the Space Station. He was still sleeping. At Barbara's invitation, Rogers had spent the night in her largish deputy commander's cabin, one of the two private habitations on the US Space Station. The other belonged to General Robbins, the Space Station commander. Barbara's room was in Habitation Module #1, adjacent to the Service Module where the garbage and toilet wastes were stored along with the expendables – water, fuel and food. General Robbins had given Barbara her choice of this cabin or of the private cabin in Habitation Module #2, adjacent to the Guidance and Control and Communications Module.

At the time, she had said, "Jack, if you don't mind, I'll take the cabin near the garbage. I want to be as far away from the racket of the Com and G&C Module as possible when I'm sleeping." Privately she thought, *I also want to get as far away from the commander as possible in case I want to entertain some of the boys in my cabin.* Last night she had taken advantage of the privacy of her cabin to engage in her favorite recreation in space. NASA regulations were silent on sex in space – neither allowed it nor prohibited it. Barbara figured, *If they don't say it's illegal, then I guess it's legal.* So she was taking advantage of the loophole in the rules when she invited one or another of the macho astronauts to her cabin. She liked them all, but Billie Joe Johnson, the commander of Columbia, was still her favorite of all the men aboard the Space Station. But, since she was the only sexually active female aboard, she thought she should spread the joy around.

Last night at dinner in the lunch room in Habitation Module #2, Barbara had whispered her invitation to Rogers. He had whispered back his delighted assent! Since the orbital period of the Space Station was 89.5 minutes, the eight hour 'night' they spent together was actually five nights. That is, the Space Station passed through the Earth's shadow five times. As Barbara was waking up to go on duty, she thought about last night's activities.

When she and Rogers had walked into her cabin the evening before, she had said, "Just a minute, Dick, until I get into something more comfortable. Will you lock the door please? I like privacy while I'm having fun."

Rogers had laughed as he carried out her wishes, "You definitely should have privacy. We don't want any of those other guys floating in here."

The Space Station was pressurized so there was no need to wear pressurized suits inside. Barbara had quickly shed her clothes and tucked them into her laundry bag with Velcro fasteners to keep them from floating around her cabin. She then retired to her 'head' (or bathroom), which was little more than a corner of the cabin with a curtain to mask it off. There were two bathroom fixtures for handling bodily excretions cleanly. They were a little awkward to use, but Barbara was used to them by now. The fixtures took bodily wastes by vacuum and dumped them into a holding tank next door in the Service Module. There was another vacuum fixture for brushing teeth and another gadget for getting a drink of water. A bag was used for taking a shower. The astronaut climbed into the bag and sealed it around the neck. A push button allowed a spray of soap and water to be controlled individually. It made quite a good shower.

Barbara had finished using her toilet and shower and had floated out in the nude, "Dick, you can have it now. That shower sure felt good. And that toilet fixture is better than a bidet. I like the sensuous feel of its warm water wash. You know, I think I'll try to market that gadget after I retire from NASA. Do you think people would like it?"

Rogers shrugged his broad shoulders, "It may work OK for a woman, but it's a bit awkward for men. I don't think the designers figured the shape for a man without sex for a month who's looking at a nude woman with big breasts floating by."

Barbara giggled, "Just give me time. I'll design a special size for you."

Rogers hurried to finish his toilet and floated back into the center of the cabin, nude, all ready for his first night with a woman in space. He asked, "How in the world does this procedure work? I never thought of the physics of doing this while weightless! They didn't prepare us for this in astronaut training."

Barbara smiled knowingly, "Let's take one step at a time," and she floated slowly over to Rogers. "Just grab hold of me and enjoy touching, stroking and massaging bare skin. We can't do that in our space gear. And don't worry about bumping into anything sticking out from the walls – I've put some kind of protective padding on each sharp corner, just for this activity."

He had wondered why she had a padded bra covering the faucet handles.

"Now, for the next phase," she continued. "Here we need some mechanical aids." She put two Velcro loops around her ankles and fastened each to a Velcro patch on the wall, holding her in place. Then she said, passionately, "Come to baby now. Just float over and I'll grab you."

Rogers pushed off from the wall but that gave him too much momentum and he nearly knocked Barbara off the Velcro 'anchors'. He recovered quickly and grabbed her buttocks to hold on. That worked well and they were able to stay coupled even after their fun and games. They continued holding on to each other and had floated off into a deep sleep, both completely satisfied.

Rogers woke up two hours later and they had a sweet reprise. When they finished a second time, Barbara remarked sleepily, "You know, I've never slept with a Russian. I wonder who the commander of the Russian shuttle will be? I sure hope he's handsome. I think I'll teach him what I taught you tonight!"

Rogers answered back, "I'll bet you will. You're a great teacher, Barbara."

They had both drifted back into a relaxed sleep, this time in Barbara's sleeping bag connected to the wall by Velcro.

Barbara reached over and gently nudged Rogers awake. She breathed in his ear, "Dick, you better get up now. We've got a meeting with Houston and Irvine this morning. Richards and Ford are going to give us the official word on the Russian rescue launch."

Rogers answered sleepily, "OK, I guess we better get dressed. General Robbins probably wouldn't allow nude astronauts in the meeting."

They dressed quickly and floated over to the commissary for breakfast. They had orange juice, hot coffee, scrambled eggs, and banana puree with strawberry yogurt, served though spouts. It was almost like eating from five nipples.

The meeting started promptly at 8 am California time, 10 am Houston time. General Robbins, Dr. Barbara Rosen, and the two shuttle commanders, Billie Joe Johnson and Richard Rogers, gathered in the Space Station communication room in the G&C and Com Module, sandwiched between Habitation Module #2 and the Docking Module. It was the nerve center of the Space Station: computers, guidance and control apparatus, communication transceivers, etc., were all neatly packaged in the module. The com room had a large TV screen with four sections displaying the UAC conference room with Dr. Richards' face on the screen, the NASA Houston conference room with Gus Ford, and the NASA Washington conference room with Dr. Bill Adams and the Presidential Science Advisor, Dr. John Davidson. The fourth screen had Dr. Lina Gorlovka and Colonel Georgi Gusev from the Russian Space Institute in Novosibirsk.

General Robbins opened the meeting, "Don and Gus, we're on pins and needles waiting to hear the official word on when we're going to get rescued by the Russians."

Richards replied, "General Robbins, we've got all the right parties on your TV screen now. I believe you've met everyone but Dr. Gorlovka and Colonel Gusev at Novosibirsk. They both speak good English and are on the screen. I'll let them introduce themselves."

Lina Gorlovka spoke up, "Hello everyone. I am Dr. Lina Gorlovka. I'm the deputy director of the Russian Space Shuttle program and with me here is the commander of the Russian space shuttle, Colonel Georgi Gusev. To answer your question, Professor Dr. Chekhov has approved a launch date of 8 August 1992."

Barbara Rosen broke in, "Dr. Gorlovka – Lina – hi! This is Dr. Barbara Rosen. I'm deputy director of the Space Station. I hope Colonel Gusev – hi, Georgi! – is bringing another three months of expendables when he comes. We don't expect your shuttle will break, but we have enough other broken shuttles floating around up here that it's always possible!"

Lina replied, "Barbara, don't worry. Dr. Richards insisted that more expendables be brought up with our first launch. That is part of our approved plan now."

Barbara answered happily, "Good! And, Georgi, we're going to have a welcoming party for you and your crew when you arrive. What do you like to drink?"

Gusev smiled, "Barbara, I drink vodka, but I assume your Space Station is like our MIR: no vodka. So I'll have orange juice!"

General Robbins interrupted, and said officiously, "Barbara is right. We will have a warm welcome for you when you arrive in August, Colonel Gusev. But first, tell me about the plans for hooking up the Russian shuttle to our docking module. Just how are you going to do that?"

Colonel Gusev replied in a serious tone, "General Robbins, please don't worry about that detail. We have two of the best men in the business working that problem: Yuli Litvinov, who is here with us in Novosibirsk, and Bucky Woods, whom I see on the screen with Dr. Richards in California. They designed the docking module for the Soyuz-Apollo link up and I'm sure they can do it again."

Litvinov interrupted, "Hi there, Bucky. I'm leaving Friday to fly to California to meet with you." Then he addressed General Robbins' question, "General Robbins, this is Yuli here. Bucky Woods and I are meeting next Monday to work out the design and details of the adapter for the docking module. Then Bucky is coming to Novosibirsk for a month. Believe me, we will have the design finished and the adapter fabricated before Bucky goes back to America. That won't hold up the launch!"

Richards resumed control of the meeting, "I know that Dr. Davidson, in Washington, wants to get more details so he can keep President Williamson informed of our progress. I've prepared a briefing summarizing the details of the rescue mission we worked out with the Russians in Novosibirsk last week. I'll present it now. Then we'll have questions after that."

As Richards launched into his briefing, Barbara whispered in Colonel Rogers' ear, "Oh, no! Another of Richards' boring briefings! Well, anyway, Georgi Gusev is a gorgeous hunk! I can hardly wait for that welcoming party to be over so I can really get to know him!"

Chapter 36

Docking Adapter

Richards was in his office on Monday morning, the 28th of April. He had been back from Russia a little over a week and was settling back into the routine of working in his own office for a while. Just before 8:30, his secretary buzzed him on the intercom phone, "Dr. Richards, Mr. Woods is here with your Russian visitor.

He answered, "Thanks, June. Show them in and then please bring our guests some coffee and some of those gummy gooey chocolate cookies out of your cupboard."

A few seconds later, Yuli and Bucky Woods entered Richards' office. Richards surprised himself by immediately going up to Yuli and they hugged and kissed each other on each cheek in the Russian custom. "Welcome to America, Comrade Yuli."

Yuli replied happily, "It's nice to be back in California. I forgot how nice and warm it is here, and how smoggy! Bucky took me to Catalina Island on his power boat Saturday afternoon. We had a great time skin diving and fishing. No smog at Catalina. Just sun and beautiful girls!"

Richards smiled, I'm glad you're getting into the California life style." He turned to Bucky, "Now that you're retired, I guess you can go to Catalina any time you feel like it, can't you?"

Bucky grinned happily, "You betcha, Don. Retirement is the greatest! No time schedules. I can do just what I feel like doing. I spend most of my summers over at Catalina on my boat. I cook on the boat and have a different young chick every night."

Yuli protested, "Now, Bucky, at our age, you really mean once or twice a week, don't you?"

Bucky laughed energetically, "Well, as often as I can! Anyway, the young girls flock to my big boat like bees to honey. They're nice to have around."

Richards, able to relax a bit for the first time in a couple of months, gets in the mood of these two good friends, "Hey, Bucky, when are you going to take me out on your boat?"

"As soon as I get back from Russia, Don. Yuli and I are going to fly there Sunday morning on that new Russian SST. We leave from Vancouver. The US won't let it land here. Damn bureaucrats! I understand it's real fast!"

"Yeah, it sure is. You're in for a real treat. Say, that's a good idea, leaving from Vancouver. I took the old 747 work horse from Tokyo. Really slow compared to the Russian SST!"

Yuli interrupted, "Don, I remember you're supposed to return to Novosibirsk the end of June for a progress review meeting, to see how we're coming on the rescue launch plans. Why don't you come the way we're going. You'll be in Novosibirsk before you know it!"

Richards checked his calendar, "Wow, that's not very long from now. I think I'll do that. Thanks for the tip."

Yuli replied, "I'll do better than that, Don. I'll have Lina send you round trip tickets, Vancouver to Novosibirsk and return, courtesy of the Russian government."

"Comrade Yuli, you talked me into it, you smooth talking devil, you!"

They all laughed. Richards interrupted the joviality with a question for Yuli and Bucky, "Now, to get serious for a moment, when are you two going to have the docking adapter finished?"

Bucky responded enthusiastically, "Hey, Don, that's easy. We'll have the whole thing all built by the time you get to Novosibirsk, the end of June."

Yuli interjected, "Yes, for sure. Why, Bucky and I sketched the design out on his boat Sunday morning while we were waiting for the fish to bite. It's amazingly close to the old Soyuz-Apollo docking adapter."

Bucky asked, "You mean Apollo-Soyuz, don't you?"

Yuli answered, "No, when a Russian is talking, it's called the Soyuz-Apollo. When one of you Americans is talking, it becomes the Apollo-Soyuz!"

Bucky responded, "You're right, Comrade." Then he added, "You know, Don, with these fancy computer aided design tools, sort of a take-off on the old Macintosh computer, we'll have the engineering drawings finished by Thursday. Plenty of time before we leave for Russia."

Yuli interrupted, "We're going to finish by Thursday so Bucky and I can go back to Catalina Island on Friday and Saturday. We've got two gorgeous blondes waiting for us. That's enough incentive to work fast!"

Just then June carried in an enormous tray of petit fours, beautifully iced with multi colors, but mostly chocolate.

Richards looked at the elaborate goodies and exclaimed, "What happened to the cookies? These are gorgeous."

June smiled happily, "Dr. Richards, you told me about the wonderful chocolate confections they served you in Russia. I went to my favorite bakery in Newport Beach and ordered these last Friday. I wanted Comrade Litvinov to know we have good chocolate delicacies in America, too."

Yuli chose a treat from the tray, tasted it, grinned, "I'll have to admit your capitalist chocolate delicacies are as good as our communist chocolate confections."

They all laughed at Yuli's joke.

A moment later June brought in a second tray with a carafe of coffee and fancy china cups and put them on the coffee table in the sitting area of Richards' office. The trio moved to the couch and its adjacent soft chairs to enjoy their chocolate and coffee feast.

Richards realized the business part of the meeting was over. He was certain these two old friends from the Apollo-Soyuz project would do a good job. He would not have to worry about the docking adapter any more. He could turn his management attention over the next two months to the larger issues of the rescue mission. Still in a relaxed mood, he asked the two men, "Tell me, you two, how does it feel to be back to work after having been retired for a while?"

Bucky replied first, "Don, I don't consider this back at work. Since I retired, I'm in a completely different frame of mind. I just do what I want to do. I never get uptight about anything any more, like I used to. When June called me last week and said you wanted me to come and help on this adapter thing, I asked myself, *Bucky, what do you want to do? You don't have to do this, you know.* I thought about it for a while and concluded, *I would really like to do this thing. It'll give me a chance to work with an old friend,*

*Yuli. And maybe, just maybe, we can help improve the relations
between our two countries!* So anyway, I decided, *Hell, yes, I'll do
it.* I told June I'd come in the next day and start."

Yuli answered, "I'm like Bucky. I do just what I want to do
now, too. None of that old bureaucratic business of meeting the
plan. I never paid any attention to the so-called plan, anyway.
Most creative people are driven by an inner urge to get things
done. The plan's for the bureaucrats to talk about. I don't
consider this work either. It's just doing something I wanted to do.
I also thought it would be fun to work with my old friend, Bucky,
here, one more time. We had a ball on the Soyuz-Apollo project,
didn't we, Bucky?"

Bucky laughed in agreement, "You bet your bottom dollar, we
did, Yuli. Remember when we took the Russian Apollo-Soyuz
team on a tour of our plants here in the LA-Orange County area?"

Yuli got a serious look on his face, "Yes, I remember that tour
group very well! I particularly remember the tour we took of the
Minuteman guidance system building over in Anaheim. We
walked through this big building with the aerospace company
marketing man showing us the inertial guidance system being built
by all those workers in white coats. They looked like doctors or
something. Then we went through the Minuteman guidance
computer assembly area, same marketing man. It was like he was
trying to sell us, the Soviets, these Minuteman components. Then I
had a horrible thought!"

Richards interrupted, "What thought was that, Yuli?"

Yuli paused a moment and then said very slowly and sadly, "I
suddenly realized that these fancy looking guidance computers
would be loaded with target coordinates. Coordinates of places in
Russia. Probably where I worked. Maybe where I lived. Then I
shuddered and thought to myself, *What utter madness! Here I am,
visiting a plant in American which is building guidance systems to
deliver thermonuclear weapons to rain destruction on my
homeland.* Then I realized, there was some plant in the Soviet
Union, building guidance systems for our ICBM's. And one of
them was loaded with the target coordinates for the plant I was in,
the plant where Bucky worked, and maybe the place where he
lived."

A pall fell over the gaiety that the three men had been enjoying a few minutes earlier. Bucky looked up from his coffee and into Yuli's eyes, "That's strange, Yuli. You never mentioned those thoughts at the time. Why not?"

"Bucky, I was too horrified about the implications to say anything about them before now. But, I've had recurring nightmares about it ever since. Sometimes my nightmare has an American President who decides he should make a 'first strike' to eliminate the 'communist menace'. Other times my nightmare has a Soviet Premier who decides he should make a 'first strike' to eliminate the 'capitalist menace'."

Richards, surprised and moved by this sudden emotional outpouring by Yuli, tried to lighten the situation, "And who wins? Your side or our side?"

Richards' ploy didn't work. Yuli was still sad and grim. He replied slowly, "Nobody wins! In my dreams, everyone dies. What can we do to bring reasonableness to our political leaders? I've lived in Russia all my life. I don't think there is a 'communist menace'. In fact, I think there are some great things about communism. But, I've been to America, too. I also don't think America is a 'capitalist menace'. You just have a different form of government. I'm not so sure either government is really good. Just necessary!"

Bucky replied grimly, "Yuli, I'm not sure we'll see it in our life time, but eventually I believe our political leaders will see the light and really do something about disarmament. We can't go on this way. I remember your leader, Gorbachev, had some radical suggestions back in the late 80's – about demilitarizing Europe – disbanding NATO and the Warsaw Pact – about eliminating all nuclear weapons. Our leaders just weren't ready for ideas like that."

Richards was now engaged in this grim discussion, "Really, Yuri, Bucky is right. Gorbachev made those propositions, but frankly no one in our government took them seriously. Our President and his advisors thought it was just a negotiating ploy in the stalled Geneva Disarmament talks. Our people in the Pentagon were convinced it was a trick to get the US and its NATO allies to unilaterally disarm. Meanwhile, they suspected the Soviets would just cheat – hide their nuclear arms – say they were disbanding the

Warsaw Pact, but still keep Soviet troops in those eastern European countries."

Yuli stood up and said, "Comrades, Don and Bucky. I have a toast to make."

He held his coffee cup up in the air, the other two men stood and did the same, "Here's to the hope that our political leaders come to their senses before one or the other pushes the button and destroys life on Earth!"

Richards replied, "Here! Here!" And the three drank to this intelligent and reasonable dream.

Bucky added, "Yeah, I sure as hell hope so. That nuclear fall-out would really kill the fishing over at Catalina, to say nothing of all the pretty blondes."

Finally, they all laughed at Bucky's grim humor. The meeting was over.

Chapter 37

Return to Russia

It was Wednesday, 25 June 1992. Richards strode into the video conference room at Universal Aircraft for his final project review meeting before returning to Novosibirsk. He was scheduled to leave the next Friday. The rest of the UAC Space Station crisis team were already assembled. Richards' chief engineer, Tom Rubin, was checking communications links with the far flung participants of the pending teleconference to make sure everyone could see and hear. As Richards came in, Tom reported, "Don, everyone is on the screens and the com and video connections are A-OK!"

Richards looked at the four big TV screens, one with Lina Gorlovka in Novosibirsk, then Gus Ford in Houston, Bill Adams in Washington, and General Robbins up on the Space Station. Richards opened the meeting, "We are going to review the status of the Russian rescue launch scheduled for August. First, let's have a status report from Novosibirsk on the launch preparations. Dr. Gorlovka, how does it look?"

Lina Gorlovka smiled broadly on the video screen and addressed the global audience, "Dr. Richards and my colleagues in America and on the Space Station, I'm happy to report everything is progressing nicely for the planned August launch. We expect to meet our launch commitment or even move it earlier by a few days. We will have the exact date set when Dr. Richards visits us next week. As always, the final launch date decision will be set by my comrades in Baikonur."

Richards interrupted her, "Lina, what is the status of the docking adapter?"

She replied, I have Yuli Litvinov and Bucky Woods here in the meeting room with me. I'll let them respond to your question, Don."

Litvinov's image appeared on the video screen, "Don, I'm happy to say that Comrade Woods and I have made great progress since we returned to Novosibirsk the beginning of May."

Litvinov turned to Woods, who was standing next to him on the screen, "Bucky, report to your boss how we are doing!"

Woods looked into the video camera and beamed happily, "Don, Yuli and I have the docking adapter almost finished. We'll show it to you next week. It will be ready for integration testing with the Russian shuttle down at Baikonur by the end of next week. No problem!"

Richards replied smiling, "Bucky and Yuli, that's just great. You both have done a great job getting the adapter designed and fabricated! – Lina, if that's all of your report, let's hear from General Robbins up on the Space Station."

Gorlovka responded, "Don, that's just about everything. I will have a two hour briefing ready for you when you are here in Novosibirsk next week, giving all the details. But there are no major problems. See you Saturday."

General Robbins spoke up in his officious manner, "Dr. Richards, I'll let my deputy, Dr. Rosen, give the status up here on the Station."

Barbara Rosen's beautiful, smiling face filled the screen from the Space Station, "Lina, good to hear there are no major problems. Tell Georgi we're all ready to receive him and his crew here in August."

Barbara turned slightly to face the TV screen displaying Don Richards, and continued, "Don, everything is going smoothly up here. The expendables are holding up as planned. They should last through August OK. We'll sure be glad to see that Russian shuttle docking here, with their refill of expendables. We will be getting a little anxious by the first of August when we will have only thirty days breathing left!"

Richards asked, "Barbara, do you see any problems docking the Russian shuttle?"

"No, Don. Should be a piece of cake. We've got Atlantis on the docking module and Columbia tethered. But before the Russian shuttle arrives, we'll tether Atlantis to make room. No problems. All the space experiments are going fine, too."

Bill Adams from NASA Headquarters, spoke up on his video screen, "Don, I've got Dr. Davidson here from the White House. He has a message from the President!"

John Davidson's image appeared on the NASA Washington screen. He smiled broadly, "I'm so glad to hear everything is going smoothly in preparation for the Russian rescue launch. President Williamson will be most pleased when I report the good news of your progress to him. The President asked that I relay the following message to all of you:

I want all of you Americans who are working so hard on the Space Station rescue to know that the full resources of the United States of America are behind you. If you need anything, to make this rescue successful, just ask for it. I'll see personally that you get it.

As to our Russian friends preparing to launch their shuttle to rescue our astronauts, let me just say, -- Thank you for your humanitarian help, and Godspeed!

John Davidson continued, "And, Don, please call me when you return from your visit to Russia. The President will want to know how you see things when you return."

Richards responded, "Thanks, Dr. Davidson, for the message from the President. We all appreciate his interest and concern. Certainly, I'll call you when I return from Novosibirsk. Now, Gus Ford, do you or your team down in Houston have anything to add?"

Gus Ford's image on the NASA Houston video screen replied, "No, Don. It looks to us like you're doing all the right things. Good luck on your trip to Russia."

Richards, speaking in his authoritative voice, announced, "Ladies and Gentlemen and Comrades, that completes our progress review meeting. We'll have our next video link meeting from Novosibirsk on Thursday of next week. Dr. Gorlovka and her team will present you all the details in a video briefing at that time. General Robbins, Dr. Rosen, and the rest of you up on the Station, we're going to get you down. Just try to be patient, and don't worry!"

At the end of the work day on Friday, Richards was packing his briefcase with all the papers he would need for his trip to

Novosibirsk. His secretary came into his office, "Dr. Richards, here are your airline tickets and trip cash. The tickets we received from Dr. Gorlovka for the flight from Vancouver in the Russian SST are in the envelope. It should be a fast flight! Your United flight to Vancouver leaves Los Angeles at 9 pm this evening."

Richards carefully put the tickets and money in his briefcase and replied laughingly, "Yes, June, it will be fast, but since we cross the international dateline, we lose a day flying west from here. At any rate, I'll arrive in Novosibirsk at 3 pm Saturday.

Richards boarded the sleek Russian mach 5 SST at the Vancouver Airport after a two hour flight from Los Angeles. As he settled into his window seat, the beautiful Russian stewardess offered him a glass of cold Russian champagne. Just as he finished his refreshment, the futuristic SST pushed back from the jet way and taxied to the active runway where they were given a priority take off clearance. Richards felt himself pushed back into his seat as the captain accelerated the throttles to the afterburner position. The big jet literally leapt off the runway and started its amazingly steep climb. As they passed through mach 2, Richards felt the sudden acceleration from the ramjet engine being turned on. The jet rocketed into the fringes of space at its cruise altitude of 150,000 feet and a speed of mach 5.

One hour and 54 minutes later they were descending into the airport at Novosibirsk. The big SST landed and taxied up to the terminal. Richards was among the first passengers off the aircraft. He was met by a smiling Lina Gorlovka who whisked him through the passport formalities to the waiting black Chaika limousine. Thirty minutes later they were in Lina's apartment building.

Lina said to Richards as they walked into her apartment, "Don, please be seated on the sofa. I have some refreshments prepared for you."

Richards took Lina into his arms, looked into her eyes, "Lina, I really missed you. When I see you on the video screen in our meetings, I have the urge to reach over, grab you like this, and kiss you!" He kissed her passionately.

She returned the kiss warmly, "I have exactly the same feelings about you, Don. On second thought, let's have the refreshments later. You must be tired after your flight and the time change. How about a nap before the refreshments?"

Richards replied eagerly, "That sounds like a great idea! I've been yearning for the feel of your warm body ever since I left here last April."

The two retired to Lina's bedroom, quickly shed their clothes, and climbed into bed.

Two hours later they woke up from their late afternoon nap. After they were once again dressed, Lina said, "Now, we can have the refreshments. It's a little after 1800 now. We're going to have dinner with Yuli Litvinov and Bucky Woods in the dining room of Bucky's hotel. We're supposed to be there at 2000, so we have plenty of time to relax."

"That sounds great. Can I help you fix the refreshments?"

"No, Don, they're ready now. You just go and relax on the sofa in the living room and I'll bring your goodies right away."

While the pair rested in the living room enjoying the Russian hors d'oeuvres and ice cold vodka, Richards said happily, "You make me feel like I've returned home, Lina. It seems like I belong here, with you."

"Oh, Don, it does feel nice to have you here again. America is so far away. Even when we meet on video, it's not like having you here."

Richards reached for Lina's hand, squeezed it gently, "Lina, I haven't felt this way for a very long time. I really missed you while I was in California. Every time a problem came up in the shuttle rescue planning, I found I wanted to ask you about it. Maybe you should move to the US. Then I could be with you all the time."

Lina got a worried look on her face, "Don, I could never move to America. I couldn't give up my job in Novosibirsk. In America, I could never get a position with the prestige and privileges of deputy director of the space shuttle program."

Richards looked a little surprised as he thought to himself, 'I thought all Russians were eager to leave Russia to seek the freedom of the West. I never stopped to think they value the top level recognition they get along with their positions in the communist government here.'

He responded sadly, "You are right, Lina. You would never be deputy director of the US space shuttle program, no matter how talented a woman you are. We talk a lot about equal rights in the

US, but if you were a woman or a black, you would never achieve the pinnacle of power, as you have done here."

Lina remarked, "Don't be so serious, Don. Maybe you should move to Russia. We would give you a top position in the Space Institute, even if you were a former 'capitalist pig'!"

They both laughed at Lina's light hearted comment. Richard smiled, "Maybe you're right. Just think, I might get a promotion. I'll never become president of Universal Aircraft. I'm in a dead-end job."

Richards got a serious look on his face as he thought to himself about his live-in girl friend, Dawn, *In comparison with Lina, Dawn is immature and intellectually shallow. Her main interest in life is eating out in fancy restaurants. I wish there was someone like Lina in California.*

He decided to change the subject, "Tell me Lina, how is Bucky Woods adjusting to life in communist Novosibirsk?"

Lina replied lightly, "He seems to be enjoying the benefits the Space Institute provides for our workers. We have a recreation facility on the Ob River reservoir south of here, south of Berdsk. We have a hunting and fishing lodge, a hotel, and a power boat for fishing on the lake. Bucky and Yuli go fishing every weekend. Bucky says it's almost as good as Catalina. He has at least three young, beautiful girl computer programmers at the Institute crazy over him. They think he is 'so mature'."

"That sounds like a capitalistic paradise."

"No, it's better. It's all free for our Space Institute comrades and their American guest."

Lina and Richards left the lobby of her high rise apartment building at 7:30 and were chauffeured to the Red Star Hotel in downtown Novosibirsk, a half hour drive from Lina's apartment.

Woods and Litvinov were waiting for Richards and Lina in the Red Star lobby. Woods' and Litvinov's faces showed the signs of a day fishing in the bright June sun on the Ob reservoir. The quartet greeted each other with hugs and kisses on both cheeks in the Russian/European custom.

Woods exclaimed, "Welcome to Novosibirsk, Don. The fishing's great here. Yuli and I just gave the hotel chef our 'catch of the day' so we'll have fresh fish for dinner!"

Richards said eagerly, "I can hardly wait, Bucky. I understand you're not only catching fish, but young chicks as well!"

"Oh, yes, Don. I have to fight them off. They just love to be taught to fish, and other things, too! The young girls here are attracted to Americans. The rock music tapes I brought along help with that."

"And how's the docking module coming?"

Litvinov interrupted, "Now, now, Dr. Richards, no business talk tonight. Plenty of time for that next week. We have a surprise for you."

"Yuli, please call me Don. What's the surprise?"

"You and Bucky are invited to Baikonur next week to view the Russian space shuttle."

Lina interjected, "Yuli, now it's no surprise. Don, you and Bucky will be the first Westerners invited to see our space shuttle. I think you will be amazed at the level of our technology, compared with the US shuttle. Our design is almost twenty years newer!"

Richards replied, "That's exciting! I'm really looking forward to the visit."

Yuli added, "Lina, he would have found out anyway. Let's go to our table. It should be ready now, considering the bribe of fish to the chef."

The quartet walked through the lobby to the large dining room. They were met at the entrance by the headwaiter. Litvinov and the headwaiter got involved in a heated discussion with much gesturing by both men. Richards couldn't understand the Russian conversation, but he heard the headwaiter say "Nyet! Nyet!" repeatedly. After several minutes of this impasse, the headwaiter turned to the group, smiled, and said something in Russian that sounded like, "Chatyal stolyik u akna," and he lead the four to a nice table by the window overlooking a luxuriant flower garden. He graciously seated Lina by holding her chair, gave them all menus and left.

Richards asked, with curiosity in his voice, "Yuli, what was that confrontation all about?"

Yuli laughed, "That was no confrontation, Don. The headwaiter was just showing his power. That is typical in Russian restaurants. No matter how carefully we make the reservation, the headwaiter can never find it when we arrive. He said he was sorry we could not have dinner here tonight. No tables!"

Richards said incredulously, "But the dining room is almost empty. Look! We got the best table in the room, by the window overlooking the flower garden!"

Yuli agreed, "Yes, but that is the game we Russians must play with headwaiters. It takes patience and persistence. The headwaiter must demonstrate his power to say 'nyet'. We must demonstrate our tenacity and refuse to take nyet as an answer. After a while persistence wins and we get our table. The waiter now knows he will get a big tip."

Richards was even more confused, "But, I thought tipping wasn't allowed in Russia. Aren't the waiters state employees like everyone else?"

Lina broke into a laugh, "Don, officially, tipping is not allowed. But everyone does it anyway. It's just part of the game we play. We all enjoy it."

The quartet was served a fantastic dinner featuring grilled flounder (kambalu) caught that afternoon by Yuli and Bucky.

As they were finishing their after dinner coffee, Lina remarked, "Tomorrow I am going to show Don around Novosibirsk. Would you two like to join us?"

Bucky responded, "That's mighty nice of you, Lina, but Yuli and I are going to spend Sunday fishing again."

Yuli added, "We left a few fish in the Ob. We've got to catch them tomorrow. But you two enjoy the sight seeing. We'll see you both at the Institute Monday morning, after the weekend."

Richards shook his head with disbelief as he and Lina rose to leave, "You two are really addicted to fishing! Sorry, but Lina and I have to leave now. I'm still suffering from jet lag. See you Monday."

The quartet exchanged kisses in the Russian manner as Lina and Richards left the hotel restaurant for the Chaika limousine waiting for them outside the lobby. When the limousine arrived back at Lina's building, she told the chauffeur to pick them up at noon the next day for their sight seeing tour.

Richards and Lina had an erotic reprieve of love making before falling into a peaceful sleep.

Chapter 38

Novosibirsk

When Richards woke up Sunday morning just after 9:30, he heard Lina preparing breakfast in the kitchen. He dressed quickly and hurried into the kitchen, took Lina in his arms and kissed her good morning. Lina smiled happily, "I had an English language version of *Pravda* delivered for you. It's on the coffee table in the living room. Your breakfast will be ready soon."

Richards gave a broad smile, "The breakfast smells wonderful. It must be sausage."

"Yes, sausage and poached eggs with Russian bread, butter, and jam. We also have fresh oranges flown in from Tashkent and fresh strawberries grown locally."

"I can hardly wait. I'll go in and read the communist propaganda in *Pravda* now."

An angry frown clouded Lina's face and she replied sharply, "*Pravda* doesn't print propaganda – just the truth!"

Caught off guard by Lina's angry response, Richards replied somewhat defensively, "But really, Lina, *Pravda* is printed by your government. You don't have a free press like we do in the US."

No longer able to contain herself, Lina bubbled over with her feelings about the American free press, "Don, I have traveled extensively in the US and Western Europe and have read your so-called 'American free press'. My observation is that your press presents a very distorted and prejudicial view of my country. No matter what we do in Russia, the American press attributes the darkest of motives to our actions. I was in Paris in 1986 when our Chernobyl nuclear disaster took place. The *International Herald Tribune* was extremely critical of our government for withholding information about the disaster. In fact, we were trying to cope with the disaster and save lives. The US press speculated that thousands of people died instead of the small number reported by my government. Your press was wrong. My government's numbers were honest. During the same week, a US nuclear submarine went aground near Gibraltar. Your government was very secretive about this incident and certainly didn't reveal all the facts."

Realizing he had touched on a raw nerve, Richards tried to retreat, "Well, Lina, the Western press does exaggerate disasters sometimes, but at least the reports are free to report the information as they see it."

Lina began to calm down after her outburst, "Yes, Don. They do report the information they receive. But I notice in reading the US press that your reporters often report this or that 'fact' attributed to an anonymous 'government source'. If the source doesn't have the fortitude to identify himself, how can the reader decide if the information is reliable?"

"You have a good point, Lina, but remember, government officials have to be careful about releasing sensitive information to reporters."

"Our government officials have to be careful, too. But they do release the truth. Tell me, Don, if an American reporter is hypercritical of the US administration, will these anonymous government sources feed him the information he needs for his stories?"

"Well, of course, no government enjoys being criticized by the press. If a reporter is unfairly critical, the government spokesman may not give him sensitive information."

Lina declared, with an air of winning a point, "Then the US press is no more free than *Pravda!* One way or the other, the US government gets its viewpoint printed, by using anonymous spokesmen and by withholding information from critical or uncooperative reporters."

Richards picked up on a flaw in Lina's reasoning, "Then how do you explain 'Watergate'? In that case, two reporters from the *Washington Post* forced a US President to resign and had a number of his closest advisors sent to prison."

Lina smiled, "Don, I'm not competent to explain 'Watergate'. I do believe, though, if there had not been a large number of congressmen who wanted to get rid of your President Nixon, the *Washington Post* reporters' stories would have resulted in nothing. I find it hard to believe that Nixon was the first US President to spy on the opposition – just the first to get caught!"

Richards laughed, "I'm going to have to learn not to debate with you in the future. You're too clever! Let's talk about something else – like the parks of Novosibirsk."

"Good idea; That's exactly where I'm going to take you after breakfast and after we've read the Sunday *Pravda* – to the central park in Novosibirsk. It's beautiful this time of year. The view of the Ob River and of the tall green trees is invigorating. Now, go to the table. Breakfast is ready!"

They settled themselves at the dining room table which looked out a southern facing window with a gorgeous view of the Ob reservoir stretching off into the distance. They enjoyed their delicious breakfast and discussed the beauty of the scene out the window. To the west of Novosibirsk lay the flat tundra of Siberia. To the south and east was the rising terrain from which the Ob derived its source waters.

After breakfast, they both read *Pravda* in the bright, sunny east facing living room. Richards read the English version and Lina the Russian version. Richards was surprised at the quality of the news reporting in *Pravda* after his earlier critical comments. He definitely detected the slant of the news to make Russia and the communist system of government appear favorable. But as he reflected on Lina's earlier comments, he began to appreciate that, at least in the eyes of a Russian citizen, the American press appeared to be slanted in favor of the US and its form of government.

Soon they were ready for their Sunday afternoon outing in the central park. Lina had prepared and packed a picnic lunch. They rode the elevator down to the lobby and were greeted by the door keeper, who provided security and other services to the apartment building residents. The big, black Chaika was waiting for them at the front entrance.

Lina and Richards spent the next several hours enjoying the beauties and pleasures of the Novosibirsk central park, along with a few thousand other residents of the city. Richards was impressed with the awesome size of the memorials erected to World War II. These war monuments were a constant reminder to the Soviet citizenry of the awful, catastrophic loss of lives which resulted from the invasion by the Nazi hordes in that now distant war. Richards began to understand the Russian emphasis on military power could be a response to their loss of over twenty million lives in that old war. Perhaps the Russians were more interested in preventing a recurrence of that catastrophe rather than in world conquest as was the assumption of US leaders. Richards himself was not sure.

As previously arranged, Richards and Lina were met by the Chaika limousine at the park entrance at 5 pm. They were driven to the Space Institute recreational facility south of the city on the Ob reservoir, a pleasant 25 minute cruise through the moderate Sunday afternoon traffic. The sun was still high in the sky. Novosibirsk, at a latitude of 55°, enjoyed a late evening sunset at 10:30 this time of year. It compensated for the dark winter days. The temperature was delightful, in the low 20° centigrade (low seventies Fahrenheit). The limousine let the pair out at the entrance to the main building of the recreational facility. As they entered the lobby, where Lina showed her identification badge, Richards was surprised to see Litvinov and Woods waiting for them.

After another warm greeting among the quartet in the Russian custom, Litvinov said lightly, "My chief 'spy' in the Space Institute – Lina – said you would be here about 5:30. There's still lots of sun left today. How about a motorboat ride on the reservoir. Bucky and I have already given our catch of the day to the chef for dinner tonight. We have dinner reservations for 9:30. That will give us time for a nice cruise, water skiing, and a swim."

Lina and Richards beamed, and he exclaimed, "Great. Let's go! But Lina, did you bring a bathing suit?"

Lina laughed, "I have on my bikini underwear. I noticed you're wearing the same. That's close enough to a bathing suit. I always go topless during the summer to get brown almost all over. It compensates for our long, dark winter here on the fringes of Siberia."

The four headed for the boat dock where there was an eight place water ski boat, complete with driver and water skis, waiting for them. They loaded in, left the dock and headed off shore. After going about a kilometer, the driver stopped and Litvinov said, "Don, you and Lina get to go first. Single ski or double?"

Richards replied, "I'm not very good. I'll start out double. And you, Lina?"

Lina was stripping down to her bright red bikini underwear, "Single ski, of course. It's the only way to fly!"

The pair dove off the side of the boat into the 20° centigrade water and put on their skis. The driver pulled them smoothly up out of the water from a deep water start until they were both skiing upright behind the boat at a speed of about 30 knots. Lina showed off her single ski expertise by crossing in and out of the boat's wake. Richards cautiously skied directly behind the boat, not venturing into the turbulent side wake area. The sky was blue, the water was warm, and the view of the blue hills to the east was beautiful. They were enjoying their day of recreation, courtesy of the communist government.

After a half hour of skiing, Richards and Lina climbed back into the boat and Yuli and Bucky took their turn on the skis. Later the boat driver cruised down the shore to a quiet cove surrounded by rocky cliffs with pine trees growing on the top. The water was emerald green and very clear. The quartet enjoyed an hour of swimming and diving. They all four used the scuba gear on the boat to descend into the crystal-like water where they could view the fish swimming slowly in the open waters and darting in and out of the holes in the rocky coves.

They returned to the dock after 9, but the sun was still shining brightly above the western horizon in the cloudless sky. The sun and water activities had been refreshing. They dressed and returned to the recreation building for their late evening dinner of Yuli and Bucky's freshly caught fish.

Lina and Richards walked into her apartment building just before 11. When Richards looked out the west facing kitchen window, he could still see the red glow of the recently set sun. The days were long but the nights were short in Siberia during June. The pair reveled in the pleasure of their bodies as they made love that night.

Richards and Lina arrived at the Novosibirsk Space Institute just after 8 Monday morning and hurried to the large conference room with the video screens. The room was full of the Space Institute personnel who would participate in the review of the rescue mission status. Richards and Lina were greeted at the doorway of the conference room by Yuli Litvinov and Bucky

Woods whose faces were glowing from their weekend of fishing in the bright Siberian sun.

Yuli said proudly, "Don, Bucky and I are going to give you a briefing on the docking adapter this morning. Then Colonel Gusev will show you how it interfaces with our shuttle on the video link to Baikonur where he is this week."

As they walked to the head of the long conference table, Lina added, "Professor Dr. Chekhov at the Space Institute in Moscow will also participate in our meeting this morning via video link."

Richards commented, "Video communication certainly brings the world close together now, doesn't it?"

Lina replied, "Yes, it does. And it saves a lot of airline travel, but sometimes it's good to get together face-to-face. The video teleconferences just don't substitute for personal meetings, no matter how realistic the video images are."

Richards, remembering his very personal encounters with Lina on this trip, enthusiastically underscored her statements, "You are absolutely right, Lina. Personal contact is very important."

Lina opened the meeting by introducing Richards to the live and video audience. Richards formally greeted Dr. Chekhov in Moscow and Colonel Gusev in Baikonur. Then Litvinov presented a briefing on the docking adapter mechanism he and Woods had designed and fabricated. Colonel Gusev showed the adapter connected to the Russian shuttle in Baikonur and described how the docking between the shuttle and the Space Station would take place.

After the formal teleconference meeting, Richards spent the rest of Monday and Tuesday with Lina's shuttle personnel collecting all the details of the preparations for the Russian rescue launch next August.

At the end of Tuesday, Richards and Woods met Lina and Yuli in her office. Lina's secretary served the group coffee and cookies. Richards asked, "Lina, what is the official launch date now?"

Lina replied, "Don, as I said before, the exact launch date will be set by our comrades in Baikonur. You and Bucky will fly there with Yuli tomorrow to see our shuttle first hand. Colonel Gusev will be your host there. Our final formal video conference with NASA and your Space Station will be held on Thursday morning.

At that time, Colonel will announce the firm launch date on which he will fly the rescue mission to your station."

"What time do we leave for Baikonur?"

"The Space Institute has an utility jet flight between Novosibirsk and Baikonur daily that leaves here at 9 am. The three of you have seats reserved on the Wednesday morning flight. You will return on the same jet on Thursday afternoon, getting here at 5. I'll pick you up at the airport."

Richards formally thanked Lina and Yuli for all the detailed information they had given him during the last two days, "I'm sure you are doing a thoroughly professional job. Your formal briefing Thursday to the Space Station crew will let them know they will soon be safe."

Lina grinned, "They shouldn't worry – the Russians are coming to their rescue!" Then she turned to Yuli and Bucky and invited them to dinner in her apartment that evening at 9.

Bucky grinned, "I'd love to come, but would you mind if I brought one of my new girl friends?"

Lina answered, "No, of course not. Bring her. What's her name?"

"Valerina. She's a beautiful blue eyed blonde."

Yuli smiled, "The three of us will be there at 9. See you then."

Lina and Richards took the Chaika back to her apartment where the two prepared a festive dinner for the Russian-American friends. The three guests arrived right on time. Lina served everyone a variety of Russian specialties before dinner, including butyirbrody (red caviar finger sandwiches), ikra is baklazanaf (baby artichokes stuffed with caviar), bljiny ssa ssmitanaj (tiny pancakes with sour cream), and ssjaljdj ss lukam (Herrings with onions) with plenty of ice cold vodka to wash down the hors d'oeuvres.

The Russians engaged in animated conversations in English, in deference to the visiting Americans. Valerina was beautiful and the life of the party. About 10:30 Lina served the main dinner starting with ssalat masskofsskij (Russian salad), bif sstroganaf kartofijil (Beef stroganoff with fried potato strips, like French fries), and finished with aladji ss jablakami (Apple strudel) for dessert. The after dinner conversations continued until well after midnight when the three visitors left Richards and Lina alone.

The pair took a warm shower and retired to Lina's bedroom and large bed. Richards and Lina engaged in a delightful session of passionate love before falling deeply asleep.

The next morning Lina and Richards met Woods and Litvinov at the Space Institute's flight operations office at the Novosibirsk airport. Richards kissed Lina goodbye and boarded the two engine jet, along with Woods and Litvinov for their flight to Baikonur. The austerely furnished utility jet was filled with space workers shuttling to the Russian space launch facilities. The plane taxied to the active runway and shortly was cleared for takeoff. Richards was sitting in a window seat next to Woods on the left side of the aircraft and Litvinov had an aisle seat next to Woods. Shortly after takeoff, the plane turned left onto the south westerly course to Baikonur. As they climbed out from the flat tundra north and east of Novosibirsk, they had a good view of the Ob reservoir where they had gone fishing, water skiing, and swimming last Sunday. It was a beautiful, clear, warm day, the second of July. Richards saw the rolling hills south of Novosibirsk leading to the tall mountain peaks on the border between this Russian republic and Mongolia. After reaching their cruise altitude of 39,000 feet, Richards looked down and picked out the wide Irytsch River that wound its way from the Osero (lake) Saissan to the Arctic Ocean far to the north. Their route of flight was over desert-like terrain with a few scattered villages and towns. They completed the 760 nautical mile trip in just under two hours, landing on the long, wide airstrip at the desolate desert space port. The facility reminded Richards of Edwards Air Force Base in the California Mohave Desert where the US space shuttle occasionally landed.

As they taxied up to the ramp, Richards picked out the tall, handsome figure of Cosmonaut Colonel Georgi Gusev waiting to meet them.

When the three stepped off the jet, Colonel Gusev greeted them warmly with hugs and kisses on both cheeks, saying, "Dr. Richards and Mr. Woods, welcome to Baikonur. Thanks to the permission arranged by Professor Dr. Chekhov, you are the first

Westerners allowed to view the Russian space shuttle. I will have the pleasure of showing it to you."

Richards replied, "Colonel Gusev, it is a real pleasure for Mr. Woods and me to be able to visit Baikonur and the Russian shuttle. We are truly looking forward to our visit with you and our other space colleagues here."

The group spent the rest of the day receiving briefings on the details of the Russian shuttle design and climbing through the shuttle itself. The business discussions were interrupted by an hour and a half luncheon in the executive dining room where Richards and Woods met the director of the Baikonur facility and several of the other cosmonauts.

The next morning, Thursday the third of July, the formal video conference meeting convened in the Baikonur Space Operations Center. The video screens were linked by satellite with the truly global audience attending this meeting – space travel experts in Novosibirsk, in Moscow, on the US Space Station, at NASA Houston and at NASA Headquarters in Washington, DC. Colonel Gusev opened the meeting by greeting the far flung participants to the meeting, "My dear Space Comrades, today we present our review of the detailed preparations to rescue the stranded American astronauts up on the Space Station. I am pleased to announce the five day count down for the rescue mission launch will begin on Sunday, the third of August. The launch is scheduled for Friday, the eighth of August. Also, I would like to invite Dr. Richards and Mr. Woods to be here in the launch control center for that time period. This will be the first time that Westerners have been invited to a Russian launch. This visit was approved personally by Premier Gorbachev and confirmed by the Politburo! Now, Dr. Lina Gorlovka will give a briefing on all the details of the launch plans. Dr. Gorlovka."

Lina smiled on the video monitor screen, "To my dear Space Comrades, we at the Russian Space Institute have taken all possible precautions in preparing the plans to assure success of this rescue. Furthermore, as insurance against any problems we might find, Colonel Gusev and his crew will carry enough expendables to extend life support through November 1992 for the US Space Station crew."

Barbara Rosen interrupted on the video screen, "Hooray for Colonel Gusev! We have a great big welcome party planned for you. And we really appreciate the new expendable supply. We are so glad to know that if something does go wrong – God forbid! – we can breath and eat for another several months."

Lina, a little irritated by this spontaneous interruption of her presentation, said, "And, to continue with my briefing, here are the details of the mission." She went on with her exceptionally clear and detailed explanation of all the arrangements made for the rescue mission, which took almost two hours. She summarized, "So you see, my Comrades at the Russian Space Institute, here in Novosibirsk, and in Moscow, and in Baikonur, have completed the planning. The unique hardware required – the docking module adapter – is completed and in integration testing at Baikonur, thanks to Comrades Woods and Litvinov."

Colonel Gusev added at the end, "Barbara, and the rest of you Americans up on the Space Station, my crew and I are looking forward to that party!"

Richards and Woods boarded the Russian SST at 6:30 Friday afternoon 4 July. At 10 am the same Friday morning, they arrived at Los Angeles International Airport, after a short stop over and change of planes in Vancouver. Dawn met them at the airport and drove them to the Long Beach Marina where Bucky Woods and one of his twenty-five year old girl friends took Richards and Dawn out on his power boat into the Long Beach Harbor. There in the midst of the confusion of hundreds of anchored and slowly motoring sail and power yachts they watched the spectacular and colorful fireworks in celebration of the American Independence Day.

Chapter 39

Government Debriefing on Soviet Trip

Richards spent the remainder of the long Fourth of July weekend with Dawn in their Irvine Hills condominium. They lounged around the pool on Saturday after a leisurely breakfast. They broke from their poolside activities for a lunch on their sunny patio about two in the afternoon and then took a two hour nap. After another three hours of sunning and swimming at their pool, they dressed and went out to one of the expensive restaurants in the Newport Beach area. They returned to their condo and made love. They repeated this pattern on Sunday. Richards found this relaxed life style helped him recover from the jet lag from his trip half way around the Earth in the last week.

A disturbing new factor had entered into Richards' relationship with Dawn. He kept finding himself comparing Dawn to Lina and Dawn always came out second best. This was new. In his previous amorous adventures away from home – with Cindy and Marie, with Brigitte, and with Juanita – he had kept these affairs in a different compartment of his consciousness. His away-from-home love making had never affected his relationship with Dawn. He had never compared the others with Dawn. He treated them as sexual objects, delightful and charming, but extra-domicile. His affair with Lina had been quite different. He thought of Lina as a complete person, not just a sexual toy as with the others. He was particularly impressed with Lina's professional abilities as well as her qualities as a woman in charge of her own life, living it the way she wanted to, making love because she wanted to, not just because an important man asked her to. Dawn did not seem to be aware of Richards' new feeling and developing inner conflict. She continued to enjoy their leisure together and the dining out in expensive restaurants in youthful innocence.

Monday morning after the three day weekend, the pair drove to work as usual in Richards' sports car. Dawn went to her job in the computer center. Richards went to his executive office to pick up the loose ends left over from his week long trip to Novosibirsk. He remembered as he walked into his office that Dr. Davidson, the President's science advisor, had asked Richards to call and report his feelings about his trip so Davidson could tell the President. Richards' secretary was not yet in the office so he walked over to his desk and dialed Dr. Davidson's number at the White House Annex himself.

Davidson's secretary answered with a cheery, "This is Dr. Davidson's office, Lois speaking."

Richards identified himself, "Lois, this is Dr. Richards at UAC. I just returned from Russia. Your boss wanted a personal report on the trip when I returned. Is he available?"

"Oh, how exciting, Dr. Richards. I hope none of those communist women over there, --er, tried to compromise you. Our latest security briefing explained how their women KGB agents try to compromise important visitors like you with, --er, --well, --you know, sexual favors."

Richards laughed, "Lois, I'm afraid I'm not so lucky or important to the KGB to merit such favors."

Lois replied seriously, "Well, I certainly hope not, Dr. Richards. I see Dr. Davidson just hung up from his call. I'll put him right on."

A few seconds later, Davidson came on the line, "Hi, Don. Welcome back. How was Russia? I'm really interested in your personal impressions. I just finished talking to the President's secretary. President Williamson wants me to brief the Security Council this afternoon on the status of the preparations for the Russian rescue mission. So you can see your call was very timely."

"Well, John, you heard the formal video teleconference briefing that Dr. Lina Gorlovka presented last Thursday. I could see you on the video screen with Bill Adams over in NASA Headquarters. My personal impression is that the Russians are dedicated to making a real success of the rescue mission. For example, my visit to Baikonur and my physical inspection of the Russian shuttle were personally approved by Premier Gorbachev with endorsement by the Politburo."

"That sounds great, but I have two questions. First, do you see any problems in the rescue?"

Richards thought carefully of the complexity of the rescue mission before replying, "The rescue is a very complicated operation. As you know, it will require three round trips to bring back all our astronauts. Many things could go wrong, as exemplified by the problems with our own shuttle missions. But, so far as I could tell from my meetings and probings during this trip, the Russians are doing a very professional job to make sure everything is taken care of properly. Their plans and procedures are certainly up to our standards."

"That's comforting, Don. Now, for my second question: how does their shuttle technology compare with our US shuttle technology?"

"That's a good question, John, and a difficult one to answer thoroughly. From what I could tell during my day of climbing through their shuttle and the briefings, I believe their technology is up-to-date. You know, our shuttle is late 1960's technology since that was what was available when it was built. The only significant up-date in US shuttle technology happened in the mid 1980's when the payload control station was installed. But that update didn't affect the cockpit or flight system technology. The Russians, on the other hand, used late 1980's technology throughout their design. Their flight computer, cockpit displays, and software technology were particularly impressive. They are much farther along on microelectronic technology than our previous US administration had given them credit for."

Davidson interrupted, "Don, I've got to leave for a luncheon appointment. I would appreciate it if you could send me a four or five page telex summary of your impressions addressing those two questions, before my 4 pm Security Council meeting. Be sure and send it encrypted. We wouldn't want the KGB to find out what you know!"

Richards laughed to himself at that absurdity, "OK, John. I'll get the telex off to you. You should have it by 3 pm Washington time. Have a good luncheon!"

As soon as Richards hung up, his secretary, who had arrived for work while he was on the phone, buzzed him, "Dr. Richards, good morning and welcome back from Russia. There's a gentleman in here who wishes to see you. He says it's urgent. I tried to explain that you were very busy, just being back from overseas and all, but he flashed an official government ID badge and insisted – "

Richards replied in an understanding tone, "It's OK, June. Show him in. It's probably important to him. I've already taken care of my most urgent phone call. We've got to get an encrypted telex off to Dr. Davidson before lunch though. We've got plenty of time for that."

June escorted the visitor into Richards' large office. Richards directed him to the couch in the sitting area as June took his coffee order. The visitor showed his government ID badge and said, "Dr. Richards, I'm Tom Ahrons from the CIA. I understand you just returned from the Soviet Union. The CIA Director asked me to pay you a little visit so he will be prepared for the Security Council meeting with President Williamson this afternoon."

Richards knew that the CIA agent assigned to Universal Aircraft normally interviewed UAC executives who returned from overseas trips, particularly trips to communist countries. But since Richards' duties on the Space Station usually did not involve travel to those countries, except for space symposiums, he had never met Ahrons before. But he wasn't surprised by the visit. He had half way expected it."

He smiled, "Tom, your Director is the second person attending the President's Security Council meeting who wanted a report from me today."

Ahrens, looking very serious, said, "Yes, I know you talked to the President's Science Advisor, Dr. Davidson. I would like a clear copy of your encrypted telex to him, also."

Richards was surprised at this request, "How in the world did you know I was sending him an encrypted telex?"

"We have our ways, Dr. Richards. Our exact methods are classified, of course."

Richards responded, "Of course! Yes, you may have a copy. What do you want to know about my trip? I was gone for almost a week and covered a number of issues."

"We rely a great deal on satellite coverage for intelligence about the Russian space program. We have good photos of the space shuttle in Baikonur but we have very little human intelligence about their space program. Your trip to Baikonur is a rare opportunity to hear from a knowledgeable US scientist about their space technology."

Richards found this meeting a bit distasteful and probably unnecessary. Nevertheless, he gave Ahrons a clear and concise summary of what he had learned about Russian space technology during his trip and his visit to Baikonur. Ahrons took copious notes.

Richards finished, "So you see, Tom, the Russian shuttle is using technology almost twenty years newer than the US shuttle. My telex to Dr. Davidson will summarize the details of what I have told you in this meeting. You can pick up a copy of the telex just before lunch, our time."

"Good, Dr. Richards. Thank you for your cooperation. Now the CIA Director will be prepared for his meeting with the President. We want to make sure he is knowledgeable, right?"

"Of course, Tom, of course. I hope I've answered all your questions."

"All but one. Did the Russians compromise your integrity with sexual favors?"

Richards was really surprised by this question, "Why, of course not!"

"Dr. Richards, I don't want to challenge your honesty, but we have it from a reliable source that you spent several nights in the apartment of Dr. Lina Gorlovka, a communist party official and Deputy Director of the Russian space shuttle program!"

Richards became angry with this line of questioning and said sharply, "I wasn't aware that the CIA was interested in my social life, even in Russia. Yes, I stayed in Dr. Gorlovka's apartment and slept in her bed, but I don't consider it any of your business, the CIA's business, or the US government's business. Your question was *Was my integrity compromised by sexual favors?* The answer is a firm no! That is an honest answer."

Ahrons responded somewhat officiously with a hint of a threat in his voice, "What is the US government's business is not for you to decide, Dr. Richards. I'm glad that you were honest about your affair with Dr. Gorlovka. Otherwise, you could have been indicted for giving false information to a US government official!"

Richards rose and said, being very careful to keep his voice calm and polite, "Mr. Ahrons, that's all I have to tell you at this time. As I said before, you may pick up a copy of my telex to Dr. Davidson just before twelve. Now, I have been out of my office for a week. I must get back to my other duties!"

Ahrons left without shaking hands with Richards.

Richards was distressed and upset by this intrusion by the CIA into what he considered a very private aspect of his life. As he reflected upon the meeting, particularly the last part, he could understand the questions his personal relationship with Lina might raise in the minds of government officials. He vowed, however, that he wouldn't let Ahrons' veiled threat affect his personal relationship with Lina.

Chapter 40

Reception at Novosibirsk

Richards spent the rest of July managing the myriad details connected with the upcoming rescue launch. His life fell into a comfortable routine of going to work daily at UAC and taking off the weekends. His incessant travel was in a lull. He held a weekly video teleconference with NASA and the Russian Space Institute about the progress of the preparations.

On Wednesday, 30 July, just before the last video teleconference in the UAC conference room, Richards had just finished dictating a memo to June when she said, "I received your SST tickets yesterday from Dr. Gorlovka's office for your flight from Vancouver to Novosibirsk on Friday. There were tickets for you and Mr. Woods."

Richards smiled, "Bucky is really looking forward to going fishing with Yuli Litvinov."

June reminded him gently, "You had better leave for the video conference now."

"Thanks, June. I'll get going."

As Richards walked into the conference room, Tom Rubin had all the video links operating, ready to start the meeting. As usual, NASA Headquarters and NASA Houston were on screen, and the Space Station, and, of course, Dr. Gorlovka. Richards was surprised to note Professor Dr. Chekhov was in Novosibirsk with Lina.

Richards opened the meeting, "This is the final regular progress review meeting before the launch countdown starts next Sunday." Then he acknowledged Dr. Chekhov's presence on the video screen, "Professor Dr. Chekhov, it is good to see you in Novosibirsk. How are the launch preparations going?"

"Dr. Richards, I have just completed a thorough personal review of the preparations and I am completely satisfied that everything is going well. Premier Gorbachev has a deep personal interest in this rescue mission, of course. He asked me to attend the launch and to report back to him and to the Politburo of any problems. I am pleased to announce I just informed him that we have no problems. The launch should occur as planned on Friday the 8th of August."

Richards responded, "That's good news, Professor Dr. Chekhov. Our President Williamson is also personally interested in the launch. His science advisor, Dr. Davidson, is on the video screen from Washington, DC, and I am sure he will report your favorable assessment to the President."

Davidson interrupted, "Yes, Dr. Chekhov, the President will be pleased to know everything is progressing smoothly for the count down. I understand the actual count down begins Sunday. Is that correct?"

Chekhov replied, "Yes, Dr. Davidson, that is right. And Dr. Richards, I'm pleased to confirm you and Mr. Woods are invited to witness the actual launch in Baikonur. A first for a Westerner! Also, Dr. Davidson, a note for President Williamson: Premier Gorbachev has authorized the video link of the launch to NASA Houston and the Space Station, so they can witness the rescue launch directly. Another first!"

Davidson answered, "The President will be most pleased to hear about the open communications for this most crucial rescue launch."

Richards added, "And thank you for the invitation to witness the launch. Mr. Woods and I will leave here Friday evening and arrive in Novosibirsk at 3 pm Saturday afternoon on the Russian SST."

Chekhov replied, "Fine, Dr. Richards. Dr. Gorlovka and I will meet your flight personally to welcome you and Mr. Woods. Mr. Litvinov wishes him to be present for the final check out of the docking adapter."

Richards answered enthusiastically, "Mr. Woods and I look forward to seeing you and Dr. Gorlovka Saturday."

Richards turned to the other video screens, "Are there any further reports from NASA or the Space Station?"

Gus Ford from NASA Houston said, "Everything looks good here in Houston. We really welcome the video hook up for the launch. A real courtesy from our Russian colleagues!"

General Robbins from the Space Station added, "I am most pleased that everything is going smoothly for the rescue launch. My deputy, Dr. Barbara Rosen, has made all the arrangements to receive Colonel Gusev and his gallant crew on the eighth."

Barbara Rosen, who was standing next to one of her part time lovers, Billie Joe Johnson, whispered to him, out of range of the audio microphone, "For sure, Billie Joe. I'll be ready to show my quarters to Colonel Gusev just like I did you last night!"

Johnson whispered back, "That'll be a real good reward for his rescue mission, Barbara!"

Richards and Woods left Los Angeles International Airport Friday evening, the first of August, for their slow subsonic flight to Vancouver where they boarded the Russian SST in Vancouver a half hour before midnight West Coast time. The giant jet climbed out from Vancouver on a northwesterly heading in afterburner. At an altitude of 50,000 feet and a mach number of two, Richards felt the burst of acceleration as the ramjet engine took over. They sped to their cruise altitude of 150,000 feet at mach five. From there the rising sun in the eastern sky glowed rosily.

An hour later they entered Russian airspace from the Bering Sea at the northern top of the Kamchatka Peninsula. The curvature of the Earth was clearly visible at that altitude. The sun was shining brightly on the ground and sea below. The atmosphere was so tenuous at their cruise altitude that the sky was dark and filled with bright, shining stars.

Twenty minutes later, Richards looked down at the wide Lena River carrying vast amounts of water to dump into the Arctic Ocean. As Richards watched this huge waste of fresh water, he remembered he had read about a Russian plan to divert these northern flowing rivers, such as the Lena, so that they ran southward to irrigate the arid portions of Russia. If this massive plan was ever implemented there would be an immense increase in Russian agricultural productivity. However, Richards knew the enormous amounts of money now being spent on armaments would have to be redirected to peaceful uses before the rivers could be diverted.

Another twenty minutes went by and the sleek SST covered another 1100 nautical miles and passed over another mighty

Siberian flow, the sprawling Jenissej River, fed by three hundred miles of lakes stretching from the Mongolian border to the Russian city of Krasnoyarsk. Five minutes later the fast jet was entering the landing pattern at Novosibirsk under crystal clear skies, and swooped down smoothly onto the long east-west runway aimed into a moderately strong west wind. Richards and Woods hurried to be among the first leaving the SST and headed for the international arrivals terminal. Richards spotted Lina's pretty smiling face next to the roundish, balding one of Professor Dr. Chekhov.

Dr. Chekhov hugged and kissed Richards and Woods on both cheeks, followed by a similar greeting by Dr. Lina Gorlovka. Richards returned Lina's cheek kiss with a short kiss on the lips. Dr. Chekhov lead the quartet through the VIP line for passport and customs formalities. They were quickly waived through as their fellow passengers queued-up in a long, slow moving line. As they walked through the terminal, Dr. Chekhov explained to Richards and Woods that there was an official reception waiting for them in the VIP lounge. The mayor of Novosibirsk and members of the Central Committee would be there to greet the American visitors. Richards was surprised at this official attention. Then he remembered the Wednesday video teleconference when Chekhov told him that Premier Gorbachev and the Politburo had approved Richards' impending visit to Baikonur for the rescue launch. He thought to himself, *The local politicians want to bask in the limelight of a visitor whose trip was approved by the pinnacle of Russian leadership. Well, I'll just relax and enjoy it.*

They reached the VIP lounge at the airport. It was packed with the twenty-odd official welcoming committee members. There was a buffet table set up with a glittering array of hors d'oeuvres plus two waiters serving chilled Russian champagne and ice cold straight vodka for the festive welcoming party. Professor Dr. Chekhov lead Richards and Woods, followed by Lina, through the reception line and introduced the American visitors to the city fathers. A string quartet from the Novosibirsk Philharmonic Symphony Orchestra was playing J.C. Bach's string quartet, opus 11, number 2, in the background. After a pleasant thirty minutes socializing, the mayor gave an official welcoming speech. Richards stood next to Lina so she could translate for him. She explained the mayor welcomed the distinguished American space scientists to Novosibirsk and was happy that the Novosibirsk Space Institute was playing a key role in the rescue of the American astronauts stranded on the Space Station. The mayor motioned Richards and Woods to come forward and he presented each of them with an elaborate medal hanging on a ribbon that he placed around their necks. He hugged each man and kissed each on two cheeks and the two visitors returned the greeting. Shortly afterwards the reception broke up.

As the four reached the waiting Chaika limousine, Chekhov turned to Richards and Woods, "I will leave you with Dr. Gorlovka now. I have a 5:30 flight for Moscow to catch. However, I will be with you for the launch in Baikonur by video link. Have a fruitful visit."

Richards replied, "Thank you for your welcome, Dr. Chekhov. Mr. Woods and I were deeply moved by the warm greeting of the mayor and Central Committee members. Have a good flight back to Moscow. I'll see you on the video link Friday."

Richards, Woods and Lina waved goodbye to Chekhov and climbed into the waiting limousine. A twenty minute drive through light traffic took them to Woods' hotel. Richards and Lina went into the lobby to be sure Woods' reservation was OK and found Yuli Litvinov waiting there to take Woods to the Space Institute recreational center for fishing. After exchanging the usual warm greetings, Richards said, "Yuli, you and Bucky have a good week end fishing. Lina and I will see you at the Institute launch control center Monday morning."

Yuli laughed, "No. You and Lina are invited to a party at my apartment at ten tonight. Two of Bucky's playmates will be there, too. See you then."

Lina smiled, "What a nice surprise, Yuli. Of course, Don and I will be there at ten. Good luck with your fishing."

Lina and Richards headed back to their Chaika and Lina directed the driver to stop by the special store where the upper level personnel of the Space Institute had shopping privileges. Lina showed her ID badge and the two went into a large store that had a wide variety of consumer goods. Lina said to Richards, "I want to buy some things for our weekend meals."

In the supermarket section of the store they found a grand selection of foods, very much like a US supermarket, except that the prices were much lower.   The subsidized prices in this 'company store' were one of the fringe benefits for a top Russian executive like Lina. She loaded a shopping cart full and Richards noticed the bill came to less than 4 rubles. He knew that a similar shopping cart of groceries in the US would have cost at least $50. He was beginning to understand the benefits of communism for the top echelon of the Russian system.

On the short ride in the Chaika to Lina's apartment, Richards, asked curiously, "How much do you spend per month on groceries?"

"They are the most expensive items on my budget. I spend almost 40 rubles a month. However, if I did all my shopping in the open markets rather than in the Space Institute market, it would cost twice that amount."

Richards' curiosity continued to grow, "How much are your total monthly expenses?"

"Since I have a state supplied, chauffeured limousine, I have no automobile expenses so everything comes to about 200 rubles a month, not counting my occasional large purchases, like a TV, video recorder, or CDs and tapes."

"If you don't mind telling me, what is your monthly income?"

"I don't mind. I get 1500 rubles a month, with a year end bonus of about one month's salary."

"What in the world do you do with the difference between your salary and your expenses?"

"I put that money in my bank account, of course. I get 5% interest. My savings account is over 250,000 rubles now."

Richards asked, "Isn't it unusual in this country for a person to accumulate so much money in the bank?"

"Heavens no! My savings account is small compared with those of some top executives like Professor Dr. Chekhov. He probably has a million rubles. He also owns a large chalet in the country outside Moscow."

Richards was amazed Russian scientists and managers were so wealthy.   He mentally compared his own highly leveraged financial position. He suddenly realized that his salary of $10,000 dollars a month and fixed expenses of $9,800 a month left him with precious little to save. Most of his net worth was in his condominium equity, not really a liquid asset. The high living expenses in California made it very difficult for him to accumulate capital. As a result, he remained a slave to his financial treadmill. He realized that if his salary were cut off for just a few months, he would lose everything, including his condominium and sports car. He wouldn't be able to keep up the payments. In contrast, his Russian counterparts were not leveraged at all. His previous black and white comparisons between capitalism and communism were eroding.

At Lina's apartment the Chaika limousine driver helped carry Lina's shopping bags into the elevator. She told him to pick them up at 10 for Yuli's party. In the lobby the pair exchanged greetings of 'dobryj wjatschjir' with the door keeper lady who returned the greeting as they headed for the elevator. Once inside Lina's apartment, Richards helped her put the groceries away. Then Lina showed him to the bedroom where he put his personal belongings away.

Richards took her in his arms, "Lina, I have really missed you during the past month. It is so nice to be back with you!"

She returned the embrace, looked into his eyes and whispered sweetly, "I've missed you too, Don. I'm so glad you're back!"

They kissed, at first tenderly, and then passionately. Lina pushed him back, holding him firmly with both hands and smiled, "There's plenty of time for love making when we get back from Yuli's party. Please help me prepare dinner now. Then we can relax in the living room while dinner is cooking in the oven."

Richards grinned wryly, "Well, OK. I'll wait until later."

In the kitchen, Lina pointed to the refrigerator, "I hope you'll make a California green salad like the one you made last time we were here, while I get the chicken ready for the oven."

"I'll be glad to. I even mix my own dressing."

He started collecting fresh lettuce, sliced mushrooms, red tomatoes, and an avocado in one of Lina's larger bowls. He mixed the salad dressing in a separate small glass container, starting with extra virgin olive oil and balsamic vinegar. He added black pepper, cayenne, and mustard for flavoring, and a small container of yogurt to make the dressing creamy. He put in a little catsup to give his mix a delicate pink color. He held up the jar and announced proudly, "Here's my masterpiece – salad dressing a la master chef Don! Here! Try it!"

Lina tasted it, "You better submit this work of art to the annual chef's contest in Novosibirsk. You'll probably get the Lenin Prize."

Both laughed aloud. By now, Lina had put her chicken in the oven and delicious smells were wafting into the room. The pair retired into the living room for glasses of chilled dry sherry while they read todays *Pravda*. Richards' copy was in English, of course. On page three, which featured academic items, Richards found an article announcing the countdown for the Russian space shuttle launch to rescue the stranded American astronauts would begin tomorrow, Sunday evening. He pointed out the article to Lina.

She smiled and said, "I just read that item in my Russian paper. Be sure to read the last paragraph."

He quickly scanned down to the end and found, 'American scientist Dr. Donald Richards has been invited by Premier Gorbachev to witness the rescue launch at the Baikonur spaceport. Dr. Richards will be hosted in Baikonur by Professor Dr. Nikolai Ivanovich Chekhov, program director of the space shuttle and his deputy, Dr. Lina Gorlovka. The launch is scheduled for Friday 8 August 1992. The space ship will be commanded by Colonel Georgi Andrejevich Gusev, the holder of the Red Star Medal and the Lenin Space Exploration Award. The launch will be shown on the fourth channel on Russian television."

Richards looked up, "Wow! We both made it in *Pravda*. We're famous!"

Lina's face turned serious, "Don, in Russia, space engineers are held in high esteem. The fact that your presence at the Baikonur launch has the personal approval of Premier Gorbachev and the Politburo gives you a level of prestige in my country that you probably have never had before, even in America."

Richards nodded, "Lina, you're probably right. I've certainly never been featured in a US newspaper and mentioned along with the US President."

The pair finished reading their newspapers as the mid summer Siberian sun set in the west, spreading a brilliant red glow on high cirrus clouds announcing the distant approach of a cold front. Lina served dinner on her table, beautifully set with linen and silver. She lit the four tall, white candles in silver candle holders as she handed Richards a bottle of Russian champagne to open. Richards popped the cork and poured the sparkling beverage into their chilled glasses as they seated themselves at the festive table. Their dinner conversation ranged over a wide variety of topics, from the stalled US-Russian disarmament talks to the problems associated with agriculture in the tundra region near Novosibirsk. Richards was surprised at the depth of Lina's knowledge and the scope of her understanding of complex issues. Again he found himself comparing Dawn and Lina in his mind. Lina won.

Chapter 41

Rescue Mission Countdown

Yuli's party was in full swing when Lina and Richards arrived at 10:30. Yuli had made an agreement to use this empty apartment of one of the Novosibirsk Space Institute engineers who was on a few months temporary duty in Moscow. It had been a convenient arrangement for Yuli who had left his own apartment in Wilkowo on the Black Sea during his assignment in Novosibirsk. The living quarters had helped ease his transition from retirement back to this exciting task of readying the Russian shuttle for the rescue. When Yuli opened the door to greet Richards and Lina, sounds of laughter emanated from the living room. The chords of Borodin's Symphony number 2 in E minor were floating out of the CD player in the background. The lights were low. Yuli's cheeks were glowing from the sun while fishing and from the vodka he had consumed already. He greeted them with a hearty 'dobryj notschi' and hugged and kissed Lina on the lips and then kissed Richards on both cheeks.

Yuli escorted the pair into the living room and introduced them into the two Russian playmates, Valerina and Anna, both in their mid to late twenties. Both girls were beautiful, with naturally blonde hair and blue eyes, and both spoke excellent English. After Richards and Lina were comfortably seated on the sofa, Yuli brought them each a small glass of ice cold vodka, saying, "This will loosen up your inhibitions and make the conversation flow. Don, in Russia, small intimate parties like this are our main form of entertainment. Yes, we have television to stare at, but we prefer to talk to each other – to get to know one another – intimately!"

Richards replied, smiling, "Yuli, I like your party. I love the people here and the music is great. But please, let me switch to white wine after this vodka. Otherwise we may get intimate here on your living room floor."

Yuli thought that was funny, "OK, if you insist, Don. But you will be breaking one of our cherished Russian traditions – drink vodka until one of your drinking companions passes out."

Lina broke in, "Yes, Yuli. I agree with Don. We'll break that tradition. With too much vodka, we couldn't enjoy our mid-summer weather on our day off tomorrow."

The rest of the evening, until after 2 am, the participants at Yuli's party discussed a wide range of topics including the world of music and ballet, world politics, fishing, the best places in Russia to go for summer vacations, and the upcoming rescue launch. In the intimate and friendly atmosphere of Yuli's cozy apartment, everyone felt free to express his or her opinion on any of the subjects. By the end of the party, Richards felt he knew everyone much better. He was particularly impressed that everyone engaged in the discussions, rather than breaking up into smaller groups.

Lina and Richards returned to her apartment and each took a hot shower before they climbed into Lina's big, comfortable bed. Soon they both reached a sparkling state of joy. He held her close as they relaxed and fell asleep.

On Sunday, Lina and Richards spent most of their afternoon in the Museum of Art looking at the exhibits of modern Russian painters. Later, they had dinner at the Space Institute recreation center with Yuli and Bucky.

On Monday, the day of the blast off, they arrived at the Space Institute just after 9, and Lina showed her badge to the guard in the lobby. The guard handed Richards his visitor's badge, complete with his picture, prepared during his last visit. They went on down to the control center where the launch countdown had already begun, the countdown that would continue for five days as each system and subsystem was thoroughly checked out to assure that everything was working for next Friday's scheduled launch. The pace of the long countdown was slow and laborious at this stage. It proceeded routinely, needing no special management attention from Lina. However, the Deputy Director's presence, along with that of the important American visitor, gave a big boost to the countdown crew's morale. It showed them their management and the American were interested in their work.

The video screens in the control center portrayed several groups of technicians in Baikonur huddled around the various parts of the Russian rescue shuttle. One group was checking out the huge hydraulic actuators and pumps that moved the aerodynamic control surfaces on the hypersonic aircraft. Another group was checking out the artificial intelligence software loaded in the multiple fault-tolerant flight computers. A third group was checking out the interactive cockpit displays with all their colored video screens for telling the pilots what was going on and what to do. Other groups were busily crawling all over other sections of the shuttle.

Lina gave a little speech to these diligent workers over the video link set up between Novosibirsk and Baikonur, "My dear Comrades in Baikonur, this is Dr. Gorlovka, here in Novosibirsk. I have Dr. Richards, who is the Program Director of the US Space Station, here with me. Starting tomorrow, the video link between your countdown efforts and the astronauts on the US Space Station will be established. This video link has been approved by Premier Gorbachev and the Politburo as a gesture of friendship for our American colleagues stranded in space. Good luck on your most professional work for this internationally and humanely important rescue launch."

Richards watched the pride show up in the faces of the Russian technicians. They liked the genuine interest and appreciation of their efforts by the top Russian leadership.

The countdown continued routinely for the next several days. Richards and Lina spent long hours in the Novosibirsk control center observing the smoothly flowing procedures.

Afterwards they returned home together. Richards was beginning to feel at home in this Russian way of life, which was, is many ways, quite different from the way of life in California.

Thursday morning, Richards and Lina carried their small suitcases down from the apartment to the waiting limousine to catch their afternoon flight to the space port in Baikonur, for tomorrow morning's launch. First they went to the Space Institute for another day of monitoring the countdown from the control center. As they drove along in the privacy of the back compartment, Richards asked, "Tell me, Lina. Why have you never married? Is it because of your career at the Space Institute?"

Lina shook her head, "No, of course it's not my career. It's just that I had never met the right person."

"But, if you got married and became pregnant, wouldn't that interfere with your career?"

"Not really. Many of the professional women at the Institute are married and have children. Modern childbirth practices allow a woman to be gone from her job less than two months. We have an excellent nursery at the Institute that takes care of babies and preschool children. This way, the working mothers can even visit their children during their breaks at work."

At first, Lina's response surprised Richards. Then he realized she had thought of marriage and of the possible consequences of having children while carrying out a top level career. Then he thought, *I suppose there is no reason physically or psychologically that a top professional like Lina should not get married and have children. It appears the Russian system is set up to support this dual role.*

Then he asked Lina another question, "How about the Russian husbands of working mothers. Do they help with the housework load to relieve the wife?"

Lina pointed out, "The letters-to-the-editor and human interest stories in *Pravda* often address the complaints of Russian working mothers – that the husband doesn't help her with the housekeeping duties of cooking, cleaning, washing, and shopping – that the Russian male considers these to be 'women's duties'. The husband comes home from work, sits in front of the TV , watches the news, reads the newspaper, and drinks beer – while the wife does the house work."

"If you were married, would you put up with such a husband?"

Lina responded lightly, "I would never have such a problem. I would never marry a man like that in the first place. It may be common for factory labor type men to act like that, but I don't think most professional men have such chauvinistic attitudes about women. Do you?"

Richards laughed, "Of course not! I like to help around the house with cooking and with other things. No, I wouldn't be like the typical Russian – or American – husband in that regard!"

Their increasingly intimate conversation was interrupted by their arrival at the Space Institute. They both switched their thinking over to the imposing task at hand, the rescue of the lost astronauts.

Lina and Richards spent most of Thursday morning in meetings and watching the countdown procedure on the video screen showing Baikonur. They had the typical Russian two hour luncheon in the executive dining room together with a number of the other top managers and engineers of the Space Institute. Richards listened with interest to the conversations, which were in English as a courtesy to his presence. These engineers and managers focused on their hobbies in these discussions which ranged from horseback riding to cycling to boating and soaring. He thought how similar their interests in leisure pastimes were to those of professionals in the US aerospace industry.

After lunch, Lina lead a video review meeting with the key personnel in both Novosibirsk and Baikonur. The consensus was that the countdown was progressing smoothly and the launch would occur as planned on Friday. At 3 pm, Gorlovka, Richards, Litvinov and Woods took the Chaika limousine from the headquarters building to the flight line at the airport and boarded the utility jet for the hour and forty five minute flight to Baikonur.

When the four travelers arrived at the flight strip, Richards and Lina were first off the jet followed closely by Woods and Litvinov. They were met by the chief protocol officer of Baikonur, a one star general who welcomed them to the Russian spaceport and then lead them to a waiting limousine driven by the young air force captain who would be their escort officer during their visit to Baikonur. The limousine had a Russian flag on the left fender, a three star flag in the center because Dr. Gorlovka had a protocol rank of a three star general, and an American flag on the right fender honoring the American visitors. They were driven to the VIP temporary living quarters in a lovely, tree lined area with wide green lawns surrounding the hotel-like building. The captain handed the room keys to Dr. Gorlovka and directed four uniformed non-commissioned officers to help the guests by carrying their bags to their rooms.

In the elevator on the way to the third floor, the young captain explained to Drs. Gorlovka and Richards they would be required to share a three bedroom suite, since it was the only three star general protocol room available. He apologized for the inconvenience and added that each bedroom had a connecting bathroom to insure privacy. Lina explained neither she nor Richards would be offended by the arrangement. The captain told the visitors he would return to pick them up for dinner at the officers' club at 8 pm.

Litvinov and Woods shared a more modest two bedroom suite at the opposite end of the hall from Lina and Richards' suite. The captain apologized that they would have to share the single bathroom.

Richards and Lina found their suite was quite luxurious and beautifully decorated. The living room had a king size couch and overstuffed chairs arranged for viewing a large color television in the corner. There was a well stocked bar with whiskies, liqueurs, wines, champagnes, and the inevitable Russian vodka. The refrigerator was full of assorted hors d'oeuvres – anchovies, olives, cheese spreads, caviar, and more. A nearby cupboard held assorted crackers and cookies. The three bedrooms were modestly sized with double beds. The attached bathrooms were complete with toilet, shower, bidet, and lavatory with a large, well lighted dressing mirror. Richards and Lina chose the bedroom with a view of the green lawn and gardens surrounding the VIP quarters as the one they would share. After putting away their personal effects, Richards poured each a glass of champagne and Lina prepared two plates of caviar and other snacks. She turned on the second channel and was fortunate to find the ballet, Cinderella, by S.S. Prokofiev, which provided a soothing background for their cocktail hour.

Lina and Richards dressed for dinner and were ready when their escort officer knocked at their door shortly after 8. Litvinov and Woods were with him. The four were driven by the young officer to the officer's club about a mile away. He pulled up in the circular driveway to the entrance to the club. The foursome were met by their hosts, the director of the Baikonur space port and his wife, for a formal dinner in one of the small dining rooms available for small, intimate parties.

As soon as everyone was seated at the dining table a smartly uniformed waiter served them a round of ice cold vodkas. The director presented a toast to the successful rescue launch the next morning. The waiter immediately began serving a lavish multi-course dinner which, with the lively conversation, lasted until almost 11. The quartet's escort officer drove them back to their living quarters and lead them to the elevator. Lina requested they be picked up at 6 in the morning to be driven to the launch control center. That way, they would be able to view the last crucial four hours of the countdown to the launch of the Russian shuttle.

Lina and Richards enjoyed a relaxing interlude of love making before falling asleep. Richards woke at 5:30 and found Lina was already in the bathroom dressing for the busy day ahead. Richards jumped in for a quick shower and dressed rapidly so they both were ready when the escort officer knocked on their door, with Litvinov and Woods in tow. They hurried down to the waiting limousine and were driven the ten kilometers to the launch control center where the launch teams were scurrying busily around finishing the final phases of the countdown.

As the four walked into the launch control center, they were greeted by the protocol office who took them to the VIP area. The multitude of TV cameras trained on the space shuttle and its huge launch rocket would give them an all encompassing view of the blast off. The other TV screens were linked with the Space Institutes in Moscow and Novosibirsk, the US Space Station, NASA Houston, and NASA Washington. Richards and Lina stood in front of a TV camera that projected their images onto one of the TV screens. They greeted the global audience that was linked together for the first time in this vast video teleconference, just a few short hours before the rescue launch.

Lina made a formal statement to this far flung audience, "My dear Comrades and Space Colleagues, this is Dr. Lina Gorlovka in the Baikonur control center. This is our last chance to communicate before the launch scheduled in just a little more than three hours from now. My comrades here at Baikonur have done everything humanly possible to make sure this is a successful launch. Our space shuttle is loaded with the crew and fuel for the trip to rescue our American colleagues lost in space. Our shuttle is carrying a cargo of expendables which will provide the necessary materials for life support until the end of November. As you know, we have scheduled three launches to return all our stranded American colleagues. These launches are currently scheduled three weeks apart. So by the end of September, if all goes well, all of you Americans up on the Space Station should be safely returned to Earth. I have Dr. Richards here with me. He would like to say a few words."

Richards stood in front of the TV camera and, with a serious countenance, spoke authoritatively into the speaker, "First, I would like to say that I am thoroughly impressed with the professional job being done by the Russian launch team here. General Robbins and Dr. Barbara Rosen, on the Space Station, believe me, your rescue is in able hands. Colonel Gusev and his crew are really ready for this launch and subsequent docking with the Space Station. I am convinced everything is being done to assure a successful rescue."

General Robbins spoke up, "Dr. Gorlovka, we are truly grateful to Russia for this impending rescue launch. My crew and I here on the Space Station greatly appreciate the efforts of your highly professional team to save our lives. Also, I truly believe this mission will greatly improve the understanding and friendship between our two nations!"

Next, Dr. Bill Adams from NASA Headquarters in Washington, took a turn, "This is Dr. Adams, here in Washington, with the President's science advisor, Dr. Davidson. We believe the Russian Space Institute's decision, to provide video coverage to NASA in the US of this rescue launch, is wonderful and a giant step in the direction of cooperation in space."

Dr. Davidson spoke next, "Dr. Gorlovka and all my scientific colleagues in Russia, I just spoke with President Williamson in the oval office before coming over here to NASA Headquarters. The President sends his best wishes to Russia for a successful rescue launch."

Professor Dr. Nikolai Chekhov from the Moscow Space Institute now ascended the video platform, "This is Professor Chekhov, here in Moscow. I am most happy to report I just received a message from Premier Gorbachev that I would like to read now:

To all my comrades in the Space Institute and especially to Colonel Georgi Andrejevich Gusev and his brave crew of cosmonauts:

The Russian leadership wishes you good luck and success on this humanitarian rescue mission of the unfortunate American astronauts.

May the spirit of Lenin be with you on this day!"

Lina concluded, "I would like to thank everyone for their good wishes, especially Professor Dr. Chekhov for his message from Premier Gorbachev and Dr. Davidson for his message from the American President. We are now approaching a crucial time period in the launch countdown and must clear the communication channels at this time."

Dr. Barbara Rosen, who was standing next to Billie Joe Johnson in the Space Station control center, turned to him and said, out of range of the audio speaker, "Billie Joe, now that all the *chiefs* are finished with their bullshit, maybe the *worker bees* can get on with the rescue launch!"

Colonel Johnson laughed, "Yeah, you're right, Barbara. Georgi Gusev, sitting up there in the space shuttle on top of all that explosive power that will shove him into orbit, is too busy to listen to all the formal baloney. That's one of the advantages of being an astronaut."

Barbara Rosen laughed, "I'll sure be glad to see that big machine docking out here tomorrow. It'll be really great to have a working shuttle up here! Also, it'll be super to have the expendables they're bringing!"

The countdown for the launch continued throughout the early morning hours. Finally, at just after 10, after a short technical hold, the launch controller said, for the final five seconds of countdown, "Pjat, tschjityrja, tri, dwa, adjin, -- We have lift off!"

The enormous vermillion flame from the huge launch rockets spewed forth gigantic white clouds of steam as the Russian space machine jumped off the launch pad and rapidly accelerated upward into the cloudless blue sky of the dessert-like terrain at the Baikonur spaceport.

A yell of exhilaration rose from the launch control center as everyone cheered the shuttle onward and upward. Richards and Lina had seen the flaming exhaust and felt the extremely powerful vibrations and heard the deafening engine roar of the actual launch from an observation platform three kilometers from the launch pad. Thirty seconds after the launch, the shuttle was a tiny white column supported by a glowing red streak. There was a sudden burst of white smoke as the booster rockets were expended and fell away from the shuttle as its main liquid propellant rocket engine took over for the orbital insertion. The shuttle became too small to see with the naked eye. Lina and Richards turned to the video image of the rocket taken with telescopic lenses and continued to watch until that picture also disappeared.

Colonel Gusev reported from the still accelerating shuttle in a calm, professional voice, "Baikonur control, this is Colonel Gusev. Everything looks normal here in the cockpit. A good launch! How does the telemeter look?"

"Colonel Gusev, this is Baikonur control. All telemeter signals look normal. You are cleared for orbital injection. Good luck!"

Another cheer went up in the launch control center. It was a successful launch. Everything was A-OK!

Chapter 42

Soviet Shuttle Docking

Barbara Rosen was elated over the successful launch of the Russian rescue shuttle. Even though she was officially off-watch at the time, she waited until the shuttle was safely injected into orbit before heading for her cabin. The rendezvous maneuver during which the Russian shuttle would make small corrections to match its orbit to that of the Space Station would take some 14 orbits or over 21 more hours.

Barbara had never thought much about dying, but tucked way back in her mind she knew if the Russian shuttle had exploded during launch or had to abort, there wouldn't be much hope for her or her fellow astronauts. The expendables would run out and they would all slowly die. Now, if the main engine functioned long enough to get the shuttle close to the Space Station, they would have the precious cargo of expendables which would assure life until the end of November. That would allow time for other alternatives, even if there were some kind of in-orbit failure. Even the critical docking maneuver didn't have to be successful. It would be possible to use the Space Station's free flyers – two miniature robotic space ships – to bring the expendables from the shuttle to the station if something did go wrong and the shuttle couldn't get close enough to dock (or even to be reeled in, like Atlantis).

All-in-all, Barbara was relaxed now with the nagging worry of launch failure behind her. When she was relaxed, she felt like sex. She floated over to where Colonel Richard Rogers, commander of the disabled Atlantis, was floating near the video screen in the Station's communications center. She spoke in a low voice, "Rich, how would you like to spend the night in my cabin?"

Rogers looked up with a pleasantly surprised expression on his face, "Barbie, you bet your boots I would! Let's go, Baby. There's not going to be much to do, duty-wise, until tomorrow."

Rogers and Barbara floated out of the communications center and into the G&C and Comm passageway, and passed through the number 2 Habitation Module. As they passed by the dining room, several of the crew members were sipping cold beer out of the beer nipples. That was the only alcoholic beverage allowed on the Space Station, and it was only 3.2% alcohol. No crew member was allowed more than six ounces per day which was monitored by a software program controlling the rations of the crew. Some of the crew members had tried to beat the limit, but whoever wrote the software program must have been a teetotaler from Pasadena. No one had ever figured out how to fool it!

Everyone in the dining room was in high spirits and they greeted Barbara and Rogers with cheers about the successful launch and orbital injection of the Russian shuttle. The pair decided to take their daily quota of beer and chat with the other crew members for a while before going to Barbara's private cabin.

While Barbara was suckling her beer, Billie Joe Johnson floated over to her and whispered, "You're going to get your chance at bedding a Russian tomorrow. You have to act fast, though, he'll will only be here one day!"

Barbara whispered back, "Don't worry, Billie Joe there'll be plenty of time. You want to make a bet whether I get him or not?"

Billie Joe whispered back, "Sure, I'll bet you a hundred bucks. But how can I be sure who won?"

"Easy! Come to my room just after dinner. I'll take on both you and Georgi – two at once. That way you'll know for sure!"

Billie Joe nodded, "Barbie, I can't lose! Then it's a bet?"

"Yep, it's a bet!"

Rogers, who had just finished his nipple of beer, yelled across the room, "What are you two whispering about? Planning some conspiracy?"

Barbara laughed at him, "You might say that, Rich. If you're finished with your beer, let's float on out."

The pair said good night to the dining room group and continued to float on through the Space Station toward Barbara's cabin. They passed through the two Laboratory Modules on the way and glanced at the science astronauts on duty busily working on their various space experiments. There were a number of significant microgravity experiments taking place. For example, one scientist astronaut was growing pure protein molecules. Another was growing perfect crystals of an enzyme called PNP (purine nucleoside phosphorylase) which was a catalyst for producing chemotherapy drugs used in treating cancer patients. Another was producing the hormone EPO (erythropoietin) which stimulated red blood cell production in patients with anemia or kidney disease. Another laboratory project was producing pancreatic islet cells which could be implanted into the bodies of diabetic patients to allow them to forgo the inconvenience of daily insulin injections. A billion dollar market had developed for these special medical molecules and crystalline substances produced in space.

Barbara and Rogers finally reached her private cabin in the first Habitation Module. They floated inside and locked the door. The two engaged in weightless fun and games and then fell asleep together, squeezed into Barbara's sleeping bag.

The Russian shuttle was within 50 kilometers of the Space Station when Barbara returned to duty on her next watch. It was closing the gap at five kilometers an hour, meaning the rendezvous would take place during the next ten hours. She studied the Space Station radar tracking the Russian shuttle. The radar screen showed the relative positions of space objects on the circular plan view screen, which was similar to the radar screen of an air traffic controller. The Space Station was in the center. The diameters of the concentric circles around the center were proportional to the object's distance from the station. The approaching shuttle showed up as a blip on the screen. The line from the center to the blip was the bearing or direction from the station to the shuttle. A digital read out printed on the screen gave the distance to the nearest meter and the closing velocity to the nearest hundredth of a kilometer per hour.

The Space Station had a telescope slaved to the tracking radar. The shuttle was still too far away to be seen with the naked eye. Even with all the fancy electronics and electro-optics to observe the rendezvous, the approach was not too exciting to watch – sort of like watching grass grow. The closing velocity was so slow! After absorbing the current situation, Barbara turned to her other tasks as duty officer.

About an hour into her watch, a red light and buzzer flashed on her inter-station phone. It was General Robbins, her boss, "Barbara, come on over to my conference room. I'm having an executive staff meeting to make sure everyone knows what to do during the next twelve hours. Johnson and Rogers will be here, too."

"OK, Jack, I'll be right over." Barbara turned to the other astronaut on duty and assigned him the job of temporary duty officer until she returned from the staff meeting. She floated over to Robbins' conference room in the G&C and Comm Module near the communications control center. Johnson and Rogers were already there and had the video screen switched to the Russian shuttle with Colonel Gusev on display.

General Robbins had the bizarre habit of conducting these meetings with his body upside down relative to the other participants. Barbara figured, when she first encountered this habit, that it was some deep-seated urge on Robbins' part to assert his superiority relative to his subordinates. By now she was used to the position and no longer thought it was particularly strange. The two shuttle commanders were also used to the habit by now.

General Robbins opened the meeting by stating pompously, "The next twelve hours will be very crucial in this rescue mission. I want everyone to know exactly what needs to be done. Here is a preliminary list of tasks and the assigned personnel for each task." He handed everyone a computer printout.

He looked into the video screen showing the image of Colonel Gusev, "And Colonel Gusev, how is your rendezvous maneuver proceeding?"

"Sir, everything looks good here on the shuttle. Our computer is now predicting a rendezvous with your Space Station at 0502 Greenwich Mean Time. That's some nine hours from now. We'll begin the final docking maneuver at that time. Docking should take about 15 minutes. We should be aboard by 0530 GMT."

Barbara Rosen broke in, "Colonel Gusev, your rendezvous estimate is confirmed by our tracking computer. We estimate your rendezvous at 0503. Pretty close! Our cargo master wants to start loading your cargo of expendables into our service module just as soon as you dock."

"Barbara, you can call me Georgi. My cargo master has been assigned the duty to work with your cargo master to transfer the expendables immediately upon docking. We have made sure our tubing fittings are compatible with your receptacles. Bucky Woods took care of that detail."

"Great, Georgi. It looks like we're in business. We'll be able to breathe until the end of November after the unloading."

Robbins spoke up again, "Colonel Gusev, we expect to have you ready to return within 24 hours after you dock. You'll have a chance for a good night's sleep while you're aboard the Space Station. We have six passengers identified for you to take back to Baikonur."

Barbara turned so her face could not be seen by either Robbins or any of the video cameras and gave Billie Joe a look that meant she and Billie Joe shared a secret about that 'good night's sleep' for Gusev!

"That's fine, Sir. My crew and I look forward to your hospitality. We have plenty of room for your six passengers. We could take seven if necessary."

Lina Gorlovka spoke up on the video link from Baikonur, "Georgi Andrejevich, you look great up there. The telemeter signals indicate everything looks A-OK on the shuttle. We'll have a big welcoming party for you and the American astronauts when you land here in Baikonur Sunday afternoon."

Georgi smiled, "Lina, let me get through the party waiting for me here on the Space Station before you plan the next one! Glad the telemeter signals look good. Everything looks normal here. My two crew members are all ready for the docking."

Richards interjected, "Georgi, your blast off looked spectacular. That shuttle of yours seems to accelerate even faster than the US shuttle."

"Yeah, Don, it does. We have 50% more x-axis acceleration than your space shuttle. We build bigger launch rockets than you Americans. Our shuttle weighs twice as much and will carry twice the payload as well."

Robbins frowned at all this chitter-chatter during his docking review meeting. He moved to regain control by declaring, "Now, back to the tasks that must be done to be ready for the docking. Barbara, do you have anything to add?"

"Well, Jack, I believe you have everything well defined here in your memo. As a precaution, I believe we should get the free flyers ready on standby, just in case Georgi needs any assistance at docking time. Also, we should have two crewmen suited up in the EVA (extra vehicular activity) suits, just in case."

Robbins responded, "Good thinking, Barbara. Please initiate those two tasks. Excellent back up! If we need them, we'll be ready."

Barbara added, "Georgi, your welcoming party is right after the docking. There's just barely enough room for us to crowd into the dining room, if we don't mind being cozy. We even have beer nipple access codes for you and your cosmonauts to use – almost as good as champagne up here!"

Georgi laughed, "That's a nice offer, Barbara. I'm afraid our Russian regulations don't permit drinking any alcoholic beverages on our space vehicles, not even beer."

Barbara replied, "Well, you Russian regulations don't apply on the US Space Station. It's not a Russian space vehicle."

Georgi smiled, "You're right, Barbara. So I guess the beer will be OK."

Robbins closed out the meeting, "OK, Ladies and Gentlemen. I believe we have covered everything that needs to be done for the rendezvous, docking, and post-docking operations. Meeting's adjourned. Welcome to our neighborhood, Colonel Gusev."

Barbara Rosen returned to her duty in the communications center. She spent the next few hours watching the Russian shuttle on the tracking radar screen slowly approach the Space Station. When the shuttle was ten kilometers out, Barbara could finally make out a small dot outside the observation window that faced in that direction. A jet liner flying at cruise altitude above the Earth would look about the same to a person on the ground. At its closing velocity of five kilometers per hour, the shuttle was still some two hours away from docking, since there was no way to slow down or stop the orbiting Space Station to make it wait for the shuttle.

Barbara went into the dining room for coffee and cookies. When she floated into the room, there were five other crew members taking their breaks, including Rogers and Johnson. Barbara said hi to them and punched her access code number into the dispensing machine and selected coffee with milk and sugar. She took the coffee nipple in her mouth for a swig of the hot liquid. Each crew member was limited to six cups of coffee in a 24 hour period by the food and drink dispensing software program. She also choose two cookies from the dispenser. The cookies were a special no-crumble type to avoid the mess of cookie bits floating all over the Station.

Everyone was eagerly waiting for the shuttle to arrive. The dining room video monitor showed the shuttle cockpit. Barbara said, in between coffee sips, "Are you all ready for the welcoming party, fellows?"

Billie Joe Johnson answered, "Hell, Barbie, I've been ready for this party since last February when Columbia busted up here! I'm on the first load going down, you know. I'll miss all you fine folks up here. But it will sure be good to get back down to terra firma. I really miss all those Space Bunnies that hang out at our hotel down on the Cape in Florida!"

Barbara laughed, "We'll miss you up here, Billie Joe! You've been good comic relief. Yeah, I'll bet all the Space Bunnies will be glad to see you back. You're such a good hunk!"

Billie Joe grinned, "Barbie, you're not so bad yourself. But, hell, it's really hard on an active male like me up here on the Station, especially since I hadn't planned on making this little five month detour!"

Rogers added, "Well, Barbie, you'll have me for another three weeks. I'm not scheduled to return until the second rescue mission."

Barbara replied playfully, "I need everyone I can get up here. It's the only thing that relieves the off-time boredom. Well, fellows, my break is over. See you at the welcoming party. Gusev is only about an hour away now."

Johnson and Rogers answered in unison, "See you at the party."

The shuttle was clearly in view by the time Barbara got back to the control center – only four kilometers away - about 45 minutes until the final docking maneuver began. Barbara watched the white puffs as the shuttle's reaction jets maintained the altitude of the huge vehicle. About every 30 to 60 seconds there was a larger white puff when the main engines fired to close the distance between the Station and the shuttle.

When the shuttle was less than 500 meters away, Barbara called the shuttle commander on the communications radio, "Georgi, you look good out there. I see your cosmonaut crew members have the docking adapter all set up for the docking."

"Roger, Barbara. Everything is looking good. I've entered the coordinates of the docking port into the computer. I'll switch from Rendezvous Mode to Docking Mode three minutes from now when we are 250 meters away. Then I'll reduce our closing velocity to 0.69 meters per second so we'll make a gentle hook-up. I don't want to blast too much at the last second. We might get dust in your eyes."

Barbara laughed, "Roger, Georgi. That sounds good. We'll appreciate a gentle landing. Our electro-optical apertures – our electronic eyes – get dirty if there's too much blasting around here. Then somebody has to go out in an EVA suit and clean them off."

By now, everyone not on duty was watching out the Space Station windows observing the spectacular event of the Russian shuttle docking attempt. Jokes were being made about how the pilots of long distance jets on Earth were supposed to make the roughest landings, because they didn't get as much practice as the short hop pilots. These kibitzers were hoping Gusev would not copy this pattern in his space 'landing'.

The Space Station dock master was busy getting the docking port ready to hook up with the shuttle. Later, he would help the serviceman who would direct the loading of the expendable cargo – the oxygen, water, reaction jet fuel, and food supplies – into the Service Module. Meanwhile Barbara was on duty as communications specialist. General Robbins was on duty as guidance and control specialist to maintain the Space Station's orientation as the shuttle bumped into the docking port. This crew of four would handle all the duties needed for the imminent docking attempt. The Space Station's six science astronauts, who manned the laboratory experiments, were trained to back up the four principal duty officers.

Before coming on duty for the docking maneuver some twenty minutes ago, General Robbins had made a tour of the classified laboratory in Laboratory Module #1 to make sure the lab's cipher lock was properly closed. This laboratory housed the Strategic Defense Initiative, or Star Wars, experiments that were strictly off-bounds to the Russian visitors soon to come aboard. He had already briefed the science astronaut responsible for that experiment to take the utmost security precautions to hide this activity from the prying eyes of the Russians. The Russian leadership was still upset about the decision of the US Administration to continue with the SDI program. General Robbins was sure the KGB had tasked Colonel Gusev to find out whatever he could about the SDI experiments on the Space Station. Even though these experiments are supposed to be 'Top Secret with Special Access' clearance, *Aviation Week Magazine* had published an article recently (January of 1992) detailing the SDI experiment on board the Space Station.

A few minutes later there was a gentle bump felt by everyone on board the Space Station. A cheer went up. The shuttle had docked!

Two minutes later the hatch of the shuttle opened into the docking module entry cavity. General Robbins shook Colonel Gusev's hand as he came out of the shuttle. Barbara Rosen kissed Gusev. All in view of the world on the television link of this historic event!

Chapter 43

Space Station Welcome Party for Russians

Barbara Rosen lead Colonel Gusev and his two Russian cosmonaut crewmembers to the welcoming party in the crowded Space Station dining room. General Robbins was floating with his head pointed towards Earth, as was usual during his meetings with groups. He opened this meeting, "Everyone to their beer nipples! I propose a toast to Cosmonaut Gusev and his crew of two!"

He waited for everyone to scramble to one of the beer nipples and to enter their access codes for beer. Barbara helped Gusev and his two crewmembers punch in their newly assigned beer access codes.

Robbins had also floated over to a beer nipple. He toasted, "Here's to the rescue by the Russians! Rah! Rah! Rah! Everyone, drink up!"

Everyone echoed, "Rah! Rah! Rah!" The room filled with the noise of everyone suckling simultaneously.

Then Gusev said, "Now, I have a toast to propose. Here's to the hospitality and good cheer on the American Space Station! We thank General Robbins, Dr. Rosen, the American Shuttle Commanders Johnson and Rogers, and all the American astronauts for our warm welcome! Drink! Drink!"

Again the room was filled with slurping sounds.

Then Barbara Rosen added, "I have one more toast. Here's to all the launch support provided for this rescue mission by Dr. Lina Gorlovka and her colleagues at the Russian Space Institute and Baikonur. May the nine returning tomorrow have a safe re-entry and happy landings at Baikonur! Drink up!"

The sound of beer suckling filled the room again. Then everyone began talking excitedly about today's rendezvous and docking and tomorrow's re-entry into the Earth's atmosphere for the six lucky astronauts and three cosmonauts. There was one thing missing from this cocktail party in space which was always present in Earth-bound cocktail parties – cigarette smoke. No one smoked on the Space Station. Even those crew members who were avid nicotine addicts on Earth had given up the habit. There was a feeling by all on the Space Station that their environment here was precarious. No one wanted to foul the atmosphere and air-conditioning ducts with cigarette smoke and its filthy residue of odor and sticky black tars.

After a period of partying, the crew members slowly began to disperse to the rest or work stations. Barbara Rosen floated over to Georgi Gusev, who was engaged in a pilot's conversation with Johnson and Rogers. They were busily comparing the control of the Russian shuttle with that of the American shuttle. In this typical pilots' talk, their hands were maneuvering to simulate the motions of their hypersonic space vehicles.

Barbara heard Billie Joe Johnson declare, "Yeah, Georgi. We have to control energy during re-entry by rolling first right 180 degrees and then left 180 degrees. This way we can adjust our landing range. We do that around mach 15."

Gusev replied, "Billie Joe, we do the same thing for energy control. Frankly, we copied the technique from you Americans. But we have a better scheme for yaw control during re-entry than you do. You have to use your reaction jets for direction or yaw control all the way down to mach 2."

Billie Joe asked curiously, "And what do you do?" Our rudder has no effectiveness so we have to use the reaction jets."

Gusev answered smugly, "We use the same scheme we use on our supersonic transport that flies at mach 5 at 150,000 feet. We use vortex generators to modulate the vertical tail lift on either side. It works!"

Barbara broke into this almost incomprehensible technical discussion by tapping Georgi on the shoulder and saying, "Georgi, you've been working very hard. How would you like some rest and relaxation now?"

Georgi immediately stopped his technical jargon, turned to face Barbara, smiled, and replied, "That sounds like a great idea! What do you have in mind?"

Barbara tilted her head to one side and laughed, "Come to my cabin and I'll show you how to really relax in space!"

Georgi smiled back, gave Barbara an intense look filled with sexual desire, and replied, "Let's go. You probably have learned some things about living in space that I don't know!"

The pair floated out of the dining room in Habitation Module number 2 and headed away from the Docking Module in the direction of the Service Module, where by now the precious expendables carried up by the Russian shuttle had been safely stored. On the way to her cabin, Barbara explained the layout of the Space Station, "Georgi, we have designed the station to be expandable, to evolve over a decade or so into a really huge structure. The present configuration is set up for an astronaut crew of ten permanent and ten transient crew members. We can squeeze in a few more if necessary."

"How many modules do you have so far?"

As they left Habitation Module #2 and entered Laboratory Module #2, Barbara replied, "Seven. You docked at one of them: the Docking Module. At the opposite end is the Service Module where we store the expendables and our waste products. You came through the G&C and Comm Module with our Control Center and all the antennas."

Georgi interrupted, "It looked like your dining room was in a Habitation Module. How many Hab Mods do you have?"

"Two right now. My cabin is in the other one up near the Service Module."

Georgi continued digging for information, "And the other two modules must be where you do your military experiments for Star Wars, right?"

Barbara lied in a sweet tone, "Georgi, we don't have military experiments on the Space Station. Our two laboratory modules, which we are passing through now, are dedicated to peaceful experiments, mainly medical research experiments. We also have a 100 inch telescope for astronomical observations."

At that point they were floating by the laboratory containing the SDI classified equipment which was locked with a cipher lock. The other lab rooms were open and Barbara and Georgi could look in and see the astronaut scientists working as they floated past.

Georgi looked at the locked, super-secret lab, "And I suppose peaceful experiments are going on in that locked laboratory! Look, Barbara, we read *Aviation Week* magazine. We know you're using the Space Station to develop key SDI elements. We learn more reading *Aviation Week* than we learn from our KGB!"

Barbara smiled placidly, "Georgi, you know I can neither confirm nor deny the *Aviation Week* article. That would be a clear violation of the US security regulations."

Georgi laughed, "OK, Barbara. I understand. We have the same kind of security regulations in our country. I'll stop asking embarrassing questions that you can't answer."

Barbara replied, "Georgi, neither one of us can be responsible for our government's policies. Let's forget all the official bullshit and enjoy our private lives, as Space Colleagues."

By now they had passed into Hab Mod #1 and they floated into Barbara's cabin. Georgi replied good naturedly, "You're right, Barbara. Right now, I want you, if I can figure out how to do it in space. It'll be a new experience for me!"

Barbara laughed out loud as she closed the cabin door, "Don't worry, Georgi. I'll show you how!"

"Barbara, you'll find I'm a fast learner."

Barbara was concerned about what Georgi's attitude would be when Billie Joe showed up. She decided she better explain to make sure Georgi wasn't offended. "One other thing, Georgi. I enjoy sex with two men at once. I hope you won't be offended that I have invited Billie Joe to join us."

"I don't mind at all. After all, we are colleagues in space. We can be colleagues in sex as well."

A few moments later, Billie Joe knocked on the door and Barbara let him in, "Come on in. Georgi agrees to a sexual pas d'trois as long as you don't attack him!"

It was Billie Joe's turn to laugh, "Georgi, don't worry. I want Barbara's ass, not yours."

Barbara replied in a comical tone, "Oh, Billie Joe, I love it when you talk dirty!"

The lessons began. Georgi and Billie Joe teamed up as true space colleagues to give Barbara maximum pleasure. Georgi quickly got the hang of using Velcro straps around his ankles to provide the proper lineal separation and bodily leverage. At the end of the activities, Billie Joe left for his own bunk, while Georgi and Barbara shared her sleeping bag for a nice long nap.

After their rest and recreation, Barbara and Georgi returned to duty to get the Russian shuttle ready for its re-entry into the Earth's atmosphere and subsequent landing at the Baikonur space port. These preparations required over twelve hours of intense effort. Georgi and his crew loaded the Russian shuttle computers with all the parameters needed for re-entry. The software for ascent and orbital operations were replaced by the software for re-entry and landing. The crew went through an elaborate check out to make sure all subsystems were functioning properly. They got a red light when the main engine controls were checked by the computer program. It gave the crew momentary concern, but when the test was recycled, they got a green light, indicating everything was OK, after all.

It was soon 0500 GMT, Sunday 10 August, 1992. The push off from the Space Station was scheduled for 0600 GMT. The shuttle would make one complete trip around the Earth while Colonel Gusev and his crew adjusted their orbit to begin re-entry. The re-entry trajectory took about the same amount of time as three quarters of an orbit. They were scheduled to touch down at Baikonur at 0910 GMT or 1410 local time.

Colonel Billie Joe Johnson and the other five American astronauts who were returning to Earth were already aboard and in their stations. Colonel Gusev's loadmaster had briefed them all thoroughly on the safety procedures on the Russian shuttle. *Just as if we were on a commercial airliner heading for a vacation weekend*, remarked one of the Americans. The sixty minute count down to take off was already well along and was proceeding smoothly. All systems checked out as normal. At T minus five minutes, 300 seconds before the main engine was to ignite to begin the orbital adjustment, Colonel Gusev used the reaction jets to back away from the Space Station docking port. The big ship moved ponderously away from the station. Gusev took a final mental snapshot of Barbara's smiling face in the communications control center window. She waved goodbye. Gusev returned her wave and turned his attention to the cockpit controls and displays as the count down continued.

The final five seconds of count down began. The synthetic voice generator in the shuttle cockpit said, in a smooth, seductive female voice, "Pjat, tschjityrja, tri, dwa, adjin, noj." The main engine fired up and the space shuttle slowly accelerated, moving away from the Space Station. Ten seconds later the cockpit emergency panel lit up, an alarm started ringing, and the feminine synthesizer voice said sweetly in Russian, "Your main engine has failed. Please take corrective emergency action. Code 173."

Gusev, well trained in all the emergency procedures, including code 173, immediately rotated the shuttle using the reaction jets and then used the same reaction jets to reduce the velocity with which they were separating from the station. When he completed the emergency procedure, the shuttle was about 600 meters from the station and drifting very slowly away at about 0.1 meter per second. Gusev continued to apply the reaction jets to kill this drift velocity. This took about 30 seconds. Then the drift showed as 0.0000 meters/second on his instrument panel. He was just over 600 meters away from the station.

Barbara came on the communications radio, asking the inevitable stupid question, "Shuttle, this is the Space Station. Is something wrong?"

Gusev, in his best authoritative captain's voice answered, "Affirmative, Space Station, Gusev speaking. We have a malfunction in the main engine. Looks like we will have to abort the re-entry. I've applied emergency procedure code 173 to stop our separation velocity. Otherwise, we would be lost in space!"

Lina Gorlovka came on the communication set, "Colonel Gusev, this is Dr. Gorlovka at Baikonur control center. We confirm from telemetered date that you have a hard failure of your main engine. Telemeter says all three of the redundant fuel valves for the main engine are jammed shut."

Gusev replied in a very professional voice, "Roger, Baikonur control. What can we do to recover power for the main engine?"

"Georgi, Lina here. We have the main engine technical team looking at the telemeter signals. Their team leader says you can expect an assessment in about twenty minutes."

"Roger, Lina. We'll wait for the assessment. I've killed our separation velocity so we're sitting here about 600 meters from the Space Station."

"Roger, Georgi. Please just hold."

The tension in the Russian shuttle and the Space Station was building. Barbara turned to Richard Rogers, "Rich, how many things can go wrong up here? Now we've got three busted shuttles up here, one Russian and two American."

Rogers, with a serious tone in his voice, "Well, at least we've got expendables through November stored away. If Georgi can't fix that thing, at least there's time to work on other options."

Thirty minutes later, Lina Gorlovka came on the video link and the communications channel, "Colonel Gusev and General Robbins, this is Dr. Gorlovka, I'm afraid I have some bad news. The main engine technical team reports there's no hope for the engine. It's a hard failure. No chance of fixing it in space. Looks like you'll have to wait for another shuttle to rescue you!"

Chapter 44

Russian Shuttle Back-up

Barbara Rosen rushed to dispatch the two astronauts who were wearing EVA suits, part of the standard safety procedures for shuttle re-entry activity. They took the long cable out to the Russian shuttle and connected it to a fitting over the cargo bay. The Space Station loadmaster slowly reeled in the disabled Russian shuttle. Gusev used the shuttle's reaction jets to perform the docking maneuver and the nine dejected men on the shuttle re-entered the safety of the Space Station.

A meeting was quickly organized in Baikonur after the shuttle failure. Richards and Dr. Gorlovka were on the video screen at Baikonur. Professor Dr. Chekhov's grim face was on the screen from Moscow. The other video screens were linked with Robbins and Rosen up on the Space Station, Gus Ford at NASA Houston, and Bill Adams at NASA Headquarters. The Director of the Baikonur launch facility was at the meeting, as well as Bucky Woods and Yuli Litvinov. They all looked devastated as a result of this latest failure in space.

Richards opened the meeting by stating glumly, "We've had an unbelievable string of failures. While we were waiting for the meeting to start I computed the probability of having four shuttle failures like this. Assuming each failure had a probability of 10^{-4} per hour, which is a good estimate for the redundancy we have, then the probability of four failures is 10^{-16} per hour. In other words, these four failures would occur, statistically, only once every 10^{16} hours, which is 115 billion years! The universe is only about 20 billion years old. In short, having this much bad luck is statistically impossible! But here we are anyway. Now what?"

Dr. Chekhov spoke up on the video screen from Moscow, "Dr. Richards, I agree. The bad luck we've had is unbelievable. But we must do something. We Russians have another shuttle which is not finished. I have my staff running a PERT-TIME run on the

Space Institute's computer here in Moscow to get the best estimate of how soon our second shuttle can be launched. I should state, however, it doesn't look promising. We should have the computer results in about twenty minutes."

Dr. Adams, on the video screen in Washington, DC, added, "Don, while you were in Russia, we ran another schedule exercise to evaluate the soonest possible date the Enterprise could be refurbished for launch. I'm afraid the answer came out to be February 1993. And that assumes we would get funds for the refurbishments."

General Robbins, up on the Space Station, broke in, and said grimly, "I certainly don't like the tone of what I hear so far. I would like to remind you all, we run out of expendables up here the end of November. Something must be done by then or we're dead ducks!"

Chekhov replied, somewhat testily, "General Robbins, may I remind you we now have three Russian cosmonauts stranded on your Space Station. Let me assure you, my country will do everything within its power to save your astronauts and our cosmonauts."

Robbins spoke again, "Yes, Dr. Chekhov. I understand that very well. It's surprising how one's point of view is affected by the situation one is in. You can be very objective about the whole thing, treating it as an intellectual exercise. However, we twenty souls up here on the station see the situation at a visceral, not an intellectual, level. It's a matter of life or death to us!"

Richards, recovering his composure after the awful shock of this latest failure, broke in, "Now, wait a minute! Let me remind you all that we do have expendables to last through November now. Regardless of the answer from Dr. Chekhov's computer, you up on the Space Station are going to be saved. The European space shuttle can be launched in October. That was their estimate last March when their launch rocket exploded. We must get that date confirmed, of course. But an October launch would be plenty of time. They could even be a month late and you would still be OK. So don't give up hope!"

Notable relief was displayed on everyone's expressions.

Barbara Rosen exclaimed excitedly, "Don, you're right! We all almost forgot about the European option. Of course, they can save us!"

Richards went on, "Look, everyone, I have an idea. I have Jacques Dubois' home phone number in Toulouse. I'll call him now and see what he says."

Richards turned to Lina, "Is there a phone I can use to call Toulouse, France?"

Lina got a sad look on her face, "I'm sorry, Don. But we're not permitted to make international calls from the base here. Too many national security matters at risk!"

Dr. Chekhov overheard this interchange and beamed happily on his screen, "Look, Dr. Richards. Give me Dr. Dubois' phone number. I will phone him from here in Moscow and plug him into the audio here. Then you can speak to him over the video link."
"Great, Dr. Chekhov. That's a good solution. Here's his number." Richards gave Dubois' home phone number to Chekhov, who then placed the call.

A few minutes later, Chekhov reported, "Dr. Richards, I reached Dr. Dubois' wife. He just went out to the boulangerie for some bread. He should be back within 20 minutes. She promised to have him call my number just as soon as he returns home."

Richard thought to himself, *Here are people all over the world waiting breathlessly for Dr. Dubois to return home after buying two four and a half franc loaves of bread!* He then replied, "Thank you, Dr. Chekhov. And have you got your PERT time computer print out yet?"

Chekhov replied happily, "Yes, yes! It just arrived. Let me look at it for a moment."

Everyone waited with tense anticipation while Chekhov pushed his reading glasses up on his nose to see the figures better and scanned through the computer print out for the estimate of when the next Russian shuttle could be launched. It seemed like an eternity before he spoke again.

Finally he said, "Ah, yes, here it is. The computer says the very earliest we can launch the next shuttle will be 3 March 1993. The most probable date is 13 April 1993. Sorry, Dr. Richards, we can't support the rescue in time."

A groan of disappointment rose from the global TV audience when they heard this late launch date.

Just then Chekhov called out excitedly, "It's my phone ringing. Maybe this is Dr. Dubois in Toulouse."

He left the TV screen for a few moments. When he returned he said happily, "Dr. Richards, Dr. Dubois is on the line. He should be able to hear you if you speak into the TV microphone."

"Jacques, this is Don Richards.   How is everything in Toulouse?"

"Everything is fine here, Don.   My wife just told me she saw the failure of the Russian shuttle on the TV while I was out at the boulangerie. Really tough luck. Where are you anyway?"

"Jacques, I'm in Baikonur, in Russia. Your voice is plugged into our global TV conference. Even the folks up on the Space Station can hear you.   Now, for the sixty-four billion dollar question – when can you launch a rescue mission with the European shuttle?"

"Don, you know I can't answer that question officially without getting several layers of approvals. I can say, though, that we have replaced all the defective steel in Ariane III so that won't hold up the launch date. The earliest I can give you an official answer is next Wednesday afternoon."

There was a loud, clearly-audible groan following Dr. Dubois' response. He heard the disappointment and tried to soften it by adding, "Don, I can tell you un-officially, that the last launch date we gave you can probably be met.   Remember, that's not a commitment though!"

Richards said, "You mean mid-October?"

"Yes. That's the launch date we gave you last March. Call me Wednesday. I'll confirm the date officially then."

A cheer rose from the audience, smiles covered all the faces. Morale was up. The inhabitants on the Space Station were now confident they would be saved.

Chapter 45

Back to California on SST

After the meeting in Baikonur, Richards, Gorlovka, Litvinov, and Woods flew back to Novosibirsk, arriving at 4 pm. At the airport, Richards asked Lina, "Can you get us reservations on the 6:30 pm SST to Vancouver today?"

"I can't be sure, Don, but I'll try."

Lina led Richards and Woods to the Aeroflot counter and, after several minutes of heated discussion with the clerk, she turned to Richards, "You're in luck. You and Bucky have seats on the 6:30 SST to Vancouver. You are also confirmed on your connecting United Airlines flight. You will arrive in Los Angeles at 10 am today, eight and a half hours before you leave."

"Lina, you're a paragon of efficiency. Thanks. That'll give me all week to get the next rescue mission organized."

Lina smiled, "Good luck, Don. We Russians have a vested interest in your success now since we have three cosmonauts lost in space."

Richards replied confidently, "Don't worry, Lina. We'll get all of them back, including your cosmonauts."

"I'm sure you will, Don. I have all the confidence in the world in you – and the European shuttle."

Richards and Woods boarded the SST flight at 6 after they both gave their goodbyes and kisses to Litvinov and Lina. The sleek supersonic plane departed on time and turned to the great circle route from Novosibirsk to Vancouver. The big bird was moving away from the sun, so darkness descended shortly after takeoff. Richards was exhausted from the tensions of this harrowing day of yet another failure in space. He realized it was once again up to him to save the twenty people stranded up on the Space Station. He vowed to himself that he would get everything arranged for the new rescue mission within a week. A lot of people would have to get into the act – his boss, NASA, the White House, and, of course, the European Space Agency, who would conduct the rescue mission. He thought of the dizzying round of meetings he would have to attend and of the business trips he would have to make during the next week as he fell into a restless slumber on the comfortable, reclining seat of the mach 5 transport.

Richards woke up to the Captain's announcement that they were descending for landing at Vancouver Airport. Richards offered a good morning to Bucky Woods, who was wide awake, having just finished breakfast. Richards looked out the window at the luxuriant green forests and blue water that surrounded the beautiful city of Vancouver. Ten minutes later they were on the ground.

While they were clearing passport control and customs, Woods said to Richards, "Don, we're going to have a second Sunday because of crossing the International Date Line and flying on the SST. I hope this Sunday goes better than the one we just finished in Russia. How would you and Dawn like to join me for dinner at Bahia Corinthian Yacht Club this evening? I'm a member and what with all this travel connected with making the docking adapter, I haven't been able to use the dining room there for a long time."

"I'm sure Dawn would love to. I'm going to call her now to ask her to meet our flight. I'll confirm dinner after I talk to her, OK?

"Sure, Don, there's a phone booth right over there."

Richards dialed Dawn at their condominium. It was only 7 am on the West Coast and he woke her up.

She said sleepily, "Hello, who is it?"

Don laughed, "I'm sorry to wake you up, Dawn but Bucky Woods and I will arrive in LAX at 10 this morning, the same United flight as last time, from Vancouver. Can you pick us up?"

Dawn, becoming more awake, exclaimed happily, "Of course I will. I better bring the Honda. There's not enough room in your sports car if Bucky's going to ride back with us."

"Good thinking. Bucky invited us out to the Bahia Corinthian Yacht Club for dinner this evening. You want to go?"

"Of course, I'd love to. Tell Bucky thanks for the invitation!"

"OK, Darling. See you at 10."

"I'll see you there, goodbye."

Richards and Woods were among the first off the United DC-10 with their carry-on bags in hand. As they walked out the jet way into the United terminal, Richards saw Dawn's smiling face in the crowd. As he rushed over to grab her, he thought to himself fleetingly, *How can I love two women, Lina and Dawn, at the same time?*

Richards hugged and kissed Dawn. She returned his kiss lovingly. Then Woods kissed Dawn on both cheeks. The trio left the terminal, took the overpass to the parking lot, and found the waiting Honda. With Richards driving they exited the airport, got on the San Diego freeway and headed south to beautiful Orange County. On the way to Irvine, Richards said to Woods, "Bucky, why don't you just lounge around our pool today? Then we'll take you home after dinner at the yacht club."

"Sounds great to me, Don. But you don't have to take me home. My boat's on the dock at the yacht club. I'll sleep on board tonight and head for Catalina tomorrow. Maybe I can find a couple of young boat bunnies around the club to go with me."

Richards laughed, "What a life, Bucky! It must be nice to be retired!"

Woods answered, "Yeah, Don, it is really fantastic. I enjoyed my several month stint back in the saddle helping with the Russian rescue mission. But it'll be nice to forget about schedules again. Don, you really ought to take early retirement after you get all this Space Station mess cleared up."

Richards smiled, "Oh, Bucky. I'm much too young to think about early retirement. Maybe in another ten years or so."

Bucky got a serious tone in his voice, "Don I'm really serious. You only live once. Don't burn yourself out in this high pressure job of yours. It sounds like fun and the money's good – but there's more to life than working all the time, believe me!"

"Well, Bucky, I'm not ready to retire yet. I'd like to get one more big project under my belt first."

"OK, but I hope you don't die of a coronary first. You're under terrific stress, you know. Stress kills!"

Richards agreed, "You're probably right. I'll have to learn to cultivate a calmer life style. Today, we'll concentrate on relaxing – first around our pool and then over at your yacht club later."

A short time later, Richards took the freeway exit and wound up the green hillside road to the condominium he shared with Dawn. He parked the Honda in his two car garage next to his sports car, and they took the elevator up to their condo. Dawn showed Bucky where to put his luggage in the guest room. They all donned their swim suits and headed for the condominium pool. At a little after one, Dawn served a fruit salad with avocado sandwiches and champagne beside the sparkling water. They all spent the afternoon soaking up the beautiful California sunshine and splashing in the refreshing blue pool waters.

About 5:30 the trio dressed in informal clothes and drove the twenty minutes to the Bahia Corinthian Yacht Club on beautiful Balboa Bay in Newport. They used Bucky's plastic card key to open the gate and parked the Honda in the lot in front of the club. They headed down to the docks for a look at Bucky's boat and then spent an hour drinking martinis in the bar and admiring the glittering blue waters of the bay and the myriad of sleek yachts returning to home port at the end of a weekend.

Finally, a little after 7, they moved on to the dining room where they had combination steak and lobster dinners, accompanied by two bottles of Corbel brut champagne. As the three were preparing to leave their table to go home, two young girls, one blonde, one redheaded, rushed up.

The blonde exclaimed, "Oh, Bucky! You're back from Russia. We have really missed you and your boat. We hope you'll take us to Catalina this week."

Bucky smiled happily, "Girls, meet Don and Dawn. Vicky and Ginny. Sure. Go get on the boat and we'll leave right now."

The redhead, Ginny, answered, "How wonderful. We'll go down to the locker room and get our bags. See you on the boat."

After they left, Bucky smiled broadly, "See, Don. I'm set for the week. Thanks for the temporary job. Glad I'm finished. Good luck on the rescue. I know you'll be successful!"

"So long, Bucky. Have fun. Thanks for all your help. We really needed your expertise."

Dawn kissed Bucky goodbye on both cheeks. Then Richards and Dawn left together for their condo.

Chapter 46

White House Meeting

Richards walked into his office just before 8 on Monday, 11 August 1992. His secretary, June, was already there. She greeted Richards with a happy, "Welcome back from Russia, Dr. Richards. Sorry about the Russian shuttle failure. I saw it on TV. Mr. Moore wants to see you right away in his office. Says it's urgent!"

Richards answered, "Good to be back, June. There's no rest for the wicked. See you later."

Richards rushed over to his boss's office. Moore's secretary greeted Richards as he walked into the outer office of UAC's president, "You better go right in, Dr. Richards. I better warn you, he's upset about something."

Moore was standing behind his desk, glowering, as Richards entered. He yelled at Richards, "What the hell is going on? I see this Russian shuttle failure on TV and not a word from you. Not one God damn word! Now, what's up? What are you going to do now? Your communication is rotten. Am I going to have to fire you for not keeping me informed?"

Richards was somewhat disgusted by his boss's emotional reaction. "For Christ's sake, calm down, Dave. You're going to have a heart attack. Now look! First, I couldn't phone from the space landing station at Baikonur because they don't allow any international phone calls, for Russian security reasons. But I didn't think I should discuss the situation over the phone anyway, for US security reasons. I flew half way around the world yesterday to get home so I could tell you what happened in person. Now, here I am. Are you ready to listen?"

Moore, calming down perceptibly when he saw Richards wasn't going to take his verbal abuse, said a little apologetically, "Don, I'm sorry. The Board of Directors is after my ass. The Chairman called me after he saw the failure on TV yesterday and said, *Moore, if you don't get this Space Station mess solved right away, I'm going to ask the Board to find UAC another president!*

So you see, Don, I'm under a lot of pressure. We can't let the corporation look like fools. If those twenty people up there die on *our* Space Station, our stock will plummet. Besides, I'll be fired. And, by God, if I'm fired – you're fired!"

Richards replied calmly with self confidence in his voice, "Don't worry, Dave. Nobody's going to get fired. We're going to go back to the European option. That's what President Williamson wanted in the first place. I've already called Dr. Dubois in Toulouse. He couldn't give us an *official* launch date, but *unofficially* he said they could meet a mid October launch date."

Moore looked greatly relieved, "That's good, but is October soon enough? Will the expendables last that long?"

"Yes, Dave. The Russian shuttle loaded enough expendables aboard last Saturday when it docked to provide life support through the end of November. A mid October launch would give us plenty of safety margin. Besides, that launch can take up another four months expendables to give us additional life support margin."

Moore was now beginning to relax and act self confidently once again, "What is the next step, Don?"

"Well, first we've got to get the White House to concur with asking the Europeans again. Once the President injects himself into these matters, he has to stay in. While I was in Novosibirsk, I kept his Science advisor up to date."

Moore smiled, "Hell, it's before noon in Washington right now. I'll call the President myself, now, and make sure he goes along. I called him before to get him to agree to the Russian option, remember?"

"Of course I remember. That's a great idea. Call him!"

Moore buzzed his secretary and asked her to get President Williamson for him, that it was urgent – about the Space Station rescue."

A few minutes later, Moore's secretary buzzed him on the intercom, "Mr. Moore, I have President Williamson's secretary on the line now. Go ahead."

Moore said, with charm exuding from his voice, "Good morning, Mary Jane. I need to explain the Space Station situation to the President. Is he available?"

"Yes, Mr. Moore, he certainly is. He asked me to call Dr. Richards' office a few moments ago, but Dr. Richards' secretary said he was in your office. Your timing is perfect. I'll put President Williamson right on!"

Moore turned to Richards, "I'll put the President on the speaker box. He may want to hear from you, too."

A few moments later, the familiar voice of the President of the United States of America boomed over the speaker phone, "Good morning, Dave. This is the President. What's the next step with the Space Station rescue? I'm terribly distressed over the Russian shuttle failure to return home."

Moore replied self confidently, "Good morning, Mr. President. Please don't worry. We here at Universal Aircraft have everything under control. Our Dr. Richards has already talked to Dr. Dubois of the European space shuttle. That's our option now. It looks as though they can launch in October."

"But is that soon enough? Won't all those astronauts run out of air by then?"

"Mr. President, October is soon enough. The Space Station has enough expendables now to last until the end of November. The Russian shuttle brought them new supplies."

"Dave, that sounds pretty good, but would you ask Dr. Richards to brief Dr. Davidson here in Washington, tomorrow? We need to have all the details for a National Security Council meeting."

Moore looked questioningly at Richards, who nodded his agreement to make the trip.

"Yes, Mr. President. Dr. Richards is here with me now. He'll be in Washington to brief Dr. Davidson first thing tomorrow morning."

"Thank you, Dave. That takes a big load off my mind. Good luck!"

"Goodbye, Mr. President."

Richards spent the rest of the day preparing a briefing summarizing the complete situation relative to the Russian shuttle failure in orbit and the rescue option using the European shuttle.

Right in the middle of this very complex job, he was interrupted by another visit from Tom Ahrons, the CIA man who insisted on debriefing Richards on all the information he found out during his visit to Baikonur. Richards had to spend almost an hour giving Ahrons the details he asked about.

Monday evening at 9 Richards took the helicopter from the rooftop helipad above his office. He carried his small carry-on bag, packed and delivered by Dawn, and his briefcase stuffed with the briefing, typed, printed, illustrated, and assembled by his competent Space Station group, for Dr. Davidson, the President's Science advisor. As the helicopter lifted off the pad, the bright lights of Orange County glittered to the West. The helicopter headed along the Pacific Ocean beaches, heading towards the glowing lights of Los Angeles Harbor with the lights of Palos Verdes in the background on beyond. The chopper turned northwesterly towards Los Angeles International Airport. A few minutes later, the chopper landed next to the American Airlines DC-10 that would carry Richards to Washington Dulles Airport. He scrambled up the stairways, proceeded to the Admirals Club, and picked up his first class boarding pass. He had time for one martini before going downstairs to get on the Washington *red eye flight*.

A few minutes before 10, Richards boarded the huge DC-10 and settled into his window seat in first class. The pretty stewardess served him a glass of champagne and handed him his sleeping slippers and a blanket for his four hour nap. A few minutes later the big jet pushed back from the jet way, taxied to the active runway, and roared down the concrete for take off. By now low clouds had drifted onto the airport from the chilly Pacific Ocean. As the wide body jet climbed out over the Pacific, Richards looked back to see the city lights glowing eerily through the thin, low clouds blanketing the Los Angeles basin. He fell into a deep slumber in the big sleeper seat.

Richards woke up when the felt the jolt of the DC-10 undercarriage touching down on the Dulles runway. He boarded the transporter that carried him and the other briefcase laden passengers into the Dulles terminal.

The first person he saw was Dr. Davidson waiting for him at this early hour to drive him into Washington. He strode over to Dr. Davidsen, shook his hand, "I'm surprised to see you here, John."

Davidson smiled back, "President Williamson said I should pick you up. So here I am. We have a government limousine waiting right outside."

The two walked through the terminal and took the escalator downstairs. They exited outside to a big, black Cadillac limousine. A smartly dressed African American chauffer was waiting to drive them to the city. The hordes of traffic cops standing on the curbs there ignored the illegally parked limousine. They knew it was a White House limo and didn't have to follow the parking rules.

The early morning traffic on the George Washington Parkway was light. They were lucky to be in front of the commuter crush of bureaucrats which would soon be rushing into Washington, DC, from the Virginia suburbs. They reached the White House Annex by 7:30. Davidson escorted Richards through the lobby security, where Richards left his carry-on bag, and on up to Davidson's office.

His secretary, Lois, was already there. She said perkily, "Good morning. You're both in the office bright and early today. Welcome back from Russia, Dr. Richards. Too bad about the Russian shuttle. How do you take your coffee?"

"Good morning, Lois. This early in the morning, I take it black, please."

The two men went into Davidson's large, comfortable office and seated themselves in the corner of the room, which was furnished with a red leather couch and overstuffed chairs. Davidson opened the meeting, "Don, I understand your boss, Dave Moore, called the President yesterday. Right?"

Lois came in bringing two cups of coffee served in china cups and saucers. She also served a plate of chocolate petit fours and then unobtrusively left the room.

Richards responded to Davidson's question, "Yes, John, Dave called President Williamson yesterday morning about 11:15 your time. He explained to the President that the European shuttle option is the only possibility now to rescue the twenty people stranded up on the Space Station."

"And what was his reaction?"

"He seemed to accept the situation, but said he would have to have a meeting with the NSC because of the sensitivity of the situation. He asked that I give you a complete briefing so you could fill in any details the NSC needed during their meeting."

Davidson replied, "Yes, the President's secretary, Mary Jane, called me just before lunch and told me you would be coming to Washington to brief me. She gave me your flight number and asked me to meet the flight - in the President's limousine."

"So that's why the cops at the airport were so nice. No ticket for illegal parking."

Davidson laughed, "Yes, Washington cops rarely ticket the President's limousine!"

Richards laughed too, "John, I'm suitably impressed. Look, I have an hour briefing on 35 millimeter slides. Here are the hard copies of the briefing, in color."

"Don, please go through the briefing with me now. I have to brief the National Security Council at 10, so we have plenty of time. May I borrow your slides for the NSC meeting?"

"Of course, John. I'll put the slide cartridge in your projector over there."

"Good, Don. Here's the remote control for the slide projector so you can relax here while you give the presentation. By the way, we have a 1 pm meeting with the NASA Director. The President wants NASA to concur with the European option."

Richards remarked, "It looks like we're going to be busy today."

Davidson laughed, "Always a hectic pace here in the White House. I would appreciate it if you would wait here until I return from the NSC meeting. That way, if there are any questions about the briefing, I can call you here on the secure phone. I'll come back here after the NSC meeting and then we'll take a White House limousine over to the NASA meeting. Now, let's have the briefing."

Richards began, "As shown by these first few slides, everything went beautifully with the Russian rescue mission until they fired up the main engine to re-enter the atmosphere and return to Earth."

Davidson asked, "Couldn't they repair the engine in orbit? We've got lots of tools on the Space Station, don't we?"

"No, John. The Russian technical team looked at the possibility of an orbital repair. The telemeter signals showed the damage resulting from the failure was too major to repair in orbit. Then we looked into how soon the next Russian shuttle could be launched for a back up rescue. The answer came back, March at the earliest. That's too late. The newly replenished expendables run out the end of November."

Richards continued, covering all the salient points. Davidson interrupted frequently to ask penetrating questions. Because of the interruptions, the briefing finished at 9:45.

Davidson looked at his watch, "I better leave now for the NSC meeting in the White House The bottom line is – we've got to get the Europeans to use their shuttle for the rescue, right?"

"Right, John. And it looks like they can launch in October. I'm to call Dr. Dubois tomorrow to confirm the launch date."

"Got it, Don. I'll be back about 12:30. Lois can bring you lunch from the cafeteria. See you then."

"Good luck with your NSC briefing, John."

Davidson returned from the NSC meeting at 12:20. Richards was just finishing a steak sandwich Lois had brought him. He asked, "How did the briefing go, John?"

"The briefing went fine, but the NSC is worried about getting cooperation from the Europeans."

Richards looked quizzically at Davidson, "Certainly the Europeans wouldn't stand by and let twenty human beings perish in space, would they?"

"No, but the President and NSC are worried about the political price we may have to pay. The Europeans are still furious that the outgoing Republican President ordered the bombing of Damascus last January. The air raid which was supposed to *emasculate terrorism* in the Middle East killed almost 2,000 civilians near the terrorist training camps outside Damascus. They're also mad about the continuing *trade war* going on between the EEC and the US."

"But, John, what has all this got to do with rescuing astronauts?"

"The Secretary of State predicts the Europeans will ask for two things as part of their agreement to rescue our astronauts and the Russian cosmonauts. First, that the US will consult the European allies before attacking third world countries, such as

Syria.   Second, that the US will stop its trade war against the European Economic Community, the EEC. The Europeans want us to stop what they call *the protectionist trade policies erected by ultra conservative previous presidents.*   This would include stabilizing the dollar relative to the EEC currencies. The EEC thinks it is ridiculous that the dollar reached parity with the West German Mark in January this year."

Richards was confused by these global politics which were beyond his comprehension. "Well, John, I hope the President and his advisors can cope with these problems. Otherwise twenty people are going to die in space, in full view of world television, while the politicians squabble!"

Davidson looked at his watch and decided there wasn't time to educate Don about these global issues, "Don, we better go or else we'll be late for your 1 pm briefing. The NASA Administrator is an egotistical bastard. He doesn't like his meetings to start late. The limousine is waiting downstairs."

The two men grabbed their briefcases containing the briefing slides and rushed down to the White House Annex lobby where they quickly cleared security. They hurried out of the old building to the waiting black limousine.

Chapter 47

Dinner at Trader Vic's

The limousine driver wound through the crowded Washington streets at high speed, expertly maneuvering around the traffic until they reached NASA Headquarters on Constitution Avenue. The driver let Davidson and Richards out at the back entrance. They walked quickly into the lobby where they were confronted by a cantankerous guard who insisted on physically inspecting – very slowly – each and every paper in their briefcases.

Davidson, becoming impatient, said to the guard, "Look, here! I'm President Williamson's Science advisor. Here's my badge."

The hugely overweight guard turned around, looked slowly at the badge, and said, "Mister, I don't care if you're Abraham Lincoln. My job is to keep terrorist bombs out of NASA! And that's what I aim to do!"

The guard then searched the briefcases even more slowly, taking over ten minutes to complete his inspection. He finally waved the two by the security check point and on into the lobby with a grumpy, "OK, you're clean!"

The two men walked quickly to the elevator and punched the button for the sixth floor. By now, it was seven minutes after one. They were good and late for the one o'clock meeting. The elevator ascended very slowly, stopping at every floor as the crowd of NASA employees returned late from lunch. The two finally reached the sixth floor and walked rapidly down to the end of the hall where the NASA Administrator's office and conference room were located. They went into the Administrator's outer office. His secretary had a frantic look on her face.

She said, "Go right in. The Administrator is upset you're late for the meeting. He just had me call your office, Dr. Davidson, to find out what happened to you. Lois said you left thirty minutes ago."

Richards laughed, "We met a guard in your lobby who was convinced we were terrorists carrying in bombs!"

The secretary smiled, "Oh, that's Henry. The Administrator told him and the other guards to watch out for terrorists after the bombing of Damascus. I'm afraid he's over-zealous. But then, I guess that's better than us being bombed."

Richards and Davidson walked into the NASA Administrator's conference room. He was sitting at the head of the long conference table. He glowered at the two men as they entered, "It's about time you got here. My staff and I have been waiting here for over ten minutes."

Davidson replied diplomatically, "I'm sorry, Sir. The noon time traffic from the White House was quite heavy. Besides, we had a very thorough check of our briefcases by the lobby security."

The Administrator said, "You should have shown Henry your White House ID badge. That would have sped things up."

Davidson smiled serenely and said, "I did! That just slowed things down!"

The Administrator cleared his throat, "Harrumph. I guess I'll have to have a word with Henry. Well, anyway, get on with your briefing."

Richards spent the next hour going through the presentation. At the end, he declared, "So you see, Mr. Administrator, the only hope is to use the European space shuttle to rescue the crew stranded on the Space Station."

Davidson stood up, "And Mr. Administrator, the President would like your endorsement of the European option."

The Administrator stood, "Dr. Davidson, you will get my endorsement, but first, I'd like to be convinced it's a real option. Dr. Richards mentioned in his briefing that he didn't have an official position from the Europeans on the October launch date."

Richards stood also, "Yes, Mr. Administrator, that's right. Dr. Dubois said he had to get upper level approvals before he could commit to the launch date. He expected to have the approvals by tomorrow, Wednesday."

The Administrator replied, "Dr. Richards, I think you ought to call Dr. Dubois now. I guess he would be home since it's after seven in Toulouse. We should know how the approvals are coming. I don't want to stick my neck out with the President and endorse an option that isn't real."

Richards answered, "All I can do is try. Here. I'll give Dr. Dubois' home phone number to your secretary to call for me, OK?"

"Sure. That's fine. I'll buzz her."

The NASA Administrators' secretary came in. Richards handed her a slip of paper with Dubois' phone number on it and explained the urgency of the call. She went out of the room and returned a few minutes later, "I have Dr. Dubois' wife on the phone. She says he went to the boulangerie for bread and should be back any minute now."

Richards said authoritatively, "Tell her we will hold while we wait for Dr. Dubois to return."

The group of some twenty scientists, engineers, and top government managers sat in the conference room waiting for Dr. Dubois to return with two loaves of bread!

A few minutes later, the secretary came back into the conference room with the message, "Dr. Dubois is on the flashing line. You can switch him on to your speaker phone on the conference table."

Richards pushed the button and said, "Jacques, this is Don Richards again. I'm in Washington in the office of the NASA Administrator. President Williamson's science advisor, Dr. Davidson, is with me. The pressure is building up here in Washington to get your answer on the launch date."

"Don, you really travel around. You called me from Russia Sunday and now you're in Washington. I'm afraid I have some bad news for you. The President of the EEC, Mr. Lopez, wouldn't sign the launch date approval. He said he must talk to President Williamson about some political matters before he could sign the approval."

Richards replied, "That is bad news. But can you answer a technical question?"

"Yes, what is it?"

"Is there any technical reason you can't meet an October launch date?"

"No, no technical reason. It's a political question now!"

Richards thought for a moment, "Would it be possible for the President to call Mr. Lopez today to resolve these political questions?"

"No, I'm afraid not. He's en-route back from the Middle East. He's been visiting the president of Syria. Something about the aftermath of the US bombing of Damascus. He will be back in his office tomorrow, though."

Richards replied, "OK. Thanks, Jacques. I appreciate the information."

"You're welcome. Hope to see you in Toulouse soon, if these political questions can be resolved. Goodbye."

"Goodbye, Jacques. See you soon, I hope!"

Richards turned to the Administrator, looked him squarely in the eye, "Mr. Administrator, you heard from Dr. Dubois that they can technically support the October rescue launch if the political problem can be resolved. I think it most important that you endorse the European option! Will you?"

The Administrator, somewhat flustered by this complex situation, replied, "Yes, Dr. Richards, I'll endorse the European option. I'll call the President this afternoon. Thank you for the briefing."

The Administrator rose, the sign the meeting was over. Everyone rose and filed out of the room, except the Administrator, Richards, and Davidson.

Davidson addressed the Administrator, "Thank you for your endorsement, Mr. Administrator. I told Mary Jane you would call just as soon as our meeting broke up. Please call now."

The Administrator turned slowly to face Davidson, "Don't worry, Dr. Davidson. I'll call him now. You can listen if you wish."

"No, that isn't necessary. I'll return to my office now. Please call me later to confirm you reached the President."

"OK, I will."

Richards and Davidson left the conference room. The Administrator stood alone with a grim look on his face. Richards thought to himself, *I think the Administrator realizes he will either be fired or have to resign when the commission, which will surely be set up in the future to investigate the string of space failures, submits its findings to the President. That's life in Washington. There always have to be scapegoats for tragedies.*

The limousine was waiting for Davidson and Richards at the main entrance to NASA Headquarters. On the way back to the

White House Annex, Davidson asked, "And where are you staying tonight, Don?"

"I have reservations at the Hilton."

"I would like you to join me for dinner tonight, if you don't have other plans. And I want to meet with you again tomorrow morning at 9."

Richards answered in a friendly tone, "No, I have no plans, John. Dinner would be fine. How about Trader Vic's there at the Hilton? Do you like Polynesian food?"

"I love the Polynesian food at Trader Vic's. I'll have Lois call and reserve a private dining room for us there at 8. That way we can discuss the events of the day freely. I'll have the driver drop you off at your hotel after we get back to the White House Annex."

"That is very nice of you, John."

The limousine pulled up to the entrance to the White House Annex. Davidson told the driver to drop Richards off at the Hilton while Richards dashed inside to retrieve his carry-on bag from the security guard and rushed outside again.

Davidson said, "See you at ten minutes to eight in the Hilton lobby, Don."

"So long, John. See you then," Richards called back.

Richards woke up from a nap in his hotel room and looked at his watch. 7:30. He took a quick shower and dressed, ready to go down to the lobby. The phone rang. It was Davidson.

"Don, this is John Davidson. I hoped I would get you before you left the room. I'm already down in the dining room at Trader Vic's. My secret service escort didn't want us to meet in the lobby. Too much risk of terrorists in the crowd there. Just take the elevator down to the basement level. Tell the hostess at Trader Vic's to take you to John Jones' table."

"John, you're being mysterious, but OK. I'll see you shortly."

Richards took the elevator as directed to the basement level, marked Trader Vic's. He walked over to the entrance and was greeted by an exotic Polynesian beauty who was the hostess. He said, "Miss, I'm with John Jones' party in one of the private dining rooms."

"Oh, yes. Mr. Jones said to bring you right in. Dr. Richards, isn't it?"

"Yes, miss."

"Please follow me."

She led Richards to the private dining room, opened the door and ushered him in, handing him one of Trader Vic's elaborate menus. As Richards entered the room, he saw a beautiful girl about thirty years old with long red hair flowing down to her waist. She was seated next to Davidson at the Japanese style table.

Richards said, "John, I didn't realize you were bringing your wife."

Davidson laughed, "Don, this is Tanya, my Secret Service escort, not my wife."

Tanya smiled, "Dr. Richards, I'm not married. With all the terrorist threats against members of the Administration, anyone at Dr. Davidson's level who goes out in Washington at night must have a Secret Service escort."

Richards was greatly surprised at Tanya's appearance, "But, I thought all Secret Service agents wore dark blue suits, had crew cuts, and carried revolvers."

Tanya laughed, "The era of the all male Secret Service has gone as the women's rights movement accelerated. President Williamson insisted the Secret Service have at least 10% women. I'm one of the token women, but I do carry a revolver and I know how to use it."

Davidson said authoritatively, "Now with all that resolved, let's decide on dinner and drinks."

Richard agreed, "Good idea, John." Then he turned to Tanya, "Tanya, the security you provide is truly comforting. I don't know when I've ever had a more competent – or beautiful – protector."

Tanya got a serious look on her face, "Dr. Richards, don't let my looks deceive you. I'm tough and authorized to kill without asking questions if anyone under my protection is threatened. My protection tonight includes you."

With a matching serious look, Richards said, "Tanya, I'm impressed, but please call me Don."

Tanya grinned, "OK, Don, but just remember why I'm here. To protect you life."

Richards smiled, "OK, Tanya, but now I would like to have a Navy Grog. How about you?"

Tanya replied coolly, "I'm sorry, but I don't drink while on duty. I'll take Schweppes Tonic with lime. They can serve it in a Navy Grog type glass."

Just then a Polynesian clad waitress appeared to take their orders. Davidson ordered for the group, "Miss, two Navy Grogs and a Schweppes Tonic with lime, in a Navy Grog glass. We'll have the assortment of Polynesian tidbits for hors d'oeuvres. Then bring us steak and lobster with all the Polynesian fixings.

The waitress responded, "Sir, that's an excellent choice. I'm sure you will enjoy that. Your drinks and Polynesian tidbits will be right here."

The Polynesian feast was a true delight. The two men ordered refills for their rum drinks. Both were glad to have the delightful company of their Secret Service agent, Tanya During dinner, Davidson reported he had a message when he returned to his office that the NASA Administrator had called the President and had endorsed the European option.

As they were leaving, and while Davidson was busy paying the bill with his credit card, Tanya leaned over and whispered in Richard's ear, "Don, with those three Navy Grogs you drank, you're going to need *special protection* tonight. I'll be up to your room 2014 just as soon as I get Davidson safely home to his Georgetown townhouse. See you in about 40 minutes."

Richards' speech was slightly slurred after the three potent rum drinks, "I do need help tonight. Knock SS in Morse code so I'll know it's you, not a terrorist."

"OK, SS is the code!"

Richards returned to his room, took a shower, climbed into bed, and started to read the *Wall Street Journal* he had picked up in the lobby. He heard a knock on the door, dot dot dot, a short space, dot, dot, dot – the Morse code for SS. He jumped up, opened the door, and the beautiful Tanya walked in. She put her revolver on the night table, quickly undressed and slipped into bed. They enjoyed a fantastic hour until falling into a relaxed sleep.

At six am, Tanya rolled over, kissed Richards goodbye, whispered, "Thanks for a fantastic time in bed. It helps relieve the tension of being a Secret Service agent. I've got to get to work now. Be careful!"

Chapter 48

Oval Office

A government limousine picked up Richards at the entrance to the Washington Hilton Hotel at 8:30 am. Richards was surprised to find Davidson in the back seat. "Good morning, John. I thought you would be in your office waiting for me."

"I had quite a headache from all those Navy Grogs at Trader Vic's last night. I'm running a little behind so I decided I better have my driver pick you up on the way in from Georgetown."

The chauffer expertly steered through the early morning Washington traffic. Richards was surprised that the limousine entered the main gate of the White House rather than pulling up to the old White House Annex building as usual.

Richards asked, with a note of curiosity in his voice, "Where is our meeting this morning, John? I assumed it was going to be in your office."

Davidson smiled, "No, Don, not this time. There's been an escalation of level. We're meeting in the main White House today."

Richards followed Davidson into the entrance of the White House. The guard smiled recognition of Davidson and waved the two men inside the building. As Richards walked through the corridors of this world wide symbol of American power, he thought of how many times he had seen either a picture or a cartoon of the White House in the news media. It was a benevolent symbol for the friends of America, but a malevolent one for the enemies and detractors of America. Richards thoughts were interrupted by their arrival at Mary Jane's desk.

She looked up, "Good morning, Dr. Davidson. And you must be Dr. Richards. Please go right in. The President is ready to see you."

Richards was amazed. He had no idea their meeting was with the President himself. The two entered the Oval Office. The President was sitting behind his big desk signing papers being handed to him by one of the presidential assistants.

The President looked up, smiled, stood up, and said, "You must be Dr. Richards." He extended his hand and Richards approached him and shook his hand. The President continued, "Looks like we have a mess with the situation on the Space Shuttle, but you've been doing a terrific job to straighten it out, Don. Believe me, I appreciate your efforts."

Richards was extremely flattered by the President's comments, "Mr. President, I am trying to do my best. The most urgent matter now is to get the President of the EEC to sign the approval for an October rescue launch of the European shuttle."

"That's what I understand from Dr. Davidson and the NASA Administrator. Mr. Lopez is going to use this emergency to extract a little political *blood* from Uncle Sam. Well, let me just say, I'm not too proud of what my predecessors did before I took office: bombing Damascus and launching a trade war against the EEC. But I'm mad as hell that Lopez would pick this issue to try to blackmail us into an agreement under pressure."

Richards smiled sympathetically, "Mr. President, I can't imagine the EEC would withhold a humane rescue of those twenty astronauts on the Space Shuttle for political reasons. After all, they agreed to launch in March!"

The president laughed out loud, "Don, being a scientist, you probably don't realize how nasty politics can get. The situation has escalated since March. Now there are both Russians and Americans up there. Mr. Lopez now views the situation as one of political opportunity. He hopes to make some *points* before saying yes. Don't worry, he *will* say yes."

Davidson asked, "Mr. President, are there any questions we can answer about the rescue situation?"

"No, John. I believe I understand the situation clearly. We have enough life support up on the Space Station to last through November. The Europeans have the capability to launch their shuttle in October. Now, the only matter left is for me to call Mr. Lopez and get him to sign the launch approval. Right?"

Davidson replied, "That's an accurate summary of the situation, Mr. President."

The President stated confidently, "I wanted you two scientists to be present while I call Mr. Lopez in case some technical question comes up. I can handle the political end. Mary Jane has already checked with Lopez's office. He is ready to receive my call. She's placing the call now."

Mary Jane's voice sounded on the President's speaker phone, "Mr. President, I have President Lopez on the line."

The President pushed the flashing light on his phone and pressed the button so he was communicating with his speaker phone. He said in his deep baritone voice, "Good evening, President Lopez. This is Jack Williamson calling from the White House here in Washington."

"And good morning to you, Mr. President. What can I do for you?"

Irritation showed in the President's voice, "President Lopez, you know exactly why I'm calling. I want you to approve the launch of the European shuttle to rescue the seventeen Americans and three Russians up there on our Space Station!"

López replied, "But, Mr. President, you know there are some important open issues between the EEC and the USA. There's the matter of consultation with your European allies before you attack countries outside the area – and there is the matter of the trade war that has broken out because of your country's protectionist policies."

The President, speaking very forcefully now, replied, "President Lopez, I realize there are some open issues between the EEC and the US, but certainly you're not going to couple these issues with your approval of this humane rescue mission. Are you?"

Lopez replied, "Mr. President, we in the EEC believe this is an opportune time to resolve these festering issues. Don't you agree?"

The President replied firmly and calmly, "President Lopez, If you insist on coupling this humane rescue mission with other political questions, I will tell you what I will do."

"What, Mr. President? Agree to resolve the open issues?"

"No! Premier Gorbachev and I will hold a joint television press conference. There should be at least a half billion people in the world who would watch this unique press conference, including 200 million people in Europe. We will denounce you on world television as being a political opportunist. How long do you think you'll remain president of the EEC?"

López, his voice betraying his weakening resolve, responded, "But, how can we resolve these open issues. They are very important to us Europeans."

The President sensed he was winning. "President López, these issues are very important to me as well. The resolution of them is very high on my international political agenda. But I must absolutely insist that agreement on these issues not be coupled with your agreement to rescue the twenty human beings lost in space."

López responded, "All right, Mr. President. I agree to approve the rescue launch using the European shuttle. The launch will be sometime in October. The European Space Council must decide on the exact date. Now, I would like to see you move in the direction of resolving the open issues."

The President smiled happily, "I greatly appreciate your approval of the rescue launch. I'm sure Premier Gorbachev will endorse your humane decision as well. Now, as far as the other open issues between the US and the EEC are concerned, I will instruct my Secretary of State to set up a meeting with you within the next thirty days to resolve these issues amicably. Thank you, President Lopez."

Thank you, Mr. President. I am pleased that the European Community can rescue the astronauts and cosmonauts of the world's two superpowers. I will advise the European Space Council to meet with your delegate next week to set the exact launch date."

"My delegate is Dr. Richards, who is here with me now. He will meet with your Space Council in Toulouse next Monday, if that date is OK."

"Dr. Dubois, chairman of the Space Council, is here with me. That date is fine. Dr. Richards will be welcome in Toulouse. Goodbye, Mr. President."

"Goodbye, President López."

The President rose from his desk, turned to face Richards and Davidson, grinned widely, and said, "Gentlemen! That's how international politics works! Have a good trip to Toulouse, Don."

Chapter 49

Life on the Space Station

It was Thursday, the 14th of August 1992. Barbara Rosen was on duty in the Space Station's communications control center. She received a call from NASA Houston. Gus Ford said, "Barbara, Gus here in Houston. We're going to have a video teleconference in thirty minutes. Don Richards is back in California after three days in Washington and he's going to update everyone on the status of the rescue mission."

"OK, Gus. We're anxious to hear how things are working out. It's pretty crowded up here now with so many people floating around. I'll try to round up everyone for the meeting."

It had been five and a half months since the first of the chain of space failures.   The population of the Space Station had doubled. Ten of the twenty were there because of the three in-orbit failures of the one Russian and two American shuttles. In the four days since the latest failure, life had begun to settle down into a routine. Barbara now had three part time lovers: Gusev, Rogers, and Johnson, the three shuttle commanders whose disabled crafts were floating helplessly outside, tethered to the station.   The shuttle community was relieved the European shuttle was technically capable of rescuing them.   There was a growing tension, an uneasiness, that they didn't have official word of the approval of the European shuttle launch, just the unofficial word from Dr. Dubois that it was possible to launch in October. So there was unusually high interest in the upcoming video teleconference. Everyone on the Space Station wanted to be there.

Barbara called all the work stations and announced the conference was scheduled for 8:30 am, California time. When she reached General Robbins, he surprised her by announcing, "Barbara, we have to limit the attendance at this video teleconference to just you and me and the three shuttle commanders: Johnson, Rogers, and Gusev." He always mentioned the three in that order, the order of their seniority of residence on the Station.

Barbara protested, "But, General Robbins, everyone would like to hear first hand what's happening with the rescue!"

She resorted to his formal title instead of his first name when she wanted a concession from him. It usually worked, but this time he replied, "Barbara, that is my final answer. Just the five of us. Everyone else has to stay on duty."

When Barbara explained Robbins' restriction of attendance to the three shuttle commanders, who were talking about flying while slurping from the coffee nipples in the dining room, they were all three furious. They believed everyone should be allowed to come to the meeting. They quickly voted Billie Joe to be their spokesman to protest Robbins' decision.

Colonel Gusev flatly stated, "Billie Joe, tell the general we three refuse to come to the meeting unless he allows the rest of the crew to come also!"

Johnson answered, "OK, Georgi. That's a good idea. Let me go talk to the old geezer now. Sometimes he can really be stubborn over nothing."

Johnson floated over to Robbins cabin and knocked on the door. Robbins yelled, "Please enter!"

Johnson floated into Robbins large private cabin, "Jack, I understand you're restricting attendance at the teleconference meeting."

"That's right, Billie Joe. Just you three shuttle commanders, my deputy, Barbara Rosen, and me. Everyone else should attend to their duties."

"I've been selected to speak for the shuttle commanders. We don't think that's right, Jack. Everyone is worried about what's going to happen. They have a right to attend the meeting. If everyone isn't invited, then we three shuttle commanders won't come either. We're no better than they are."

Robbins was surprised by this confrontation. He backed down with a compromise, "Well, OK. I'm willing to be adaptable, but someone has to stand emergency watch. What if something happened and we had a breakdown and the Station began to tumble? We'd be in a hell of a mess."

"OK, Jack. We'll draw straws to see who stands emergency watch. Is that fair?"

"Sure. I'll buy that. Just make sure the crew member selected knows what to do!"

"Jack, everyone on the Station knows the emergency procedures. Their lives might depend on them!"

Billie Joe hurried back to the dining room and announced, "General Robbins agreed everyone could attend, except we have to choose someone to be on emergency duty."

Rogers spoke up, "Oh, hell, I'll volunteer. I'm sure everything's going to be OK anyway. Just fill me in later on what happened."

Barbara put her arm around Rogers, pulled him close to her, and breathed quietly in his ear, "That's mighty nice of you, Rich. Just for that, you get an extra night in my cabin this week."

All three shuttle commanders guffawed!

Barbara went back to the communications control center and announced on the Station broadcast system, "Everyone is invited to the Control Center for a video teleconference that begins in five minutes. Colonel Richard Rogers will be on emergency duty watch during the meeting."

Everyone squeezed into the control center and crowded around the video screens showing Baikonur, Washington, DC, Novosibirsk, Houston, and Richards in the UAC conference room in Irvine, California.

Richards opened the meeting by saying, "I know you are all anxious to hear the official word on the rescue launch. I'm pleased to announce that I met with President Williamson in the White House yesterday. While I was there the President talked directly to Mr. Lopez, president of the EEC. President Lopez agreed to approve the rescue launch of the European space shuttle to save our twenty colleagues stranded on the Space Station. The exact date hasn't been set yet, but it will be in October sometime. I am scheduled to meet with the European Space Council in Toulouse next Monday morning and the launch date will be set at that time."

A cheer went up in the Space Station control center from the nineteen crew members crowded around Richards' image.

Richards added, "We'll set up a video teleconference from Toulouse, so you can all hear what the exact launch date will be."

General Robbins responded, "Dr. Richards, on behalf of my brave American and Russian crew up here on the Space Station, thanks for a job well done. Our thanks also go out to President Williamson and President Lopez for making the European shuttle launch possible."

There were a few intellectual questions from scientific members of the vast audience and few more laudatory speeches similar to General Robbins' from people who wanted to collect some attention to themselves. With that, the meeting broke up.

Barbara wafted by Gusev, "Georgi, let's float over to my cabin now and celebrate the official word with a little sex. OK?"

Georgi replied, smiling broadly, "You talked me into it, you smooth talking beauty!"

Chapter 50

Aerospatiale in Toulouse

The captain of the non-stop Air France flight from Los Angeles to Paris announced in French and then in English, "Ladies and Gentlemen, we will be landing at Charles De Gaulle Airport in ten minutes. There are some scattered thunderstorms this morning near Paris. Otherwise, the weather is warm and clear. It is 23 degrees centigrade. Please fasten your seat belts.

The announcement woke Richards from his deep slumber. He was so behind on sleep that he had slept right through the breakfast service. The last week, flying first from Novosibirsk to Los Angeles and then a round trip to Washington, had left his body confused as to what time zone it was in. Now, he was arriving in Paris where the time difference was nine hours later than Los Angeles. He looked at his watch. It was just before 4 pm Paris time on Saturday the sixteenth of August. It had been almost 11 hours since the jumbo jet took off from Los Angeles last night. He had a 5:30 connecting flight to Toulouse. Richards had called Dr. Dubois Friday morning to tell him of his arrival time in Toulouse. Dubois had told him Dr. Juanita Gonzalez, who happened to be in his office when Richards phoned, would pick him up at the airport. She was staying in the Toulouse Grand Hotel where Richards also had reservations.

The Air France 747 landed just after 4 pm. Richards quickly cleared passport control and customs. He took the airline bus to the domestic terminal at De Gaulle and caught his Toulouse flight. The French airliner landed at Toulouse at 6:45, a little late due to departure delays in Paris.

Richards exited the plane onto the tarmac. He was happy to see the beautiful, sun tanned Juanita Gonzalez waiting for him just outside the exit gate. He rushed over and kissed her on both cheeks, in the Spanish style.

She turned her head so their lips met and kissed him passionately. "Oh, Don, I've really missed you. It's been four months since I last saw you."

Richards replied happily, "It's great to be back with you, Juanita. I understand we are both staying in the Grand Hotel again."

Juanita smiled, "Yes, here's your key. I've already checked you in. We have adjoining rooms again. We won't be using one of the beds, will we?"

Richards squeezed her hand as they started walking toward the exit leading to the parking lot, "No, Juanita, dear. We only need one 'matrimonio cama'."

Juanita exclaimed happily, "Oh, you're learning Spanish. Good, because we'll be going to my office in Malaga Tuesday."

"Why in the world do we have to go to Malaga?"

They continued across the street to the parking lot where Juanita's rental car was parked. She replied, "We need a specification for the rendezvous software module I'm writing. Dr. Dubois said you should review the preliminary spec and software on site in Malaga where I'm working on it."

As they walked up to her Hertz car, Richards asked, "Why is it so important to review the rendezvous software?"

"The rendezvous and docking software is the only new software needed for the rescue mission. It shows up on the PERT chart as time critical. I believe you Americans call it the 'long pole in the tent'! Anyway, Dr. Dubois wants to make sure there's no problem with the software spec."

Climbing into Juanita's car, Richards replied, "Sounds like a good investment of my time. We can't afford to have any schedule slips."

Juanita laughed as she started up the car, "Enough of business talk until Monday. You need a European type weekend – relaxed. I think you Americans don't spend enough time relaxing. Dr. Dubois mentioned your recent travels: Novosibirsk last Sunday, Tuesday in Washington, DC, Los Angeles yesterday, Toulouse today!"

"You are so right, Juanita! Too much dashing around, but, because of the failure of the Russian shuttle, I'm afraid it's all necessary. I'm in the hot seat to make sure the rescue comes off.

We've got so many people stranded up there on the Space Station now: seventeen Americans and three Russians."

Juanita answered sympathetically while heading out of the parking lot, "I know, Don. You are under a lot of pressure. That's why you need a restful weekend."

"I'm ready for that!"

Juanita pulled up in front of the Grand Hotel in the center of Toulouse some twenty minutes later. As they walked into the lobby, Juanita said, "The registration desk needs your passport. I didn't remember the number when I registered you."

Richards took care of this minor task and the two took the elevator to the fifth floor. Juanita was in room 518 and Richards was next door in 516. At Richards' door, Juanita said, "Don, you go in and open the connecting door. I'll do the same on my side."

Moments later the doors were open. Richards took Juanita into his arms, "How about a nap before dinner?"

Juanita looked at her watch, "It's 7 now. I'll call the L'Orient Restaurant and make reservations for 9. It's the only three star restaurant in Toulouse. It's very nice"

Richards liked the suggestion. They undressed and climbed into the double bed in her room. Richards kissed her warmly and she kissed him back. What they did next was hidden under the covers. They soon dropped into an entwined sleep.

Richards woke up at 8:30 pm. Juanita was already up, showered and almost dressed. Richards quickly showered and dressed. The L'Orient Restaurant was only a short walk from their hotel. Their route took them along the canal that flowed through Toulouse and they stopped a short while to watch the boats moored there.

The headwaiter showed them to their table for two, set with linen and silver, with a vase of red roses. The ambience of the restaurant was exquisite and very French. Richards asked the waiter to bring a bottle of Mumms Champagne to enjoy instead of the usual cocktails before dinner. While the pair were deciding on their gastronomic delights from the long menu, they sipped their bubbly champagne from ice cold glasses. They both settled for white flounder cooked in a delicate lemon sauce for the main course.

As they finished their dessert of strawberries with fresh, thick 'creme chantilly,' Richards commented, "I can see why L'Orient rates three stars. The food here is out of this world."

"Don, enjoy these expensive French restaurants while we're in Toulouse this weekend. Next week, you're going to stay in my 'piso' in Malaga and I'm going to cook at home for you, using the fresh vegetables, fruit and fish available in my ancient city."

Richards reached for Juanita's hand, kissed it, "Juanita, I'm sure your home cooked meals will be better than a five star restaurant!"

But in France, three stars is the maximum!"

"Yes, I know."

They had Tia Maria liqueur with their after dinner coffee. They strolled back to their hotel and had a reprise of their earlier activities.

It was almost 10 when Richards and Juanita woke up Sunday morning. They decided to have a leisurely continental breakfast served in their room. While eating, Juanita suggested, "It's such a beautiful day, let's drive over to Carcassonne and visit the fortified medieval city there. It's only about an hour's drive on the autopista from here."

"That sounds great. I like to wander around in ancient buildings. The oldest things in the US are 200 years old, except for some Indian ruins."

Soon they were driving out of the city and onto the toll road to Carcassonne, some 90 kilometers southeast of Toulouse. They left the toll road and followed the signs to the medieval city. Richards was fascinated by the old community which was still functioning, with shops and residents. They walked all around the restored city and its ancient fortifications, stopping for a late lunch at a sidewalk café.

Then they headed back to Toulouse and spent the rest of the afternoon strolling through the beautiful Toulousain Park on an island in the Garonne River. That night, Richards and Juanita had dinner in the Grand Hotel and retired to their connecting rooms for a delightful evening and night together. Richards had caught up on his sleep, relaxed from his hectic racing from one space shuttle site to another, and was ready to start again overseeing the problems associated with trying to rescue the twenty space prisoners.

Monday morning, Richards and Juanita met the other out-of-town members of the European Space Council for breakfast in the Grand Hotel dining room.   Dr. Heinz Zinn was there from Munchen, Professor Dr. Tom Shepherd from Milton Keynes, UK, and Dr. Enrique Rodriguez from Madrid.   Professor Shepherd invited the group to ride to the meeting in his Jaguar sedan. Of course everyone agreed to enjoy the luxury of the professor's car which he had driven from England via the ferry across the English Channel from Dover to Calais. The beautiful white machine was parked near the front entrance to the hotel. They all climbed in the right hand drive auto and Shepherd drove to the Aerospatiale plant, following the banks of the Garonne River.

At the guard gate, Professor Shepherd showed his Space Council ID badge and the guard waved the Jaguar inside and directed them to the visitors' parking next to the building where the meeting was to be held. Dr. Dubois greeted the group in the lobby and handed Richards his photo identity badge, the same badge he had used during his visit in the Spring. Dubois led all the visitors up to the conference room full of video links. By pre-arrangement, there were links with NASA Houston, NASA Headquarters, the Space Station, and the Russian Space Institute in Novosibirsk.

Dr. Dubois opened the meeting with a formal prepared statement which he read in French.   Two women simultaneous translators changed his message into English and into Russian for the wide spread audience, "Ladies and Gentlemen, I am pleased to announce that the EEC President Lopez has approved the launch of the European space shuttle to rescue our colleagues lost in space on the US Space Station. The problem which caused the loss of the Ariane III launcher on the first of April has been fixed. It was necessary for us to change the elements which used the defective Japanese steel. A subsequent test firing has been accomplished to prove that the fix was satisfactory.

"Now for the launch date that you've all been waiting for. The Technical Committee of the European Space Council, which consists of myself, Dr. Dubois of Aerospatiale, as Chairman;

Professor Dr. Tom Shepherd of the Cranfield Institute in the UK; Dr. Heinz Zinn of Siemens in München; Dr. Enrique Rodriguez of Iber Avion Spacio in Madrid; and Professora Dr. Juanita Gonzalez of Fujitsu España in Malaga, had our meeting last Saturday morning to decide on the exact launch date. I must be honest with you. We uncovered one threat to a launch date in October. It is one of the key software modules required for the rescue mission, one that we don't normally require for our own shuttle missions."

The tension had been building among those on the Space Station during Dubois' long statement until finally Barbara Rosen couldn't stand it any longer and interrupted impatiently, "Dr. Dubois, this is Dr. Rosen up on the Space Station. Can you just tell us when the launch date is? Are you going to be able to launch in October or not?"

Dr. Dubois was visibly upset about this interruption of his prepared statement. He regained his composure and replied, "Dr. Rosen, if you will be patient for just a few more moments, I'll answer the question. But first, I must describe the schedule threat."

Barbara Rosen, with exasperation in her voice, said, "OK, but please hurry with the bottom line. We twenty souls up here are on pins and needles to hear the launch date."

Dubois cleared his throat and then said, "Now, if I may continue, -- as I just stated before Dr. Rosen's outburst, we, the Technical Committee of the ESC, met Saturday and identified a software threat to the launch date. The rendezvous and docking software modules to permit our shuttle to meet your Space Station in orbit and then to dock with it, have not been written and verified yet. Our Technical Committee member, Professora Dr. Gonzalez, is responsible for this software and has a preliminary specification for the required rendezvous/docking software module. I am going to ask Dr. Richards to spend the rest of the week in Dr. Gonzalez' office in Malaga preparing the final specifications for this critical module. Assuming there are no unforeseen problems with the development of this rendezvous/docking software module – we call it the RDSM – then we can commit to a launch date of 12 October 1992."

Barbara Rosen was still unsure of Dr. Dubois' meaning. She quizzed him, "Dr. Dubois, please make sure I understand. Is the bottom line the twelfth of October? Is that the launch date or isn't it?"

"Yes, Dr. Rosen. The twelfth of October is the launch date!"

A yelp of joy rose from the crew on the Space Station. General Robbins responded to Dubois' prepared statement and launch date commitment, "Dr. Dubois, this is General Robbins, commander of the Space Station. On behalf of my American and Russian colleagues up here on the Space Station, we would like to thank you and the EEC for committing to this launch date of twelve October. We can certainly breathe easier up here. And, Sir, one other very important point – please bring another three or four months' expendables during your first rescue launch, for safety and back-up."

Dubois responded, "Yes, General Robbins. We plan to include expendables on each rescue mission. We will work out the exact details of the expendable cargo with Dr. Richards during our meeting with him today here in Toulouse."

Robbins added, "One other important point, Sir. I have decided that all twenty of the people on the Space Station will be returning to Earth during your rescue missions. The Station crew was originally scheduled to remain up here only a year, a date which has long since passed. We will have a fresh crew of four brought up on your last rescue mission to act as a caretaker crew. We need to end up with enough expendables for at least nine months for the caretaker crew to live up here."

Gus Ford from NASA broke in, "Yes, Dr. Dubois. NASA has officially approved General Robbins' request to send up a fresh caretaker crew. That item should be part of your mission planning."

Dr. Dubois relied, "I see no problem in complying with this new requirement. Be assured, your request will be incorporated in our mission planning."

Richards spoke up, "Gus Ford and General Robbins, I would just like to say that I'm sure Dr. Gonzalez and I will be able to finish the rendezvous and docking software spec this next week. Dr. Gonzalez assures me she will be able to finish coding and validating the software if she has a good specification. Fortunately, along with all the stuff I carried over here in my briefcase, I brought the rendezvous/docking software listing and spec for the US Space Shuttle. That should be a great help to Dr. Gonzalez. Right, Juanita?"

"Yes, Don. I've had a few minutes to look at the documents you brought. I am confident this software can be completed before the end of September now. That gives us a two week schedule pad."

General Robbins said, "Dr. Richards and Dr. Gonzalez, your words are comforting."

Dr. Dubois interrupted, "As program director of the European Space Shuttle, I would like to warn you that what you have heard from Doctors Richards and Gonzalez is not official, just their opinions." He then formally announced the end of the teleconference meeting.

Dr. Dubois turned to the two software experts, "I would like to have the two of you meet with me here in Toulouse a week from today to review your progress on the program for this new software module we need for the rescue."

The two nodded their agreement.

Chapter 51

Software in Málaga

The captain of the Iberia Airlines jetliner announced, first in Spanish and then in English, "Ladies and Gentlemen, please fasten your seat belts for our approach and landing into the beautiful city of Malaga on the Costa del Sol. The temperature is 28 degrees centigrade and the weather is crystal clear. Thank you for flying Iberia and have a nice stay on the Costa del Sol."

Richards looked out the window by his seat for his first sight of the blue Mediterranean Sea and the spectacular coastline near the city of Malaga. The jetliner passed over the hills east of the city, descended over the Mediterranean Sea, and then turned west for the straight in approach to the long runway 25 at the Malaga International Airport. Juanita pointed out the port area, "My piso is near the port over there overlooking the playa and the mar."

Richards looked where she was pointing, "What a beautiful view you must have from your apartment!"

The jet landed just after 4 pm Tuesday, the 19th of August. It taxied up to the terminal and Richards and Juanita were among the first passengers off the aircraft. They each had one small carry-on bag and a briefcase so they quickly cleared customs and took the airport bus to downtown Malaga where Juanita lived within walking distance of the end of the bus line. Twenty five minutes later they exited the bus in front of the centuries old Malaga Cathedral.

Juanita said, "This famous Catedral de Malaga was built beginning in 1528, some 36 years after Columbus sailed from Benalmadena Costa, just west of here, to America."

Don answered, "I'd like to see it sometime. I'll bet it's beautiful inside."

"It is. Maybe we can attend Sunday Mass on the way to the airport. We will be catching the bus right here next Sunday morning as the first step on our return to Toulouse."

"Good idea. I'd like that, Juanita."

Juanita led Richards past the Palacio Hotel to the beautiful Paseo del Parque – a broad avenue with wide tree-shaded tile sidewalks on either side. Paralleling the more southerly sidewalk was a large park filled with subtropical plantings. They walked to the end of the park to the Plaza del General Torrijos, which featured a beautiful, large fountain in the center. They crossed here to the other side of the Paseo del Parque.

Juanita pointed out the ancient Gibralfaro, an old fortified edifice on top of the high hill above Malaga. She told Richards it was built from 1333 to 1354 by the Moors, who occupied this part of Spain during the first millennia after Christ. Lower down the mountain, overlooking the port of Malaga, was the exotic Alcazaba, a palace constructed by the Berber king Badis of Granada, from 1052 to 1063.

Juanita explained, "This is considered the recent history of Malaga. Some one thousand years before Christ, Malaga was founded by the seagoing people from Tyre on the coast of Lebanon. This city which became a center of trade on the Mediterranean Sea."

They continued walking along the street leading to her nearby apartment. Richards responded, "What an old city! More than 3000 years old!"

"Right, Don. After the people from Tyre founded the city, the Phoenicians came, and then the Cartegenians. Then the Romans conquered Malaga from the Cartegenians. There are ruins of an old Roman theater near the Alcazaba."

"Juanita, you're a real historian!"

"When you live a city as memorable as Malaga, you naturally become interested in its history."

Soon the pair arrived at the high rise apartment building where Juanita lived. As they entered the lobby they were greeted by the portero, or doorman, "Buenos tardes, Dona Juanita. Welcome back from Francia."

"Hola. Buenos tardes, Francisco. Por favor, encontras mi amigo, Senor Doctor Don Richards."

Francisco responded happily, "Hola, Don Richards. Welcome to Malaga. I hope you enjoy our Costa del Sol."

"Thank you, Francisco. I'm sure I will."

The pair took the elevator to the tenth floor where Juanita led Richards into her luxurious four bedroom flat.   The master bedroom and the living room opened onto a marble floored patio-balcony with a spectacular view of the blue Mediterranean Sea and the beaches of Malaga extending to the east of the port. The walls were paneled in richly grained wood. The floors were all tiled in marble, except the bedrooms which had carpets.

Richards was amazed at the beauty and luxury of the apartment. He asked, "If you don't mind my asking, how much rent do you pay for this flat, Juanita?"

"No, I don't mind. I don't rent it. I bought it for 3,500,000 pesetas, or about 25,000 US dollars. But other apartments similar to mine are rented to tenants in this building and cost about 50,000 pesetas per month, or about 350 US dollars per month."

Richards got a surprised look on his face. "Wow! In Newport, California, a flat or condominium like this would cost 750,000 US dollars and would rent for about 1500 or 2000 US dollars a month!"

Juanita laughed, "We Malaguenos can't even conceive of such costs, Don. Maybe you should move to Espana."

"Maybe I should."

After Don and Juanita unpacked their bags, Juanita said, "We should go to my office now and get our work for the weekend organized."

Richards glanced at his watch, saw that it was just after 4 pm. "What are your work hours here in Málaga anyway?"

"We work in the morning from 10 am to 1:30. We then take time off for lunch and a siesta and return to work from 4 to 8 pm. We usually have dinner about 11 pm."

"That's quite a different schedule.   But it sounds nice and relaxed."

Juanita laughed, "Don, a study by our National Health Institute showed people who sleep twice a day live longer. That means, all factors being the same, espanoles should live longer than norteamericanos."

"You're probably right. Where is your office?"

"It's just around the corner on Avenida Canovas del Castillo, a couple of blocks away. We walked right by it getting to my piso.

I was so busy explaining the history of Malaga I forgot to show it to you."

"Well, first things first. Let's go. I'll bring the rendezvous software listing and spec."

"Good idea. Those documents could save a lot of time in developing my new rendezvous/docking software. I'll look at them closely when we get to the office."

They left the piso, took the elevator down to the ground level and walked over to Juanita's office. As they walked along, she explained the main Fujitsu España, S.A., plant was near the airport, but her software development office was here in the center of the city, close to her academic office at the El Ejido (college) about two kilometers to the north. She added, "This central location for the software office is convenient for me and it makes it easier to hire good software people. They prefer the city surroundings to the factory environment of the main plant."

"How many employees do you have?"

"Twenty here, doing our shuttle software. Usually five are off-site at Aerospatiale in Toulouse or at Iber Avion Spacio in Madrid, performing software integration testing. But here is where the creative work takes place."

Juanita led Richards back to her smallish but beautifully furnished office where she had several lovely paintings of scenes of the sea, mountains, and pastorals of the Andalusian area of which Malaga is the capital. She had a computer terminal with a color video monitor and separate keyboard on her modernistic desk. There was a printer on a table next to her desk connected to the computer.

Richards exclaimed, "This office has everything needed for a software person to create software."

Juanita got a take-charge attitude, "Don, let me see the software listing. I have an idea."

She studied the long computer printout Richards handed her, "It looks to me as though we can use this software code 'as is' in my rendezvous/docking software. You used the programming language Jovial. We use the language Pascal. Fortunately, I have a Jovial to Pascal translator program. Look. We can really speed up the process."

Richards was amazed at Juanita's rapid grasp of the complex ten page computer program on the printout. He asked, "How can you speed it up?"

Juanita smiled, "See that little gadget connected to my computer terminal?"

Richards looked at it carefully, "Yes, it looks like a wand connected to a cord."

"That's what it is. A wand for reading printed matter and entering it into the computer memory. I can use it to scan your software listing and soon we'll have the listing in my computer."

She picked up the wand, touched it to the paper, running it along the words on the listing document line-by-line, and, as if by magic, each line of software code was printed out on the screen of her computer terminal. The complete document that Richards brought with the software program that controlled rendezvous and docking procedures of the US space shuttle with the Space Station was entered into Juanita's computer.

Juanita said, "Now, let me run a check to make sure the 'magic wand' read your program correctly."

She pushed a few keys on her keyboard and then scanned the document a second time. She announced, "The check program says it's right. Now to run the translation program to translate the Jovial language of your computer into the Pascal language of my computer. This will take some time, but it's automatic so after I get the computer started on the translation we'll leave the machine to do it's work and I'll give you a tour of my software development facility."

Juanita pushed a few keys again, and then announced, "I now have Pedro the Computer working on the translation. Let's tour."

Juanita led Richards through the facility, stopping briefly at each software engineer's office to introduce Richards to her staff. The staff was roughly half and half female/male. Everyone was dressed in informal clothes. Most of the men had beards and wore sandals. The women were unusually beautiful, most with long hair. They were dressed mainly in colorful, tight fitting pants that showed off their curves in a most revealing fashion. Each of the staff members had a computer terminal on his or her desk.

Next, Juanita led Richards into a large laboratory which had a mock-up of the European space shuttle cockpit with all of its fancy controls and displays.   Like the Russian shuttle, the European shuttle also had color TV video displays for telling the pilot what to do and what the shuttle was doing.   In front of the cockpit was a rack full of four flight computers with a mass of cabling leading to the cockpit.   The room had a large Fujitsu computer with cables leading to the flight computers.   Richards commented, "This looks like a simulation laboratory."

Juanita smiled proudly, "Yes, Don.   That's exactly what it is. Here we use the large Fujitsu computer to simulate or play like it is the shuttle vehicle in flight.   It was built so the flight displays in the cockpit look exactly like they would during an actual flight of the shuttle."

Richards interrupted, "And the four flight computers over there -- they are for checking out your flight software?"

"Exactly, Don.   We use four computers on our shuttle.   That way we can have three computers fail and it will still fly.   It's worked great so far.   Anyway, this laboratory is where we will check out the rendezvous/docking software as soon as we have it finished.   After we finish eliminating all the bugs we can find, then we deliver it to Aerospatiale in Toulouse where it will be loaded into the actual shuttle computer and tested more thoroughly with the actual European shuttle spacecraft."

Juanita continued showing Richards the rest of the facility and then they went back to her office.   She looked at the computer terminal and called out, "Voila!   The translation from Jovial to Pascal language is complete.   Now to see if there are any errors in the translation.   I have a program that checks for syntax errors – like grammar errors – and fixes any it finds.   Let me get it started."

She spent a few more minutes at her computer terminal pushing keys, and then said again, "Voilà!   Now, while Pedro the Computer is working, let's take a break and have coffee con leche."

She led Richards to an attractive lunch room near her office where the software employees prepared snacks and had coffee or beer during their work breaks.   As they sat down to enjoy a cup of hot coffee with hot milk, Juanita asked, "Tell me, Don, if we already have the rendezvous/docking program in the computer and it works, why do we need to write a spec?"

Richards stammered, "Well, Juanita, in the US we always write a computer spec before we write the software code. That way, we know what the software program should do.

Juanita persisted, "Just because its done that way in the US doesn't mean we have to do it that way. Besides, if this Pascal language version of the program works, it will be the same as the one on your space shuttle. If we have to take a spec back to Dr. Dubois, why don't we use the same spec that was used to develop your program in the first place?"

Richards thought for a moment, smiled and nodded, "That's a very good idea, Juanita. I brought a copy of the US specs with me. It's here in my briefcase. And if you have to make some changes to the software to make it work, then we can change the spec to agree with those changes."

Juanita got very excited, "Guess what, Don?"

He looked at her curiously, "What, Juanita?"

She laughed, "I think we just saved over a month of the time needed to complete my rendezvous/docking software. I think we can take a working software module – not just the spec – with us when we return to Toulouse Sunday."

Richards caught the excitement of Juanita's brilliant idea for saving time. "If we can, that should convince even Dr. Dubois that there's no schedule threat to the 12 October launch date."

"You're right, Don. He's a real worry-wart. If I hand him a tape with the functioning software on it and say, *Now it's ready to integrate with the shuttle,* he will agree the schedule threat is gone."

Richards was getting really excited now. "Do you really think we can finish by Sunday?"

"I think we can finish Friday. Then you and I can spend a day at the Playa de Pedragalejo, swimming, sunning, and relaxing Saturday, like Malaguenos."

Richards responded, "Great, let's try to do it."

Juanita laughed again, "OK. Pedro the Computer should be finished checking the grammar errors now. Let's go see."

They hurried back to Juanita's office, both elated that they had eliminated the software schedule threat.

Juanita checked the computer screen on her desk, "Pedro was busy while we were gone. He tells me he found 103 errors and fixed all but two. He didn't know how to fix those two, but he knew where they were."

On the screen were two lines of computer code that Pedro knew were wrong. Juanita looked at them carefully, then said, "Of course! These semi-colons should have been colons. Voila. They're fixed now. Pedro is not too good on punctuation, sometimes."

Richards exclaimed, "You mean to tell me you have the complete computer program for rendezvous and docking translated into Pascal now?"

"Yes, Don. Now we have to see if it works. I can put a computer program in Pedro with a thousand test cases in it. These test cases cover a wide range of conditions that the shuttle may encounter while trying to find your Space Station. Let's put Pedro to work again. He's really slow at this. We'll have time for a stroll along the beach while he's working."

Juanita again pushed a few keys and said again, "Voila. Now Pedro is checking to see if the rendezvous and docking software really makes the shuttle find the Space Station. We can go now."

"Right. Why should we sit around worrying while Pedro's working?"

Richards and Juanita left the office building and headed south, back towards the beach in front of her piso. They strolled east along the broad Paseo Maritimo sidewalk that bordered the beautiful blue Mediterranean Sea. The seawall was dotted with young lovers enjoying their kissing games in the environment of the soft, cooling breezes from the sea. As Juanita and Richards strolled along, numerous joggers passed them by, panting and sweating with their late afternoon exercise.

After a half hour stroll, they returned to Juanita's office. She studied the screen on her computer and said, "I have a message from Pedro. He says the software works for all the test cases."

Richards smiled, "What's the next step? Certainly you're not through already!"

Juanita answered, "No, unfortunately. The next step is to load the software program into the flight simulation computer we saw in the laboratory. Then we get an engineer to act as the shuttle pilot. He will fly the simulation shuttle on ten practice rendezvous flights to see if it works. Since each rendezvous flight takes about one and a half hours, that's a little over two days work."

"And who is the pilot? You?"

Juanita laughed and said, "I can fly soaring planes, but not shuttles. One of my software engineers, Jose Espejo, will act as the pilot. I'll call him in now and explain what needs to be done."

Juanita called Jose on the intercom. He came to her office where she explained the task in rapid Spanish for about five minutes. Then she said, "Entiendes, Jose?"

"Si. Si. Hasta luego!" and Jose left for the laboratory.

Juanita told Don, "Jose understands what needs to be done and will run the first rendezvous simulation now. He thinks he can get one finished before quitting time."

"Great. Can we go and watch him fly the simulator?"

"Sure. It'll take him a few minutes to load the program into the flight computer and get everything going."

Richards and Juanita joined Jose in the simulation laboratory where they watched him 'fly' the first rendezvous and docking mission. Jose kept careful watch on the shuttle cockpit instruments during the intricate maneuvers which simulated the actual flight of the European shuttle as it adjusted its orbit to match up with the orbit of the simulated Space Station orbit.

Just before 8 pm José exclaimed, "It all works. The rendezvous and docking software worked perfectly on this test case."

Juanita turned to Richards and said, with a wide grin on her face, "Don, I think we've got it made! Now we merely have to check the other nine test cases using this simulator. Then we will have verified that the rendezvous/docking software works."

Richards beamed happily, "Looks like we are well along the way to eliminating the software schedule threat."

Juanita answered, "Yes, Don. The computer printout of the US shuttle software you brought was the key. You've saved over a month's time!"

Chapter 52

Final European Shuttle Launch Plans

Richards reached over and gently squeezed Juanita's hand as they leaned back in their first class seats. He gazed out the left window as the Iberia Airlines jet turned north toward Madrid. He watched the beach along the Paseo de Maritimo leading to the high rise apartment building where Juanita lived. He fondly remembered their five delicious nights of love making in her big matrimonio cama. He thought of the restful naps they had taken nude in the sun on her patio balcony during their afternoon siestas. The beautiful, late evening dinners she cooked using the fresh vegetables, fruits and fish they bought together in the Mercado Central lingered on in his memories of beautiful Malaga as the plane climbed up into the cloudless blue sky of southern Spain – the Andalusian Costa del Sol. They had celebrated finishing the rendezvous/docking software on Saturday by lying on the beach at Pedragalejo, a short three kilometer walk east from Juanita's piso. Every time they got too hot, they plunged into the cooling Mediterranean waters. Richards was relaxed, tanned, and happy with their personal relationship and with the professional accomplishments in Malaga.

Juanita turned to Richards, smiled happily, held up a small magnetic computer tape cartridge, "Here it is. The software program for rendezvous and docking is stored on this tape. We even have the specification that Dr. Dubois wanted stored on this tape. Remember how easy it was to prepare?"

"Yes, you just took the US spec I brought, entered it to your computer with your 'magic wand', spent some time editing it. Then, voila! You copied it onto that tape you have in your hand to carry to Dr. Dubois! For the spec we have a printed copy, too."

Juanita looked Richards directly in the eye, "Don, do you see how relaxing life in Europe can be – and still get a lot done?"

Richards laughed and replied, "Right. In the US we would have had a panic, around-the-clock effort for weeks to accomplish what we did – what you and your small technical team did – this one week. We even finished by siesta time on Friday."

"Yes, it was a good productive week, and so pleasurable. I will miss you when you return to the US next Tuesday."

Richards squeezed Juanita's hand, reached over and kissed her, "Juanita, I'll miss you – and your relaxed life style."

They arrived at the Aerospatiale plant in Toulouse at 8 am Monday the 25th of August. Juanita led Richards up to Dr. Dubois' office on the third floor. Dr. Dubois' secretary greeted them and escorted them into Dr. Dubois' comfortable office. She seated them in the corner on a couch facing a coffee table. Dr. Dubois was on the phone talking to the shuttle launch facility at the space center in Kourou in French Guiana. His secretary served Richards and Juanita coffee while they waited for the end of the phone call.

A few moments later, Dubois joined the pair in the sitting area, "That was our space center down in Guiana. They just had another successful launch of an Ariane III. That bodes well for our 12 October launch since we use that rocket. Well, did you two finish the specification for the rendezvous and docking software?"

Juanita grinned broadly, pulled the computer tape cartridge out of her pocket, "Jacques, we did better than that. We finished the software module and tested it on our simulator in Malaga. Everything works. The program is stored on this tape, all ready for installation on the European shuttle spacecraft here in Toulouse.

Richards added, "And for good measure, here's a print out of the specification as well. The spec is also on the tape."

Dubois got a dumbfounded look on his face, then recovered enough to ask, "How in the world did you finish the whole rendezvous/docking software module in one week? I thought it would take until the end of September?"

Juanita exclaimed happily, "We were able to adapt the listing of the rendezvous/docking software module for the US space shuttle that Don brought along with him."

Richards added, "The 'magic' software tools that Juanita had in her Malaga office did the trick. I was also amazed. But I witnessed the tests. It really works. Juanita and her software team are really talented and super efficient."

It finally sunk in to Dubois what the pair accomplished in Malaga. Dubois smiled broadly, "Well, this computer tape eliminates any threat to our 12 October launch date. We can validate this software on our shuttle spacecraft here by the end of the week."

Dubois looked at his watch, "We've been busy here in Toulouse, too. We have an 8:30 video teleconference all set up. We better get up to the conference room. You will hear how we have all the final schedule details worked out."

Dubois led Richards and Juanita to the conference room where all the global participants were already visible on the multiple video screens. Dubois strode to the TV camera and opened the meeting, "My colleagues at NASA in the US, at the Space Institute in Novosibirsk, and you twenty up on the Space Station: we have great news to report today. First, Dr. Juanita Gonzalez and Dr. Don Richards just handed me the computer tape with the new software for our shuttle stored on it. That schedule threat has been removed. Second, we have completed all the detailed launch plans."

He launched into a short briefing, which he finished by saying, "So, as I hope you have seen, we have all the plans for the three launch missions completed. We will carry up extra expendables with each of the three rescue launches and on the last launch we will carry up the four members of the replacement crew for the Space Station. They will then have enough expendables stored for a full year!"

General Robbins responded from the Space Station, "Dr. Dubois, it certainly sounds like you have all the 'ducks lined up' for rescuing us. We can all relax now and enjoy our last month and a half in space. Now that those nagging worries about our rescue have been put away, we can enjoy the beauty of this immense universe we can see so well from up here. We have something to announce as well, but I'm going to let Dr. Barbara Rosen tell you that news."

Barbara came on the screen, smiled broadly, "Using the 100 inch telescope – part of our scientific equipment – we have discovered a planet circling Alpha Centari. We have strong evidence of intelligent life on that planet. We have been able to correlate radio signals received from the exact direction of that planet as being modulated with a signal that could only be produced by a highly intelligent civilization. Their message was, 'We know you are there. We would like to communicate with you.' It was in English! That means they have learned our language from radio intercepts!"

Richards arrived back in Los Angeles at 4 pm Tuesday the 26th of August 1992. As he strode off the Air France 747, he saw Dawn waving happily from the crowd. He rushed over, took her in his arms and kissed her warmly.

Dawn kissed him back and said, "Welcome home, Darling. I have dinner reservations for us at Captain Jack's in Huntington Beach."

Richards, stuffed with the superb French cuisine served to him and his fellow first class passengers on the long, non-stop flight from Paris, hid his feelings about another dinner and exclaimed, "That's wonderful, Dawn. Let's go!"

When Richards awoke the next morning after a vigorous night of lovemaking, he was surprised to find the bed empty of Dawn but with a note on the bedside table that read:

Dear Don,

I've enjoyed those times we did get together, but I can't stand your being away so much of the time. I've met a younger man who has kept me company during your absences. Please remember me lovingly.

Dawn

Richards was truly astounded. All the time he had been thinking about how Lina was a more interesting personality than Dawn, it had never occurred to him that Dawn might be unhappy in her relationship with him. He looked around his apartment. It seemed empty and uninteresting suddenly. He was glad his work would help him adapt to this life change.

Chapter 53

Final European Shuttle Launch

Sunday, 12 October 1992

Everyone on the Space Station was awake early. The launch of the European space shuttle was less than ten minutes away. The count down had been unusually smooth. There had been one temporary hold for an apparent software 'bug' last night but Dr. Juanita Gonzalez found the problem and solved it quickly. Dr. Barbara Rosen was on duty as communications officer this morning. The video was linked with the European space center in Kourou, French Guiana, as well as the control center at Aerospatiale in Toulouse, the NASA Houston control center for Space Station Operations, and the Russian Space Institute in Novosibirsk. Most of the Space Station crew members were crowded into the communications control center to watch the last minutes of the count down.

Barbara remarked to Georgi Gusev, standing next to her, "Georgi, I think the European shuttle is going to work. It's about time we had a successful round trip mission to the Space Station."

Gusev whispered softly to Barbara, out of earshot of the others, "Actually, Barbara, I'm beginning to like it up here on the Space Station. I'm glad you and I are scheduled for the last launch. After Rogers and Johnson return to Earth, I'll have you all to myself for a while. I'm really going to miss you when I get back to Novosibirsk!"

Barbara smiled and then replied quietly and seriously, "Georgi, maybe we can figure out some way to get together, after you return to Russia."

"I hope so!"

The count down continued. The launch controller reached the last five seconds and counted in English, "Five, four, three, two, one, launch! We have a successful lift off. All telemeter signals look good!"

A cheer went up in the Space Station communications control center. The TV cameras trained on the shuttle showed it flying into space on a tail of flame. A few moments later the launch controller announced, "Commander Bourgain, this is Eurospace Control. All telemeter signals look normal. Your trajectory is within limits. You are cleared for orbital injection. Bon voyage!"

Another roar went up from the crowd on the Space Station!

During the last two months since the rescue mission was scheduled, the Space Station crew, including the three stranded shuttle crews, had slipped into a relaxed routine on board. The scientific experiments had continued. The duty watches had gone on. There had been several EVA expeditions outside the Space Station to get more detailed information about the breakdowns of the three space shuttles tethered to the Station. The details about the US Shuttles had been transmitted to NASA and those about the Russian shuttle to the Russian Space Institute. The ground crews used this information to assess just how repairs could be made in the future to recover these three broken spacecraft.

The detailed rescue plans called for three rescue missions. The first two trips would carry down seven astronauts each. The first return flight would include the Columbia's commander, Billie Joe Johnson and his crew, since he was the first shuttle to be stranded. Several of the Space Station personnel would go with them. The second return flight would take down the Atlantis' commander, Richard Rogers and his crew, again with several people from the Station crew. General Robbins would also return on the second flight since he had been on duty longer than Barbara Rosen. That would leave Barbara Rosen as commander of the Space Station until she returned to Earth on the third flight along with the Russian shuttle's commander, Georgi Gusev and his crew plus the Space Station dock master and the last G&C specialist. The third rescue mission expected to bring up four fresh astronauts who would man the Space Station until the three shuttles could be repaired and returned to Earth. At that time, the Space Station crew would be increased to its full compliment.

The rescue plans included replenishing the expendables during each of the three rescues. The expendable inventory would be adequate to maintain life for the four new astronauts plus the repair specialists for a full year.

Thirty minutes into the flight, the European shuttle launch controller announced, "Commander Bourgain, you are now cleared for orbit and rendezvous with the Space Station. All telemeter systems look normal. Your orbital parameters are all within the nominal range. Twenty minutes to your first orbital adjustment."

Commander Yvon Bourgain looked at his cockpit instruments, "Roger, Kourou Control. Everything looks good here in the cockpit. We are beginning our twenty minute countdown for first orbital adjustment. The Earth looks beautiful from up here!"

This was European Shuttle Commander Bourgain's first orbital flight. He had flown the shuttle simulator in Malaga and Toulouse so often he felt completely at home as commander. He was full of self confidence as he manipulated the shuttle controls and read the information from the color TV displays and other instruments. He felt as much at home flying the shuttle as he did driving his Citroen on the magnificent autoroutes of France. He usually cruised along those super highways at 180 kilometers per hour. Today he was orbiting in the European shuttle at 27,680 kilometers per hour or over 150 times faster than he drove his Citroen. He found the experience exhilarating, well worth the long years of working 12 to 14 hours a day to prepare for his role as European space shuttle commander. He was glad he had been chosen for this mission and proud to be able to rescue his space colleagues stranded up here. His stopover would be short: one day or sixteen orbits of the Space Station.

Bourgain read the distance to the Station using his radar. He was 2,810 nautical miles away. He punched this distance into his computer console on the front panel. He selected the orbital adjustment mode so that when he fired the main shuttle engine, the computer would apply enough impulse power from the engine in the proper direction to achieve rendezvous with the Space Station in fourteen orbits. His closing speed with the Space Station would be 200 knots or 334 meters per second. That meant the rendezvous with the Station was twenty hours and fifty three minutes from the time of engine firing, about seven minutes from now.

Bourgain called Kourou Control and reported, "Kourou Control, this is Commander Bourgain in the Shuttle. My on-board computer indicates rendezvous with the Space Station will be twenty hours and fifty three minutes from engine fire. Please confirm."

"Roger, Commander Bourgain, this is Kourou Control. Our ground computer confirms your on-board computer's computation. Six minutes and thirty seconds to main engine pulse."

"Roger, Kourou Control. Now six minutes and fifteen seconds to engine pulse. We have the countdown and engine turn-on under computer control at this time."

At the time the main engine was fired, the European shuttle entered the rendezvous mode under the control of the rendezvous/docking software that Drs. Gonzalez and Richards prepared in Malaga last month. The final operational test of the software would take place soon. The ground testing had assured it would work with a 99.999% probability.

The main engine countdown continued. At five minutes before engine firing, the attitude control system turned the spacecraft to the proper orientation relative to the orbit of the Space Station. The last ten seconds were counted out by the cockpit voice synthesizer as in the Russian shuttle. However, this pleasant female voice counted down in English, the official language of the European shuttle, "ten, nine, -- two, one, fire!"

Yvon Bourgain and his crew felt the acceleration force on the spacecraft. They were pushed back into their seats for the time period necessary to give the amount of impulse power to achieve rendezvous. After the engine stopped firing, Bourgain looked at his rendezvous radar and it read the distance to the space station as 2790 nautical miles with distance decreasing at 200 knots or about ten times faster than the Formula 40 catamarans he had watched on TV in the Grand Prix Race in Cherbourg the week before he flew to French Guiana for the launch.

After the engine firing, the launch control center called, "Commander Bourgain, this is Kourou Control. Everything looks normal. Our ground computer estimates rendezvous at 1000 GMT (Greenwich Mean Time) on Monday 13 October.

"Roger, Kourou Control. Commander Bourgain here. Our on-board computer agrees with the ground computer. Everything looks A-OK here.   Request permission to contact the Space Station."

"Roger, permission granted."

Bourgain called the Station on the spatial communication frequency of 156.15 MHz and said, "Space Station, this is Commander Bourgain on the European shuttle."

Barbara Rosen replied, "Commander Bourgain, this is Dr. Rosen, communications officer on the Space Station. Please call me Barbara."

"Roger, Barbara.   Please call me Yvon.   We have a rendezvous date at 1000 GMT tomorrow."

"Roger, Yvon. We read you at just less than 2800 nautical miles away, about the distance from Washington, DC, to Los Angeles. Our radar indicates you are closing at 200 knots or 334 meters per second. We're all waiting to welcome your arrival."

"Roger, Barbara. My crew and I will be glad to get there. Everything has gone very smoothly so far."

At 1000 GMT, the European shuttle arrived at its rendezvous point ten kilometers away from the Space Station. Commander Bourgain selected the docking mode, which fired the main engine to slow down for the docking maneuver, some sixty minutes away.

Chapter 54

Docking and Re-entry

At 1100 GMT, Barbara Rosen felt the gentle bump of the European Space Shuttle hooking up at the Space Station Docking Module port. She announced over the communication channel to the shuttle, "Welcome to the US Space Station, Yvon and crew. Our dockmaster says you may exit into the pressurized lock in two minutes, if you're ready."

"Roger, Barbara. It will take about five minutes to shut down our systems and secure everything ready to board your Station. Glad to be here."

A few minutes later, Commander Yvon Bourgain and his crew of two astronauts, boarded the US Space Station. They were welcomed by a floating reception line. First in line was General Robbins. Next was Barbara Rosen who kissed each of the three astronauts warmly. Then the three shuttle commanders, Johnson, Rogers, and Gusev, greeted the newcomers warmly with hugs and hand shakes.

At the end of the line, Commander Bourgain and his two crewmen were led to the dining room for the combination welcoming and going away party. General Robbins opened the formal part of the fiesta by saying, "On behalf of the Space Station crew, we would like to extend a formal welcome to Commander Yvon Bourgain and his two crew members from the European space shuttle. Congratulations for a successful launch, rendezvous and docking. And, may I say, we all fervently wish you a successful re-entry and landing on Earth tomorrow!"

The astronauts and cosmonauts clapped loudly, with yells of 'bravo!' among the group. Then Yvon Bourgain responded, "To my fellow space colleagues, my brave crew and I are pleased to be here. We will carry seven of you back to Earth tomorrow – without fail! In recognition of this festive occasion, the president of the EEC, President Lorenzo Felipe Lopez, asked me to bring these gifts to be used during our celebration."

Bourgain opened a bag he was carrying and held up a split of champagne with a special valve/nipple on it for imbibing the bubbly liquid in space. A cheer went up from everyone as they saw there was a small Moet champagne bottle for each of them!

General Robbins said, somewhat stuffily, "Ordinarily our regulations do not permit alcoholic beverages, except for a small portion of 3.2 beer. However – in view of the special circumstances of this happy event – I hereby declare a one-time-only exception. Cheers! Drink up!"

Robbins set an example by opening the valve on this space-champagne bottle and taking a fizzy swig of the precious liquid. All the rest followed suit, and then gave out a chorus of happy cheers.

After thirty minutes of convivial fellowship, General Robbins interrupted the party, "It is now time to have the drawing for those unassigned crew members who will be given berths to return to Earth tomorrow. By our return criteria, the Columbia crew are already assigned to return tomorrow. The Atlantis crew are assigned to return on the second return flight, which will also be taking me. The service and dockmaster astronauts and the Russian cosmonauts will return on the third return flight along with Dr. Barbara Rosen. That leaves the six science astronauts unassigned. The three winning the lottery today will return on the flight tomorrow. The remaining three science astronauts will return on the second flight. Is that clear?"

Barbara, standing next to Colonel Gusev, whispered, "About as clear as mud!"

Gusev laughed and replied quietly, "The General is sometimes too formal."

Robbins added, "I have the six names on slips of paper in this can."

He turned to Gusev, "Colonel Gusev, since you are an objective third party, please reach in the can and draw out three names."

When Robbins opened the can, two slips of paper floated out. Gusev grabbed them and took one more from the can. Robbins quickly snapped the lid back on the can and read the three names from the papers Gusev handed him.

As he pronounced the three names, those three astronauts smiled happily and the group applauded their selection. Robbins then closed out his interruption of the party, "Well, that defines the returnees for each of the three return flights. With that formality over, please enjoy the party. Remember, though, we have a lot of work ahead of us to get ready for tomorrow's return. So, let's break up within twenty minutes."

The party went on for a while and then the various crew members left to return to their duties. The European shuttle crew were given cabins where they could sleep undisturbed to be fresh for their return trip. The Station loadmaster directed the unloading and storing of the precious expendables.

The next morning, Colonel Billie Joe Johnson and his six fellow American astronauts joined Commander Yvon Bourgain and the two European astronauts in the European shuttle. Commander Bourgain received a command on his cockpit director display to push back from the Space Station using his reaction jets. As soon as he was a safe distance from the Station, the on-board computer began the countdown which would lead to the firing of the main engine with an impulse sufficient to remove orbital energy and to start the long, high speed re-entry into the Earth's atmosphere. By pre-arrangement with NASA, the space shuttle would land at Edwards Air Force Base near Lancaster, California, in the high desert. A special adapter had been built for the piggy-back Boeing 747 to fly the European shuttle south to Kourou, French Guiana, for the second rescue launch.

The sweet, feminine, synthesized voice in the cockpit said, "At the tone, it will be exactly five seconds until the main engine ignites to initiate re-entry to Earth. Your Earth destination is Edwards Air Force Base, latitude 34°37.6' north, longitude 117°15.7' west. If this destination is not correct, please push the red abort button.."

Yvon Bourgain turned to Billie Joe Johnson, who was the honorary co-pilot, "Billie Joe, we're about ready to start the re-entry. Hope everything works!"

At that moment the tone sounded and the voice synthesizer said, "Five, four, three, two, one, fire! Your re-entry into the Earth's atmosphere is now beginning. Your estimated time of arrival at Edwards Air Force Base is 1703 GMT or 1003 local Pacific Daylight Time."

The crew felt the strong acceleration of the main engine firing. The spacecraft was oriented so that the engine impulse slowed the big vehicle down to make it begin descending from orbit.

Billie Joe called out, "Yippee, Yvon. We're on our way now. I jes' hope that re-entry computer of yours doesn't make a mistake. I would hate to be burned to a crisp after getting this far!"

Yvon replied seriously, "Billie Joe, I hope so, too! We do have to fly through a narrow 'safe corridor.' If we go too low, we'll go too fast and burn up. If we go too high, our angle of attack will be too great and we'll burn up."

Billie Joe added, "Yeah, Yvon, we have the same limits on our shuttle. I worry about 'crisping' every time we re-enter. I wish we astronauts could talk NASA into installing an emergency re-entry capsule for us to ride in to save us in case something does go wrong."

Yvon asked, "That's a good idea. Why don't they do that?"

Billie Joe responded glumly, "They say it's too expensive. After all, it's our asses that'll get burned up, not the bureaucrats or congressmen, if something goes wrong. But the ol' Yankee dollar is all important to then."

Yvon responded, "We have the same problems in Europe. Bureaucrats are the same the world over. Well, here we go. We're five minutes before communications black-out. We better talk while we can."

Bourgain called the Space Station on his communication set, "Barbara, this is Yvon. Everything looks normal here. I think we have a successful re-entry going. So long. Hope to see you again in about two weeks."

Rosen responded, "Yvon, we still see you on the radar screen. You looked good when that main engine started up. See you in two weeks. Bon voyage!"

Bourgain then called Eurospace Control, "Kourou Control, this is Commander Bourgain. We have initiated re-entry. Our on-board computer estimates EAFB at 1703 GMT. Do you confirm?"

"Affirmative, Commander Bourgain. This is Kourou Control. The ground computer has your estimated time of arrival at Edwards Air Force Base as 1703 GMT. We will notify NORAD so they won't think you are a Russian missile and launch World War III. We'll pass along your ETA to Edwards. Bon voyage!"

A few minutes later the crew in the European space shuttle watched the eerie red glow build up around the space craft caused by the ionization as the shuttle encountered the tenuous outer edges of the Earth's atmosphere. The ionized atmosphere surrounding the spacecraft also caused a communications black-out. Radio waves can't penetrate this ionized shield, or plasma. This was the most crucial part of re-entry. If something went wrong, the crew could not communicate the problem with the ground. The spacecraft and its inhabitants would be incinerated with almost no evidence left to tell the world what happened. It was a nervous time for the shuttle crew and its passengers.

The surfaces of the space craft striking the atmosphere turned a cherry red. The crew members began to feel the heat seeping into their environment through the thermal protection system, or heat shield tiles, that insulated the spacecraft from the extreme temperatures of re-entry.

During this plunging re-entry into the atmosphere, the space craft first rolled 180° to the right and then rolled 180° to the left. This controlled rolling was repeated several times. The hot time during the total forty minutes of re-entry only lasted about ten minutes, but it seemed like an eternity to the crew.

A few minutes later, the space craft slowed to mach 5 at 150,000 feet above the Pacific Ocean, the same speed as the Russian SST that Richards rode to and from Novosibirsk.

Suddenly the communications returned. They were now out of the communication black-out zone.

Bourgain called Eurospace Control, "Kourou Control, this is Commander Bourgain on the Euroshuttle. Do you read now?"

The crew were very happy to hear, "Affirmative, Commander Bourgain. Kourou Control reads you loud and clear. We have telemeter signals once again. Everything looks normal. Your trajectory to Edwards looks fine."

"Roger, Kourou Control. Everything looks fine on board. We are beginning our approach to the California Coast. We can see it in the distance."

Ten minutes later the Euroshuttle passed over the Edwards AFB Tacan station at an altitude of 50,000 feet, going east-south-east.

Bourgain called Edwards, "Edwards Control, this is Commander Bourgain in the Euroshuttle. We passed over the Tacan station at 1656 GMT. Beginning procedure turn for landing on your project runway 25."

"Roger, Commander Bourgain. This is Edwards Control. Euroshuttle is cleared to land. Runway 25. You look good on our radar. We just heard your supersonic blast."

"Roger, Edwards Control. We are cleared to land."

A few minutes later, the sleek shuttle turned onto the runway heading, still flying at 200 knots, and began the steep descent to landing. At about 500 feet above the runway, the radar altimeter on the spacecraft sent signals to its autopilot for the automatic landing flare to the runway. A few seconds later, the landing gear touched down on the cement project runway at Edwards with a puff of black smoke as its wheels accelerated up to speed, taking rubber off the tires. Bourgain braked the big craft to a stop just in front of the official greeting party.

The welcomers included the NASA Administrator, the President's science advisor, the commanding general of Edwards Air Force Base, and Dr. Donald Richards, whose hard work made the rescue possible.

After several minutes, the crew and passengers opened the door and walked down the moveable de-planing stairs to the cheers of the welcoming committee. There were dozens of television cameras documenting the exit for world TV. The officials hurried forward to shake the hands of the rescued space travelers, with broad smiles on everyone's faces. The returning space crew were herded in front of a big TV screen, a video link direct from the White House. President Williamson's image came on, and he said, "Commander Yvon Bourgain and your crew, on behalf of the American people, I thank you for your rescue of our American astronauts who have been lost in space for so many months. We thank you from the bottom of our hearts. And God bless you all!"

Chapter 55

More Rescue Launches

Sunday, 26 October 1992

The countdown for the second Euroshuttle rescue launch was proceeding smoothly. Only fifteen minutes until blast off. Don Richards and Gus Ford, in the NASA Houston Space Station control center, were staring at the video link screens displaying the Eurospace control center at Kourou, the Space Station with Barbara Rosen's face, and the Russian Space Institute in Novosibirsk with the beautiful Lina Gorlovka smiling from the monitor. Another monitor showed Yvon Bourgain, lying in the cockpit of the Euroshuttle. He looked remarkably relaxed, considering the many tons of explosive chemicals beneath him and his crew, ready to blast him into Earth orbit in several more minutes.

The countdown proceeded without any delays. Almost routine! The launch controller said, "Five, four, three, two, one, lift off!"

The huge booster rockets lumbered off the launch pad in a big cloud of white smoke. The Euroshuttle accelerated from the surface at an amazing rate, riding the bright plume of rocket exhaust into space. The launch was successful. The insertion into orbit, the rendezvous, and the docking proceeded smoothly without a hitch. A routine mission. The docking occurred at 1015 GMT on Monday, October twenty-seventh. No problems. Another happy but smaller welcoming party took place, since there were only thirteen people left on the Space Station now.

The next day, General Robbins turned over command of the Space Station to his deputy, Dr. Barbara Rosen, and boarded the Euroshuttle along with the Atlantis' commander, Richard Rogers, and the other passengers, leaving six people on the Space Station. The Euroshuttle commander, Yvon Bourgain, invited Rogers to be his honorary co-pilot during the re-entry and landing maneuver.

The push back, retro-fire of the main engines, re-entry and landing went exactly as planned.

This second rescue flight with its crew of three plus seven more of the stranded American astronauts landed at Edwards Air Force Base in California just after 8 am West Coast Local Time. The returning astronauts were welcomed by a smaller, and less prestigious party than the first return, but the welcome was warm and happy.   Richards was there again to welcome General Robbins, Colonel Rogers, and the others.   Standing alongside Richards were the Edwards Base Commander, a two star general in the US Air Force, and Dr. Bill Adams, there to represent NASA Headquarters.

The third launch was accomplished on the tenth of November 1992.   It was equally successful and the Euroshuttle carried as passengers, four fresh American astronauts to man the Space Station while those on the ground figured out how to repair and rescue the three shuttles tethered there.   At that time, the normal complement of Space Station crew members would be sent up. The re-entry went without any problems.   The last of the original American astronauts led by Dr. Barbara Rosen, as well as Colonel Georgi and his two Russian crewmen, were returned safely to Earth, again landing at Edwards Air Force Base.

Richards was joined by Dr. Lina Gorlovka to welcome Colonel Gusev, Dr. Rosen, and the others on their return from space.   During the welcoming party that followed the official speeches given for TV, Richards cornered Gorlovka, Rosen, Gusev, and Bourgain, and proposed there be a big celebration party the following week in some convenient location in Europe for all the astronauts, cosmonauts, and key people who contributed to the success of the rescue.   They enthusiastically endorsed Richards' idea.   They all agreed, after much discussion of the November temperature and weather in various places, to hold the celebration in Malaga.   They also agreed that Dr. Juanita Gonzalez should organize the party, with help from Yvon Bourgain.

Don Richards arrived at the Malaga Airport after a two hour flight from Paris. He was met by Dr. Juanita Gonzalez and Yvon Bourgain, who, Richards noted, were holding hands. Richards rushed over to greet Juanita and Yvon. He hugged them both and kissed Juanita on each cheek.

Juanita exclaimed happily, "Don, your idea for a celebration party was wonderful. Yvon and I have been working very hard to get the party organized and make sure everyone gets here."

Yvon added happily, "Yes, we worked so well together, I asked Juanita to marry me. And she said yes!"

Richards was surprised, but he forced a smile and replied, "But, isn't that a rather short courtship?"

Juanita blushed, smiled, and said, "No, Don, not really. You see, I spent over a month working with Yvon while he was training in the simulator here, learning to use the rendezvous/docking software. We got – you know – very close during that time. Yvon is going to move to Malaga and commute to Toulouse and the other places he has to travel to."

Richards regained his composure and exclaimed happily, "Well, congratulations, Yvon! And all the happiness in the world, Juanita. Please invite me to your wedding!"

Juanita grinned, "You are invited. Just stay over here after the party. We're getting married at noon Saturday – in the Catedral de Malaga."

Just then they heard a loudspeaker announcement of a Swiss Air flight arriving from Zurich. Juanita said, "Don, let's go over to the gate where that flight is arriving. There are some people coming to the party that you know."

"And who can that be?"

Juanita smiled, "Just wait. You'll see!"

Several minutes later, Richards saw three people exiting through the customs gate from the Zurich flight. Colonel Gusev was leading Dr. Barbara Rosen by the hand, followed closely by Dr. Lina Gorlovka. Richards rushed up, grabbed Lina, hugged her and kissed her warmly on the lips. He greeted Gusev and Rosen and then asked, "How in the world did you three get together?"

Lina laughed, "Well, I'm on the flight because there's good airline service between Moscow and Zürich with a good connection to Malaga. I met these two – Barbara and Georgi – hugging and kissing in the Swiss Air departure lounge, just like teenage lovers."

Barbara laughed, "Thanks for the compliment, Lina, but Georgi and I are almost twenty years out of our teens. We took a non-stop from Los Angeles to Zurich last Friday and have spent several days touring Switzerland together. We visited the glacier on Jungfrau Mountain near Interlaken and Georgi checked in with the Russian Embassy in Berne to keep the bureaucrats happy. Then we spent a couple of days in the Dolder Hotel in Zurich – a beautiful hotel in a beautiful city! Then we took the Malaga flight today, and ran into Lina at the airport!"

Richards laughed and took Lina's hand, "Well, now I understand everything, almost!"

Barbara said, "Don't look so scandalized, Dr. Richards. Georgi and I had a great time doing it in space. We just decided we would see if it's as much fun when there's gravity!"

Everyone in the party laughed hilariously. They all proceeded to the airport bus that took them to the old Catedral de Malaga where Juanita and Yvon were to be married on Saturday. Everyone was staying at the Hotel Palacio, a short block south of the Catedral. Tomorrow's party was planned for the roof top restaurant in the Palacio. The warm Malaga weather was ideal for the mid November gala.

The big celebration party started at the very non-Spanish time of 6 pm, in deference to the habits of the foreign guests. All of the twenty astronauts who were lost in space for so long were there. The European Space Council technical committee headed by Dr. Jacques Dubois was there. The key NASA executives were there: Dr. Bill Adams and Gus Ford. Bucky Woods and Yuli Litvinov, who were sunburned because they had been fishing all afternoon, were there. Professor Dr. Chekhov had come from Moscow. And finally, Dr. John Davidson, the US President's science advisor was there. Several of the married party-goes had brought their wives. And some had brought girl friends. Quite a large group.

The champagne flowed freely. There were many toasts drunk. The hors d'oeuvres were marvelous and the buffet dinner was outstanding. General Robbins and Dr. John Davidson both made boring after dinner speeches. The crowd pretended politely to listen. The party was a huge success.

Richards and Lina slipped away from the crowd just after 1 am and retired to their suite overlooking Malaga harbor with the moon glistening on the dark Mediterranean Sea. After a strenuous and satisfying session of love making, Richards turned to Lina and said sleepily, "I love loving communists."

She looked into his eyes and replied, "That's good, because I love loving capitalists."

EPILOGUE

President Williamson and Premier Gorbachev met in Geneva for three days beginning 1 July 1993. On the third of July, the two leaders of the superpowers announced a break-through in the disarmament talks that had been going on for almost a year. The two signed an agreement that would eliminate all nuclear weapons by the year 2000. In the meantime, there would be an immediate fifty percent reduction in warheads. To assure compliance, each country would convert the plutonium in their warheads into nuclear fuel rods for burning in the nuclear furnaces of the world's peaceful nuclear power plants. This accord implemented an idea suggested by Dr. Simon Ramo almost a decade earlier to dispose of nuclear warheads peacefully, with an absolute check on compliance. The process would be supervised by a joint committee composed of European Economic Community country delegates.

Premier Gorbachev gave his blessing to the expansion of the EEC by the inclusion of Russia's communist state allies as well as the independently minded Yugoslavs and Albanians, if they wished to join. All had indicated they did wish to become part of the European Community.

As part of the Disarmament Agreement, President Williamson agreed to stop the Strategic Defense Initiative program. Instead, the US and Russia together with the newly expanded EEC signed a joint treaty to begin a Joint Space Program to colonize the planet Mars by the year 2020. As part of the new joint space program, the US and Russia agreed to a joint shuttle salvage program to repair the broken shuttles sitting in space and to return them to Earth for re-use. In addition, the US, Russia and the EEC agreed to internationalize the US and Russian Space Stations and to pool resources for re-supply and operations.

President Williamson announced all the details of the agreements with the Russians in a Fourth of July address to the American people. He had feared that his popularity would drop if he signed such sweeping disarmament and cooperation agreements with the Russians. He found instead that his popularity ratings soared – not only in the US but in Europe as well.

Dr. Don Richards applied for permission to emigrate to Russia so he could marry Dr. Lina Gorlovka. He was granted permission in December 1993. He and Lina were married in a simple ceremony in the Moscow City Hall during the last week of 1993. Richards became a scientist in the Russian Space Institute. Dr. Gorlovka was promoted to Director of the Institute and Richards was named a Special Deputy Director to oversea the Russian participation in the recently signed International Space Treaty.

Colonel Georgi Gusev married Dr. Barbara Rosen. She was named Commander of the International Space Station. He was named Deputy Commander.   A new regulation permitted cohabitation in space by married crew members. In their spare time, the couple co-authored a book titled, "How to Enjoy Sex though Weightless." It became a best seller!

On Tuesday, December 23, 2008, the Internet carried the following news: NASA has awarded a pair of contracts worth $3.5 billion through 2016 to two private aerospace firms seeking to haul vital supplies (expendables) to and from the International Space Station, the space agency announced late Tuesday.

NASA has been seeking commercial U.S. cargo delivery services to the space station to reduce reliance on its international partners during the anticipated five-year gap between the 2010 retirement of its aging space shuttles and the first operational flights of their successor, the Orion Crew Exploration Vehicle.

NASA said it is absolutely vital that SpaceX and Orbital come through with their cargo launch and return pledges to support the space station's full, six-person crews in the future. Ultimately, the companies are expected to provide between 40 percent and 70 percent of NASA's space station cargo each year.

The Hawthorne, Calif.-based firm Space Exploration Technologies (SpaceX) and Orbital Sciences Corp., of Dulles, Va., beat a third competitor for NASA's Commercial Resupply Services contracts with their proposals to privately develop and launch spacecraft capable of delivering cargo to the space station and returning supplies back to Earth.

NASA's Commercial Resupply Services plan calls for SpaceX and Orbital Sciences to haul 20 tons of cargo to the space station through 2016. NASA has agreed to pay $1.6 billion for 12 flights of SpaceX's planned Dragon spacecraft and their Falcon 9 boosters. The agency has also doled out $1.9 billion to Orbital for eight flights of its Cygnus spacecraft.

SpaceX plans to launch its Dragon spacecraft atop a Falcon 9 rocket from Florida's Cape Canaveral Air Force Station, while Orbital Sciences is developing its Cygnus vehicle to fly atop its Taurus 2 booster from NASA's Wallops Flight Facility on the eastern coast of Virginia.